IF CROWS KNOW BEST

Mage of Merced Volume I

By Aimee L. Gross

Moon Road Press
Topeka, Kansas

This is a work of fiction. All of the characters, names, places and events are products of the author's imagination, and any similarity to actual persons, living or dead, is purely coincidental.

First Edition
First Printing: 2014

ISBN:0990968103
ISBN-13:978-0-9909681-0-8

Library of Congress Number: 2014919945

Moon Road Press
6501 SW Vorse Road
Auburn, KS 66402

Dedication:

To my husband, a good man who just keeps getting better.
Also to our children, who loved all the stories and clamored
for more.

CHAPTER 1

What possessed my brother Wils to want to get married, I never claimed to know, but he did ask Annora to come to our mountain and be his wife. I went with him the day he first met her. That morning was the start of my life being turned over like a drying hay-row, and me getting tasked with the care and keeping of his bride. Along with a great deal more, besides.

I walked around the corner of the shed and saw him snatch up the hind leg of the smallest kid in the goat pen.

"What are you doing with the puny one?" I asked him. "You're not going to butcher it, are you?"

"I'm taking it down to the village, to that girl I heard cures animals," he said, swinging the squirming kid onto his shoulders. "Get the gate, can you?"

I opened the gate and stuck out my leg to keep the other goats from barging through with Wils. "She's going to fix it with magic? I'm coming, too."

"I don't know what you'd be needed for, Judian. You can do my chores while I'm gone, soon as you finish yours."

"And I don't know why I'd want to do your work—I want to see her do magic. If we can get a decent goat for a sickly one, that is worth seeing. What if I could learn how to fix animals?"

Wils sighed and gave over arguing with me quicker than

usual. So, we set off together down the sloping track to the village. Morie saw us go by the yard and came running over from the barn, calling out that she wanted to come along.

"Your legs are too short," I told her, true enough because of being only four years old. "I'm not carrying you back up here. You need to take water out to Da come noon, anyway." I pointed at the midmorning sun. "When you see the sun straight overhead."

She pouted while we walked on. Wils shifted the bleating kid and held its hooves in either hand on his chest so it would be still. Soon its head hung low, drowsing. A scrawny thing, it never had fed well although the nanny had plenty of milk.

A warm breeze made walking pleasant, and for a further pleasure I would see something new instead of doing the same old chores at home. When I said as much, Wils rolled his eyes and said, "You always think you have to do more than your share, anyway." As it was perfectly true that I was the most burdened with work, I ignored Wils and listened instead to crows mobbing an owl in the trees beside the road. Three of them, cawing like mad and rushing at the branch where the owl perched, hunched and glowering. The crows never give up until an owl flees, I knew, no matter how long they must torment the larger bird. Da once said that crows think they have final say in all matters.

Wils told me as we walked how Annora had come to the village to live with her Uncle Werrel and Aunt Lorneh when her grandmother passed, and how before long folks were saying if you had a sick calf or dog or any sort of animal, take it to see Annora; she has "a way" with all manner of creature. As if animals told her what ailed them. When we came upon her home place, she stood in the kitchen garden, picking herbs, with the sun on her hair and her skirts tucked up to keep dry. I saw the look on Wils's face, as if he'd been struck on the temple with a thick branch. And that was the end of him having any sense, exactly then.

"Bring her over by the shed, there's a bench," Annora said.

How did she know the kid was a female? Before she even

looked?

So, over we went, and she sat and ran her hands over the kid while we stood, and Wils started talking to her like I never heard him talk to another person inside our family or out of it. The kid nudged her hands and bleated at her like she was its mother, and she let it suck her fingers while Wils yattered on until he said something that made her laugh. I heard him talking to Da about it later that night by the hearth fire. The way he would have given anything to make her laugh again, it was so fair to hear. Da nodding and smoking his pipe.

She never said what was wrong with our kid that first day, but she gave it a dose of spicy-smelling brew by dipping a rag in the bowl and letting the kid suck it off the twisted end. If Wils had been quiet for a moment *ever,* I could have asked her, maybe, what was in the stuff. Or if it was even magic, because it didn't give off sparks or mist or anything. She told us that one dose would fix our kid, and didn't it scamper around and suck up like mad when we got home. Wils never noticed, pining already for Annora, I reckon. From then on, if he wasn't down there trailing around after her, he was at home being utterly useless. Staring off down the town road and wishing, I'm supposing, that he was in her company.

Wils making tracks to the village to see her every chance he could meant he was never at hand, for tending goats and all the other work that fell on me instead. Da just laughed whenever I would huff about it, and told me, "Judian, he's a fine full-grown lad and she's caught his heart. And isn't she better than all the village girls who've been up here making calf's eyes at him?"

That would always make me snort, to remember the other village girls trailing around and sighing after Wils. He didn't give them much to hope for one way or another, Da said, but to me Wils never seemed as put out with them as he should have been. As I would have been. As I *was* when Da said girls would soon be coming up to trail around after me. For every time Wils came round a corner or looked up from cutting feed, there lurked another girl, simpering, "Hullo, Wils, isn't it hot?" Or "windy" or "wet" or anything plainly obvious. So, at least Annora never did that, which made me like the idea of her some better. And, she could do magic.

After I'd done most all the work around our place for the entire summer, then he decides to ask her to be his wife. Apples and pears were coming on, even Morie was supposed to be helping in the orchard, though she was generally more of a hazard. A couple of village girls had come up to see Wils, but word about him becoming an idiot had spread round and they looked a bit pouty when they told him it was a warm day, wasn't it.

"It is," he allowed. "I hope the weather holds for my wedding, and all."

That went over well.

"They say she's talking to animals all the time. Don't you know what that makes her?" said the dark girl, whose name was Jilly.

"You must be bewitched," suggested her friend, who had a shiny pink face—Gefretta, the smithy's daughter.

"I expect I am bewitched, then." Wils went on picking apples.

"You're never really marrying her, are you?" said Jilly.

"Is she coming to live here?" asked Morie, eyes wide with fear. Wils lets her get away with anything, while Da's out working fields. What if she had to mind? And do chores?

"Is anybody going to pick up any apples? And who cares where you live, I'll still end up doing everything," I said.

"She'll come here," Wils told Morie.

"Splendid," I said. "Maybe she can witch apples into their baskets. And turn little sisters into rabbits."

Morie shrieked and threw her apron over her head, together with the paltry few apples in it, one of which clapped the pink-faced girl in the nose. That marked the first time I heard Wils laugh since he became a fool over Annora. Wils offered his handkerchief to help the girl mop up, her nose was gushing buckets of blood. The two girls tried to act dignified instead of furious, but as Wils

4

kept laughing (and I did, too) they gave us up and stalked off down to the village road. Morie watched them go, and said "She has a lots of blood," which made us laugh again.

Annora's Uncle Werrel made the long climb up to talk with Da about Wils's offer for his niece. He was the hairiest man I ever saw; sandy red hair fuzzed out from his head and chin and up out of the neck of his tunic, front *and back*. His arms were frizzy, his fingers, his knuckles even. His face flushed red and dripped sweat, for it was a warm day. Da gave him apple cider and a seat in the shade of the nut tree. I busied myself setting onions out to dry near enough to hear them work around to what he came to discuss.

"You do understand she brings no dowry? She lived all those years with her gran, after her folks died in the South War."

"Bad times," agreed Da.

"Her father was my brother, but she went to live with the grandmother on his wife's side, no blood relation to us. She hadn't much to come to our doorstep with, and no bride price tucked in the hem of her skirt."

"That is not news to deter Wils, I believe."

"He does seem to have a bad dose of it, eh?" Werrel said with satisfaction. "Not that her skills with stock won't be an asset wherever she lands."

"Oh, has she been turning a profit for your homestead these months?" Da asked mildly.

"Nah," he hurried to say. "All and sundry drag animals to her and she doesn't ask a copper for the cures. Some come round without animals, or with sound ones, as she is a treat to look on." He gave what I thought was a sly wink.

"So Wils says," nodded Da.

"And she seems to think he's a match. I have no reason to stand in the way of the young ones' plans, see."

He indeed seemed all too ready to be shed of her, to my mind.

"Shall they plan the wedding for a month from now?" Da said in the same even, affable way as ever he had, while squinting out over the stony slope to the road.

"Well, to be sure, if that's what they wish. My wife and I won't be able to put on a wedding for them, see. We haven't the means to set it out. And her being the niece and all, and not the daughter of the house…" he let his voice trail off with a shrug.

"Likely they'll marry in Bale Harbour then, and come on up here to settle in. We'll have a bit of a gathering for them, if you and Lorneh would like to come up and raise a glass to the newlyweds." Da paused. *For Werrel to squirm?* "Nothing fancy, just a table under the trees, some of the young wine and a wedding meal."

"Ah, of course if you think so, we'll do our best to join in." Werrel wanted to go now—he was stirring in his wooden chair. He drained his cup and held it out.

"More?" said Da, imperturbable as ever. Like a thick tree in the wind. But Werrel was on his way before I set another onion out, fanning himself with his hat and stepping double-quick.

"Where's your brother?" asked Da, watching our visitor's back.

"Up in the northeast pasture fixing fence."

"Go along up and tell him he's to be married in a month. With the blessing of all concerned, by the gods."

"And the good riddance for his bride from others, it seemed like."

"Mmm. We'll not look for good grace where there is none to be found. Off you go then, Judian."

###

So, the month passed, all of us were scrubbed raw, the wagon decorated with bittersweet vines and stalks of grain and the lot of us drove down to collect his bride. Virda, our neighbor downslope for many years, came to help set out the wedding meal for later. Since Mum passed, Virda often came and kept Morie and me when Da and Wils went off to markets. She was stout and practical and had raised a dozen sons who all went off to sea like their da. She

6

annoyed me by calling me a "poor lamb" since I had no mum anymore, but she was a fine cook.

Wils had told me his thoughts about getting married, when I asked him if he would get any sense and purpose after since he surely had none now. He couldn't laugh enough, and said I'd learn one day what it meant to want someone there at the open and close of every day, to tell things to that you never thought you'd tell anyone. I will avoid it, if that means mooning around like Wils. He said it wasn't as if the village girls all came up to flirt with him because he was such a good-looking man. Though he is, tall and lean with dark wavy hair and black-dark eyes. All of us are dark. He said it was because we had the largest, richest place in the province, and he looked to inherit it. I had not thought of this. "Does Annora want to be the richest matron in the land, then?"

"No," he said, "she doesn't seem to care at all. She likes the idea of coming here, but mostly just because of me." That led him to blush, which honestly I had never seen before. It was disturbing.

He seemed quite as imperturbable as Da driving down to get her, though. All the dark looks we got going through the village, from the girls who watched him slipping away, did not even catch his eye. On we passed between the high brushy banks of the harbour town road, to her Uncle's place on the north side at the edge of our village, with Wils and Da straight-backed on the seat, and Morie drowsing with her head on my knees in the wagon bed.

Annora stepped out of Werrel and Lorneh's gate without a backward look. Her uncle and aunt stood in the doorway and raised hands in greeting our way, but made no move to come out to see her off. Her cousins were nowhere in view. And if she felt slighted she gave no sign. Wils vaulted off to help her board the wagon, grinning down at her upturned face. She had found white flowers and pale green ribbons to plait in her gold hair, but wore the same linen blouse and bodice and brown woolen skirt she had been wearing the first time we saw her—when we brought her the sickly kid. She smiled and handed over a package of what must be her personal things, clothes and all. Wils handed the packet to me, *why would I want it?* I passed it to Morie, who hugged it to her chest and watched, with her lips in a round "O" as Wils lifted Annora up into the wagon.

Morie stared at her unblinking, until I thought Annora would catch fire from the glare of it.

"Are you a magic princess?" Morie breathed.

"She is a magic princess, well and truly," Wils laughed, and his bride turned rosy-pink. Soon as we set off again, Morie wheedled some flowers and a bit of ribbon for her own hair, and Annora sat her in her lap and prettied her up. There would be no living with Morie now, I thought. The magic bride had petted her.

Town fair teemed with people when we rolled in. Da drove to a chapel on the rise above the market street—crumbly yellow stone with a dusty yard shaded by a huge oak. Crows crackled and cawed to each other in its twisted branches. Some perched on the bell tower, above the great bronze bell. The chapel apostate within spoke the joining ceremony in a lispy voice that made Morie giggle. He had particular trouble saying "Wils." The bridal couple knelt facing each other as the apostate walked the circuit around them calling down the blessings from the five gods. At the end, Wils took Annora's face in his hands and kissed her.

"See, now we can go home," said Morie. "And I'll show you my kitten."

Annora laughed as she hugged each of us in turn. Da kissed the top of her head and welcomed her to the Lebannen family. "We'll do our best to give you a good life and a full heart," he said, as he wiped away a tear. And I found I was lying back when I said I didn't know what possessed Wils to want to get married. Because I thought right then that Annora was the prettiest thing that ever drew breath.

Da gave the apostate a donation for the chapel, which must have been more than the usual, from the way the man's eyes widened. The town grew ever louder, noise from the street below the chapel gushed in when we opened the heavy oak doors to leave. "Is it some festival?" wondered Da. "The ships shoving off?"

"The tholdiers have been coming in from parts west for the past three days," the apostate told him. "There's been thuch rumors! King's troops gathering in the borderland, raiding parties reported all along the river. Look how many helmeted men you thee in the threet!" He shifted uneasily. "All the best to the newly joined." He wanted to shut the door, I saw, and he edged us out into the dappled shade on the steps.

"Judian, bring the wagon around." Da shaded his eyes and looked out to the harbour.

I went round and untied the team, and hoisted myself up to drive them to the door.

"You!" shouted one of the helmeted men. "How old are you?"

"It's my da's wagon. He told me to get it."

"Leave it, Boon. This one's voice hasn't broken yet," his companion growled.

"We're to bring any we can use. Boys can be of use!" They were already walking on, though.

"Of use for what?" I called after, but they did not turn, so I clucked to the horses and we rolled to the steps that went up to the chapel.

"What are the soldiers looking for?" I asked Da.

He sighed. "Soldiers are always hungry."

"What, they wanted food?" I said, uncertain that was what they were about.

"Always hungry. And not just for food." He handed Morie up and gestured to Wils and Annora to come, and me to get down in the bed so he could climb onto the seat and drive. "We'll want to get out now and back to our own lands."

"Why?" I persisted. The apostate began to ring the chapel bell to mark the joining he had just officiated. I had to wait until the echoing clangs faded before adding, "What's happening?"

"Da thinks the soldiers have come to press men into service because there looks to be a war," Wils answered. He and Annora climbed aboard and we set off.

Da drove through narrow, packed streets. People were calling out, the crowd surged and eddied. Da looked more and more grim. Morie crept into Annora's lap and held her hands over her ears. I knew the look, she'd be sniveling soon. She hates loud noise and crowds. Annora settled her chin on Morie's head and crooned "Hush, shhhh." Wils kept his arm tight round the two, and I sat opposite hugging my knees.

Wils tried to get up on the bench seat beside Da when we slowed and stopped in the thronging, rushing people.

"No!" Da said sharply. "Get down low, so it looks like only the girls are there. Put the sides down."

"I won't!" I said. "They can't take us! What are we hiding for?"

Da didn't turn round. "Do it now."

I did it, but grumbled to Wils, "I'm not a baby."

"Be glad if they think you are," he hissed. He and I untied the heavy canvas rolled up above the wagon bed and drew down the panels that secured to cleats on the sides. Our wedding decorations were shredding and trailing away as the people pressed close to go by. I could still see through slits between the panels, few soldiers, mostly town folk shouting and pushing past us. I could make out snatches of what different people called to each other:

"Bring my sword!"

"They'll give you a sword—"

"—and all the dried meat you can pack in it—"

"Aren't there any more blankets? Bring them all!"

The younger horse, Sollen, began tossing its head and tried to sidle in the traces, snorting. There was no turning round, or even turning off the main street. Annora handed a quivering Morie to Wils and jumped down to stand at the gelding's head, whispering and touching her hand to its lips and cheek.

I could tell Wils didn't like it, her down there on the cobbles with frenzied folk pushing at her, but the horse stood still and, except for breathing fast, seemed to steady.

"Can you lead him on, girl?" Da said, leaning forward to peer ahead.

She stepped out with a hand on its neck, not the harness. Again and again, she drew the team forward. "Where do we want to end up?" she asked, calling over her shoulder. I could see now the tide of folk had shifted, most of them were going the same way as we were, burdened with packs and armfuls of goods.

"We'll have to go along with them," Da said. He looked out the back of the wagon and saw Wils and me. Wils was up on one knee with Morie perched on the other with her face buried in his shirt. I knelt and swayed just behind the bench seat so I could see. "We'll end up where the soldiers are driving us. I've seen the conscription before."

He had fought in a war years ago, I knew. Before he married Mum and had us. He still had a sword at home and other gear. "What will happen?" I asked Da. "Will they take us all?" I didn't mean Morie and Annora of course—girls can't go off and fight.

"There'll be soldiers in the town square, organizing this mess into ranks, I expect. The soldiers in charge are the ones I want to talk to." He set his jaw and held tight to the reins while Annora led on.

Wils patted Morie and did not take his eyes off of his new wife, drawing our team step-by-step through the throng. Every time someone pressed too near Annora, Morie would yelp "Not so hard!" into his shirt-front.

"Give her to me, if you're going to whack her." I only had to ask once—he thrust her at me and put his head up by Da's hip to watch out for Annora.

"You're choking me," I told Morie, so she clung round my chest then, instead of my neck.

"I want to go home now," she whispered.

When the street opened onto the square, we could see helmeted men with pikes herding town men into files, checking what stuff they had carried in. Shouting and swearing, they pushed them toward the far side of the square. Most of the women seen earlier in the streets were gone now, and I saw men of every age. Some of them surely too old to march?

"Stop it here, under the inn sign. Wils, you're with me. Judian, you, too." He vaulted down, and Annora climbed up to take Morie from me, so I could go. "Don't let them take the wagon!" Da called over his shoulder to her.

"And how would she stop them?" Wils snapped, but he put out a hand to help me down and we set off after Da.

Men got out of his way. He's like a big old bear, heavy built. Men just moved aside until he came to the man he wanted. This one was a taller soldier in a tan tunic, where the others wore green. He had silver braid on his shoulders and other soldiers surrounded him, vying for his glance to ask him questions.

"Yah, Coulier," said Da, for that was this man's rank, "What is this you're organizing? What orders?"

The Coulier snapped his head round, to tell Da to go where he was wanted, I think, but then saw his face.

"Blast me if it isn't Fenn Lebannen!" he shouted, his voice hoarse from all his other shouting so far today, maybe. "Have you come to help me wet-nurse this lot of whelps?"

"Not I. I came to town to see my son married, and went from chapel into your war-drive. What's the word, Dub?"

"War is upon us. Troops massing on the western border, readying an assault. We're to gather as many as we can equip and march out to meet them. It looks to be huge." Dub ignored the soldiers hurrying up to him, leaving them shifting foot-to-foot as they waited.

"But by the gods, why would Keltane want to attack us now? It's madness to start a war with winter coming on. In a month, the passes will be snowed-in and their army will be cut off from supplies and reinforcements."

"What I hear is their king is god-touched and says to his advisors that the gods told him it's his destiny to march on us."

"Bah, the gods told him he needs a decent harbour, more like," said Da. "But why now, in the name of sweet reason?"

Dub shrugged. "Help us sort it out. Bring your boys, there, and come see the troop marshal. You outrank him."

"I did."

To the men pressing around us, Dub announced, "Here's Paladin Fenn Lebannen, come to set us all on the right path. Make way!"

Da, the paladin in the old war? That I never knew. Wils and I made to go with him, but he put up a hand. "Let me see my younger boy back to the bride and my little daughter. Wils and I will come with you then." Dub waved assent and turned to the other soldiers jostling him. We set off, following Da as he cut across the square filled with shoving, stamping men. I could scarcely keep pace with Da, and turned to Wils beside me.

"I'm not getting left behind as if I was a girl and no use!"

"Shut up, can't you? I need you to get Annora home. She's never even been to our place." Wils pushed me toward the wagon.

"Why do you get to go with Da?"

"Who's older? Don't you think I'd rather go eat my wedding feast?"

"You do that, then, and I'll go with him and be a soldier."

"You must be thinking they'd want you!"

Da forged ahead through men gradually filing into columns. We found Annora standing on the wagon bench, Morie clutching at her skirts, and the team digging in their hooves while two great hulking soldiers swore and dragged at their harness. It was all too apparent they would have taken our wagon if they could have, and left Morie and Annora standing on the grass by the square without anything but the clothes they wore.

"Leave go of it." When Da sounded like that, no one would

cross him. They let the harness go.

"We have supplies to load," the first one started.

"We need the rig. She won't get out," put in the other, pointing angrily at Annora.

"And these horses are rooted here," said his fellow with a rude oath.

"Da won't like you to swear," Morie scolded him, clearly sure with Da's return, our side was winning.

"He's Paladin Fenn Lebannen," I said. "Are you going to tell him to give over his wagon?"

Both of them stammered and flushed, and got away quick. Da smiled at me but said, "Don't toss that around too free. I'm not paladin now, that's past."

"Didn't it work, though?"

"I'm thinking Annora wouldn't have let the horses set a step forward. It's so isn't it, girl?"

Annora nodded. "Still, I'm that glad to see you back." She reached for Wils, who helped her down and held her to him.

"Da and I are setting off with the soldiers, love. You and Judian and Morie are to go home now. Look for us as soon as we get things sorted."

"Please, you can't mean you're going to war? Today? Not today."

Da looked across the square. "Today's the day to find out what's been set in motion. And why."

"You picked a bad day to get married," I said to Wils, still smarting about being left behind.

"Come aside, Judian, and let them say good bye." Da led me around the back of the wagon. "When you can do so unobserved, you gather supplies at home. Water, food, arrows, knives. Take my sword, you know where it is. All this you take to three separate caves up in the mountain, close in and further up as well. Enough you can take Morie and Annora there and last a week and more. Pack it safe from animals and other foragers. Do you understand what I'm telling you to do?"

"When will you be coming back? How far away is this marshal they want you to see? Won't you and Wils be back tomorrow?"

"There's no telling at present. We could be gone a week, a month, longer still. I need to know you can keep safe at home if war comes our way." He sighed. "This makes no sense on the face of it. I want you to have a secure place to go to ground if soldiers come to the mountain. Do you know where to prepare places out of the way?"

I nodded. "I know good caves to use."

"I know you'll take it seriously. Don't let anyone know—the village folk—no one. If it comes to that, and you want to take Virda up as well, I leave it to you."

Laid on me, deciding to let soldiers murder Virda or not? This was too much to hear at once. "Am I to let Annora know?" I said this quietly, pretending to look at the backboard of the wagon for damage. I couldn't meet his eye just then, I felt too tight in the throat.

Da bent to look with me. "I leave that to you as well. She has her wits close by her, but may be that wrought up over Wils being off to war on their wedding day—maybe you'll tell her when you've done."

Morie had just figured out that Da and Wils were leaving and set up a screeching wail. Da made sure I had no more to ask before he went round to her, though. I could not help but feel proud—and burdened.

Morie cried all the way out the streets to the edge of town. "I want Da!" over and over, even Annora could not soothe her. Which was just silly to expect, I knew, since Morie saw her for the first time only hours ago. But I had to drive the team, so Annora held her as she hiccoughed and sniveled. Annora did not cry. It tore at me to see her, with the ribbons trailing out of her hair, looking back down the road with dry eyes. The soldiers would march west we had learned; we set off home on the village road north. I planned my cave havens as the miles rolled past.

CHAPTER 2

Virda had the wedding meal set in back under the willows when we drew up to the barn. She bustled over wiping her hands on her apron, smiling until she counted heads. "Whatever—" was all she managed to say before Morie scrambled down onto her, sobbing all over again. I hopped down and helped Annora onto the ground.

"You tell her," I said, "while I see to the horses."

By the time I put all the gear away and watered and fed the team, I felt a little less like my head was stuffed with fluff. I carried Annora's packet of things over to where the women were seated at the long table. Annora sat at the head, with Wils's empty place beside her. Virda cradled Morie on her lap, feeding her bits from her own plate, like when she was a baby.

I sat on the other side and took some sausage and bread. I looked close at what was laid out, thinking what would keep in a mountain cave. Would it be best to start packing tonight?

"Poor lamb, and on your wedding day!" Virda sighed. *Good, someone else can be poor lamb now.*

"Will you help me learn what needs doing here? I've never been at such a big place," Annora said softly.

"Of course, dear. There's lots to do to make ready for winter. But, they'll be back before then, of course they will," she said quickly, as Annora's eyes shifted to look off the way we'd come.

A couple of Virda's sons, on dry land for a change, came up to play their feddles for the dancing that wasn't to be. They plucked the strings and twisted the knobs to tune them to each other. We lit the fire Virda laid, and warmed ourselves while they played sea-songs under the trees. The stars glowed and a fox came sniffing by the edge of the grass. "No chickens for you," I heard Annora say to it, but the fox just sat and let its tongue loll out to one side.

Annora and Virda cleared up the food, and I showed Annora the washhouse. Morie showed her Murr the yellow kitten, and Annora made over it to Morie's satisfaction. I checked all the stock and shut up the henhouse. We said farewells to Virda and her sons, as they set off down the slope carrying a lantern. We three went inside then, and I realized I had no idea where to put Annora. She would have been supposed to share a bed with Wils, but she could hardly sleep in the loft room I shared with him. Da's room? It seemed too strange for her to sleep in his bed. But maybe that had been the plan, for Wils and Annora to have the room behind the stairs, which had been Mum and Da's. No one thought to tell me. I stood at a loss, but Morie took Annora's hand and led her to the top of the stairs.

"You can sleep in my bed," she chattered. "There hasn't been enough girls here until now."

"Thank you, Morie. Is that all right, Judian?"

I hadn't thought to be asked. "That should be fine."

"What about you? Do you sleep upstairs as well?"

"I'll stay down here by the fire for now."

She looked as if she had something else to say, but Morie was tugging on her hand.

"I'll wake you in the morning when it's time to start the chores," I said.

"Good night then, Judian."

"Yes," I said. If I should have said something else, I didn't know what.

###

Once the girls had shut their door, I went to the big oak chair Da sat in every night by the fire. I felt very small sitting there. I poked the fire a bit, and then rested my chin on my pulled-up knees. If I gathered some food and packed it by the back door, I could take it up to the cave I had picked out, first thing tomorrow. Virda planned to come help Annora, and I could tell them I must go up to check fence, or whatever made sense as a reason for heading up the track with a loaded pack.

I was deep into my plans, and starting to drowse in the fire's glow, too, when I heard a thud at the door. I leaped to my feet, snatching for the poker when it came again, a single low blow on the outside of the door.

"Who's there?" I managed to say as deep as my voice would go.

No answer from the outside, but Annora's voice quietly from the top of the stairs, "Judian? What is it?"

"Shh." I crossed to the window that looked out on the porch. Another thump made me jerk back my hand from the curtain, but I stretched it out again to draw the corner of the curtain aside. In the moonlight, on the stones crouched the biggest black dog I had ever seen. I'd have thought it was a bear if it hadn't had a long flag of a tail. As I watched, it lurched forward and butted its huge blocky head against the door. Annora sucked in her breath behind me, having crept to the bottom of the stairs.

"Do you have a dog?" I asked faintly.

"No. Is that a *dog* making that noise?"

"Mmm." I wanted to sit down.

"Are you going to let her in?" Annora walked to the window beside me, and twitched the curtain aside.

"Are you going to tell me you're sure it won't eat us all?"

"She wants to come in, it's cold out." *Thump*, and the beast began wagging madly, too.

"Have you seen it before? I've never seen it, it's huge. Annora, wait—"

19

She drew back the bolt and swung the door wide. The bear-dog sat back and waited, a mass of matted black hair hanging from its broad chest. It had feet the size of horse hooves.

"Come on, then." Annora stood aside. The dog rose, and walked in straight to the rug by the hearth, where it circled and lay down with a deep sigh.

"In the morning, we'll clean her up. She smells a bit now." Annora wrinkled her nose, then smiled at me. "Animals turn up quite often where I am."

"If it eats Morie's kitten I'm not going to be the one to tell her."

Annora smiled again, as if this was the least likely thing she had ever heard, and went off up the stairs, lifting her nightshift in both fists. I watched her for a moment, her long plait swinging as she walked.

"You'll tell me if you're expecting anything else?" I said, as I crossed over to Da's chair. The dog opened one eye as I sat down. I showed it the poker I still gripped, and it sighed again and closed its dark eye.

"Fine," I said. "Just stay right there and don't do anything but sleep." I echoed its sigh. "That's what I wish I could do."

But presently, I did sleep, though I kept the poker across my lap.

CHAPTER 3

I woke to Morie jabbing me in the shoulder, saying, "You should see our dog. She likes me." I tried to turn my head to her, but my neck felt like it had a wire strung through one side. I looked back the other way to find the dog regarding me placidly an inch away from my nose. "Gaah!"

"You'll scare her!" Morie shook her finger at me.

"That's likely." The dog hadn't moved, though I had lurched up and wrenched my neck all the worse.

Annora put a steaming mug in my hand. "Virda hasn't come yet. Is there anything I should start besides breakfast? What do you like?"

"Oat gruel!" sang Morie. "With honey, please."

"Anything." I took a pull on the brew. "I'll milk and feed. Morie can gather eggs."

"You come too." Morie patted the broad black head, and the dog thumped its tail on the floor.

"Morie, some dogs chase chickens. You can take Murr." I stretched my shoulders. Tonight I'd sleep in a bed.

"And Annora," Morie assured me. "She wants to get the eggs too."

"I've no doubt."

"And Virda," Morie prattled happily as she went off to get her boots by the back door.

"Ask Virda if she wants a dog," I said, eyeing the massive shaggy thing. It seemed to look at me with gentle reproach. "Only she is a widow alone, after all."

###

When I carried the milk back to the house, I found Virda and Annora exploring the kitchen garden, and Morie teasing Murr with a strand of twine on the back stoop. The dog sat with dignity next to the steps, ignoring the kitten's occasional scrambles across her paws.

"Her name is Wieser," Morie told me confidently.

"What, she told you? Now you can talk to animals, too?"

Morie nodded, bouncing her dark curls. "Like Annora."

"Well, Wieser, you need to come over to the pump and get a wash to cut the smell. Morie, go get a comb in the barn. You can get some of Wieser's snarls out." I went in the kitchen for a sliver of soap, and to set the milk bucket next to Morie's basket of eggs. Wieser rose when I stepped back out and followed me to the pump without prompting.

She had to have been on her own for some time judging from the look of her coat, which hung clotted with mud and matted around burrs and twigs. She was not thin, however, and stood patiently while we sluiced her with cold water and dragged at her fur with the comb. Annora came over, too, and worked at the tangles. Some we had to cut away, but most Annora teased out with slim fingers. Wieser shook herself when we finally stepped back, and the sun gleamed on her curly black coat.

Next I packed up torches, lanterns and oil in the barn instead of packing foodstuffs, since everyone else gathered in the kitchen and larder after Wieser's bath. An axe and shovel were the largest items, so I had to start strapping everything onto Dink, our mule. I had a leather pack stuffed full, and figured I could carry no more than one pack at a time without raising questions. I had many trips up into the hills ahead of me, if I was to stock three caves with a week's provisions. I started a list of what I took, figuring it would soon challenge memory to recall what I placed where. Dink pulled wisps from his hay net. I was writing an inventory of the first pack when I heard a sound behind me, a soft cough.

I jumped and spun about as though doing something guilt-worthy, and found Annora holding out a paper-wrapped packet and a water jug.

"Some food. You're going up to the high pasture? Virda said you and Wils have brought all the animals down. Maybe you want to take Wieser with you?"

I almost said "Why?", but realized she meant since I didn't have Wils. No doubt she didn't know I'd been doing it alone all summer while Wils courted her. Wieser herself appeared at Annora's side just on cue.

"I'll go by myself as I generally do—thanks though. Lots of stockmen use dogs, I'm surprised a calm one like Wieser isn't working a herd somewhere. Although, black dogs scare the stock, you need a dog with some white on it, but not all white or the herd won't pay it any mind." To my ears, I sounded just as idiotic as Wils had become.

"She's come to us now, to stay," Annora said. "Judian, how will we get news of your da and Wils? Should we expect they will send word where they are? Should we go back to the town to see if we can find out … anything?"

"We can rely on Virda, she knows all the news and gossip anyone can hope to learn. She's down to the village at least every few days for this and that, though not all the way to the harbour town. There's often merchant traffic coming through there. She'll be sure to nose out any developments recounted. And she'll carry every tale she can back up here to us, be certain."

"Have they gone to war? Or just to find out what's happening, as Fenn said?"

I raised my shoulders. "I wish I could say."

"So," she brushed straw off her skirt, "do you come back for supper? We'll wait for you, if you will be back by dark."

"Yes, I'll be back by nightfall. Have Virda stay until I come down, and I'll carry her home in the small cart. Ahh … she'll mother you ragged if you let her." I did feel I should warn her.

I got a sunny smile in response. "I quite like her. She's been nothing but kind. She thought a lot of your mother." She paused to look about her. "I do know how to muck out stalls, if that needs doing."

I nodded toward the pitchfork and stuffed the list paper in my pocket. I had to hold the food packet after tying Dink's pack shut, for I left no room in it. "It seems there's enough food here for both Wieser and me," I said, hefting the packet. "So you'd better come with, dog. Let's go." I took a walking staff from next to the door. "We'll be back. Don't let Morie worry you to a frazzle."

Annora waved as I led the way upslope and Wieser followed, placidly padding alongside Dink.

I went to the closest cave first, not far from the upper meadow. I figured we needed one we could reach quickly from the house. Wils—when he used to work—and I were often up in the meadow with the goats and our few sheep, keeping watch over them while they looked for ways to die. Our shelter there, truly more of a hut, would not do for a hiding place. But the cave he and I had explored could not be seen easily, back in the trees and boulders on the north side of the meadow. I led Dink to the entrance, and tied him while I pulled the pack from his back. Then I led him back to the meadow and tied him near the stream so he could drink. Wieser felt compelled, for whatever dog reason she had, to splash in the pool and get soaked and sloppy while getting her own drink and then shaking all over me. "How many baths a day are you used to?" I asked while I wiped my eyes.

I placed everything deep inside the cave and up on a ledge as high as I could reach. I thought about digging the trench for the fire. Wouldn't it be better to do that after I had hauled everything we needed to all the caves? I remembered a tin trunk at home, and thought that would help keep mice out of the food I brought up. I had heard of folk who dug deep holes to hide clay pots filled with food, before disguising the trap doors above. How deep could I dig in the cave floor before I hit stone? I think the folk that did that must have lived in the plains, where the grass-covered soil runs deep, instead of the mountains. Up here, the bones of the earth rest closer to the surface.

I knelt at the back wall and scratched the symbol for the kavsprit there with my knife. The wise always leave deep-earth creatures some offering to thank them for allowing folk to share their dark places, so they make no mischief. I put some pine nuts and wildflower seeds in a palm-sized linen pouch beneath the sign, and water in a thimble of clay. Both would be empty when I returned, but I didn't expect to see the creatures themselves. Few folk ever had. They kept hidden whenever men came about, and dwelled ever with no light at all.

Next I took the axe out to the trees and gathered and chopped dry wood to keep at the back behind a rock, so a firewood stash couldn't be seen from the mouth of the cave. I would also have to bring some pots or jugs to store additional water.

"What would you suggest?" I asked Wieser. "Maybe you could be fitted with panniers like the dogs in Da's one book." Wieser had a broad back, and was surely strong. Really, not a bad idea to have her haul with me. I shared the hard-cooked eggs, bread and cheese Annora had sent, since none of it would keep in the cave.

"Blankets," I said to Wieser, because back inside just a short way the air grew damp and chill. I knew it would always stay the same within, whether hot outside or bitter cold. A draft wafted from deeper in, but the passage soon narrowed so much there was no way to go further. Wils and I had tried to explore more last spring, but were blocked by crowding, dark rock. Likely there was a whole network through the mountain, all interconnected. Usually I liked to imagine things such as that, but just then the thought made me glad for Wieser's sturdy presence.

I left the water jug at the back of the cave, refilled from the stream, and strapped the empty pack onto Dink. I felt I had done a good day's work but still had plans and lists coiling and flexing in my mind all the way down to home.

When Wieser, Dink and I emerged from the meadow trail, smoke curled from the kitchen chimney, and gold evening light touched the stone walls. *It's a good house,* I thought. Rambling and large enough to have quiet places to be alone and good rooms for all of us together to eat and read by the fire. I felt a rush of missing Da and Wils and wanting war to stay far away from our house and lands. I put Dink away and readied the little cart, but found the evening barn chores already done, with the horses pulling at their hay nets and the water trough full. Wieser and I came to the back door, where I heard Annora singing, in a clear rich voice that put me in mind of my mum singing to us when we were small.

Wieser wanted to go in, probably because something smelled delicious in the kitchen, but I stood for a bit and listened, my heart beating in time to her music.

CHAPTER 4

I worked around the regular chores to find time to carry my packets up to the caves. Of an evening, after Morie and Annora went up to bed, I crept around the house gathering lamp oil and dried meat and fruit and all such like items. Annora sometimes stood and puzzled at a shelf which had become less laden from my dark-of-night raiding, but she did not ask any questions.

She sewed smocks and leggings for Morie, and taught her to whipstitch the edges of a felted vest. I came in one evening to find her working on a soft leather vest for me. Generally, I got Wils's old clothing—cut down if I looked to trip over it or snag it on fenceposts. I'm not sure I ever had anything made for me before, being the second son. I wondered at it, soft and supple, made with two wool-lined pockets for hand warming.

"How did you learn to make such a thing?" I asked her. I could have been more polite, but she smiled wide for she could see I liked it well.

"It was easy to work up, such soft leather. Is it goatskin? I've used deerskin before. My gran taught me simple leatherwork. I can even make boots, just light ones, not like soldiers' boots. Good for walking in the woods."

Which she surmised my absences to be? "That would be useful. Is there leather enough?"

Annora nodded, firelight glinting on her hair, and bent to her work. Morie teased Murr with a bit of yarn, and scolded when he went for the finger that twitched it instead of the end of the tuft. He rolled on his back with claws up-stretched, purring so loud I could hear him over the pop and crackle of the fire.

Da taught me how to read by the fire of an evening, my eyes following as he moved his long, strong finger along a line of letters until I could make sound and sense out of the words. We owned any number of books. I loved them all, and balanced favorite ones on my lap to read aloud to Da when I had learned enough to be fluent. Morie had been read to, but was not yet learning to read herself when Da and Wils left us. Annora used paper and ink to make little books for her, and drew the pictures of the animals and flower sprites she wrote about. Morie was enchanted, as if she hadn't already thought the sun rose for nobody but Annora.

Morie read her books to Murr and Wieser, and she tried to read them to me. One story told about rabbits dancing in the moonlight. Morie assured me Annora had made the meadow rabbits dance, on a night with an early moonrise. And perhaps Annora could make rabbits dance. She proved able to milk Noda, our ill-tempered nanny, without the useless thing stepping in a full bucket or sneaking in a kick. Which I had never been able to do in all my years of chores.

Annora made a doll for Morie—a poppet stuffed with lamb's wool and dressed in a miniature smock like Morie's own. It seemed to be bound to Morie with invisible twine, and collected eggs with her every morning.

"What's her name, then?" I asked wearily, sitting down to a supper of lentils and bread. Up and down the trail every day was wearing on me.

"Her name is Iggle. She likes her name," crooned Morie. "Judian, when are Da and Wils coming home? Iggle is missing them."

"Yeah, I can tell. What if I tell her as soon as somebody tells me." I stared into my bowl for a bit. "I miss them, too."

"Oh, me too," breathed Annora. But still she didn't cry. Nor did she look up from the needlework in her hands.

###

As the weather grew colder, folk began to bring animals up to Annora on the mountain, since she did not dwell at the village edge any longer. I often brought Dink to the barn on my return from the high country and found somebody's milk cow with a caked udder being tended by Annora in a lantern's glow, or an injured hawk with a bandaged wing. She used some of the garden herbs I hadn't known the proper use of to concoct her broths and tisanes. Many plants hung in the kitchen rafters, drying in bunches for the first time since my mum had gathered them.

It was one such cool evening when the smith's wife came to our door. Annora and I trooped out to her little cart, where her son of about eight years old sat holding the reins and looking sullen.

"I don't know what to do," said the wife, loosening her shawl from about her head and shoulders. "Bar's gone off with the men folk to war, and it's just me and the little ones trying to keep things going at the forge. Ticker here took it in his head to go hunting and you see what's come of it. We can't have any more bad luck!" She drew a square of canvas away from the cart bed, uncovering a dead vixen with swollen teats, an arrow wound in her chest. Ticker hung his head lower still.

"You've found her litter, though?" Annora pointed at a basket I hadn't noted, tucked up under the cart seat. This brought a little spark to Ticker, who hurried to take the basket up and proffer it to Annora as he climbed to the ground.

"I had to look for the den a long time. I looked and looked before I found it. I didn't mean to kill a mother fox. I shot her before I realized. I wouldn't have taken her if I had known!" He shot a look at his glowering mother.

"It is strange," Annora said kindly as she knelt in front of the

29

boy. "The vixen was ill-favored, bearing so far out of her season. This should be a spring litter. You wouldn't expect to find her with young kits now." She lifted the woven lid and looked at the tangle of small fuzzy bodies.

"Can you take them to foster?" asked the wife. "We can't afford the bad luck, killing a mother. You know how that follows a person. Idiot child!"

Annora likely would have taken the kits in any case, but faced with the distress of both the hunter and his mother, I stepped forward and took the basket.

"We'll see to them as best we can," I said. "They're very young," I added doubtfully. The basket was hardly heavier than if packed with feathers.

"I'll find a wet-nurse for them," Annora confirmed. And in fact, I expect the mother and son had not traveled back to the village forge, by the time Annora had the kits tucked up with Wieser in the barn, in a wooden box lined with fresh straw.

"She hasn't any milk," I pointed out.

"She will by morning," replied Annora, holding a bowl of some kind of milky-colored herb sap for Wieser to drink.

"Will she be tied to home, then?" I had gotten used to her company.

"I'll find a vixen, so they don't grow up not knowing their proper ways. Here, we need to keep it dark for them now, like the den." She took up the lantern as Wieser began to lick the nearest kit, which wriggled and squeaked. I counted six altogether, and sent up a prayer to the gods that the ill-luck of the smithy's wife and son would not be visited on us instead. It *was* strange, the vixen bearing so late in the year.

When we returned to the front steps, we found the little vixen's body, still in its pitiful square of canvas, laid on the bottom step.

"They do want it all to be far from their own door, don't they?" Annora said, with the first touch of annoyance I had heard in her voice since she came to the mountain.

"I'll bury her. The smell of blood will make the stock restless. I'll go get the shovel and carry her over beyond the apple trees."

"Do you want help?"

"No, no need."

When I returned to stow the shovel, I saw Annora's silhouette in the moonlight, standing at the edge of the larch grove with her arms outstretched. I could hear her humming softly but could not make out if she sang words.

Three days later, a sleek red vixen was curled up with the kits when I went into the barn for morning chores, and Wieser was sitting by Dink's stall. I put my head out the door and called to Annora as she passed by with the full egg basket. "Is this the fox that was sitting out here the night of your wedding dinner?"

"That was a dog fox. Not much good for nursing kits. I called this one from farther away, though she's been that one's mate before," she said as she walked on through the dewy grass.

"Yah, of course," I muttered, taking up the pitchfork. "Probably brought her bloodstock certificate all written out. Chapel apostate probably signed the paperwork for the mating. Matter of record. You could look it up." I kept grumbling while I worked, but the foster-mother did not stir from her charges, and Wieser waited patiently for me to get Dink ready for our journey to the caves.

###

Some three weeks later, on a drizzly, grey afternoon I saw the soldiers as I rounded the east ridge on my way down from the nearest cave. Not Da, but a big man wearing a bluegrey Mercedian officer's tunic, mounted on a bay horse, followed by six soldiers on foot who wore green tunics. They would come to the house on the road they were on, and before I could get there and chivvy everyone up to the cave, too. Wieser walked with me as usual. "I wish I could talk to you like Annora," I said to her. She gave me the look of exaggerated patience she saved just for me. "Run down to the house and warn them, then!"

She shot off instantly, out of sight down the path and back into the trees. I knew what Annora and Morie would be doing at home. Sitting in their small clothes drying their hair before the fire, because today was the day Annora laundered clothes and washed herself and Morie—she went through these ablutions every week without fail, and I had learned when to come home to avoid catching them at it.

I fairly flew down the path, for I had not brought the mule and wasn't laden on the way down the mountain. Rain-slicked rocks sent me sprawling twice, scrambling and snatching my way back to my feet. Chest bursting, I careered into the back garden and swatted open the gate. Would they all be murdered? Should I find some sort of weapon? Blast all, why had Da and Wils gone off and left us up here like orphan cubs in a den?

Wieser came bounding around the corner of the house. She looked back over her shoulder, then looked pointedly at me. So I followed her around the stone corner, to find Annora standing on the porch with Morie peeking from behind her skirts. The big man stood in the yard holding his horse's reins, with his men ranged behind him.

All eyes shifted to me. "Come, Wieser," I said, still gasping a bit. I mounted the steps to stand by Annora, and felt Morie grasp the back of my trouser leg. Wieser stood beside me. Head lowered, she lifted her lips to bare white teeth and gave a low rumble.

"Yet more children!" the officer exclaimed. "How many does Fenn Lebannen have?"

"Get behind me," Annora said softly.

"No," I said back.

"I've come up here to speak to Paladin Lebannen. I thought he had sons, grown ones by now." He scratched his forehead with a gloved hand and looked up at us. "We need to look to my mount and put my men up for tonight. Is your da expected by dark, then?"

I wasn't going to answer that, and it seemed Annora had not

made free with information, either. Why didn't he know where Da was, if this soldier was on our side? "Who are you?" I asked.

He sketched the fist-to-heart salute of our military, with a corner of his mouth twisted up. "I am Fieldmaster Behring. These are my men, and I've been sent to speak with your father, boy. I served with him before."

"You might meet him coming from the harbour town road," I suggested, this being my first thought of getting them far away from in front of our house.

"We came up on the coast road and saw no one." The men standing behind him were large to my eyes, too, though younger and not so hard-looking as the officer. He looked like a dark hawk, with a sharp nose and big yellow teeth. I saw their clothes looked as mud-flecked and spattered as my own, and the young foot soldiers sagged with fatigue. The fieldmaster's bay hung its head in the drizzle.

The officer sighed and looked over our heads at the mountain. "We'll stay here tonight. It won't do to go down the trail in the dark. What's your name, Donatta?" he said to Annora, as proper to address a maiden.

"I'm Donah Annora Lebannen," she said, correcting him about her status. "These are my husband's brother and sister, Judian and Morie."

He inclined his head. "Judian. Take my horse in out of the chill, if you would. He needs fed and his feet seen to."

"Don't your men do that?"

"They'll be getting ready to be fed themselves. Whatever Donah Lebannen can pull out of the larder for us." His smile might have been meant to be friendly, but I would not be sent apart from Annora and Morie. Not when it was my job to protect them. Soldiers are always hungry, Da had said. And not just for food … they might be our troops but still, they were soldiers.

I made no move. Actually, I couldn't, as Morie had such tight grip on the back of my leg. "You'll find an empty stall, and hay and grain," I nodded toward the barn. "Set your men to making themselves comfortable in the stable loft and I'll bring food out. You see the water well, just there. And there's a vixen and her litter with a den dug in the southwest corner of the barn. They won't bother you."

"Ah, son. We'll want to be by the fire on a damp, cold night like this promises to be. Your da will find us inside when he comes. I know he'll expect to." And I saw he wasn't fooled about Da being on his way home tonight. Whatever I did that showed I had realized this, Wieser's growl resumed and louder, and the hair on her back rose. When the fieldmaster held out his reins to me, Wieser snarled and stepped from my side to stand in front of us.

"Call it off." Fieldmaster Behring showed no fear of her, but the men drew back and his horse stamped a hind foot. "Do it now, boy."

Well, what now? Wieser couldn't take on seven soldiers—one of them would put a quarrel or a knife in her. I couldn't get the girls out of here and up to the cave with the lot of them in the house staring at us. Dark was coming.

"I can have some soup ready for your men," Annora said suddenly. "There won't be room for them all in the house to sleep, but we can accommodate them for a meal. Let them see to your horse, it needs out of the weather and fed a hot mash. The men will sleep warm enough in the loft straw, we've blankets if they don't. You'll come in, please, to wait for Donar Lebannen and my husband and the rest."

"And the rest," he repeated. He didn't look as though he believed that, but I found it a good try. I laid a hand on Wieser's head. She licked her lips and sat, but never took her eyes from the fieldmaster and the hand he held outstretched toward me.

He moved without looking behind him, and swung his gloved hand aside to his men. One of them stepped up and took the reins. He led the horse toward the stable; the rest of the men followed. Fieldmaster Behring pulled off his gloves as he mounted the steps.

He reached past us to push open the door, then stood back to let Annora go first.

I have to get rid of them, I thought, as I went through the door with Wieser at my side and Morie still stuck like a burr to the back of my knee.

CHAPTER 5

I indicated a chair by the fire—not Da's chair—for the officer. I detached Morie gently and sent her following after Annora, and took Da's chair with Wieser sitting at my feet. Behring and I surveyed each other while Annora set about clanking and chopping in the kitchen.

He leaned forward to say, "You see, son—" when Annora brought a kettle to hang over the fire, stepping between us. Just as well, as my back went up instantly when he spoke.

I was not his son.

"Judian, can you bring more wood?" she asked, turning from the hearth to face me, her back to him. She fixed me with some kind of meaningful look, but I wasn't sure what she wanted.

I saw she had the kettle full of vegetables to boil, which I expected she planned to add to our supper of beans and smoked meat that simmered over the coals. Annora always made us a flavorful meal out of bits of meat and herbs with a rich bean broth, but even with the addition of her kettle of chopped parsnips, onions and carrots, I couldn't see it feeding so many.

"Please, let my men bring your wood, Donah." Behring said with a broad smile, and continued, "I can have them split more for you, to compensate for their meal."

"There's no need," I said. I chopped all the wood we used. The officer had already risen to go call out to his men, though, so

Annora and I seized the moment to whisper to each other.

"We have to think of a way to get rid of them," I murmured.

Annora nodded and reached to stir the beans, saying softly, "If we can just get them all out in the barn and off down the road at dawn, that's the best we can hope."

"If only they knew something about Da and Wils. I think it's strange, our own soldiers coming to look for him at home—"

Behring returned to the hearth then, so we could say no more.

Thus, shortly the lot of them settled before our blazing fire, wet woolens stinking and steaming on their backs, while Annora moved about with bowls and spoons and mugs of brew and the soup bubbled busily in the biggest kettle we had.

I saw the young soldiers watch Annora like dogs watch meat as it turns on a spit; their eyes followed her everywhere. When she bent to stir the pot, one nudged another and said something that caused the fellow to snigger. The fieldmaster stood behind the two of them sipping his hot drink, and shoved the speaker in the back with his knee. The man slopped brew in his lap and studied his cup, still smirking.

I had to get shed of them.

"That really smells grand, Donah," said one who was polite at least. He accepted a slab of hearth-loaf and butter from her.

Morie huddled by the table with a strangle hold on Murr and Iggle, both. I felt my brain churning, but I couldn't form a reasonable thought about getting them gone from here. All I could think was, their presence would bring more soldiers—maybe even an encampment in our orchard and troops from all over coming here to stage their campaign. And then the enemy would come and fight the war on our doorstep. The heat from our built up fire made me sweat and feel queasy, or maybe it came from feeling frantic but being unable to *do* anything.

"Judian, would you get more bread cut?" Annora asked.

They certainly eat a great lot, I thought as I stood and abruptly swayed on my feet, feeling dizzy.

"Are you all right? Judian?" Annora stepped toward me, the ladle in her hand dripping soup that the fellow she was serving tried to catch in his bowl by leaning after her.

"I need some air," I said as I made for the back door. On the back stoop, breathing cool air as deep as I could, I heard the clink of spoons on bowls and soft voices. The fieldmaster seeing to the needs of his men. And it came to me: The officer would want to get his men away from contagion. Of course he would. So, I began to retch loudly. I carried on a bit, then decided someone might check, and stuck a finger down my throat to make something actually come up. Disgusting. Further, I hadn't eaten since some dried fruit and boiled egg up at the cave. Not much to show, but at least I had been demonstrably sick.

I pushed open the door just as Annora came to check on me. "Judian, what—"

I stumbled a little walking over to the pallet by the fire. This was in fact where Wieser slept, but I collapsed on it heavily. "Oh, give me a blanket. I've got to lie down."

"Are you ill?" fussed Annora, spreading a lap quilt and feeling my forehead with the backs of her cool fingers.

"I'll be all right in a little." I made myself shiver just a bit. A couple of the soldiers were watching, one with a spoon halfway to his mouth. The fieldmaster had sat in Da's chair when I left the room, I noted. He watched me too, but without much interest. I retched again, annoyed.

"Morie, hand me the scrap bowl," Annora called. Morie sidled up with it, and set it in front of my chin.

I lay there and willed Annora to get what I was trying to do. She paced about finishing up meal tasks, and I shivered and coughed now and then. Morie regarded me soberly, but Wieser came to lie down next to me and fell asleep.

"Judian, do you want to hold Iggle?" Morie whispered.

"No, Morie. I do not want to hold a doll."

"Only she makes me feel better."

"That's fine. You hold her. Can you go away?"

She nodded and put her thumb in her mouth. I hadn't seen her do that in a long time.

"What's amiss with you, boy?" The officer stood over me. I grunted. Annora knelt beside me with a steaming mug of herbs.

"Do try a little," she coaxed.

I moaned and turned my head away. "I can't now." *Please, Annora. Understand. Come on.*

"Oh!" One hand flew to her lips. "Oh, I hope it's not River Fever. Oh, no. Why does everything have to happen when the men are away?" *Ah, good girl!* She wrung her hands and looked near tears. She reached for the officer's sleeve. "Did they have Fever in the south?" she asked him urgently.

"We came down the coast from Chartin. We haven't been south of Bale Harbour." He had backed up a step, I was pleased to note.

"It's the wrong time of year—the Fever comes after the spring floods. Oh, but he acts just like it, how it comes over folks so sudden. He was fine! What am I going to do?" She looked down at me in such despair, I hoped she was just acting along. I coughed for effect, and shuddered. I took a certain savage satisfaction in seeing four of the men stand and inch toward the door. I flailed about to get my face closer to the fire to heat my skin, should some one of them want to feel for a fever.

Annora continued to fret. "So many things happening out of their season. The fox's litter. Did you see the pear tree? It's leafing out, and winter is coming." She tucked the quilt about me. "Even the birds are confused. The ones that should be gone south are hanging about, and the winter birds are—"

"Perhaps the boy should be put to bed," the officer suggested as he scrubbed at his chin with his knuckles. "Do you need help to shift him?"

"No. I can manage. You and your men should go and get settled. If it's River Fever ... " She drew the covering aside and

40

bent to help me to my feet.

"As you wish, Donah," he said, turning to the men now standing in a clump by the door. He ushered them out as Annora walked beside me to the room under the stairs. And if only we'd given a thought about where Morie had got to, our ruse would have had them all out of the house and reluctant to have any more to do with us.

CHAPTER 6

S o happy to hear the front door close on the officer and his squad, I almost said, "Yes!" or some such sound of triumph. I coughed instead, but perhaps a bit smugly. When Annora helped me reach the edge of the bed, she put her lips close to my ear and said, "Judian, do you think they'll go tonight for fear of Fever?"

"No, it's dark of the moon even if it wasn't raining. Too dark to head down a steep, unfamiliar road. But they'll be gone at dawn, thinking we have Fever here, and are no good for a site to fortify. Or stage a battle."

"What a blessing that you're clever."

That made me feel warm in the face. "I had just thought of any sort of contagion. You were great to think of River Fever. That scares everyone witless."

"I've seen it. I lived in the South with my family before I came to Uncle Werrel and Aunt Lorneh's. The Fever takes many folk every spring."

I nodded, and lay on the bed quilt, playing my part if anyone cared to look. We kept our voices low, still wary.

"Call Wieser in and tell her to keep watch. I want to know if any of them step foot out of the barn."

"You can tell her what you want her to do," Annora said with a smile.

"You're the one who can talk to animals," I said.

"Anyone can talk to them. Can you hear what the animals answer back—that's the difference." She walked to the bedroom door, and swung it open to admit Wieser, who waited just outside.

"And does she know what I want her to do, having listened at the keyhole?" I asked.

Wieser looked from one to the other of us, wagged her tail, and set out toward the front door. Annora went to open it for her.

"I'd say so," I answered myself, then sat up to pull off my boots.

Annora said she would get a candle for my bedside, but she reappeared at the bedroom door without one just as Wieser gave her signature thump on the front door. "Where's Morie?" Annora said. "She's not by the fire and Murr is in his basket."

I leapt to my feet and in three strides, crossed to yank the front door open. Wieser paced on the porch, panting, agitated. "Where's Morie?" I asked her, thinking about earlier—telling Morie to go away while I acted ill by the fire. Wieser whined.

"Take me to Morie," I said, as Annora shoved my boots into my hand.

I pulled them on, hopping to keep balance, and followed Wieser out into the drizzle. She led me across the yard to the washhouse. Annora followed close behind with a lantern held aloft.

Under the eaves of the washhouse, we found Fieldmaster Behring seated on the stump chair kept there, with Morie on his knee. She held Iggle up to dance on her lap while she told him earnestly all about Da and Wils and the soldiers they went away with, and how "—we've been waiting and waiting and we haven't seen them in such a long time." I wiped a wet hand over my face, and felt as if a swallowed stone dropped to the pit of my stomach as the officer looked up and met my gaze.

"Now we'll go in to sit by the fire and talk," he said. And what else was there to do?

The officer carried Morie back up the porch steps and into the house, trailed by Wieser, Annora and me. I was sure my thoughts were the blackest of us all. Behring handed Morie off to Annora, telling her to dry her and put her to bed. I jerked out a chair at the scrubbed kitchen table and indicated the officer should sit in it, while I took the one opposite.

Annora returned to find us staring at one another like a pair of tom cats, though neither of us had a tail to twitch.

"That's low," I said, "using a little child—"

"Feeling better, are you?" he asked dryly.

"No. In fact, I feel worse, just now."

"I learned long ago how observant a child can be. No one thinks to ask them what they know."

"She's four years old! She doesn't understand what's going on!" I protested.

"Neither do you," he said, scowling. "But I'm about to tell you, as you are in danger here."

"How can you think I don't know that?"

Annora drew a chair to sit by my side. "What can you tell us? We are in desperate need of news."

"As am I," he sighed.

"Yes clearly, if you've come here to speak to a man who is months-gone to the western borderlands." Annora laid a hand on my arm, and she was right. I had to get myself reined in; my flash of anger aided us in no way at all.

His lips twisted in a grimace. "Our military is some time out of the business of war, and more suited to rendering help in times of natural disaster. We are more constabulary than warriors, these days. Rounding up brigands, sand bagging against rising floodwaters—such are our tasks nowadays. Our ranks are depleted, thus the conscription drive the little one described. Communication is not what it should be."

I grunted agreement with that.

He continued, "If Fenn Lebannen marched with them to see

the marshal at the border fort, word was not sent to us farther up the coast. Now, was this because he did not arrive, or because our couriers have not spread the necessary messages to all troops? We have heard nothing from the western border since word that Keltanese troops were gathering in preparation for attack."

"I'm feeling worse all the time," I said.

He laid his right hand palm down on the table. "This is Merced, and this, where you live near the northwest border." He indicated the top knuckle on his first finger. He laid the other hand alongside the first, thumbs butted together. "Here is the neighboring country of Keltane, landlocked for most of its breadth with only steep cliffs where it comes to the sea, well to the north of Merced. Long have their sovereigns coveted our deep water harbour, so that their trade need not be transported through the mountain passes and delayed so by treaties and letters of passage permit."

"Has it not been so for many years?" Annora said, looking down at his hands.

"Indeed, Donah. Yet the word we have received tells that Keltane moves against us, their king claims it is their right and destiny to take our country as part of their own. We will fight to avoid conquest and occupation."

He sat silent for a moment, looking at his own hands. Then, "Trade goes through the western pass, in large part. If that way of attack is met by our massed troops, such as we can muster, then lesser passes will be used by our enemy. And you," here he lifted his first finger on his right hand, where he had said we lived, "are in the path of that line of attack, with the northwest pass in the mountains above you."

Would Da have left us here if that was the likeliest way of the coming battle? I wondered. He had told me how to prepare, though, and counted on me to keep Annora and Morie safe.

"What did you want with Da?" I asked.

"In fact, I was sent to ask him for his insight, and to request he accompany my troops to the west to learn what transpires there. As paladin, he has experience we sorely need. I must know what he told you, boy, and whether his plan was to send your brother back with news for you." Behring set his palms together at his chin and rested his elbows on the table, waiting.

Annora gave a soft moan. Thinking what it meant that we had seen nothing of Wils's return with any message? In any case, that was what came to my mind.

I made my decision. "Da told me he went to find out from the marshal what was happening to the west. He did not say why he brought Wils along, but I thought it was to fight if war was what they found. He told me to prepare places to go to ground near here, if it came to that. If fighting came near to home. But I don't think he believed it so likely, since the northwest pass is the highest. It is the first to snow in, and the last to clear in the spring."

"Yet we have such unseasonable weather," the officer mused. "It suggests the uncanny. When are the first snows usually come?"

"Most years, a month past. Or more."

"And you mentioned, Donah, so many occurrences out of season. Aside from River Fever." This remark caused me to grimace. "A boy, and a woman and child are not safe here. You must pack only the barest necessities and head for the coast. Else how will Fenn Lebannen greet me when I find him, if I must tell him I left his family in harm's way?"

"How can we leave? We have stock and work to do—"

"Who will care for your stock when you are gone to ground?" he countered. "Boy, you cannot hide from an army in some shepherd's hut. If the attack should come from over the mountains; the safest place for you is away down to the sea."

He'll be leaving in the morning, anyway, I thought. If enemy soldiers were going to come pouring over the pass, at least it would not happen in the dark tonight. He still had his task of finding Da; he and his men were not the ones who would set up an encampment here. "Will our army send troops here, to block an attack over the pass?" I asked.

"I cannot say with any certainty, but I would suppose that some fortification will be thought wise, if there are enough men to spare. It falls to others in our army to make such decisions. And to implement them."

"Please," Annora burst out. "Do you at least know if fighting has started west? Could my husband have been hurt? Or … or killed?"

"Donah, I can only say we have not been told of their troops crossing the border. Not yet. Keep him in your prayers."

"Always," she whispered. But I'm sure she heard, as I did, that Behring didn't say he knew the fighting had not started, he said he had not been *told* that it had.

"Give us the night to think on our plan," I said. "If we must move, we will."

He seemed to accept this as evidence he had persuaded us, and stood to leave for the stable. "I would that I could offer to guard your journey. My orders point another way. I have always thought high of your father, boy, and wish I could do him that favor." He sketched the hand-to-heart salute, and turned to go through the front door into a gust of cold damp.

"Stop calling me boy," I said to the closed door. And to Annora, "Go on up to bed. I'll make sure Wieser is put on watch, and we'll talk about this more at dawn. Send them off with cheese and apples, not a hot meal, eh?"

"I know I fed them over well," Annora said. "Only I hoped someone, somewhere might be doing the same for Wils, is all."

CHAPTER 7

I endured a restless night, though Wieser sounded no alarm. As I rolled over yet again, I mulled my options. Da would not have left us here if he thought the pass was a threat to our safe havens out of war's way at the caves. True, Da had not been here to see the past months' curious happenings. Neither had Behring, he just noted the snows were overdue. Further, the officer had chased up here to talk to a man long gone to the west border. His information was cold hash indeed, to my mind. I would not rely on it.

At first suggestion of light, I met Annora at the kitchen garden gate, each of us setting about our morning tasks as customary. In no longer than it took to cross the yard together, I told her about the caves and supplies, that I wanted to bring Virda up with us, and that I wanted the soldiers to think we were getting ready this morning to head to the coast as directed. "I trust what Da told me to do for you and Morie, more than I trust any other," I said.

"I agree," she said at once. "What shall we do to send them off with the impression we make ready to travel?"

"You get their food ready, then pack food for us where they will see you setting it out. Gather some clothes for yourself and Morie, as well. I'll let the goats into the hayfield, and decide what to do with the chickens, all that." I put out my hand to touch her arm as she turned away, and said when she turned back to me, "I cannot offer to bring your aunt and uncle and cousins with us. I'm sorry. I don't think we can even get word to them of what's happening today."

"The last thought they gave to me was when I went out their front gate, Judian. This is my family now."

She gave me a nod and set off to collect eggs. I pulled the cover off the wagon and let down the latched back as though I prepared to load. Soldiers began to yawn and stretch their way out the barn door, on the way to wash up at the pump. As they seemed unsurprised to see me up and about, I supposed the officer had told them not to fear River Fever would spread to them from me. Several nodded to me, and I returned the wordless greeting. *You'll soon be on your way*, I thought, *and happy I am to see the back of you.*

We passed an uncomfortable hour while they made ready to set out. The polite soldier thanked Annora again for feeding him and his fellows, as if she had been playing hostess. But perhaps she thought again of Wils having to rely on strangers' kindness somewhere, so she sent a distracted smile in his direction while gathering our cloaks and woolens. He stared after her too long as she walked away. *Better for me if she was not so pretty, she attracts too much regard*, I thought sourly.

I found the lidded basket used for the fox kits on their journey to us, and gave it to Morie as transport for Murr.

"Where are we going?" she asked, yawning hugely. "Murr won't like being in a basket for long."

"He'll take a lot of naps," I told her. "This way he won't get lost."

"Are we going to find Da and Wils with the soldier man?"

"No. Don't ask so many questions, or you'll use up all your allotted talking for the day before the sun even rises all the way." I certainly wasn't going to tell her anything she could pass on to her soldier man friend.

Loath to admit she did not know what a talking allotment

50

might be, or that she had one, she dubiously put the basket over her arm and went to look for Murr.

This must be said for Officer Behring: he organized his men and mounted his horse in quick order. They headed down the steep stony path to the road before the morning mist began to clear. The last thing he said to us was, "Do not linger. Make your start as soon as ever you can!" He raised a hand to us and pulled his horse's head around to the road, not waiting for an answer.

My next tasks—turn the mule, horses and goats out, and shoo the chickens into the garden where they could forage in our absence. Annora gathered the remaining cheese and bread to bring with us. I decided to take us to the nearest cave, which was the farthest from the pass route but closest to a cliff that overlooked it. Once I settled Annora and Morie there, I would return for Virda and we would all be tucked up by nightfall.

"I don't want to walk, I want to ride in the wagon," Morie said. Her lower lip pushed out.

"I can't be saving your life all the time without you helping along a little," I groused, picking her up to carry. Annora handed her Iggle, newly dressed in a small cloak to match Morie's own. This so delighted Morie that she let me put her atop my shoulders and set off up the trail, with Annora toting Murr in his basket and Wieser walking alongside. I looked over for a last glimpse of home before we lost sight entering the trees, and said a prayer we would find it as we left it, on our return.

Morie found the cave an adventure, and set her bedroll and candle on a rock shelf, with a scrap of wool spread next to her for Iggle. Murr stalked shadows and pounced on dust motes at our feet while I showed Annora where I stowed our supplies. She astonished me by hugging me of a sudden and saying, "Oh, Judian, you are a wonder!" I left as quick as I could to go fetch Virda.

I left Wieser on guard at the cave, so I had no one to hear me practice what I would say to Virda, not wanting to walk down the path talking to myself. Talking to a dog was perhaps no better, if I had met anyone, but I was alone the whole way. Our soldiers were long gone, and none of the enemy troops marched on the trail, yet.

I found Virda washing clothes, which I hoped were not the clothes she would want to bring. To her credit, she listened to my hurried tale of soldiers and the threat of the northwest pass, nodded once and made ready to travel. Her geese and goats I turned out as I had our stock. "As long as nothing happens, I'll come down to check things at your place and ours, from time to time. Mayhaps we'll move your animals up by ours to make it easier to keep track of them," I told her as she bustled about. She set her wet clothes over the line in a trice, and put out the hearth fire.

"I'll just bring a tin with some herbs to brew," she said, "as it does my bones good of an evening."

"We can bring your kettle, too," I offered, because I had forgotten to think of one.

We set off up the hill, and though she puffed a little as we climbed, she never complained. And not once did she call me poor lamb. I could not help but feel I was making the right choice, in taking us all to the cave.

CHAPTER 8

W e passed the time until the moon waxed full, cooking stealthily once I determined the fire's smoke could not be seen. The cave's draft drew it deeper into the mountain. The earth spirit-folk left us be, and Virda became the one in charge of refilling their water cup and seed bag. Murr might have found some of them a time or two, but his yowl and hiss as he erupted out of the dark corners told me the kavsprit could fend for themselves where he was concerned.

I feared Morie would be frightened living in the cave, but she took to it as if we shared a home of charming comfort. She never complained of the night chill or of having to go out into the woods to tend to herself. Always, Annora or Virda went with her, to keep watch over her and make sure she did not do her necessaries too close to the watershed for the stream we used for water.

I began to feel safe in our haven. Evening was coming on one day, and Annora had taken Morie out to the woods just before I set off to walk the perimeter with Wieser. I heard Virda humming as I left, while she prepared simple food for us in the cave, expecting us back before sunset.

I always walked far enough to see our side of the pass once each day, to be sure no troops advanced on us. I had seen no activity there save for deer and crows, and found no boot prints or shod hoof prints when I ventured closer to the track. This day, I was behind my usual time and did not go close enough to check the path for spoor, but only looked from the high ground. Wieser and I turned to make our way back as the shadows lengthened, and the twilight chill began to gather.

We swung wide around the meadow below the cave entrance, where the stream was met by a freshet in a deep creek bed. We crossed on a downed tree trunk that spanned the banks, and continued through the woods, noting nothing unusual.

It wasn't until Wieser and I turned north again, just coming out of the trees into the meadow, that I saw them. Two soldiers on horseback, in the wine-colored tabards of Keltane. Armed. Wieser and I stopped as one, and faded back into the trees. We were downslope and downwind. That much was good. They were not far from where Annora and Morie might yet be in the woods' edge. That made my heart mount up my throat.

I sank behind a wide rock and nearby tree bole, and spoke softly to Wieser. "Go back across the creek and get to the cave from behind. Keep Virda inside out of sight. I'll find Annora and Morie." She gave me that look of understanding I would never be able to explain to anyone who hadn't seen it, and slipped back the way we had come. She made no sound as she moved. I hoped I could do the same.

I edged around the meadow's verge, keeping to the dappled dimness in the trees. The soldiers rode across the grass toward the stream, and let their horses lower their heads to drink, just where Annora often lay on her belly and convinced fish to leap on the bank to become our supper. I was behind the horsemen now, but with too much open country between me and the path to the cave. If Annora and Morie were still in the woods, their route back to the cave would cross the soldiers' line of sight. My hands were shaking when I rubbed them on my thighs. How to keep us all safe?

The horses lifted their heads, trailing drops from their lips in

54

the slanting light. One made a try for a mouthful of grass but was jerked up short by its rider. No time to browse, because they were scouting?

Why only two men? Where were others, if there was a troop? I faded further back as the two turned toward the northwest pass. When they started across the meadow I doubled back to the side where the girls might be. If only I knew if the two girls were already back at the cave. Their whereabouts were what I should have asked Wieser to find out, I realized too late.

I went deeper into the trees so I could move faster, since the horsemen were taking their time going across the meadow. I reached a downed tree laying in the beginnings of the grass and found Annora crouched behind it, frantic-eyed. Morie was not with her.

"Where?" I whispered, sinking beside her. "Morie?" I said, when she did not answer. Annora pointed to the boulder at the stream's opposite bank. I could just see Morie's brown curls at its crest. "She was sitting in the sun when they came. I had crossed to fill the jar." She gestured at her feet where the water jar lay on its side. "I only had time to signal to her to hide. I've been holding my breath, since I can't see where they've gone."

"Headed to the pass. If we just stay hidden, all will be well."

"No—" Annora seized my arm. "Oh, baby, stay down ...stay down."

Morie had lifted her head to peek over the boulder's top. The men would see her, if they chanced to look back. And as if the gods were distracted and not attending to my fervent prayers, both soldiers swung their mounts about and began to patrol back our way.

I erupted from behind the log with a shout, shoving Annora down with the arm she still grasped. Answering shouts from the men let me know they had seen and heard me, and I hared off into the woods, away from the meadow, stream and cave path. I was already bolting into the trees as they spurred their mounts after me.

They would not be able to ride through the woods—would have to dismount to pursue. Now, if Morie did not run out to kick them in the ankles, I could lead them away.

Annora was clever, she would understand and wait in hiding until she could safely get Morie away to the cave. I had to get the men far into the wood and lose them. I had to plan to make this happen while my lungs threatened to burst. I plunged through the brush and made for the thickest cover. Soon I heard them crashing behind me, calling in Keltanese for me to stop. Now that they were dismounted, where to lead them? I swung back toward the deep creek, up the ridge. When I was out of their line of sight, I shoved a rock over the edge to thump and roll down the bank then splash in the water below. I hoped they would think I had fallen in, and switched direction to cross into deeper woods.

Only briefly fooled, they harried me harder into the tallest trees. They were hampered by swords and heavy leathers, bulky crossbows at their backs, so I could dart faster through the limbs and rocks. I fell, but found my feet again without a pause, and ate up the ground in leaping strides. No arrows flew that I could hear, but they would have been foolish to try to aim true through the growth of forest. My lead lengthened as I drew them away from both the cave and our home place. Soon I could hear they were flagging—slowing.

Then they pursued me no longer. Dark was drawing down, already darker yet in the close trees. I knew my way back to where I wanted to go. I could not but think they did not know the way back to the meadow so well as I.

Gradually I slowed to a walk and risked doubling back, while trying to slow my breath enough to hear their voices. I caught a few snatches of argument from one as he and his mate plucked grab-tights and thorns from sleeves and leggings. They turned back toward the northwest without hesitating. Thus, they showed themselves not entirely lost, as I had hoped them to be. But, giving up the chase was what I had hoped, as well. Both men began to trudge away the direction they had come.

I made no move in the gathering dark. They could be clever enough to wait for me to lead them, showing them the way to my haven. I could wait all night if need be. I could stand the coming hoarfrost, for I wore the woolen shirt and leather jerkin that Annora made for me. I said another prayer, in case the gods had turned their attention my way, that Annora and Morie and Virda were all snug in the back reaches of our cave.

I heard no more from the soldiers, but would not trust that they did not stand in equal silence nearby, waiting for me to start back. The moon had long risen, and I was thinking how worried the others would be getting, when I heard snuffling and twigs snapping behind me in the dark. In these deep woods, such sounds could mean a bear, or mountain cat. I held my stillest yet, and waited with my back pressed to the cold stone boulder.

Nearly I yelped when Wieser thrust her nose in my palm, and set about licking me. I was too weak to speak for a moment. She had been sent to bring me back, I surmised. "So," I said to her as we set out for the cave, "how is it you didn't warn me the soldiers were in the meadow, eh? Your nose should have found them before my eyes." She only wagged her tail in answer.

CHAPTER 9

I t grew dark enough that I had to grasp a handful of Wieser's scruff to avoid falling on the way back to the cave. We found Virda, Annora and Morie huddled together at the back of the sanctuary, all wide eyes in pale faces. The three of them fell on me, all gabbling at once, more than I could stand at the time.

"For sake of sanity, let me sit down!" I managed, and tried to hold Morie away from my legs so I could walk the rest of the way in.

I told my story, and heard from Annora and Morie of sneaking back to the cave after the soldiers pursued me into the forest. Then I endured Virda's scolding me for keeping them waiting on tenterhooks while darkness fell—though both she and Annora agreed I could hardly have done anything else.

"We'll go to the next cave tomorrow, just as soon as there's enough light to see our way. I'll have to go a longer route to keep checking the pass, but these men today seemed to be scouts. More will be on their heels, I reckon." I took a pull on the hot tisane I had been handed, and blessed Virda for thinking to bring it along.

Annora and Virda made ready to go in the quiet dawn, while Wieser and I made sure our route was not strewn with Keltanese soldiers lying in wait. We found no sign among the trees and boulders, and the two from yesterday were not patrolling the

59

meadow when I slipped down to check. In silence, we set out, with Murr in his traveling basket after a brief tussle. A pair of owls called to one another across the ravine we skirted, and knee-deep mist eddied among the pine trunks as we passed. I was not prone to fancy, since much used to walking in the woods and being on my own. But the morning felt eerie, and I kept turning to look behind us, unable to shake the feeling we were watched from the shadows. Wieser seemed unsettled as well, ears pricked and nose working, casting across the trail.

We drew close to the second cave when a mob of crows took wing from the tree tops just before us, cawing and flapping, creating startling noise where all had been so quiet moments before. One broke off from the half-dozen of his fellows, and dived at us. The great glossy black wings beat before Annora's face, and she flung up an arm. I swung at the bird with my walking stick, and I nearly caught Annora across the cheek. She ducked, and the huge bird dropped to the ground at her feet, shaking back its ruffled feathers. It turned its head to look first at her, then at me, cocking its head.

"Is this some message from the wild things for you?" I said, staring down at it.

"What can it want?" Annora said, trembling.

It hopped closer and shook its wings. The others still circled above, calling.

I watched it through narrowed eyes. "I thought hawks were the messengers for the gods. Hawks and owls."

The bird now hopped up and down and made a gargling noise. Annora got down on her knees before it, while Morie hid her face in Virda's skirt.

"Crows always think they know best," Annora said as she stretched out her hand toward it. It lunged at her and stretched its neck to peck at her fingers. I swept the staff across its path as Annora snatched her hand back. Its bright eyes flashed.

Indeed, what did it want? "I want us out of sight until we can get into the cave. All of you go into the brush here." I pointed. "I'll go ahead and see if our messenger is trying to warn us of trouble." Though unsure why this thought came to me, I chose not to stand exposed in the woods staring at the crow's undecipherable expression any longer. When Annora stepped away to part the limbs and push back the foliage for Morie and Virda, the bird rose and settled on a low branch at my left shoulder.

"My plan suits you, does it? Come on then." And it did, gliding from branch to branch as I walked with Wieser, as silent as we could be over the pine needles and twigs. Just as I came to the rise where I could view the cave entrance, the bird dropped at my feet. I took this to mean I must stop, and froze there with Wieser at heel. The crow flapped up to the top of a boulder on my left. I crossed behind the stone and clambered up to overlook the cave.

There, where the trees were spaced farther apart below my vantage point, two mounted Keltanese soldiers watched two more men in long dark cloaks slowly walk towards each other, then away, holding some sort of sticks or branches out in front of them as they paced. It looked to my eyes as if they measured or marked out distances along the ground, conferring every few passes while gesturing at the earth. The mounted men watched the walkers but did not scan the ridge. Or look up at my boulder, thank the gods. What purpose could there be to this ... survey? They faced away from my cave's mouth, concealed amongst grey tumbled stones. The party would have to actively explore to find it there. But, they were too close for us to gain safe entry unnoticed.

The crow hopped closer to peck me on the shoulder. I glared at it in fierce silence, for its heavy beak delivered a sharp blow. I sank back below the top of the boulder, and rummaged in my vest pocket for a bite of bread for our sentinel. For although ill-tempered, it had saved us from walking into threat. I did not offer it from my hand, though. I set it on the granite for the bird to snatch up, which it did at once. It followed as Wieser and I slunk away, and made our way back to the others.

"Two choices," I said when I crouched beside them in the thorny brush. "We can return to the first cave, or go on to the third and highest. I don't know if we can rely on Annora's messenger to keep us forewarned of more men."

"The crow didn't come for me," said Annora.

"No," Virda agreed, "that was for you, Judian. You're so like your mum, you have her gift. I've always thought it would show soon."

She might have been speaking some queer foreign tongue, what she said made so little sense to me. "My mum's gift? Annora's the one gifted with animal ways."

"Oh, your mum knew such magic. She had skills greater than anyone here-abouts. You're coming into it now, is all. The crows came for you. You called them."

"I'd have called a bear to eat the soldiers, not a crow to mystify us all."

I glanced at Morie to find her with Murr's basket planted on her lap, her chin propped on the handle. Her eyes moved from Virda to me and back again.

"You never knew about your mum? I knew right away from the sorts of herbs in her garden—" Annora began.

"Stop. Tell me more later. I'm sure to recall this bit of news. Now, I have to get you somewhere safe." I tried to steady my breath. "We're going to head for the highest cave, and sort things out from there."

Without questioning, they all rose and followed me, including our crow. His fellows had flown off. He continued his lope from branch to branch beside me, interspersed with higher flights circling above the tree tops. Wieser continued to sniff the light wind, and I tried to concentrate on leading my band of females through the forested slopes. *Later*, I thought. *Find out about Mum later*. There was no room in my head, no room at all, what with all the images of marching soldiers in my mind.

We reached the uppermost cave without encountering the Keltanese, by skirting wide from the second cave site. I could see no sign of trespass, when I, and my stealthy dog and crow, scouted ahead. None had visited, disturbing the cave or its stores. This cave was the largest and deepest of the three, with corners lost in inky black shadow and even more tumbled rocks to clamber over at its mouth. Also, likely the least accessible of the three to any prying searchers.

I brought us all within, and set the lantern where its glow did not reach the front. Virda replenished the offering gifts, Annora brought out dried fruit and nutmeats, and Morie released Murr from his basket. He puffed up like a dry milkweed pod on catching sight of the crow perched on the craggiest rock pillar. The crow shook its wings at him, cackling like a chuckle.

Wieser sniffed all the corners but found nothing to perturb her. I called Wieser to me, to come along to the spring close by where we could fill our jugs and add to the water I had stored earlier.

"Don't go!" Morie ran to me, Iggle clutched to her chest. "What if they catch you?"

"Nobody's going to catch me—nobody's looking for me. They're looking for ... well, I don't know what they were doing, but they weren't hunting for folk. Or tracking. Looking at the lay of the land, maybe."

I explained what I had seen in answer to inquiring looks from Annora and Virda. Virda clapped a hand to her mouth and said, "Gods' mercy!"

"Do you know what they were about?" I said.

"Mages. Sorcerers. In the lands my sons sail to across the sea, there are such sorcerers. My boys have told me about them, plotting the lines of power in the earth, the ley lines. They use the pathways for their magic. There are storm-casters, who can make the ocean winds shift to blow ships off course and change the currents. Sailors fear them."

I had not heard of such powers. "We aren't on the sea, though."

She shook her head. "That's what the boys know of mages. They work their magic on land, too, overseas. Why they would be on our mountain, I cannot guess."

"And observed by the Keltanes while they plot the ley lines in our land? Would the Keltane sovereign bring them here?" Annora wondered.

"I have more questions than we can number. I'll get water. No fire tonight, not until we can be sure smoke won't be noted." As I turned to go, the crow took wing, also. I nodded, glad of the extra eyes even though the walk was short to the spring.

Once Morie had fallen asleep on Annora's lap, for her earlier comfort with sleeping on her own little ledge abandoned her in this cave, I raised the question of my mother working magic.

"How is it," I asked, "that neither Da nor Wils have ever said anything about Mum being able to call animals or heal them? I only remember her doing what all the farmwives do to care for the land and creatures."

"You remember your da seemed to know what I could do with the wagon team, when we had only just met," Annora said, drawing Morie's cloak closer about her narrow shoulders and smoothing her curls.

"Your uncle came up and talked to him about your skills. And Wils couldn't still his tongue about you, either," I argued.

"Yes, and Wils told me about your mum. She had many gifts."

Virda laughed quietly. "Fenn thought the world and all of your mum, Judian. She helped me with some of my births after she came to the mountain, and I helped her when all of you were born. She had the way, and I knew some of her children would, too. The gift comes of need, sometimes. You favor her the most, to my eyes."

I could remember what she looked like, in a faded kind of vision. Morie was only just walking when Mum died. She had been helping a sick family in the village, a year with bad lung-fever. She took the fever and died down in the village, would not come back home to be nursed for fear of carrying the illness to us. All the family she was helping died, too, and the home had to be burned. I missed her so much, I thought I would go mad from it. I couldn't remember much what Wils and Da were like, but Morie cried for her often in those days. Virda came to live with us for some months after, to care for her while we all did field work, since Morie was too little to spend all day outside. I just remembered working and feeling hollow inside day after day.

"If I have this gift, how do I learn to wield it to keep you all safe? Who teaches someone so gifted how to use it?" I said finally.

"My gran taught me. I had not shown it yet, when my mum and da died," Annora said. "I can show you things I know, but the crow came to you, Judian, however you called it."

And how had I called it? For I could think of not one thought or desire that had been in my mind to bring it. "So, did Wieser come to you, or to me?" I said at last.

"To you, I must think, looking back. She seems always to center on you. You'll learn what skills you have as time goes by," Annora said.

"I need to know now. I hope I can learn faster because my need is pressing." I looked at Wieser dozing by Virda's feet, and the crow perched above us on its rock, staring into the dark distance with its feathers fluffed. "And you'd all better hope I prove to be a quick study, too."

CHAPTER 10

Annora taught me how to call a fish for supper as the days passed. It mostly involved lying on the stream bank with my hand aching in the cold water and "seeing" the fish swim into my grasp. An essential bit was thanking the fish for making itself our meal, similar to the way Da thanked a stag for being brought down for our table at the conclusion of a successful hunt.

Sometimes the magic worked, and sometimes it didn't. Wieser watched impassively. The crow seemed amused by my efforts, if that is what one could reckon by a great black bird cackling and clicking its beak while it stepped to and fro.

I would have preferred to depend on a sharp spear. Not just for the fish.

Annora also instructed me to gather spider webs to staunch a bleeding wound, and what herbs to crush in what reagent for treating stomach complaints, wheezing, trouble passing water and a whole host of other ailments I had never heard tell about. *It's a wonder people don't tip over dead at every turn*, I thought, as I pressed dew-spangled webs onto a square of linen.

I groused as I tried to learn it all, unsure how any of it would help with soldiers shooting arrows at me—until I thought maybe my mum would be the one teaching me if anyone had known how to cure lung fever that year.

The highest cave being too far east, I could not overlook the pass every day to check for the invasion's onset. I expected snows to close the northwest route any day, but still the weather held, cold yet clear. I worried we would run out of food. I worried about the stock foraging for themselves at our place and at Virda's. I wanted to take Wieser and the crow down with me to gather more supplies and check on the animals, but Annora and Virda would not hear of being left with Morie in the cave waiting to see if I made it back.

When the last bit of flour had been baked as a stick of bannock, and only a couple of dried pears remained in our tin trunk, there was no denying we must make a foray, at least to the middle cave.

Virda and Morie were persuaded to stay close to the cave and check the deadfall traps I had set. Annora and I set off with Wieser between us on the path. The black shadow of the crow spiraled across the track as the bird circled and banked over our heads.

Careful approach to the cave below raised no caws or hackles. My feeling of being watched on the way up from the first cave did not haunt me again. We found the cave the same as I had left it, and we took everything we could carry. Before we departed, I stepped into the sparse trees, where the mages earlier paced along the ley lines. I had no sensation of anything uncanny, nor any residual sense of menace from their having been there. The horse droppings left by the soldiers' mounts were of an age to suggest they left the same day and had not returned.

"Annora, can you feel anything amiss here?" I gestured her to come closer.

She walked to where I stood, shifting the packs of dried squash and barley meal in her arms. "I would have to stay here quiet for a time before I could feel the deep power. But I don't sense anything disturbed or rankled."

"Whatever they were doing, they must have done it and gone

on. Where to, I'd like to know. Tomorrow, I'm going to come down again, and check the pass. Don't look at me like that, I have to know what's coming, or I can't do what Da charged me with." I had determined my next step, and would not allow her to turn me from it. Quick-minded as ever, Annora did not try to talk me around, and quietly held up for me when I told Virda my plans.

I prepared to set out early with Wieser and the crow, with my walking staff now decorated with a shed black feather from my winged lookout.

"Your bird needs a name," Morie informed me.

I drank the last mouthful of my morning tisane, blessedly still hot. "Maybe you'd like to pick his name. You did fine with Murr and Iggle. They like their names. Wieser, too."

Morie gave the crow an assessing look, returned in kind. "His name is Gargle," she pronounced.

When I snorted, she said, "It's that noise he makes. Murr says "murr" when I pet him."

"What does Iggle say?" I teased, but Gargle seemed to suit the bird. He came when called by name, though not to put too fine a point on it, he had made a habit of accompanying me anyway on my forays. I did like a name better than calling him "the crow."

Gargle, Wieser and I took our leave, and I realized as I walked into the misty morning that both my animal aids were solid black. Although, I had never been one to believe in omens, as a rule.

The woods were full of the usual bird calls and squirrel chatter, and it struck me then that the forest where we holed up in our cave had been unnaturally quiet since our arrival. I would have to talk to Annora about it when I returned.

I became more cautious as I drew close to the pass overlook, though I neither heard nor saw any person, on foot or mounted. When I peered over the edge, keeping my head in shadow to avoid being backlit, I seized Wieser's ruff in shock—below us lay earth churned and pocked by countless hooves. When had so many mounted troops passed? Had they swept through on their way to the village and to Bale Harbour? Or were they now encamped in our orchard? Wagons could not have negotiated the steep pass, only pack trains could have done. Plenty of supplies and men could be reflected in the ravaged dirt, certainly.

Where are all those horses and their riders now?

"Gargle, can you fly where I tell you, to look for soldiers? You'd be less likely to get shot at than Wieser, I think." He turned his head to look at me with one beady eye. "How would you tell me where you found them, though? There's that to surmount. I'd go look myself—" He leapt and pecked my foot. "That even hurts through the boot, you know." I rubbed the spot. "What am I going to do if I find them, anyway? Better we get back safely to the cave and lay low. The food's replenished. We can hold out there." I grasped my stick, and had at least the presence of mind not to stand up in plain view on the ridge. I kept low to hitch back into the cover of boughs behind me, and thus lay out of sight when I heard a voice a scant few trees over say, "I swear I heard someone talking just now," in Keltanese.

Gods, was that what the peck had been for? And Wieser, just as frozen as I, had given me no signal of a man nearby. Or, I had not looked at her as I chatted about the pass. Out loud. To animals. I gritted my teeth and called myself every kind of fool, though silently now.

Gargle commenced his gurgling, muttering sound and flapped toward the voice. And scald me if he didn't sound sort of like a person, at least enough that a second voice said, "There's your talker, I think." I heard Gargle shake his feathers and click his beak, then mount to the sky, cawing raucously.

The first voice laughed and said, "Maybe it's one of the mages transformed. I heard they can change into beasts and go about. I wish they would go back where they came from. In truth, they make me feel queer whenever they're close by. As if someone's at my shoulder, but never there when I turn to look."

"Ah, you're queer enough, whether mages are nearby or not,"

said the other. "Come, back on the loop."

I heard fading sounds of them departing the cliff.

I lay in the cool boughs and blessed Gargle, and all the gods in turn, and Wieser for not barking, and my da for making me learn Keltanese. Time passed, my heart began to slow and my guts to untwist. It was a long while before I could move, though. Wieser lay beside me, while Gargle returned to perch above us, and devour a weasel carcass he brought back with him. If he'd have wanted, I'd have cooked it for him.

CHAPTER 11

"Some number of enemy troops have come through the pass," I said as soon as I entered our cave. "I heard two on patrol but saw no one else on my way back."

Annora looked up from combing Morie's hair. "You heard them?"

"Talking. Near the pass." *And they heard me too, though Gargle saved me, and I'm not telling you about that.* "They were certainly from Keltane, so our only option is to stay secreted here, and wait out whatever is coming."

"Oh, I'd give a lot to know if our troops were on the way to meet them!" said Virda.

"It doesn't matter to us now whether Keltane takes the harbour or is forced back over the border. Our only need is to keep out of the way and avoid any kind of soldier."

"You couldn't tell how many came through?" Annora asked.

"I wouldn't know how to tell—the ground was badly torn up from many horses passing, but how many? I'd only be guessing."

"If we only had a way to get word to Fieldmaster Behring or his fellows—"

"Annora, are you mad? What we want to do is keep out of it." I gaped at her, amazed at her sudden flight of wit.

"He certainly seemed in need of information when he stopped by us."

"I'll not argue that, but he hardly needs vague information from refugees in hiding, does he? How would we find him, anyway? He was off to hunt for Da, probably bound for parts west when he left us."

"Any of our troops, then. He said some thought this pass would be the enemy route. Should we not confirm that they've come?"

"No! Any message would have to go down the mountain through the enemy troops, don't you see? Our troops will find out soon enough, when they trip over them."

She sat staring toward the cave entrance. "What if I could have a message carried out to them? Putting none of us at risk?"

"Not Wieser, or Gargle, either."

"No, I was thinking of a little hawk that's been coming every day. She might carry, but where to send her?"

"Strap a note to her leg and send her to the biggest gossip in the village," I suggested, mocking her gravity.

"You said Virda was the biggest gossip," Morie said.

"I never, and Virda doesn't live in the village, and furthermore, I was not serious!" Could I feel more put upon— burdened as I was with keeping the lot of them from being killed? Wasn't that enough to be getting on with, or did I have to run the Mercedian defense as well?

I threw up my hands. "Do whatever you can manage without bringing harm to any here. I have my own duty to carry out. If you see this as your duty, then you do it without involving me."

I watched with lingering aggravation as Annora and Virda sat close to the lantern and composed a message they wrote on a scrap of paper. This scrap they rolled tightly and secured with a thin length of leather, leaving the ends free. Presumably this would be tied to the hawk's leg, pursuant to my joke proposal of delivery method. Where would Annora direct the bird to deliver it, though? I had given up wondering *how* she would direct it. I did note her sorting through her leather pouch of herbs, and taking a sprig she

74

found there to crush into a paste with some dried meat. This she patted into a small ball with the addition of flour and water, and laid to dry by the tiny fire we dared. Murr had to be shooed away from it, as well as Gargle. Annora guarded it vigilantly until it dried enough for her to wrap in a piece of cloth.

I woke to see her release the messenger hawk in the dawn light. I could not keep myself from asking where she had sent it.

"To the chapel apostate in Bale Harbour. I fed the bird a bit of the holly I picked there on my wedding day, and saved for luck. The apostate may think she is a messenger from the gods, and so look close enough to see the note. I hope."

It made as much sense as anything else that was happening. Although I thought the lisping apostate was more likely to hide in the chapel cellar than go out and look for soldiers and deliver our message, none of us had been put at risk in sending it. "I hope so, as well. I'm sorry you had to sacrifice your memento. Perhaps good will come of it."

She rewarded me with a smile so bright, I had to look away. I felt the worse for having shouted at her the night before.

We kept to the cave, and smelled smoke on the wind every day for three days. I had dream visions of burned fields and a smoking rubble that had been my home, waking at night sweating in the chill air. I would have tried to send Gargle to ride the air above our place to reconnoiter, but how would he communicate what he saw? If I had been a mage, maybe I could have flown with him by magic, and seen through his eyes. Virda said she had been told they could do such things across the sea. I envied the foreigners' power, because I felt powerless and small. I wished for someone else to be the boss of our party, or for Da to stride in and say, "Well done, Judian. I'll take us all home now."

As that didn't happen, I kept on directing the portioning of food, the use of boughs to blur our footprints stream-side, and all the other details to keep us from attracting notice. I consoled

75

myself that at least it seemed to be working. Whatever was happening farther down the mountain, we saw no one, and no one found us.

On the fourth day after Annora's messenger flew, we woke to heavy snow all about our haven. It came to Wieser's belly, and she had to bound through the drifts. Murr had never seen snow, and shook each paw as he lifted it from the cold wet. He was still light enough that he did not sink into the depths, but ventured only far enough to do his business and then scampered back into the cave and licked his feet with a passion. The snow had washed the smoke scent from the air, and the clear sharp breeze made me feel fresh despite the dismal filthy state of my clothes. *Soon the enemy will find us by our reek*, I thought.

Virda set about filling any kind of container we could spare with snow, to let it melt in the cave. This to supplement the jugs I filled so cautiously in dark of night at the spring.

Morie was yawning and putting on her cloak for a trip to the bushes with Annora. "I need my boots," she complained, as the boots she wore in the farmyard had not been brought along.

"I'll carry you, if you like," I said from where I stood in the entrance.

"You are not allowed to come with. You're a boy!"

I laughed to see her instantly scandalized, fists on her small hips. "As if I haven't taken you to the bushes a thousand and more times."

"We didn't have enough girls, then, and now we do."

"Yah, I think now we have girls aplenty."

"Judian," Annora said at my shoulder, "how long before you think we can return to the house? Food is running low again, even with the hares that Wieser brings."

I turned to her, frowning. "Better if I go see what I can scare up, while the rest of you stay here. It's possible the war has passed us by, yet equally possible we're still on the fringe of it raging. How to know?"

"Oh, I understand you think it all through. I just don't know if I can face another day of you gone and no way of knowing what's happening to you. If you didn't come back … it would be too awful to bear." Though she spoke softly, I didn't want Morie to hear, and shushed her.

"Wieser and I can travel silent and quick, and Gargle keeps watch above. I can't think how to make it safer, except if I could be invisible or turned into an animal like the mages." She looked so worried, brows drawn down over green eyes. "At need, I'll call wild boars to eat some soldiers," I said with a grin, and was gifted with her smile. Morie trundled up in her bundle of cloak and scarf, and held up her arms. Annora, still smiling, bent to gather Morie up and carry her to the brush.

"Never think of setting out before we get back," she called over her shoulder, but still quietly, as we took no chances of being overheard. Sound carries in the mountains, even though it's difficult to tell where a noise comes from, distorted as by fog. Wils had taught me that, as we played at hiding and finding one another among the tallest trees. *Where is he now*, I wondered. *Is he coming home to his bride?*

CHAPTER 12

I n the end, I went no further than the middle cave, where I gathered everything remaining and carried it up the mountain. We could not go there to stay without restocking. I replenished the offering to the kavsprit, though, so they would look favorably on us if necessity drove our party there.

More snow fell that night, as if once the sky opened itself to winter, all the snow that had been like a held breath tumbled down to smother the world. It could be deep enough now to keep more troops from crossing the border through the pass. I wished I knew how to magic an avalanche, to seal the border for certain sure.

Virda's cough came on during the night, and by the next morning she turned clammy and shaking. Annora cocooned her by the measly fire I allowed, and fed her hot broth. Her fever rose high that night, and we tucked Wieser up with Morie while Annora and I took it in turns to sit beside Virda and try to get her to drink. She sipped gamely, and slept in snatches. As Virda snored softly in the early hours after midnight, Annora came and sat beside me. "Judian, we must take her down. Living out in the weather like this, she'll only get worse."

"There's no more you can do for her here?"

"She must have a warm fire and dry bed. More substantial food, and I know you've done your best. We just must go back home."

I could not argue. I could not see Virda as a price to be paid for my peace of mind. "If she can walk down in the morning, we'll all go to the first cave. I'll scout the farm, and come back to bring her the rest of the way if all is clear."

Annora rose and began to pack up what we would carry along. When next she spelled me at Virda's side, I replaced our remaining stores into their rock crevices at the high back of the cave. I did not neglect the kavsprit, and discovered when I placed the offering that the cave creatures had left one for us, as well. A gleaming shard of obsidian, sharper than any man-forged blade. A considerable boon, for the black stone was a rare thing in our land, and valuable. I doubled what I left for them, and thanked them aloud. I might have heard whispery high voices like wind in dry leaves, or I might have only fancied I did. I wrapped the obsidian in my leather glove, and packed it carefully in my gear.

Virda walked slowly next morning, leaning heavily on my staff at first, and then on my shoulders as we neared the lowest cave. Her cough sounded deep in her chest and her breath came in wheezy gasps. I charged Annora with wiping out the footprints we left as we moved through the snow. And Morie—who for a change had seen fit *not* to complain of how much she had to carry while Annora worked and I helped Virda—led her from the entrance to lie down within. The floor was drier than the cave we had left, since no one had been tracking in snow for days. Wieser and I set out with Gargle, to make a cautious roundabout off the regular path.

The thick snow obscured any evidence of horses and men who might have passed prior to its fall. The icy edge of the stream bore only deer tracks and bear paw prints next to the black water. Swollen clouds piled overhead, leaden gray; more snow in the offing. I walked slowly, having to bough-sweep my footprints away as I went, so no one could follow my tracks back to the cave. I had left my gear there with the women, but taken Da's sword with me, though unwieldy. I was no swordsman, but better than

Annora, surely. They'd be more likely to have a sword used against them than to defend themselves successfully with it, so I told myself as I snuck through the pines. When I paused below the last ridge, which I must climb to get a view of the road and the farm, I recalled discovering the fieldmaster and his men on that very stretch of road what seemed like an age ago.

I crouched at the base of a wide trunk to catch my breath before starting up the rise. The wind stirred the branches above, and with a *whumph* snow buried me utterly. I sputtered as I fought my way to the surface, to hear Gargle cackling above me, bouncing on a branch. I had learned my lesson previously, and made no remark aloud, but did offer a rude gesture in his direction. Crows always think they know best, indeed!

I started to brush off, then thought better of it. A snow-covered figure in a gray cloak was less likely to be noted by any observer. *Still, Gargle, I could have preferred less ice water down the back of my neck.* I tossed some snow over Wieser's black coat, which she tolerated with better grace than I might have. We climbed the slope.

The road stretched past, an undisrupted expanse of white. No mud or wagon tracks marred its surface. I back tracked below the top of the ridge and moved to where I could overlook the house and barn.

Snow covered the yard and orchard, pristine. But jutting up from the pure white, the charred beams of our barn leaned and tilted awkwardly where they weren't collapsed altogether. I caught the scent of the wet burnt wood. The stones of the house still stood, the back garden and stoop covered in snow but without evidence of fire that I could see from where I cautiously peered from the trees. The house still bore its roof, the washhouse stood as before. But the chicken coop lay broken and scattered. The goat pen? I could see nothing but snow where it should be. Though I crouched a ways away, I could see no sign of folk about, no tracks in the snow leading to the pump, no smoke from the chimney, no footprints by

81

the woodpile.

"It could be worse," I whispered to Wieser. Maybe it was worse under the snow. I decided I would bring Virda down, even so. When I turned to withdraw down the ridge, I came face to face with Dink, and only barely kept from shouting. He snuffled at me, looking with his liquid brown eyes. Hooves muffled by the snow, he had made no sound coming behind me. I sent a look Wieser's way. "Just a shove with your nose would let me know something was up." She wagged her tail at me, and touched noses with Dink. I sighed, and supposed Dink was no stranger to Wieser to trigger an alarm.

"Come on, Dink. I have to suppose Virda will welcome a ride down, even bareback. Did I call you, I wonder? Perhaps I'll call some goats or chickens later." And off we went.

###

Although I furrowed my brow and tried to summon a nanny or hen from the wood, we collected no more of our stock on the way back to the house. I led Dink with Virda astride, and the others followed. We made for a rag-tag procession, and none too fast, besides. I charged Wieser and Gargle with alerting me to anyone lurking, but they raised no alarm.

We found the back door kicked in but not splintered off its hinges. Snow drifted and eddied on the kitchen floor. Snow also mixed with scattered foodstuffs in the larder. I could see anything that required cooking lay scattered, spilt and spoiled, whereas anything that could be carried away and consumed was missing. Much of the crockery lay smashed on the flagstones, but not all of it. Furnishings were overturned but not broken, for the most part. They had not troubled to knock out window panes, I was glad to see. Glass is difficult to come by, Da always said. Our leaded triangle panes kept the snow out, still.

I bade the rest of them stand by a ready escape at the back door, while Wieser and I made a tour through all the rooms. I carried the sword to stab under beds and in behind curtains. No soldiers.

Annora helped Virda to Da's big bed, after replacing the straw-stuffed mattress they had dragged off the frame. I found some dry woolens to cover her, and began to debate in my mind about the advisability of a fire. Would smoke from the chimney alert nearby Keltanese to our presence? Just how nearby were they, by this time? All the damage had been accomplished before the snows commenced, I reckoned from the lack of fresh tracks.

I decided to warm stones in a fire built in the ruin of the barn, where rising smoke might be expected past the actual blaze that consumed it. What cooking we must do could be accomplished there as well. The stones I could carry by bucket to Virda to keep her warmed, and we would all sleep in the room under the stairs.

I took Wieser along to the wood pile, and gathered enough for an armload. Wieser set up a whine, and would not go in the barn's foundation with me. "I know it's queer, Wieser. Let's just get a fire laid. It's not as if we can damage it further."

She would not come closer, though, and whined all the louder. I got the fire going, and placed my warming rocks along the edge. "Back to the house, then. You can stay with the women next time."

Murr shot out between my legs when I opened the back door, zipping into the garden under the snow-laden bean vines. Morie appeared next, anxious to chase him, but I would not hear of her wandering out alone.

"We haven't had a chance to look at the state of the place, you could fall in a hole or gods know what else could happen. You'll stay in here, and come with me when next I go out. Lay the cloaks out to see if they'll dry."

She laid Iggle's out first, of course. Wouldn't want Iggle to catch a chill. When I brought more bedding for us down the stairs, I found only Virda and I were accounted for—no Annora or Morie.

"She's wheedled Annora into going out to find Murr. She never minds!" Gargle pecked at the back window, followed by Wieser renewing her whine at the threshold. I yanked open the door, set to yell for them, when Annora appeared, dragging Morie by the arm.

"There's a soldier in the barn, Morie says." Annora, wide-eyed and out of breath, turned and pointed.

"He's maybe dead," Morie said, equally breathless.

"Did I not say to stay in the house? What makes you think he's dead?"

She would not answer, pouty since I had scolded her. Annora said, "I understood her to say she pissed in his ear."

"Morie! Did you do that?" She nodded, still refusing to speak. Morie, who would not be taken to the bushes by her brother, had pissed in the ear of an enemy soldier. I could not credit it.

"Show me!" I commanded, meaning show me where he is. Instead Morie dropped to her knees, and before I could say anything, leaned forward and said, "Pssst, are you dead?"

Annora burst out laughing, and I could not help laughing, too. "And when he didn't answer, you thought he was maybe dead?" I said, passing a hand over my brows.

"He didn't answer, he just went *unnngh*," she said, imitating a guttural moan. Relief fled as quickly as it had flooded me. I snatched my sword, snapped, "Take me to him," and strode out ahead of them. "Wieser, come on. Is that what you've been whining about? For gods' sake, you're going to have to be clearer. What's the use of vague unease? How is that a message from you?"

I stalked toward the barn, Annora and Morie with me, Wieser wagging her tail now, of all things. I quit talking and shushed everyone including Gargle, who flew over to join the procession. I crept in at the place Morie pointed, under the shelter of one of the tipped walls where snow drifted in lightly. The water trough stood with a skin of ice on it, holding up one side of the charred wall. He lay in the pallid light that filtered in, Keltanese tunic plain to see, gore-clotted cloth wrapped around his throat. I could not see if he was breathing, but Morie had claimed he made a sound. I eased

84

closer, and saw a knife lying just where it might have fallen from his grip, near his hand on the stone floor. His uniform was filthy, ripped at one shoulder. He wore one boot, and rags wrapped the other foot, the protruding toes waxy pale. Frostbite.

I pitched my voice fierce as I could, as I did not plan to piss in his ear in my turn, and said, "You! Are you living yet? You can be dead quick enough, if so." I prodded him with the sword, having first kicked his knife away from his easy reach if he showed able to move.

He moaned, tried to open his eyes, and said, "Water," in thick-voiced Keltanese. I repeated my warning in Keltanese, then, but he only repeated his request, nay plea, for water.

"Can you speak Mercedish?"

He made a minute nod, and croaked again, "water" but in our tongue. Annora, who generally had shown sense on our adventures, squatted by his side, dipped a bit of cloth in the trough, and held it to his cracked lips. She squeezed it to drip in his mouth, when he acted too weak to suck it.

"What are you thinking? Get up!" I shouted, and he was undead enough to stay her hand as she began to withdraw it. "Angel, please," he groaned. I laid hold of her arm and pulled her out of his grasp before he could hurt her, or take her hostage. Though, in truth, I had to admit he looked unable to do much at all.

I dipped the rag again, and shoved it roughly into his fingers. Preparing to withdraw with Annora and Morie, I saw him feebly shift toward his mouth with the cloth. "Bah!" I said, and lifted his hand by his cuff to set it over his lips. I chivvied the two girls and Wieser out into the dim winter light.

"What are you going to do with him?" were the first words from Annora.

"I'm going to roll him down to the town road and pin a note to his tunic telling his own to look after him," I said hotly. "What I'm not going to do is open an infirmary for all and sundry who wash up here. He's the enemy!"

85

"He's a wounded man, and freezing out here."

"Why have they gone off and left him? How far off have they gone? Maybe they'll be coming back for him, have you thought of that?"

"It looks as if they've left him for dead."

"Or, they've gone down to Virda's to get some help for him, and are bringing a litter as we stand out here arguing."

I turned in disgust and began to head for the house.

"I can't leave him out here."

I wheeled on her. "He's not Wils lying there. He's an enemy soldier, here because he's invaded our country, sacked our farm and burned our barn and we don't know what all else, yet. I haven't had time to inventory, since I'm trying to have us all keep waking up alive. What do you think you can do for him? Get him well enough he can slit our throats in the night?"

Morie began to cry, and she does not cry quietly. Her wail reached a screech when I clapped a hand over her mouth. "Take her in," I said, and shoved her toward Annora. "I'm getting him out of here alive or dead, and I do not care which. Better dead, so he can't tell any of his fellows about the angel who gave him a drink."

"They'd think him raving, I expect. Though you gave him a drink, too. Do you think you have it in you to go and stab him as he lays?" She looked at me closely over Morie's curls, while Morie burrowed her face deeper into the scarf at Annora's chin.

I did not know how to answer. If I said I could go back and push my blade into him without hesitation, she'd know I lied. Clearly, I had never killed anyone. But this was my home, I had to defend it and those I loved. "I'll be along in a minute."

She waited, unmoving.

"I won't do anything yet. Take Morie in out of the cold. Check on Virda, she's probably frantic if she's heard us carrying on out here."

She carried Morie in, then. I went back to be sure the man

86

hadn't moved. He lay as we had left him, with his hand still over his mouth with the rag. He looked grayer in the face, if anything.

I thought hard on the walk back to the house. What would Da want me to do? He had killed men when he was a soldier, surely? And not an enemy in his own barn, presenting a greater threat than one off far from home somewhere. What would Wils want? His bride protected, or mercy shown to an enemy?

Wieser walked beside me, and Gargle perched on the porch roof, muttering. "You all are no help. You may be telling me things, but I don't know *what* any of the time! I can guess at things for myself. Are there any others about the place? No? Or yes? I could wish you were more use, if you're here because I summoned you." My anger and uncertainty spilled out onto them, since I had no other ready target. Neither of them commented by sound or action. I heaved a sigh and went in the house.

"Judian, I have not opposed you in anything since I came here," Annora said as soon as soon as I set foot in the kitchen.

I looked for Morie, but she must have been persuaded to "help" Virda for a bit. "No," I acknowledged, pulling out a chair at the table. "No, you've been game for everything and a great help to me with Morie. And Virda. I'm going to ask you to tell me why you want to part ways with me now, over this man."

"I don't know, I wish I did." She crossed her arms and hugged herself, staring out the back window. "It just seems I cannot leave him out there to die. I'm no warrior. I'm only barely become a wife. But if I can heal someone, I find I must do it. I can't turn away. I know he's our enemy. I do understand how hard you've strived to keep us safe. But I can't leave him there, and I don't want you to have to kill him, and hear his ghost whisper in your ear forever more."

"What's this about his ghost?"

"Wils said your da told him he hears the ghosts of men who fell to him in battle. Has he never told you? He said they breathe in his ear at unexpected times, times when he's happy and content, or times when he's complaining about some something that isn't going as he wishes, as well. Reminding him they would be content or irritated, but cannot be either, as they are dead. By his hand."

Fine. I had not thought of bearing the burden forever of ending the man's life. I just wanted to know what to do now as my best course. I rubbed my forehead. "Can I sleep on it?"

"He'll die, I fear. He's half-frozen now. I don't think he'll survive another night while we deliberate."

She wasn't deliberating, I was. I stood abruptly. "I'm walking down to Virda's place. I want to see whether more men are there, or what they've left if they passed through. We're going to need more food. If any has been left there, I'll bring it. Give me some kind of a blanket or cloak, I'll cover him as I leave. Help Morie find Murr, if he's close by in the garden. She won't rest until he's back in. Call him for her. When I come back, I'll have decided what to do."

"All right, Judian. I know you have a burden you should never have had to bear so young."

"I don't feel young," I said. "I feel a hundred years old at least."

CHAPTER 13

V irda's house still stood, and in fact, off the direct path from ours by a short ways, had been unmolested. That is, as far as I could tell, what with the snowy cover over all. I gathered food we could well use, and lantern oil, and packed it on Dink, who found some of Virda's goats' hay a ready meal while I searched about. I had agreed to leave some kind of message for Virda's sons, should they come seeking her, saying she was safe and in hiding. I wrote a few lines and placed the paper under a candle stick on the fireside table. Perhaps I should move us all down here? But that brought us closer to the harbour town road and the village, and that much closer to trouble, I feared.

I had left Wieser and Gargle at home, set to guard all there and instructed to give clearer warnings of danger. Wieser gave her look of reproach, and Gargle hopped along the porch railing, cawing as I rode out on Dink.

My trip took perhaps two hours, and in that time I decided I could not kill a wounded man. If he had come bursting through our door waving his knife, then I would have done my best to run him through, no doubts. But when I tried to imagine standing over him, putting a blade into him as he lay there helpless, I could not finish the vision. I helped slaughter my share of pigs and goats, had wrung many a chicken neck, done time and again any of the hundred chores involving death on a farm. Hunted the slopes and taken game. If I had more practice thinking of an enemy as less than a man, maybe I could have done it. I thought of leaving him to freeze, and decided I could only have done so if I hadn't known he lay out there. Easier if I could have discovered him already frozen dead, and know the gods determined his fate rather than me.

When I brought the food in, I asked Annora to come help me move him. I told her we would put him on a pallet in the kitchen, which she prepared in a trice, using Wieser's former fireside accoutrements with no apology. He would be placed in the corner alcove, without a view of the rest of the room, where the oak barrel of ale had disappeared from when his fellows came through. He would be warmer than in the barn. She could dress his wound. We would offer him food and drink and set Wieser to guard him. If he improved under our care such that he could walk, I would blindfold him and take him out into the woods near to the road and set him loose.

"Yes, oh, Judian, I'll do whatever you direct. I'm so glad we don't have to murder him!"

"I was going to be the one to have to do murder," I protested.

"As if I'd have let you do it without helping you."

Doubly sure I had chosen well, since I did not want to take anyone else down the ghost-making path, I stood at his head to lift him under the shoulders and Annora carried his feet, and we partly dragged the soldier up the stoop and into the kitchen. He seemed barely aware of being moved, and his brow felt feverish despite his coldness to touch elsewhere. I held him propped against me while Annora unwound the cloth from his neck, soaking it where it stuck to avoid pulling loose the scabs and so set the injury bleeding anew. He bore a jagged gash across the side of his neck that curved round the back. It looked to me as if someone had tried to take his head off. He knew little of our ministrations, having utterly passed from awareness as soon as I sat him up. His pallor was shocking, in the better light of the kitchen lantern. He had lost much of his life blood.

Annora bound the wound with fragrant herbs and some of our spider web poultice. It did not seem to be festering, no odor. She did not blush as she stripped off the rest of his wet garments, and left his small clothes in place. She bade me turn him to see if further wounds had gone unnoticed, but we saw nothing else bleeding, only a multitude of scrapes and bruises. Of more concern were his frostbitten feet, and now fingers as well. She clicked her tongue as she inspected the yellowish white toes. "I hope they don't split and peel. We must warm him carefully."

I noted with unease he was young and heavily-muscled. He bore blade scars along his arms, and one crossed his left temple, visible in damp, thick black hair. I could see on his back the ends of ropy reddish whip scars at the neck of his under tunic, and looked down to see they crisscrossed his back beneath the fabric. What manner of life had he lived?

No, I wasn't going to concern myself with that. "If his hands are sore he can't hold a weapon. And if his feet are the worse for frostbite, he can't run off and bring back his fellows," I pointed out.

"I wonder if his other boot is under the snow somewhere?"

"I don't think I want to keep him in the kitchen until the spring thaw. If I set him on the road, we'll put something on his feet."

"Lay him back. He's clean, at least. When he wakes, I'll try to get some warm broth in him." I helped her drag a pair of Da's trousers and a woolen shirt onto him, and we covered him with the thick woolen blanket we used in the sleigh. It was a horrible scratchy thing, but trapped the air well. In any case, we had no sleigh now, since it had been in the barn, and no harness or horses, either. *I need a sign I've done the right thing*, I thought darkly.

I went in to Virda and Morie. I told Virda about the note I left and that her house remained in good order; this news causing her to clap her hands under her chin like a delighted child. She already looked better since arriving in a decent bed, and her cough was breaking up. Morie sat on the bed with her, with Murr curled between them and Iggle tucked under the quilt, also.

"This is important, Morie. The soldier is in the kitchen, and I want you to stay away from him. No talking to him, no showing him Iggle, nothing. He is not our friend. Wieser and I are going to watch him until he is ready to leave. Do you know what you are supposed to do?"

"Leave the soldier alone. He's mean."

"Good enough." I didn't know how mean he could be just presently, but better if she thought so. Virda was giving me a questioning look, but I didn't feel like discussing my choices any further today. "I'll bring your supper in to you soon. I believe we have turnip soup, tonight."

"I don't think I like turnips," Morie said, pursing her lips in doubt.

"I think you'll find you like them fine."

Annora knelt, spooning some of the soup into the man's mouth when I came back to the kitchen. He had a napkin tucked under his chin. He watched me with fever-bright eyes as I approached.

"I've you to thank?" he said, his voice more hoarse than in the barn, but stronger. I nodded.

"His name is Gevarr," Annora said, spooning up another mouthful for him. I didn't want to know his name. I should have given the "he's not our friend" speech in the kitchen, not the bedroom. I shrugged, and told him the same plan I had told Annora: under constant guard, out as soon as he could travel. He inclined his head to nod, then winced and said instead, "Yes."

"When you can talk, I want to know whatever you can tell us about the invasion and where things stand."

"No fresh news," he said and gestured to his throat. "Wounded early on."

"We'll talk later." He knew something, had to know more than I knew from my refuge up in the mountains. I looked out the back window to see more snow blowing. Tiny ice crystals pattered faintly on the glass. I would have to run the rope lines from house to barn and waterwell which we used during a blizzard time. It was too easy to become disoriented and freeze in one's own yard, mere feet from safety. I sent up a hopeful prayer that our ropes had not also been taken with our ale barrel.

I thought to fortify with hot soup before heading outside to warm the stones for tonight. I found two pots sitting on the cold hearth. Annora carried cooked food inside from the fire in the barn, rather than cooking indoors. But why two kettles? As I picked the ladle out of one, she appeared at my elbow. "Not that," she said in my ear, and made to serve me out of the other.

I looked aside at her, brows raised. "Later," she said, setting more bowls on a tray to take in for Virda and Morie. I followed her into the bedroom, after setting Wieser to guard the man in the kitchen, dozing after his soup.

"What?" I said as I helped hand steaming bowls around.

"Don't eat from the food I serve him. It's dosed to keep him docile and fuzzy-headed."

"Aren't you the clever girl," Virda said warmly, and I had to agree.

CHAPTER 14

I had been insulated from some of the realities of the sickroom, for Annora tended Virda. Because of my gender, it fell to me to attend to the soldier's needs, as food and drink were followed in due time with the requirement to eliminate. I helped him stand to the piss pot, but took small solace that he was able to walk with help to the washhouse by the time more compelling needs arose. I was not going to wipe his ass. I suppose I made a poor nurse. He made a poorer convalescent, though, unsteady on his rag-wrapped feet and putting most all his considerable weight on me while complaining of being unable to tend to himself.

"Be your age," I snapped. "How do you think I like it?"

Curiously, he laughed, but made no more complaints that trip. I had not been thinking to entertain the man.

Wild-blown snow piled up to the window sills, and more fell daily. The winds packed full the spot by the trough where the soldier had lain, he'd have been entombed there if Morie hadn't found him. I had to dig it out to allow Dink to blow down and melt the trough ice for drinking. My fire site would no longer do. What boards overhung it were now too burdened with snow—I did not want to be underneath tending our fire when all collapsed. I brought wood inside and we began to use the hearth for more than setting pots upon. It felt more like home, then.

The soldier began to ask questions.

"Keep him more muddled," I told Annora.

She sighed, floured to her elbows kneading bread. "He's gaining strength. And if I keep increasing the dose, he won't be able to aid you at all in getting him about."

"He aids me little enough." Yet, I did not have to drag him, and doubted I could. I compromised by stringing up a quilt to block his alcove, and forbade any traffic through the rear door besides the two of us on the way to the privy. Virda was beginning to get up and about a little, and Morie and Annora could help her outside at need, using the front door. I strung another rope, this time from the front porch to the washhouse, to guide them in blowing snow.

Morie had been sufficiently glowered at by me whenever she peeked out of the bedroom, such that our invalid had not seen her since regaining his senses. I suspected he had wits enough to count voices, though, of those unseen. Morie's high voice carried, and he must have heard Virda coughing; was of course familiar with Annora and me, his attendant.

"Where's your da?" he asked, catching me off guard when I settled him on his pallet after a trip outdoors. I didn't answer right off. I should have been more careful when we first brought him in, and tried to isolate him more while I stomped around upstairs in Da's heavy boots to make him believe he was not alone here with a boy and a passel of females. *I'm a wood-wit,* I thought.

"We got separated when we fled."

"And Annora's husband?"

I didn't like him calling her by name. He was too familiar by half. "The same."

He did not ask when I expected them back, and I fretted about how I should play my hand. Act as if they should walk in any moment, stomping snow from their boots? Then when (if!) they didn't, he would know what he wanted without asking: he was gaining strength alone with women and children who were no match for him.

I took my obsidian shard to Annora, and asked her to wrap a bone haft with tough leather and affix it so I might use it as a weapon. She marveled at it, and I found when she finished with it and handed it back that she had balanced it well, and drawn runes on the leather with a fire-heated hasp. "For stealth and protection. This is a powerful gift. You cannot doubt you are magic-touched if the spirit-folk would give you such a thing as this!"

"Is the stone magic?"

"Things from so deep under the earth are old magic, time out of mind. The kavsprit strive to keep such in their realm, and do not lightly send them up into the world above. They honor you."

"Maybe they meant to honor Virda, she was giving them their due quite regular before she took ill."

"No."

I kept it on me at all times, once she made me a sheath so as to keep it in my boot without slicing my leg open. Da's sword was too ungainly to carry constantly, but I kept it near to hand. Out of Gevarr's sight. I found as Annora continued to call him by name, I fell into the habit also. I resolved to ask him questions, since he could talk well enough to complain. He spoke Mercedish well, and seldom made any comment in Keltanese.

Annora had set him a chair so his feet could be soaked in a pan of tepid water as he sat behind his quilt barrier. I brought another chair and set it to face him. He looked up from his bleak regard of his swollen toes, and raised his brows at me, inviting me to speak, it seemed.

"How many came through the northwest pass with you?"

He considered me for a moment. "How old are you?"

"I am asking you now. Answer me true and I'll think of answering your questions later."

"Twelve? Not yet thirteen, certainly no older, I think."

"*I think* you're starting to look fit enough to be put out on the road. Storm's brewing again." I kept my voice even, and did not blink.

His face split with an infuriating grin. "A battalion, does that make you happy?"

How many men were in a battalion? It sounded like a great many. "How is it you came to be left here?"

"We raided your place as we marched for the deep water harbour on the coast. I heard talk among the officers of making this a headquarters, else you'd see more damage. Your da was wise to build a stone house. Anyway, they decided it was too far from the main road, and we went on. When we met resistance on the way to the village, I was wounded. I could not march when my squad moved on. I made my way back here over a couple of days, seeking shelter."

"Resistance from Mercedian troops?"

"Would have had to be, wouldn't they?"

"How many?"

Again the flash of white teeth. "Not enough."

"Enough to take you out of it."

He acknowledged this with a slight inclination of his head my direction.

"Were the men you met in uniform?" For Behring and his men had been, while the farmers and shopkeepers from Bale Harbour, and Da and Wils, would not have been.

This question surprised him, it seemed, and he took a moment before answering, "Yes."

"Are there other wounded around here that you know of? Did you lead others back our way?"

"Frozen and buried in snow, if so. But I made my way here without seeing anyone." He paused. "They'll think me dead. I was unconscious on the battlefield for … I'm not sure how long. All was quiet there when I woke and staggered away. They won't be looking for me, Judian."

I didn't like him calling me by name, either. Annora needed to learn to still her tongue while she cared for him. "How will you find them when I set you loose?"

"I'll go to the sea. There will be no need for me to bring any of them back here. They will have taken the harbour. You are conquered and don't know it yet."

"You don't know that."

He shrugged, then winced at the pull it caused on his neck wound. "I've been ten years a soldier. You get a sense of the way of things. Your troops were caught out by the west border build up, and left the flank unprotected. A mistake."

"And you used foreign mages to delay the closing of the northwest route, or else your invasion plan would never have worked." Then I bit my tongue and drew blood, because the idea was for me to get information from him without revealing what I knew. *Here, let me demonstrate my lack of experience with men's doings.*

His craggy features might have been carved of wood, so still did they become. I could read nothing there.

How old was he? If a soldier for ten years, perhaps ten years older than Wils, then? He looked older than twenty-eight to me. He bore signs of hard use. Ill use.

"Your tunic has the signs of rank torn away," I said, for I had noted it when I packed the uniform in the trunk upstairs.

"Demotion."

"Who put those scars on your back? And why?" *Are you a worse threat than just an enemy soldier, a criminal, too?*

"She said you were shrewd."

She says far and away too much. "Why were you whipped?"

"I disobeyed an order. I was disciplined." I waited for him to say more, unmoving. Finally, "This was before we marched on Merced, by some months. Your sharp eyes must see the marks are healed."

"That doesn't tell me what you did to get them."

"I refused to throw my men away on a useless gesture, and thus appease the vanity of a petty lord advisor to the king. In the end, they were just as dead, and I was no longer anything but another foot soldier in the ranks. Sent here to be wounded and kept in a farmer's kitchen like an old tom cat, past use in catching mice." He seemed to have said more than he planned, and grunted. "That's my side of it, others might tell another."

Annora then appeared around the corner of the quilt to collect his foot bath, which had to be unpleasantly chilly by now. He likely could not feel it, for the throbbing of his feet. Coming out of frostbite is painful, I'd been taught. I helped him out of the chair after she patted his feet dry and re-wrapped them, and the two of us settled him on his pallet together. He was careful not to lean too heavily on her, I saw.

When she let the quilt fall back into place as she withdrew, his gaze lingered after her. "Your brother is a lucky man, to have such as her waiting his return."

I sighed. Wils couldn't have found a plain bride? I certainly would look for such if ever I thought to marry. "No one waits for you?" I asked.

He snorted. "No woman has concerned herself with my comings and goings for as long as I can recall. No. No one waits."

I turned to go. His voice stopped me. "In fact, I've no reason to want to leave here at all."

His remark knocked my breath back down my throat, and I had to take a moment before I could say, "It's not a matter of what you want." I pushed the quilt barrier aside and went looking for Annora.

CHAPTER 15

Likely a good thing Annora was not immediately to hand, with my blood fair roaring in my ears. Not enough that we had an invalid enemy soldier installed in our kitchen, she had to nurse him so tenderly that now he was smitten and didn't want to part from her. Because I had seen that look before, the way Gevarr watched her move. I had seen Wils look at her the same way—and wouldn't my brother be delighted to come home to this hearthside scene? How he would thank me! I felt like kicking the hearth, but remembered in time how much more that hurts with a cold foot.

Annora wasn't in the house, so I set Wieser to guard Gevarr and sought her outside. Wrapped in her cloak, she stood swinging the axe to chop ice from the trough for Dink. "Do you think we should fix him some shelter?" she asked when she saw me. Then she looked at my face closer. "What is it?"

"Gevarr sees no reason to leave us. I think you have been altogether too kind to him *considering he's our enemy!*" I choked out. "I think you'd better knock him out with one of your concoctions so I can load him on Dink and take him off somewhere to figure his own way home."

"I take it you don't think he's going to murder us all, then?"

"Only some of us. You're likely to be safe."

Her eyes flashed. "You think he's in love with me? No. He's

adrift, without a life to go back to that he wants any longer. It's only natural he would look at us all and want to stay where family cares for one another."

"You've *known* he doesn't want to leave? And when did you plan to say something to me about it?" I sputtered.

"I didn't really think you'd be like this about it. I thought you could use his help around here when he's well enough."

"Gods' mercy! He's not a stray pup! He's double my weight, and age, too. And you think you can bid him do this and that, and he'll be docile as a—as a—"

"Judian, take a breath! I don't object to his staying on, but if you do, well, he can't stay if you don't trust him."

"Trust him? Why by gods' teeth would I trust him?"

"He'd have to earn your trust, of course," she said with maddening serenity.

"Are you still on your "I hope someone's doing the same for Wils somewhere" buggy ride? Because I keep reminding you— he's not Wils by any stretch. He's made a ten year career out of killing people!"

"If you're going to condemn him just for being a soldier, I remind you your da was one, too."

"Da fought for our side! Gevarr's part of the invasion! I can't see how you think this could ever be wise, letting him stay."

"I haven't said I advocate letting him stay. I just don't object to it out of hand. He can't leave yet, in any case. He's weeks from being able to walk. There's time to discuss it and decide. Just let's go in out of the cold, can't we?"

That at least *was* a reasonable thought. I had come out without any heavy clothes, and could not feel my hands. Annora's teeth were chattering. Wieser began to bark as I turned to head to the house, and it was no easy feat to get through the snow and up the back steps in only seconds, but I did it with Annora on my heels.

Gevarr had managed to stand with the aid of my walking stick, and pulled open the back door when I arrived on the stoop. Wieser ceased barking when she saw we had responded to her alarm, and sat. "That's the kind of warning that does some good," I told her. She swept the floor with her tail.

"I'm the cause of some new trouble, I hear," Gevarr said.

"Actually, you've been nothing but trouble from the first," I said. I pointed back to his alcove, and took the stick from him.

"I heard you fighting." He looked only at Annora. I took his elbow to steer him back to the pallet.

"I'll tell you anything you need to know about it," I said. "In fact, I'll be doing all your care from now on. Move."

He did so, but gods knew I could not have made him if he set his mind against me. It was going to require some careful thought on my part, how to proceed.

It would be a good time for Da and Wils to come home.

Annora settled Morie and Virda, who, according to our drill, had barricaded themselves in the bedroom when Wieser sounded off. At least *that* had happened as I directed.

I set Wieser on duty again, and went into the bedroom. Annora, Virda and Morie were sitting on the bed in a row, looking toward the door as I entered. I was just preparing to lay out my misgivings about our patient when Wieser yipped.

"Can the man not just stay where he's set?" I came out of the bedroom, but a knock at the front door told me Wieser's different bark was "Company's come" not "Soldier on the move." She clicked across the stone floor and met me at the front window. Ticker, the smith's son who had brought us the fox litter, stood on our porch.

"What's the trouble?" I said when I opened the door to him, for certainly he would not have waded through the snow to us unless compelled by urgent need.

"My mum," he said, ashen pale. "The baby's coming, but it's taking too long, it won't come down, she says. I couldn't find the midwife at home." Indeed not, since she was recuperating in our bedroom. "So, I came up to see if the lady here would come. She knows lore, Mum thinks."

Annora came out to us, saying "Of course, we must help her." I hadn't noticed the woman was carrying when they had brought the dead vixen and her litter to us. How long ago was that? Must have been middle days for her term then. And, no wonder she so strongly desired to ward off the ill-luck of killing a mother animal.

"Do you know birthing? Or can I take Virda down?" I was thinking fast, who to leave and who to take, and what to do about Gevarr if we had to be gone.

"I don't think Virda's recovered enough to be out. She can stay here with Morie and you and I will go."

She was thinking fast, too, and did not mention Gevarr. "Gather what you need," I told her, and, leaving Ticker standing at the door, went to Gevarr's alcove with a length of rope.

"I'm going to hobble you, now."

"Am I not hobbled enough already? What's happened?"

"Put your hands out." I bound his wrists, in front of him, though, so he could lie on the pallet. His fingers were swollen enough that I did not believe he could pick out the knots. His ankles likewise, I tied so that he could lie but not maneuver to stand. I set Wieser on guard. "If you need a trip to the privy, you'll have to wait until I get back and take you—or not and you'll deal with cleaning up later. Don't ask the others for help."

"Where are you off to?"

"Woman's … work, gone ill in the village. I can't let Annora go alone."

"No, better you go with her. I won't make trouble."

I nodded, and set about putting on my heaviest winter gear. Tinker had brought their sleigh at least, so we would ride down to the village, but we would need everything we had to combat the cold. I brought along the sword and a lantern, thinking we may not return by dark. Morie chattered about a baby and wanted to come down and see it. Annora packed her herbs and some other mysterious things into a bag, under constant narration from Virda.

104

It was a relief to shut the door and step into the freshening wind.

Ticker bundled us into the sleigh and set off, with a constant refrain of, "It's my fault, it's the ill-luck from the fox. Mum has to be alright, oh, we have to hurry," in time to the muffled hoof beats of the stocky cob which pulled us along. I noted rags wrapped about the harness bells to silence them, and questioned him.

"It's so the soldiers can't hear. Ranks of them came through on the way to the harbour, but Mum thinks some may yet be about on patrol. They'd take the sleigh, they took so many wagons and such. Mum didn't want to send me out, she waited overlong, but then she said I just had to go. We have to hurry!" He clucked to the horse, already trotting, and traveling as fast as was safe coming down the steep road on runners. I heard wing beats overhead, and Gargle settled on the back of the sleigh.

"Bad omen!" cried Ticker, lifting his whip to strike the bird.

I caught his wrist. "No, no omen. This crow has been living with us for months, sort of a watch dog."

"But I saw you had a dog."

"Yes, but I had to leave her for Virda and Morie. This crow will sound off if soldiers are about."

"You can train a crow to do that? We need one, too," Ticker decided, glancing aside at Gargle. The bird, for its part, seemed to relish the rush of cold air in its face without the work of flying. I suspected laziness.

"Ticker, how long has your mum been laboring?" Annora asked, voice hard to hear through the scarf she held to her face. "Is the baby early, or is it time?"

"Two days," he said miserably. "It only took short hours overnight for my two younger brothers. I woke up and they were born already. I think it's about her time, midwinter or so."

Annora did not ask more, but met my eyes with worry in her own. Ticker took up his "we have to hurry" chorus again, while I wished I was on some other errand. Such as one I knew anything about.

Ticker unloaded us at the side door to the forge, and took the sleigh around back to hide it. Not a soul stirred in the village, and no candles glowed in the windows that faced the road. Annora and I went in and through to the living quarters attached to the smithy's shop, and I called out, "Hullo, the house! We've come to help you."

The miller's wife, red-faced with wisps of gray hair escaping from her linen cap, reached out the door to pull us in. "Where's Midwife Virda? What's this?"

"I've attended my share of births. Virda is too ill herself to come tonight," Annora said as she unwound her scarf.

"You'll need all your skill with this one. Come with me," she said, and left me standing just inside what proved to be the keeping room, while she took Annora's bag and led her to the door opposite.

Ticker's two younger brothers sat on a bench facing the hearth, eyes dark with fear. The older brother paced to and fro behind the bench without pause. There was a sister or two, as well, I remembered, but they would likely be aiding their mother. It was warm with a bright fire in the grate, so I began to take off my heavy clothes.

Ticker came in, stamping snow off his boots. "Has it come?" he asked immediately. All the heads shook in response.

"She's not crying out any more," the oldest boy said. He looked a couple of years older than me. I wondered if her silence was a good sign, or ill. I had never been to a birth, and avoided listening if ever Mum talked of any with Virda within my hearing. I gathered there were hazards for both mother and babe, and that some births were easier while others were made difficult by any number of problems. Virda once said what war was to men folk, birthing was for women. I did remember that, sitting there, and then wished I hadn't.

We were comfortable by the hearth, until the daughter Gefretta, one of those who used to come up to trail about after

Wils, came bustling in. She threw open the window and swung wide the door to the shop. She then took up the knife from the block—"To cut the pain," she said—and hurried back toward the bedroom. One of the boys stood to close the window, and she snapped, "It's to open the way for the baby!"

I did not see how this would help, since the baby would not come through window or door, but I had no experience in birth chambers and was not going to contradict. Instead, I handed my cloak and scarf and other gear around, so we didn't freeze while waiting.

Annora came out to boil water and rummage in her herb bag, brows drawn down and lips pursed. She stirred herbs into the kettle, and lifted it by the bail with her hands wrapped in a fold of her skirt.

"How goes it?" I asked quietly.

"The baby's turned sidelying, and her waters are gone. I must unclench her womb enough to shift the baby, if I can. Her strength is … challenged, working so long." She looked at all the anxious faces. "Feed them something. It's long since they have eaten, I gather."

All said they were not hungry, but when I set Ticker and his elder brother, Tarn, to cooking porridge, the smaller ones found the butter and even a few dried apples to add in. Just as we settled close to the fire with our bowls, we heard their mother begin to groan and strain in the other room.

In between the pains, I could hear Annora calling to the baby, "Come down and meet us!" And to the mother, "Bring your baby to life!" The miller's wife, and then the mother herself echoed the call, "Come out, baby, come!" And following one huge bear-like roar from the laboring mother, I heard a thin wail. There came a lot of sobbing and thanking of the gods, and then Gefretta reappeared, slammed the window and trilled, "It's a girl!" I met her at the door, meaning to shut it since its magic was no longer needed, if indeed leaving us to shiver had magic at all, and the girl said to me,

"Wils's wife really is a witch, just like I heard."

Irritated by the accusation in her voice, I said, "Maybe you'd like her to put the baby back, then."

She huffed out a breath and turned on her heel to go back to her mother. Ticker brought me my bowl of porridge with an apologetic look, and I gave him a grin, to show it wasn't he who rankled me.

Annora brought out a loaf-sized bundle with a tiny, pinched pink face, and showed it around to all the brothers. "Your mum is doing well. Take her in some porridge with honey. Put another log on the fire to warm the house for your sister."

"She's not very pretty," said the youngest dubiously.

"Neither were you," Ticker told him.

The younger boys made a show of getting their mother's bowl ready, while Annora took the baby back into the bedroom. The next bit of our errand of mercy involved carrying out a lot of bloody straw and the afterbirth, which we placed on the burn pile in the forge.

"It's better to burn it now, so it doesn't draw rats," Annora told Tarn, so that became his contribution to the process.

The mother was so relieved by her safe delivery that she insisted on Ticker carrying us home in the sleigh, even though that would get him back home after full dark. I prepared one of their lanterns so I wouldn't have to send him home with ours. Her largess grew with passing minutes as the babe latched and fed, and she insisted on giving us a sack of oats, a jug of milk, a basket of eggs—and would have kept going, I think, but she fell asleep when the baby did, both exhausted after their effort.

I heard the miller's wife gushing over Annora's knowledge and skill with such a harrowing birth, but I never did hear the daughter thank Annora at all. I felt very glad Wils hadn't picked *that* one to wed. *Imagine dragging her around to live in mountain caves.*

When Ticker, Annora and I bundled up again and headed out

the side door of the forge, we saw a trio of soldiers in the square, in Keltane's colors. We hung back and watched them erect a window-sized board held up by posts to either side, with a narrow roof jutting out above, and then nail a parchment onto it. Once they had mounted their horses and ridden away on the road toward the coast, I carried the lantern out to look at the notice.

In thick black lettering, in our language, the notice proclaimed that all the lands from the western mountain range to the sea were now a part of Keltane, and under the rule of the sovereign king. Our council was dissolved, and all our citizens owed allegiance and fealty to King Aerelon the Sixth. Signed with illegible flourishes, the parchment trailed scarlet ribbons from a saucer-sized purple wax seal.

I didn't feel any different, now that I was Keltanese. We had a quiet ride back up to our house, each of us lost in our own thought, including Gargle, as far as I could tell.

CHAPTER 16

With relief I found all as we had left it. Annora bade Ticker farewell, and I hurried to loose Gevarr and help him to the privy. He had the good grace to be grateful for my service, and say so. I told him he had been right.

"We are conquered, as you said. I saw them post a notice in the village."

"Ah. Was there much damage, did you see?"

"No, but folks' goods have been taken, and all the villagers are keeping off the streets and out of sight."

"Our forces would want to preserve the village and road, the better for uninterrupted trade. An occupying force needs food and shelter, so there's little sense in destroying the services needed."

"Or those who provide the services?"

"How did the mother fare?" he asked, instead of answering me.

"Well enough under Annora's care. I think she and the babe would have died, else. Do you know anything about turned babies?"

"Do I look like a man who knows anything about women's work?"

"No."

"You're lucky not to have to worry about getting a baby

birthed of Annora up here on this mountainside. Lucky your brother went off and left her a kissless bride, though I doubt he'd agree."

"He kissed her—I saw him!"

"That's … not what that means."

I felt my ears burn after I thought a moment. She really did share overmuch with the man. Or else he deduced overmuch. "Do you have any children?"

"Not as far as I know. A soldier's general experience with women is camp followers, not ladies and wives."

"Well, some of them have to be married."

"The camp followers? Hardly."

"No, the soldiers! My da was a soldier, and he married and had us." *And that is what comes of me letting my guard down.*

Between one shuffling step and the next, I saw his expression change from a grimace of concentration and pain to one of avid interest. On the heels of my light-hearted remark, he wanted to know all about it.

"When was he a soldier? Does he have maps and gear here?"

My turn to be wooden-faced. "He went for a soldier when he was young."

"Is he gone off soldiering now?"

"I told you, we were separated when we had to flee the invasion. Perhaps you should tell us what you know about the Keltanese plan, so we know if we should remain here or no. You will not be fit for travel for some time, Annora says. Bad to walk much on thawing feet. Hard to tell at first how much damage was done deep. *Really* bad if they freeze again. I wonder if we'll have to get some bone-setter to cut your feet off?" I knew I babbled, and hoped I could think and talk at the same time. No luck.

He was laughing at me when Annora met us at the door. "I'm fixing some bread and cider for the others. Will you have some? What is funny?"

Gevarr only shook his head and tottered over to the pallet.

After all my nagging of Annora to keep her tongue back of her teeth, I didn't want to say I had blurted out news that Gevarr might use, or pass on, to our harm.

I said yes to bread and jam and hot cider, and helped her fix it. I first put the poker into the fire to heat, then I carried the pitcher down into the cellar to collect the cider. By lack of time during their raid, or oversight, the troops had not pulled up the trap door in the kitchen floor, and emptied the cellar of stored food. Our root crops, parsnips, turnips and the like, still rested in their baskets. A keg of dried beans, another of flour, some honeycombs in jars all remained on the dusty shelves or standing on the dirt floor. A lovely big barrel of cider stood on blocks in one corner. We always put by a large store of food for the winter, since commonly snowed in for considerable stretches. I poked about while I waited for the pitcher to fill, and was amazed to find some small baskets of soft fruit, raspberries and blueberries, sitting fresh as when picked on the shelves. I hadn't noticed them before.

"Oh, that's an easy-enough spell," Annora said, when I carried some up to show her.

"You did this? You can work spell craft?"

"Yes, I'll teach you. It's easier than drying fruits or making preserves to put it by."

I wondered if Wils knew all the sorts of magic she could do. My mum had not fed us summer fruit in the shortened days of winter; I would have remembered. I wanted to find out what all her gran had taught her, and learn it, too.

I plunged the hot poker into the cider and it hissed fragrant steam. A treat on a frigid night, and the cider was not too hard yet for Morie to drink. It would be stout by spring.

As according to my new rules, I took Gevarr's to him, a generous portion as he had no supper. I determined to direct the conversation, not liking how it felt to be on the defensive after my blunder about Da.

"Do you think you might be able to walk on snow frames?

Some call them snow shoes. We have some stored below, to keep the mice from eating the gut laces. So they weren't lost in the barn fire."

"I came from warmer climate down south. What are they for?"

"To keep a man from sinking into the snow. It is kind of a paddle strapped to your boot, and spreads out your weight."

"I'll try one in the morning."

"You wear them two at a time. Or, one on each foot, I mean. We could have pulled you on the sled, but that did burn in the barn."

"Where is it you're taking me?"

"Remains to be seen," I said, and backed out of the alcove with his empty cup. In truth, I suppose I only wanted to give him something to ponder besides my da the soldier. And my brother's unkissed bride.

I chose to carry some of the supplies from the smithy's wife down to the cellar. It wouldn't do to have it all stolen if we were overrun again. The milk and eggs were welcome, and Annora stored them in the cool north corner of the larder. I longed for a bit of butter, and thought maybe we should ask for that if someone else needed a birth managed.

"Do you think his toes and fingers will be of full use in the end?" I asked Annora when I had finished stowing the goods.

She considered. "It is a good sign that the fluid in the blisters stays clear, and not bloody. Nothing blackens so far. It's early days yet, after the injury. Frostbite takes its time showing the full extent of the damage. You say you don't want to keep him until spring, but it may be spring before he's sorted."

I didn't like to hear that. "If he is able, I'd like to have him help me put up some kind of shelter for Dink. I believe our horses must have been taken by the troops, and our goats and chickens are eaten or run wild. I'd like to haul some hay from the field for Dink and keep him close here. We might have sudden need of better transport than our feet alone."

"If you can knock together some manner of sled, I can get the hay and drag it back."

"I'll look tomorrow for some barn wood with enough strength, and lash it together. Good that our store of rope was generous. And left for us. Nails are going to be hard to come by. Maybe the smith's wife would spare us some, if I went to the village."

"I should check on her within the week, to make sure she has no sign of childbed fever. Ticker will come fetch me. I think she'd give me whatever I asked," Annora said with a smile. I thought so, too.

Come a morning clear for once, I lugged an armload of snow frames up from the cellar. I settled Gevarr on the back stoop, and strapped a pair on his feet. Since his single boot would not fit his swollen foot, and none of Da's would fit him either, I had wrapped his rag-bound feet with leather and secured that with twine.

"This is how to walk in them," I said, after I strapped on my own. I paced heel-toe lifting them high, and used the snow poles in either hand to aid my balance. "It is not a fast way to travel, but faster than sinking to the belly with each step."

I pulled him upright and gave him poles. He proved no more able to walk in the frames than I would prove able to fly if I jumped off the roof. It takes time to get the way of it, and he could not keep on his feet. He ended in a tumble, with Gargle cackling so at him that the bird fell off the eaves and landed with a soft plop in the drifted bank below, scaly black feet uppermost.

I laughed so hard at Gargle that tears came to my eyes. Gevarr perhaps thought I made sport of him, and threw one of the poles away with a disgusted grunt. He tried to rise again using the other, and I went to help him up. When I had him swaying on his feet, I pulled Gargle out by his stick-like legs, still laughing. Gargle tried to peck me, then shook off snow and flapped to the porch rail to perch and preen, grumbling.

I gave it up as hopeless, and removed the frames for Gevarr. "When you are better, we'll try another lesson with boots. It takes practice."

"I heard you planning for Annora to go fetch hay."

"We had plenty of stored hay in the loft," I said, pointing at the black ruin of our barn.

"Do not let her go alone."

"Do you think there are troops on the mountain, still?"

He looked off over the snow pack, upslope. "Maybe, or maybe not. But she is at risk if any should discover her. Even wrapped in heavy winter gear, enough of that fresh young face can be seen. And the way she moves marks her a woman." He brushed snow off his knees with clumsy, thick-wrapped hands. "You have kept her safe up 'til now, and must have good sense for a half-grown boy to have done so. Still … where is my knife?"

"I have a knife." *Bah, how easily I am surprised into revealing what I should keep to myself.* "Yours is put away."

"Give mine to her. If I'm no use to go with her, at least both of you should be armed. Take your sword, too. The one half again as big as you, if you can wield it. It must be your da's, eh?"

My breath huffed out in a cloud, and I did not speak for a bit. Into that pause the door opened, and Annora stood on the threshold wearing a pair of Wils's trousers. Both of us stared at her, jaws hanging.

"You think it's easy to snow shoe in a skirt? Help me strap them on, Judian, and we'll go look for sled wood in the barn."

Gevarr waved me away when I made to shift him back inside. "I'll wait here and see if I can be of any use in sled-making. I might be able to keep the boards from moving by lying on them as you secure them. A dead weight may be all I'm good for." He was thinking, then, to aid me in keeping the others safe? Or, thinking if I gave Annora his knife he'd have no trouble taking it from her? I could not trust him easily. I called Wieser to watch him before making my way to the barn with Annora.

We used the axe to bang loose enough boards for a five plank sled, and some shorter pieces for bracing. I was able to salvage a handful of the square-headed nails that had held our fine barn together. I despaired of raising another half so large and snug, when men came home and folk got about the business of living again.

Annora dragged the wood over to the porch, where I had shoveled the drifts away to clear a space to assemble the sled. I continued deconstructing the sagging east barn wall, to free up lumber for a shelter for Dink. I stacked these boards by the trough.

She laid out boards, and helped Gevarr to stand when I returned from my stack of lumber.

"You go in, we'll manage this," I told her.

"Another pair of hands will make it go faster," she said.

"Aye, since my pair of hands are good for nothing," Gevarr allowed.

"You must take care not to pull on the scar at your neck," she said. "It's lucky you didn't start bleeding again, trying the snow walking."

"No one likes a scold," he said mildly.

No, and I didn't like their easy way with each other. We all worked together in the end, though. Because it was true that all three of us could finish the work quicker than a crippled man and a *half-grown boy*. Before long we had a lashed-together, cobbled sled I could pull with a length of rope looped over my shoulders. Annora, born in the wide-river land to the south, said it put her in mind of a raft.

"May it float over the snow, then. I need a tarp and more rope, so we don't shed all the loaded hay as we make our way back from the field." I helped Gevarr back into his alcove, and then went upstairs while Annora searched for a canvas tarp and lashing rope.

When I met her in the kitchen, I handed her Gevarr's blade.

CHAPTER 17

A good thing nothing pursued us to the hay field, since there was no way to rush. Wieser bounded beside us; Gevarr swore we needed her senses more than he needed guarding. He even offered to be tied again, so I yielded and left him in the kitchen, with Virda and Morie in their bed chamber with the door locked. Wieser made many detours to plow her nose into small animal runs along the meadow edge. Likely she would bring us a brace of rabbits for the stew pot, so I did nothing to discourage her. Morie carried fond thoughts of the dancing rabbits from this meadow, but if she encountered the meat already butchered and in the gravy she might not recall the twilight magic of months ago.

Gargle tried to ride standing on the sled, but couldn't keep his balance, so gave up, cawing as he mounted to the sky above us.

We found the remaining haystacks trampled about with horse and deer prints, snow dug away from the bases so the fodder could be reached. *I should try to take a deer*, I thought. It not being good to live too long on rabbit—not enough fat. I would have a job field dressing a decent-sized deer, though, and getting it back to the house by myself. If I brought the shovel and buried what I couldn't carry, perhaps. Or built a cairn for the rest of the meat, since the ground was frozen and other predators would find meat buried only in snow. A hunt would take some planning …

Piling armfuls of hay on our sled became a game, as we slipped and slid even in our snow frames. We couldn't use the poles with loaded arms, and often joined the hay when we tried to throw it onto the sled. I had fed the ropes underneath the planking before we started, and when the pile looked like it would feed Dink for several days, we spread the canvas overtop and secured it.

Gargle had some purchase to steady his ride, then, and settled in with feet gripping the rope for the return journey. "That rabbit is not for you. Leave it be, and get fed at home," I told him. Wieser had brought one to us while we loaded, and set off on the hunt again. The wind ruffled the rabbit's fur where it laid, tied next to Gargle's perch. "Watch him while I pull," I said to Annora. "He keeps sneaking looks at our supper."

We traveled no faster going back, though the loaded sled pulled almost like the un-laden, or fair at best. Between my puffing breath and wool-wrapped head, for a wonder I heard the sound in the trees south of the meadow.

The clang of metal-on-metal carries remarkable well.

I halted and wheeled, with a finger to where my lips lay under my scarf. Annora stopped at once and voiced no question. I pointed to the north side of the sled and crouched there with her.

"Did you hear? It sounded like swordplay in the trees there. I want Wieser back from hunting, so I can take her along to check. You stay here out of sight."

"The sled is sure to stand out if anyone's looking this way."

"There's nowhere to hide it quickly. You have your knife?" She nodded as a sharp clank came again on the frigid air. Wieser came to my side, panting, and whined softly by my ear. "I know," I said. "We have to go see who's there."

The powdery snow did not crunch as I made my way to the edge of the trees. I had to abandon the snow frames there, and crawl forward to peer through the fir boughs and bare larch limbs. I hoped I could find the right place; no more sounds came as Wieser and I approached.

I saw three men under the lower branches of a bare tree, hunched over trying to light a fire with flint and striker. A sword stood hilt-uppermost, jammed in the snow beside them. A fourth man foundered up, arms full of tinder and small fuel. They did not wear uniforms of either Merced or Keltane, but seemed to have blankets and rags drawn about them rather than cloaks.

Were they renegades? I could hear that they spoke, it seemed sharply, to one another, but could make out no words. I would get Annora back to the house and ask Gevarr what he made of it, I decided. I backed out of my position, and had just pushed up to stand when a cold hand covered my mouth and strong arm gripped me from behind.

I wrenched around, shoving with my left arm and digging through layers of wool with my right for the knife at my waist. Wieser launched herself at the man, setting her jaws on the arm he had slung around me. He cursed, and I over-balanced as he released me, pulling my knife free as I fell backwards. I looked up at him as he wrestled with Wieser, and the face I saw, I knew.

It was Wils.

"Wieser stop!" She loosed her hold on his arm and I struggled to my feet. He was breathing too hard to speak, it seemed. I flung my arms round him, then as quickly pushed him away. "Gods, you stink! Is Da with you?"

"See—" he panted, "how good—you smell after—blast all, Judian, you're tall! What's this hulking great dog? No, Da's still at the border fort, as far as I know. Can we get my men in out of the weather? I've been down scouting the house. I reckoned you'd be up at the caves, and thought the chimney smoke was Keltanese troops. They burned the barn?"

"I cannot tell you months of news standing here. Those are your men yonder? Get them and we'll bring the sled in. Annora will be wondering what's become of me, she's over there—"

"You brought her out in the field?"

Moments home and already complaining.

121

"You get to see her that much sooner," I started, but he was already setting off where I had pointed. "Tell her it's you, with the beard and all, she may get her knife out when she sees you coming!"

As I was delayed by collecting my snow frames at the edge of the wood, by the time I got to the sled I found the two intertwined and laughing. "Shush, there may still be renegades out here. Can you get your men and come on?"

I sat on the hay to put my snow frames back on, and found Gargle looking over my shoulder. "I can't think what use you were in this. Ah, and I see you've opened our rabbit while you were waiting, too. Though it wouldn't have fed so many men, I know." Gargle croaked as if to say, "well, of course not, so I kept it from going to waste" and hopped back into position on top of the load, ready to be saved the effort of flying home. "Crows know best," I said to Wieser, mocking him. "Or think they do." I gave Gargle what I hoped was a repressive look, and went to take up my tow rope.

When he returned from the woods with his men, Wils directed two of them to pull the sled, so I walked behind with the rest. I had been trying to raise the subject of Gevarr without success at getting a word in, besides it being hard to wade through the snow and talk. When we came within sight of the house, I grabbed Wils's arm. "Let me go ahead. Annora, tell Wils about our—" What was he? Not a guest, an enemy but it seemed not our enemy? "—eh, whatever he is. I'll make sure he doesn't think we're hostages."

She turned to Wils and I went on. Gevarr met me at the door with the poker in one hand and a piece of firewood in the other. Why had I not thought to hide the fireplace tools?

"Give me that." I put my hand out for the poker. "My brother's home, and has some of his men with him."

"His *men*? Who went with him when your *family* fled and you all got separated?" Gevarr said, holding the poker behind his head out of reach.

I stomped a foot. "Are you going to make a stand and crack my head open with all of them outside? Give me the poker, and no, I haven't told you everything. You are outnumbered now, and not fit, besides. Give it to me."

He did so, and dropped his club, too. "I wonder what I did in life to warrant this punishment of being bossed about by a boy and a bunch of women?" He glared my way.

"Just go lie down and act like you can't get up on your own. Wils is going to have plenty to say in my ear about you being here, I'm certain. I'll go tell Virda and Morie they're coming."

"You'll find them in the cellar," Gevarr said. In answer to my swinging back to face him, he continued, "I saw a man hanging about outside. I was cursing sending both animals with you, leaving me no way to warn you about him, and persuaded the two to hide in the cellar, in case there was trouble."

It was going to be a relief to hand all this to Wils. See if he could get this bunch of wood-wits to stay organized and do what he said. I'd just watch. I shook my head, and let Virda and Morie up out of the cellar. Once I shuttled them back to the bedroom, I draped my cloak over the back of Da's chair. Then I squared my shoulders and waited to face Wils when he came in through the back door.

CHAPTER 18

W ils cast a dark look at the quilt-hung corner, and shed his blankets and rags. He took Annora by the hand, told the men who filed in after him to shout if the soldier moved, and said to me, "Upstairs."

He began as soon as I shut the door on the three of us.

"After you went to all that trouble to avoid the enemy, why did you bring one in to sit by the fire?"

I told him my side of the story from his wedding until he attacked me in the wood, and finished with "… and if you think you could have done better, here's your chance, because I'm done. If they all do what *you* tell them, it may be because you have four other men that I did not have, just think of that when you're in charge."

We glowered at each other until Annora said, "Wils, you know he's done a fine job in spite of our … being a lot to manage. And you'll be wanting to question Ge—the soldier and see if he has information you can pass on." She won a grudging nod. "Tell us what's befallen you since you left us. Unless you want me to see to your men first? They must be hungry." I suspected so, they all looked drawn and pale, Wils maybe most of all. He shook his head, though.

He drew her down to sit with him on the bare frame of the bed she shared with Morie before we were refugees. We had since carried the ticking to the bedchamber below. Annora still had on his trousers, with the knife tucked in the belt of her blouse and her fair hair straying from the coiled plait at her neck. He smiled at her and cupped her chin in his grimy hand.

"How I've longed to look at you," he said, voice as soft as his gaze. I'd have left them alone, but there was no chance of me missing what he had to say about what had happened to him. So, I sat on the floor and drew my knees up.

Wils began his story. "We went west out of Bale Harbour, marching with all the men you saw. The marshal Da was seeking traveled ahead of us, delegating conscription teams and troops to gather supplies. Da and I went from officer to officer, pointing out that a mounted man could never be caught up by pursuers on foot. After days of this, finally one of the procurers found Da a mount— a leggy grey stallion, a fine horse. I hope he has him still. For me, they found a plow horse that shook my teeth loose trying to keep pace with Da. Our new speed brought us closer to the marshal, but always we heard:"Yesterday noon the last of them left," or "If only you'd been here when they were delayed by rain, day before last." The procurers were like locusts, stripping orchards and mills, and the folk began to flee for the coast, fearing what worse was coming from the west. So, the tide of refugees began to impede us. They had misadventures at the ferries, and had to be rescued from the current. They broke axles from overloading, they slid off the road trying to travel in foul weather. Da and I tried to help as we could, and persuade them to leave all the stuff they had packed so carefully … their own safety had to be all, in these times.

"Like your Fieldmaster Behring, no one seemed to know if the Keltanese were attacking, or if war only threatened and we sought to turn it aside. Messengers came and went, but who could say if their information was true? Or fresh? Da and I waylaid any couriers we saw, but which had news we could act on with any confidence? There was no way to know. Some folk argued the winter was too close for an actual invasion, others saw the uncanny autumn lingering as a sign the enemy was too powerful to resist, and advocated surrender. We kept seeking the marshal. Da thought he would know, if anyone did, what was truly happening."

Wils paused a moment, and in the silence I heard a spoon tapped on the rim of a pot and chairs scrape. Savory smells wafted up to us, as well.

"Virda has a nose for hungry men," Annora smiled. "Because she has all those sons. She'll see to feeding them below. Do you want something now?"

I did, but Wils shook his head and continued. "We chased that blasted marshal all the way to the border. There, we found he established a massive encampment on our side of the pass, and ran him to ground at the fort that overlooks the trade road. Immense place, built up out of the very bedrock. He seized on Da to lead a negotiating party. They planned to invite the Keltanese over the pass to the fort, Hasseron, it's called, and threaten to close the road and void all transit treaties if the troops on their side of the mountains were not dispersed. Scouts said they outnumbered us three to one. Those who made it back.

"Da chose the rest of his party but forbade me to come. The other soldiers had thought of me as Da's adjutant or assistant, few of them knew me for his son until then. I remained at the fort, and had the worst two days of my life, fretting over him. I nearly brushed the coat off his grey stallion. The party took heavier mounts over the pass.

"Late the second night, he and two of the twelve he had left with came tearing up on blown horses, calling for the gates to be opened to them. We turned away their pursuers from the ramparts, before our troops on the valley floor even had time to muster. Da marched straight to the hall and seized hold of the marshal by the tunic-front, shouting it was a ruse, to send the army to the harbour, that Keltane would attack from the northwest route. It was all lies that so many enemy waited over the border at the pass. A show of camps and troops spread thin, with fires and tents multiplied by some magic to fool us. The summer raids along the border, all events were designed to suggest the threat lay in the west.

"I'd never seen Da in such a fury. He had every officer from the fort rousted and sent down to get the troops ready to travel. It was dark, deep night, and he rode down himself to organize breaking camp and loading all of it for dawn departure. By the gods, he had them moving! They were funneling onto the road east when he came to me in the morning. "You know what this means," he said to me. "Keltane will come right over the top of our place on the way to the sea." He looked haunted. I said you would surely be holed up in the cave by now, because I couldn't stand to think otherwise. But he said you'd never be expecting the northwest route, why would you, when the military hadn't even seen this knife before their face."

Here he passed a hand over his eyes, and Annora smoothed his hair. "We were safe. Judian had us snug and away from the route. We never saw but a few of the enemy."

She meant this to be soothing, but he gave me a fierce look and said, "Until you chose to adopt one."

"As you weren't here to ask, I had to make a choice and live with it," I said shortly. "Did you and Da set out for home then, when the troops moved out?"

"I wanted to. I was packing. Da advised the fort commander to close the pass, and the old sot wanted Da's help to do it. They were preparing their teams for the climb to the high ground—to loose the rocks that would make the road impassable. Then Keltane made their move, and in the space of a few hours, we were under siege and the few troops Keltane had on the border were enough to pin us within the fort.

"Da had been through a siege in the South War. He directed the fort in conserving water and rationing food. I thought I'd go mad as weeks passed. That's when I gathered the men I've brought. An old groom told me he heard tell of a tunnel or cave that came out in the valley, and I conscripted these four to search for it with me. The fort is a warren, and we scrabbled in every corner. The place is built on bedrock, as I said, so there was no thought of digging a way out. Down in the depths by the cisterns, we discovered the old tunnel. It appeared mostly natural, very steep and low-ceilinged in places, enlarged by pick and shovel in the worst spots. We cleared some of the rubble, brought what supplies we could cadge and our gear, and waited for full moon.

"It was hard to tell Da I was going, but he understood. He gave me messages to carry to our troops in the east, and bade us good fortune. He said to tell you he would come when he could, that they had means to hold out for a long time. If as you say, we are already conquered, perhaps he'll come soon."

"I've hoped for that," I said. "For both of you to get home safe at last."

He didn't seem able to stop once he had started his tale, and spoke on in a weary voice I hardly recognized. "We came here on foot through desolation, traveling mostly at night and sleeping in shifts during the day. I hope I never have to eat another dirt-crusted turnip dug out of an abandoned garden. The snows started as we closed on Leverton. Our troops had passed long before us, and we only saw signs of battle near the village road just before we turned north to home. When I saw the barn had been burned, I sent the men into the wood and skulked about trying to tell who was home. The rest, you know."

Annora stood. "Come, you must eat now, while I heat some wash water for you and get you clean clothes." His smell *was* penetrating in closed quarters. "Judian, carry the mattress back up here, please, and arrange some pallets for the men downstairs—"

"I need to question the soldier you're keeping," Wils interrupted.

"He'll be there tomorrow. He won't forget any news overnight," she said briskly. She put one hand on her hip and held out the other when he remained sitting, so with a rueful smile he rose.

"Don't boss me about in front of my men, or I'll be made

sport of from here forward. They've already given me grief enough about how hard I've driven them to get back to you."

I made ready to escort Gevarr out to the privy when we got below, but Wils said, "Let Perk take him." The burliest of the four rose from his place by the fire, not eagerly.

"I've been taking him all along. Surely your man is only just getting warm after living outside for weeks," I said.

"If I overpowered him, where would I go?" came Gevarr's voice from behind the quilt.

Wils's men all looked at each other, then at Wils. "I thought you said he was kept muddled," said Wils. "He sounds clear enough to me."

"That was at first, when he was the most ill and we were deciding what to do with him," Annora said.

"As opposed to now, when he's better and can have the run of the place?" Wils said, voice rising.

"He's not running anytime soon when he still needs aid to the privy." I put on my cloak. "I'll take Wieser if that makes you feel better. Come at a run if she barks."

"Mmm," Wils said around a mouthful of barley gruel. "By all means, take the hell-hound with you. Gods but hot food is good." Annora grinned at me over her shoulder, having just put the bowl in his hands.

Morie had been allowed out of the bedroom when Virda came out to feed Wils's men, but she was shy of them and I hadn't heard her voice while we had been upstairs. Now she saw Wils, however, she recovered the power of speech. She took up position on his lap and gabbled at him while he nodded and spooned in his supper. I slipped behind the quilt with a cloak for Gevarr over my arm.

"You'd be wise to seem feeble," I told him, as I helped him stand and put his arm round my shoulders.

"As compared to you?"

I jabbed him in the ribs with my shoulder, making him grunt. "Do you think you will like living in the cellar tied to a pole? Wils

130

has reason to be wary of Keltanese in any condition."

Gevarr was docile enough on the way to and from; and did not meet the many eyes that followed his every shuffling step. I gave him his bowl of barley when he was propped back on his pallet.

"Will he interrogate me tonight or tomorrow?" he asked as I turned to go.

"In the morning, likely."

He nodded. "That's what I'd do, if I were him."

I planned to sit in on that session. I made myself busy getting bedding, and what might pass for it, together for the men. Our store of blankets and quilts was thin, what with some of it still up in the caves and one larger one hanging in the kitchen corner. Morie fell asleep and was carried in to bed. Virda next went to lie down, tired from cooking for the group. She wasn't well yet, I reminded myself sternly. I'd have to see to it she didn't feel compelled to take care of these men as if they were her sons.

How were we going to feed them all, anyway? Gevarr already made a dent in our stores. Five more men? How did armies get fed? By stealing food, it seemed, but that couldn't go on once an army stopped marching. There was only so much food to go around in any one place.

I was musing like this while I spread a rug by the hearth. Perk got up to help me, perhaps grateful that I saved him a trip outside. He had dark-tanned skin like folk from the far south, and a barrel chest. I liked his wide, easy smile. He had a tendency to squint—as if he was always looking into the sun. He seemed delighted to have come along home with Wils, shown by his eagerness to be useful.

Perk claimed the first place I made, and the next man stepped up to help and introduced himself as Cobbel. He was tall, ginger-haired and abundantly freckled. He was made, to my eyes, out of knee bones, knuckles and elbows, with a beaky nose. He looked to me like the sort of thin man who could eat tremendous amounts of food. He settled into the second space with a tug at his forelock.

The last two were sharing mugs of brewed herbs and quiet

131

words with Wils, who sat in Da's chair with Annora leaning her hip on the oaken arm. Both men had wide foreheads and flat noses, and the resemblance made me think they must be related, although one was fair and the other sallow. The fair one noticed my regard and jerked a thumb at his chest. "Beckta," he said, and then pointed at the other man. "He's Miskin. I don't want to say I'm glad your barn was gutted, but Wils had told us to expect to be sleeping in the hayloft. I'm not that sorry to be by a fire and within four walls."

"Are you brothers?"

"Cousins. We served the fort's horsemaster, until your brother recruited us for courier work."

This remark caused Wils's gaze to sharpen; he made a snap of a nod toward the alcove and Beckta looked chastised. "Can I help you with our beds now?"

Once they were all set up, I banked the fire for the night. I told Wieser to guard Gevarr, but Miskin carried a chair to the back door. He drew his smelly blanket around his shoulders and said, "Wils told me to take first watch."

I looked about for Wils but found he and Annora were missing. "Leave 'em be," said Miskin with a grin. "They managed to get away upstairs without calling too much attention to themselves."

"Aye," came Perk's voice from the dim light by the hearth. "He's waited long enough. And we've had miles to hear about how long he's waited, too."

Another man laughed, must have been Beckta, because Cobbel's voice said, "He never talked ... unseemly."

This drew a hoot from Miskin. "It was more what he didn't say. Go to sleep."

A sound idea, I decided, and turned to go to my own bed. At least there would be no more talk of kissless brides, because I knew Gevarr was listening, too, from behind his barrier.

CHAPTER 19

When I went in to Gevarr on waking, he told me the dawn watch had already seen him to the washhouse. "I'm being readied for my interview, it seems."

Wils left him in the corner while we made short work of the smithy's eggs and some griddle cakes Annora and Virda served to appreciative appetites. Morie was indulged with extra honey on hers, and I felt a twinge for Gevarr when I carried him in another bowl of barley gruel. He accepted it with no ill-humor. I supposed Wils was putting him in his place.

When the breakfast dishes were cleared away, Perk and Cobbel brought Gevarr to the table and seated him facing Wils. The women were banished to the bedroom. Wils's men took places on his side of the table. I refused to be sent to the other room and planted myself at the end of the table nearest the cellar. Gevarr folded his reddened, swollen hands on the scrubbed wood and waited.

It will never be known how Wils meant to start his questioning, because Wieser at that moment sprang up barking with her hair standing up along her spine. Gargle began a frenzied pecking at the front window, and continued window-to-window around the house.

Men flew instantly to every curtain, peering out cautiously to avoid being seen in return. I opened the cellar, and Wils appeared carrying Morie, leading the others.

"Three enemy, leading a pack mule up from the road. No weapons drawn," reported Cobbel from the front window. I brought Gevarr to the cellar steps, and turned to yank down his quilt barrier. Blast all, pallets lay about everywhere in plain view.

Wils tossed cloth down to Annora below, saying, "Gag him."

"Not necessary," Gevarr said as he started down.

Wils gave a savage shake of his head. "You gag him, Miskin."

The other men were gathered for their descent when three loud bangs echoed from the front door. At least they weren't kicking it in. Yet.

Who should answer? The others disappeared down the steps and Wils closed the trapdoor on Perk, who remained on the steep, twisting stairs just below the floor. Wils and I looked at each other as the bangs came again. I pointed at myself and Wieser, and Wils nodded and stepped back into the corner so he couldn't be seen from the front door. I saw the gleam of a long knife in his hand as I turned to go answer the knocking.

Wieser growled loud as I shouted through the wood, "Who's there? What do you want?"

"Open the door, boy. By order of the King."

I opened it just wide enough for Wieser to put her head through, snarling. Foam dripped from her jaws. Two of them took a step back, but the third was the one in charge.

"We're here to take food for the guard." He put his arm to the door, but Wieser shoved against the edge with her shoulders, straining to get at him.

"Wait and I'll bring it. I can't hold her." I shut the door before he could speak, and Wieser launched herself at it, clawing and howling. Next she leapt at the window as a soldier tried to peer through it; his oath as he jumped back was one I hoped Morie didn't hear. I snagged several cabbages and a small sack of meal and shoved all in a cloth bag.

"This is all I can spare," I said, as I contrived to shove the bag out while making a show of barely holding Wieser within.

"Are you alone up here, boy?"

"No, I have the dog." The pitch of her barking increased to the point I could hardly shout over it.

"And what does the beast eat?" he inquired, looking into the bag without much enthusiasm. I felt the same way about cabbages, that's why he was getting them.

"She catches her own, of late."

He handed the bag to one of the others to carry to the mule. Which, I saw with relief, was not our Dink. I sent a wish for Dink to make himself scarce, and hoped whatever magic I had was working.

"We need hay for our horses, as well."

"Our hay was burned with our barn." *No, it won't do to antagonize.* "There's a few haystacks in the field east. You're welcome to what you can get there."

"Bring it down to the village livery," he called over Wieser's tireless assault.

"I can't. The sled was in the barn," I called in response.

He spat out an oath of his own. "Then I'll send some men back up to fetch it. How much hay is left there?"

I made him repeat his question, claiming I couldn't hear over Wieser's racket, then shouted, "Not much since the deer have been at it," with my hands cupped to my mouth.

"Useless folk—achh, a pax on them all!" He wheeled away and waved the other two back to the mule. Wieser continued to sound crazed; gobs of foam flecked the floor and wall. *May they give us up as too much trouble for too little return,* I thought, and leaned my forehead on the door and closed my eyes. When I opened them, Wils stood close, looking at me with narrowed eyes.

"Glad you two are on our side," he said, and went to let the others up from the cellar.

When next we attempted to begin with Gevarr, I did not have to make my own way to the table. Wils pulled out a chair for me.

Again, the first question had not been asked when Wieser gave her yipping cry. I tried to explain to Wils that this had a different meaning to the last alarm, but he insisted on repeating the drill. I saw Gevarr trying to keep from laughing aloud as he was shuttled to the cellar for the second time.

"It'll likely be Ticker," I told Wils, reminding him that Annora would be expected to go check the mother and baby in the village.

"Cannot Virda go in her stead?"

He looked so uneasy, I felt for him. I remembered Virda needing to rest after fixing a simple meal the day before, though. I proposed Annora and I go and take along Wieser and Gargle to guard us, since Wieser need not be left at home to look to Gevarr.

"The smith's family will likely give us food, which we need more than ever now."

He gave his consent as Ticker mounted the front steps. The boy was beaming. His mum felt stronger every day and the baby proved an easy feeder. He was only too happy to have Gargle atop the back of the sleigh watching for soldiers, when he learned we had been visited. He must have just missed the trio on his way to us. Wieser made us crowded in the sleigh, but did provide some extra warmth with her wooly coat. She seemed to enjoy the wind in her face as much as Gargle did, and worked her nose the whole ride.

Annora went in to check that all was in order with mother and infant. The younger boys fussed over Wieser, and fed her bits of cheese that I would have liked to have eaten myself, but she rated a treat for her performance of the morning. I pocketed a couple of bits for Gargle, who deserved reward, as well.

Either the food-collectors had not visited the smithy, or they had been given short shrift if they had, because their larder lacked nothing that I could see. As soon as Annora declared the pair fit, Donah Estegg began directing Ticker to load the sleigh for us. We were gifted with more eggs and milk, plus a haunch of venison that bespoke a better-favored hunting excursion than the one that had first brought the boy and his mother to us. A box of salted fish and a keg of nails completed our load. I couldn't thank them enough, and prayed we wouldn't run across the three soldiers on our way home in the sleigh.

When we swung around to the high road, the miller's wife waved us into her yard. She and her broad-backed daughter hefted a sack of flour into the back of the sleigh. She clasped Annora's hand, and laid a finger over her lips. "We have no wagon to get goods to the harbour, so better this goes with you."

The village was still unnaturally quiet. I reflected that it would not be long before the soldiers suspected folk of holding out on them, and began to bring more men along so they could search out our villagers' stores and take what they found.

"Ticker, when you get back home, you and Tarn would be wise to hide your supplies, in several places. Well hidden. Then can you go about town and advise others to do the same, but keep it very secret?"

"Like spies?" he asked, shifty-eyed.

"Much like. The soldiers who came to our place looking to take food and hay, are sure to make the rounds to you, as well. Better they find empty shelves and apparent want than leave your family really without means. Soldiers are always hungry, my da says. They won't care if they leave enough for you."

"But you must be careful," Annora put in.

Ticker nodded and clucked to his horse. Wieser and Gargle both seemed more interested in what was in the back of the sleigh under the canvas than in smelling the air on the way back. Even if they were distracted from their guard duty, we in any case met no one on our road home.

Ticker helped unload and asked good questions about potential hiding places. Rafters? Under the floor planks in the forge? I shared my methods of keeping out mice and vermin. He seemed eager to get about his task. As I had been, preparing the caves, I thought. Didn't that seem longer ago than it was!

Annora carried the eggs and milk, and I went in to corral some help in carrying the heavy things to the cellar. We found Virda and Morie braiding loaves on the kitchen table.

And no one else at home at all.

CHAPTER 20

Annora called after me when I banged out of the back door. "Oh, please wait, Judian! You don't know they took him away to be rid of him. Wils would have told Virda something, surely!"

They had left none of the snow shoes, and taken Gevarr on the sled, apparently. *Fine, look for me at your backs*, I thought grimly, and set off staggering in the sled track. Wieser and Gargle joined me, but I sent Wieser back. Annora stood on the stoop where I pointed. "Wieser, you must stay. Nobody is home but the women. What if the soldiers come again?" She wagged at me, and turned for home with the bounding, leaping way that made her look like a shaggy horse jumping hedgerows. Annora lifted a hand, in acknowledgment that I would not be dissuaded, I guessed.

I floundered on, thoughts pumping as furiously as my heart. What could Wils be thinking, not waiting for me? Why drag him so far into the wilderness to kill him, if that was what they were about? Had Gevarr been obstinate when Wils questioned him? Or, worse, said something about Annora to enrage Wils? By gods' teeth, this was hard going. Was Gevarr already murdered? To think I had once considered murdering him myself, and now I prayed to all the gods I would be in time to save him.

Gargle flew ahead from one treetop to the next. He swooped to my shoulder when I struggled to the top of a ridge.

"Don't peck!" I panted, when he seemed to be choosing a place to poke his beak. "Do you mean you see them?" He squawked in my ear and took wing again. As I crested the ridge I saw four men pulling a fifth, who was sitting upright, praise gods for good fortune. They were having a job dragging him up slope. I was faster coming down to them, found Wils first and shoved him hard in the chest.

"What madness is this? I'm not gone an hour and you're leaving Virda and Morie alone to chase off into the woods?"

Wils shoved me back, but lost his balance and fell sideways onto Gevarr.

"*Somebody* grab him by the scruff of the neck, will you?" Wils said to his mates.

"If you think you can catch me." I glared at them all. None of them reached for me, so I turned again on Wils. "Tell me what's happening right now!"

"Gevarr led us to a cache the invaders left. You're a bit full of yourself since you've been on your own," Wils snarled, trying to shift an arm under himself to rise.

"I haven't been on my own, have I? I've been hauling your wife and sister around the mountain trying to keep us all alive. Towing Gevarr around in the cold is only going to set him back. And what did you all have to come for? Where is Cobbel?" For I noted now he was the one not among the party.

The others said nothing, but opened their cloaks to show arrows, knives and swords tucked about their persons; the weapons from the cache they had been led to, I surmised. Wils regained his footing, with a solicitous push from Gevarr, whose mouth was twitching.

"Shut it, Judian. This doesn't involve you," Wils said harshly.

I had plenty to say about that, and drew breath to begin, but Gevarr said, "Not prudent to be out here shouting." He looked about him at the drifting snow. "I think if Merced had an army of boys like Judian, things might have gone another way."

Perk laughed, and got a look from under Wils's brows that could have scorched a plank.

"Yah, they have some fierce boy warriors in these parts, I've heard," Beckta said, lips twisting. "I've never seen anybody get close enough to strike you first blow, Wils," he continued with exaggerated innocence.

Wils cast his eyes skywards, and the two hauling on Gevarr's sled took up the rope again. I fell in behind, and we toiled uphill.

"Are you all right? Have you gotten too cold?" I asked Gevarr.

"You sound like somebody's mother. Hot stone," he nodded toward his feet, then held up his wool-swathed hands, "and baked whole squash. I've been coddled, in truth."

Did having more weapons do any good if you had no more hands to wield them? I remembered thinking I was happy to hand all my responsibilities over to Wils now he had returned. Believing he'd be better at it than he was proving to be … I schemed to find him alone and prise his plans from him. He must have something in mind besides hanging about the farm with his lot of men through winter solstice. Beckta had said Wils recruited them for couriers. I would find out about that. Perhaps Cobbel was on such an errand now, and they didn't like to say in front of Gevarr.

As usual when I returned from anywhere of late, Virda and Annora were frantic and Moric wasn't sure what the fuss was about, but was pleased to whine as her contribution. Murr, grown lean and leggy now, found the charged atmosphere ideal for stalking people's feet and pouncing on their skirts, and so stirred the pot of distress that attended our arrival.

"Glad to be home?" I overheard Gevarr say in Wils's ear as my brother helped him to his pallet. I only barely caught the remark, since everyone else chattered at us in high female voices that made my head squeeze.

Just as Wils bellowed "Enough!" the other three men came in. They had hidden the scavenged weaponry somewhere outside, I gathered. Next, Wils pointed at me and then at the ceiling.

I headed up the stairs and heard Wils trying to put Annora off from coming along. "Oh, no. At least you must be kept from fratricide," she said as she swept past him to follow me. We three faced each other in the watery winter light slanting into the bedroom.

Wils opened his mouth but I spoke first. "Where's Cobbel? Gone on a courier errand?"

It appeared this wasn't the start Wils expected. "Gevarr warned me you don't miss much. I told him not to tell me about my own brother, and he predicted I'd underestimate you to my peril." Wils sat on the bed. "I was trying to let Gevarr think Cobbel stayed home with Virda and Morie, until you came plowing up to announce the women were left alone. Did you really think we took Gevarr out to kill him?"

"I thought you might. He's too valuable, as you have discovered in time. He's not told nearly all he knows, no matter how much he gave you when you questioned him. Did he tell you about the mages?"

He had not, evidently, so I did. "That's the only reason their plan to use the northwest pass worked. Virda thinks the sorcerers came from across the sea to help Keltane delay the snow and keep the pass open. I've never heard of any skilled with weather-working who come from Keltane or Merced."

"You've not heard of many things, being only twelve."

"Have you heard of any?" I said, stung.

He shook his head. "I sent Cobbel to deliver a message to any of our troops he can find in the cliffs above Bale Harbour."

I thought it more likely he would find some Keltanese troops there. "Did you know Annora can send messages with hawks, and direct the birds where to deliver them by magic?" I might have sprouted another nose, the way he looked at me. "Wouldn't it be better to put your messages in code and send them by animal courier, than risk your men each time?"

His head swiveled to Annora, who said eagerly, "I will just

need a bit of something that comes from where I'm sending the bird, so I can feed that to them with the proper spell."

"Have I come to the right house?" Wils wondered aloud.

"We may not be able to fight in a battle, but we can fight in other ways. You don't have to do this work alone," she told him.

"Apparently not, what with you two suborning enemy soldiers for the greater glory of Merced. Gevarr told us their scouts chased a boy in the forest one day. He thinks that must have been you. Was it?"

"Likely, yah. You see? Gevarr never told me he knew of that or suspected it was me." Had I forgotten to mention that incident when I told Wils our story? "Does Cobbel know his way? It's far to walk in this heavy weather."

"I put him up on Dink and gave him one of Da's maps. He has a good sense of direction, better than most."

"Send me along next time. I have Wieser and Gargle to aid with direction, and also with avoiding enemy troops."

"So I should send my younger brother out into hostile territory?"

"A boy traveling is less likely to attract notice than a soldier-age man, I think."

"I think you can count on Judian, at least until we work out the ways I can help," Annora suggested, taking his hand. He never actually said yes, but allowed her to pull him to his feet. She walked us back belowstairs to the fireside and gave us hot drinks. Beckta, Miskin and Perk had stowed the smithy's gifts I left standing out when I took off after them. Each of them gave me a grin, I think glad to see me reappear without blacked eyes or swollen, cuffed ears.

Virda gazed out the back window, waiting for the braided bread to finish proofing. "Just look, will you? Gods' teeth and toenails, the spring melt is going to be havoc this year. I never remember seeing such snows. It's blowing up again."

I sent a wish for Dink to make it home safe with Cobbel

astride, and sipped my mug. Morie came and climbed on my lap with one of her books Annora had made for her, rediscovered on the hearth. It was the tale of the dancing rabbits, and I read it to her, thinking all the while of how to help Wils and keep us all safe, as well.

CHAPTER 21

W ils ultimately agreed to send me along with Perk on the next search for Mercedian troops. Luckless Cobbel had returned from the first trip saying he heard the army was disbanded and everyone who served now considered outlaws, since King Aerelon ruled us all.

Wils and the other men pored over codes they might devise. Perk and I were charged with making contact. Failing that, I was to collect bark or brush that Annora could use for her sending spells. She called owls and hawks to visit us daily, and got them used to being fed by her and gentled to handling so she could tie on messages. Beckta and Miskin, especially, watched her and marveled. Few did magic where they came from. We kept Gevarr from observing any of it. He was another one who missed nothing and had a shrewd mind.

But, Perk and I proved to have no better luck than Cobbel. We traveled east at least once a week until mud season, and then the way turned impassable, as Virda predicted. Wils decided we would scavenge and barter for enough lumber to rebuild the barn, and stay home for a time. Dink kept well enough in the lean-to Wils and the men made out of the scorched lumber from the barn ruin, but Wils wanted to give the impression we were occupied with farming by getting more stock. A few chickens and geese, maybe some goats. Not enough to attract Keltanese scavengers, though.

Chicks and goslings were in short supply, he found, and no one would part with a goat if they had so far kept it from the enemy troops. Our part of Merced seemed locked away behind doors, with folk suspicious and fearful. I could not blame them.

Virda wanted to return to her place, but Wils and Annora argued it was not safe for a woman alone. She worried that the mothers-in-waiting could not find her. Miskin, Beckta and Perk were dispatched with me to collect all her remaining goods, and post a notice that those needing a midwife should seek her at the Lebannen place.

Wils sent us less frequently, but could not rest for too long without us searching the cliffs for any of our troops in hiding. One rainy night when Perk and I returned from our wanderings on the soaked cliffs above the harbour town, I was out-of-sorts and wet to the skin. I went to Wils wringing out my tunic hem, and asked him, "I don't see that much difference between life as a Mercedian and life as a Keltanese. Tell me why we are spending all this effort to try to get rid of the invaders now they are entrenched? The soldiers haven't been back to take more of our food. The villagers say transport goes a pace whenever the road is passable. We have our farm. Why doesn't everyone surrender and Da come home?"

"You don't know anything about politics."

"And you do?"

"I heard plenty along the road west and at Fort Hasseron. Merced is, or was, ruled by the Council of Elders, with representatives from all the provinces. We had many freedoms, to make our living and choose to move here or there as we pleased. We owned our farm. We traveled to trade our goods and get the things we could not make for ourselves. That is not the way Keltane is governed."

"What do they do? Gevarr says he came to northern Keltane when he wanted to be a soldier, after growing up in the south."

"In Keltane the King owns everything. Not just the land, but the game and the crops. He can give our farm to some lord who does him a favor, and we have to stay and work, owned by the King. Not free men."

"That is just ridiculous. Not our house—the King owns it? The hay we scythe and stack is the King's hay?"

"I couldn't believe it either. You'd think the Keltanese would be begging us to invade them and govern them our way." He shook his head. "But that's why we have to find what's left of our army, and resist the occupation."

"I think the Keltanese are clever enough to make sure there isn't army left to find. We're probably better off trying to recruit a new, secret army. The one we had was sparse and disorganized, according to the fieldmaster who came here."

"How are we going to find new soldiers?"

"Right now we're not finding the old ones. I can look for boys my age to carry out tasks for us. They attract less notice, I keep telling you. Ticker and Tarn from the village have done a fine job of keeping supplies out of the occupation's stores."

"All right, true enough. I'm worried about more than that, though. The fort cannot be abandoned, or we lose all hope of controlling the pass. And the siege has gone on for so long. I must make plans to get fresh supplies to them, maybe through our escape route. Even if I can get supplies, I have no wagons or horses, and how do I smuggle goods in plain sight along the trade road?" He let out a frustrated growl, and began to pace.

"Unless we let Keltane load the wagons and send them down the road for us, then we supplant their drivers along the way in some remote stretch, and take the goods on to our own destination."

"You," he said with relish, "have developed a devious mind. Where are Da's maps of the western territory?"

We put our heads together by the fire, and worked long into the night. Eventually, my clothes dried, still on me. Perk and the others gathered around us, looking for good spots to stage an ambush in the hinterlands. At last it felt as if we could do something meaningful to strike a blow against the invaders.

Annora found enough leather to fashion some boots for Gevarr, and he began to help with chores. He got about well enough, I supposed, but his long convalescence had left him out of condition, and he fatigued easily. Annora set him tasks in the garden, preparing for planting and clearing away old vines. He was leaning on his hoe when I went out to fetch water one morning.

"I'm no farmer," he said ruefully. "I'd be better suited to hunting for the table."

"I don't think Wils is going to hand you a weapon any day soon. What did you do before you were a soldier?"

"My family were tanners. You use more furs in this climate. We did smooth leathers, in the south. My older brother went into the business with our father, but I couldn't stand the stink of it. And, my father and I didn't get on."

"Just the one brother?"

"No." He chopped a bit with the hoe at a stubborn root. "No, I had a younger brother, a late-in-life child for my mother. One of those who don't have ... all the wits they should. He was sweet-natured, though. It fell to me to keep care of him most of the time. My mother helped along at the tannery."

I put my bucket down. "So you are the middle child, too?"

He flashed white teeth. "Aye, pushed from both sides, aren't we? Anyway, my younger brother had a weak heart, and took ill with River Fever one spring. After he died, I packed up and went for a soldier. My father spat on the ground at my heels. I've never been back."

When I stood there not knowing what to say, he grinned again. "You'll be getting no further revelations from me today. Why I tell you such things is a puzzle. Did you ever think of a posting as an apostate?"

"What, me?" I scoffed. "You just have a loose tongue, now you've given up soldiering."

I worked every night to convince Wils to send me with Wieser to Bale Harbour. I wanted to see how the cargo arrived and was routed away west, who watched the inventory and assigned the wagons and drivers. Whether guards accompanied the shipments on the way.

"Information is power, it's all about getting information, and who has the information we need. We've had months of rumor and false tales. If Merced had a working way to communicate crucial information, we wouldn't be conquered now!"

"Be that as it may, and I don't say you're wrong, it is a separate issue from me sending my younger brother into only gods know what danger. You don't know your way around the harbor."

"I know my way well," came Virda's sturdy voice. "I've traveled there many times, what with my husband and sons setting sail over the years."

"Now, that is madness. Send a boy and a woman into the enemy camp." Wils clenched his fists.

"My friend Guthy runs a boarding house there for sailors waiting ashore for their next berth," Virda continued, shaking out her cloth after wiping dishes.

We ate in shifts, since we numbered so many and a lot of our crockery had been smashed by the soldiers. Wils and I were arguing while awaiting our turn.

"Your friend Guthy likely has a house full of Keltanese soldiers, by now. Do not look at me like that, Annora. I know you think Judian can do anything, but how are you going to feel if they go down there and never come back? And you never know what befalls them?" Wils accepted a bowl and spoon from his now solemn-faced wife.

Cobbel spoke up, a rare event. "We're unable to act on anything until we know more. Won't we have to take a risk before we can plan action? How long can we stay holed-up on this mountain?"

"We're free men, put it to a vote," I suggested.

"A vote!" Wils said, the way you would say "A dog turd!" when you stepped in it. Gevarr burst out laughing. We sometimes forgot ourselves, and discussed plans in the kitchen by his alcove that we should have talked over out of his earshot. Still, he often contributed a thought on what Keltanese military protocol might be employed by the occupation force, as if it was neither here nor there to him what we did about it.

"All those in favor?" I pressed. Virda, Perk, Cobbel, Miskin, and I put our hands up. Annora and Wils crossed their arms, and Beckta looked uncertain. Gevarr stuck his hand out of his barrier quilt, and Wils snapped, "You don't get to vote." He withdrew it with a smothered snort.

"The ayes still carry the day," Perk said, eyes glinting. Wils grabbed handfuls of hair on either side of his head and groaned.

The next fair day, Virda, Wieser and I set out for Bale Harbour.

CHAPTER 22

D eep ruts from wagon tracks marked the Harbour Road as soon as we walked east of the village. We had not wanted to risk having Dink taken from us, so traveled on foot. At least the mud had a dried crust atop, so we did not have too hard a way to make.

Virda carried a large bag of spun yarn which she would say, to any who asked, that she planned to trade for needles and yard goods. I carried pelts to trade for woodworking tools, which would be scarce, I knew. Wieser walked beside me, never straying. Though to be sure there were lots of new smells she would have investigated if left on her own. Her nose twitched like mad. Several times we had to clamber up the weedy banks to let large cargo wagons pass. Each outbound one had two mounted soldiers behind.

We entered town the way we had left it after the wedding, discovering as we did so a stone wall being erected over the ruins of a slap-dash wooden barricade at the edge of town. More wagons rumbled past us, loud on the cobbles. Virda led the way through busy folk hurrying here and there. Watchful soldiers walked in pairs among them. We were descending to the wharves when she turned aside into a street of shops topped by leaning overstoreys supported by timbers. Whitewashed walls surrounded small windows. Halfway up the street, she stopped and knocked on a peeling green door.

"Guthy," she called, and the door flung open to show a cloud of frizzy, ash-grey hair above a round, beaming face. The lady within pulled Virda into a rib-crunching embrace in the doorway, and waved me through from behind Virda's back. While Virda and Guthy yattered about wrinkles, waistlines and new grey hair, I set down my pelts, bade Wieser sit, and looked about.

Guthy's place seemed like a cross between an inn and a home. The large room where we stood held a long table with a dozen chairs, instead of smaller round tables with a few chairs around each. I had never stayed at an inn, but Wils described them to me after he and Da traveled to markets. A fire burned in a wide deep hearth, where a pot hung suspended over the flames. Pitchers stood on the mantel, along with fat tallow candles in greenish copper candlesticks. A door stood open across the room, where stairs rose into the shadows. Beside the stairway, a swing-hinged half door led through to the kitchen. The place smelled of meat roasting and lye soap. Wieser licked her lips, but not for the soap scent, I reckoned.

"But this can't be another of your boys, Virda. Are you sending the rest of the village sons to sea now?" Guthy chuckled, and seized me by the shoulders.

"The sea has had enough from me! This is my neighbor's boy. Judian, say hello to Donah Guthy."

I ducked my head and said, "How do you do, Donah." She squinted into my eyes, and nodded at whatever she saw there.

"Let's get you settled upstairs, and then think where you can trade your goods. A person has to tread wisely these days, I'm telling you." Guthy let go of me and bustled toward the door to the upper floor.

"Will it be all right for my dog to come with us?" I asked. "She is too valuable to leave in the street or board in a stable."

"Guthy's place making room for country dogs," Guthy mused. "And why not, since I've had to make room for Keltanese dogs often enough of late." She looked over her shoulder, as if she checked for some unwelcome listener, and led on.

I waited until she showed us into a tiny, gabled room above the front door before asking, "Are some of the troops staying here, as well?"

"The officers bided with Guthy for a while. The rank and file are bedded in stables and halls all over the town. Surly they are, too. Eat like warehouse rats, from what I hear. The officers had some better manners, but no one paid Guthy a copper for their keep. They took over one of the big merchant's houses on the hill. The better to oversee things in the harbour, I have been told." Guthy pulled back a worn counterpane from the single narrow bed. "I'll have the kitchen girl bring you up a pallet, young man. And you'll both be wanting to wash off the road grime before you come down and eat. I'll send her with wash water and toweling, too."

I was well pleased with our chatty hostess, and shocked Virda by flinging my arm round her shoulders once we were alone. "We're going to find out all sorts of useful information here. You had a brilliant idea, coming to Guthy's!" She was still flustered when the kitchen girl knocked softly on our door.

A frail-looking, mousy, doe-eyed girl stood at the door. She shrank away when Wieser came to sniff her. The pitcher of water she carried seemed almost too heavy for her to balance, since she was draped with blankets and towels in addition. I took the pitcher. Virda relieved her of the blankets and the rest. She gave a vague curtsey, then stammered, "D-did you see the battle when the s-soldiers came? They fought our troops further west, we heard. M-my da and brothers might have been there …"

"Were your men folk in uniform? Or conscripted by our army to march west in the fall?" I said.

The girl looked in a pitiful state. Virda commenced *tsk-tsking* and murmured "poor lamb" under her breath.

"No-n-no uniforms, when they left."

"Then they did not fight the invaders on the west road. That

153

was near Roicer, the village by our home. Our troops were in uniform there. Was there a battle here, when they reached the harbour?"

"On the edge of town, our troops t-tried to turn the invaders away, but were too few. The barricade they put up w-was easily overcome. All was finished before the morning was out, and the other soldiers streaming through the streets, shouting and jeering. They t-took all of our soldiers away and locked them up in a warehouse near the docks. There were not many men left." She dashed the back of her hand across her eyes, and curtseyed again. "Please to come down to the k-kitchen when you are ready. My mistress has some tea brewing."

We took our tea in the kitchen instead of the keeping room, and it felt more homey to me. Still, I was excited to be in the town and to have a job to do, rather than feeling homesick already. Tea at Guthy's wasn't only a hot drink, I found, but meat pies and savory bread and honey cakes, too. How much would our keep set us back? I had brought some coin, on Virda's instruction, but began to wonder if I carried enough. I might have to sell my pelts, if any would buy, just so as to have more currency—and come home with no tools at all.

We stepped into the street with our goods, directed by Guthy where to take them for the best value. Wieser and I followed Virda, who truly did know her way street and alley through the town. We were easily marked as country folk, with Virda's shawl over her head and tucked into her waist after swathing her shoulders. I did not see town women wearing theirs that way, but only loosely over the shoulders instead. I wore a lighter weight wool cloak, and rough weave tunic and trousers. I saw finer cloth on the town folk. I had left my walking staff in our room, but carried my knife in my knee high boot.

I smelled the sea, and fish mongers. Gulls called above, and I thought of Gargle. I had left him with stern instructions to perch on the highest part of the new barn frame, and warn the men if anyone approached. It would not do for soldiers to find five able men working at the Lebannen place. He hopped on the porch rail and clacked his beak as I walked away, but flew to his post before we left the yard. I had told Annora to give him treats if he did his job well—and if he quit harassing the hawks and owls answering Annora's summons for courier training.

I goggled at the forest of ship masts that came into view as we descended the stone steps to what Virda said was the quayside. I did not see how it could be less busy under the occupation, because if there had been more activity before, folk must have been jostling each other off the docks into the water below.

Huge nets bulging with crates or sacks hung above the dock planks. Sweat-coated men drove creaking drays piled high with trunks. Bewildered oxen bellowed, swung in a sling over one ship's railing. Sheep bleated from knocked together ramshackle pens on the back of another ship. *How do they keep track of which is coming in to unload, and which to carry goods away*, I wondered. I had never seen the like. I heard Mercedish spoken, of course, and also Keltanese. But many other tongues reached my ears in snatches, none of which I knew.

"Virda, are they come from all over the world?" I asked.

"Oh, aye. The ships do not need to anchor off shore here, and ferry cargo to and from land. This is the best port along the eastern shore for a great many miles." She was smiling into the ocean breeze, wind lifting her hair where it strayed from her shawl. "My Davini was a ship's master, and sailed the exploration voyages that opened trade routes across the sea. Oh, he was handsome in his shipmaster's hat, carrying his scope glass. I lived in Bale Harbour, you see, before you were born, and raised my oldest sons here. When I had so many we were crowded, Davini bought us our mountain home."

"Are your sons shipmasters, too?"

"No, no. But Lichan is a first officer, on the *Moon Road*." I took this to be the name of his ship, as I saw lettering on the front sides of those we passed. "I'm that proud of him. Of them all, of course."

I made myself break off thinking what it would be like to sail all over the ocean seeing new sights, and attend to the work I had to do here. "Do you think we can find where our troops are being held?"

"We can walk through the warehouse district, and see if we can tell. This way."

We spotted the prison used to hold our defeated soldiers, after we reached the looming brick buildings. Only one had maroon uniforms stationed at the wide wooden sliding doors. I worried we would draw notice, but there were just as many folks scurrying about their business on these streets, and we blended well enough. I drew Virda into the alley behind, where no guards watched since there was no door. I looked for something to collect to guide Annora's messenger birds. No shrub or bush sprouted, nor even blade of grass poked up, between the cobbles and packed dirt. There was a window ledge overhead, with bars a bird might fit through. With Virda and Wieser posted at either corner, I climbed teetering empty crates to the window. Noisome smell wafted from inside. I hoped they were not all dead in there, but dare not call out for fear of being discovered clinging at the window. After scouring the ledge for something I might take to the birds, I pulled out my handkerchief and spit on it, then rubbed up some of the grime that coated the mortar ledge. I hoped it would be sufficient, and clambered down.

"Remember Guthy said we must be back by curfew at dusk," Virda said. I took back the pelts I had handed off to her for my climb.

"Let's at least try one of the places she suggested for your bartering, so we can say we did some of our business."

The yard good merchant's storefront was well kept, but his shelves showed more space than goods. "More cloth is sent overseas than comes in, this season." The toothy, bald shopkeeper fingered Virda's yarn, and tugged on a strand to test its strength as he spoke. "I do not have linen, but I can give you a nice length of linsey-woolsey, and ten packets of pins, plus two packets of needles."

Virda bargained for more needles in greater variety and fewer pins altogether, then wanted to see the fabric and confirm how long a length he offered. Wieser and I watched out the shop window, observing the crowd and most especially the pairs of soldiers patrolling on foot. I would have liked to have overheard the orders they were sent out with—what were they supposed to watch for?

Virda and the shopkeeper concluded their wrangling, and she packed her bag. I shouldered my pelts, and decided we ought to hang onto them so we would have an excuse for more exploring tomorrow.

"Be sure to be back in your lodgings by curfew," he called after us. "And bring me any more of your spinning in future."

"He must think he made out to his advantage," I said to Virda as I helped her across a rut puddle.

"He did no better than he ought. He needs goods. Too much is exported or sent west, he said. He has to rely on small country crafters to have anything to sell."

I was mulling this over, scanning the people who strode by us, when I saw a familiar man. Huddled in the doorway just across the street, was the polite soldier who had thanked Annora for feeding him at our place. He hadn't seen me, or didn't recognize me if he had. He stepped out of his doorway and down the opposite side of the street.

"Walk this way, Virda. There's someone I want to catch up." We crossed as soon as traffic would allow, and followed his brown cloak. We had to walk faster and faster, maybe he could tell he was being pursued, though there were plenty of folk all around on the cobbles. I almost lost him when he turned abruptly into the close by the stockyards. I stepped after him into the dark, narrow alley, and Virda caught my arm.

"This isn't the best of places for a woman and child to be." Brave Virda, she did not say she would not go in.

"You wait here with Wieser," I offered. "I'll see if I can find him nearby." I left them and stepped farther into the dank yellowish light. I had gone a dozen paces when I heard the scrape of a boot and a sharp breath. I ducked low, and avoided an arm across my throat. It was the soldier, wild-eyed and armed with a wooden club.

"I just want to talk to you," I said, backing up. "Remember, you were at our farm in the mountains?"

He peered closer at my face, then brightened. "How fares your brother's wife?"

I knew he was taken with her. "She's well. We avoided the invasion and got by with only a burned barn. How did you and your fellows fare?"

"Mostly killed or captured. I got away, barely. Behring was dispatched west with mounted troops to go after your da. My squad was to aid in blockading the road into town, and more troops were to arrive to oppose the invaders if they came from the northwest. I don't think any more of our men ever arrived. We were outmanned from the start." He looked up at what little could be seen of the sky. "You have to get out of here before dark."

"I'm staying in town tonight. Can you meet me tomorrow at the doorway where I saw you just now? There is more I want to talk to you about."

He looked about him, left and right, then sighed. "I'll be there at midmorning. Walk past and I'll fall in with you. Don't speak to me first, and if I do not fall in, walk on past and don't come back."

As good as I was going to get, I saw. I nodded and clasped his hand, and said no more. Virda and Wieser both appeared eager to be collected for our walk to Guthy's warm fire. My thoughts ground away the whole route, working out how to get best advantage from what I learned hour by hour in Bale Harbour.

CHAPTER 23

G uthy scolded us for cutting the time too fine when we arrived at her door, worry plain in her eyes.

"What do they do to people caught out after curfew?" I asked her.

"Who can say? The soldiers take them and they are seen no more. The harbour still works the night through, but no folk whatever are allowed on the streets."

We ate our supper at the long table in the keeping room, joined by old men of varying degrees of toothlessness. There were six of them, and I could judge their number of teeth because they kept leering at Virda. I fairly choked on their pipe smoke after we finished the excellent goose. It would have been worth it if the fellows had been saying anything useful as they smoked, but most of their talk centered on days long gone by.

I went to the kitchen to fix Wieser her share of food. The kitchen girl left off scrubbing a large soup pot, and found a meaty bone for my dog. She bade me give it to Wieser, though, seeming still unsure of her.

"What's your name?" I asked by way of easing her nerves.

"I'm Honni Emeral." She almost whispered, her eyes fixed on Wieser's white teeth gnawing.

"Do you live here, so you don't have to go home after dark?"

"Yes. After the invasion, my mum asked Guthy to keep me

nights."

"I know you're worried about your da and brothers. My da is gone west, too. My brother made it home, though." Did Guthy feed the girl? She would cast a stick shadow. "I was watching today, at the quayside. Do you know who keeps track of all the ships and the cargoes?"

"The harbourmaster," she said promptly.

"Is it the same man as before the invasion, or did the Keltanese replace him with their own?"

Her focus shifted to me in earnest. "How would they have a harbourmaster experienced in such things, since they've n-never had a harbour?" There was more of a mind in there than she let on at first, and more spirit.

"How do they get the Mercedian harbourmaster to do what they want? It seems such a big job, endless details. How would the Keltanese know if he kept goods back or deceived them in other ways?"

"I heard they have his f-family imprisoned. His lady wife, and son and his wife, and their little boy. My friend worked in their house, and told me about when the soldiers came and t-took them away. Horrible!"

I wanted to ask more, and see if I might have a chance to talk to her friend, but loud male voices sounded from the keeping room. Wieser abandoned her bone at once to come with me and see what the fuss might be.

Four helmeted Keltanese had barged in, and wanted Guthy to give them tankards of ale and a wheel of cheese. "Let's have a nice loaf of bread, too, eh?" said the tallest. He seemed the only one who spoke Mercedish, the others made rude remarks in Keltanese. I gave no sign of understanding.

Wieser started to growl, but I bumped her with my knee. Guthy gathered the cheese and bread, and Virda drew off the ale from a tun in the corner. The old men glowered but made no move. I hated feeling powerless while people minding their own business

160

were robbed. I stood gritting my teeth, when the tall one pointed his pike at me.

"Come along and carry this for us, boy."

Virda protested at once, "My nephew isn't from here, he doesn't know his way about—"

I took the chance to whisper to Wieser, "Follow after."

"Shut it, woman," the man growled. "That way maybe you'll get him back after."

I slung the sack with the loaf and cheese over my arm, and took two tankards in each hand. Guthy wrung her hands, and Virda had bitten her lip so hard it bled onto her chin. I followed the soldiers out the door, and went along the cobbles with them. We tramped down the deserted street to the corner, and turned toward the waterfront.

As we walked, the men complained in Keltanese about having to be out in the night patrolling. "It's not as if this lot of idiots could mount any counter attack."

"There isn't a backbone among them. We're not going to have resistance here. Once the fort is taken, maybe most of us can go home."

"I hate this damp and fish-stink. Bah, what a place!"

"You have better quarters than me—hardly any rats! The bastards gnaw my toes when I sleep!"

Alongside the main road, a fire burned in a ring of stones. Crates upended next to the fire made seats for them, and they settled there and held their hands out for their food and drink. I'd have liked to fling it in their faces, but that wouldn't prove wise. After handing it all over, I stood at the edge of the firelight as they tore chunks of bread and passed cheese they hacked off the wheel with long knives.

"Find your way home, if you can," said the tall one who spoke Mercedish.

"Could I have Guthy's sack?" I said.

He balled it in his fist and drew back to throw it in the fire, but another snatched it away and tossed it to me. I turned tail and loped back the way I had come. "Hah, coward!" the tall one called after me.

I gave a thought to wandering a little further to see if I could find out more about what happened here at night. If the patrol was sitting by their fire, maybe I would never have a better chance. It could be that there were other patrols, though, and I would be picked up and locked away. What I had learned so far meant nothing if I could not return to Wils and the others to share it.

I turned up Guthy's street when a heavy hand fell on my shoulder. I was jerked around roughly to face another helmeted soldier; a second stood close aiming his pike at my chest.

"After curfew," said the one holding me, in a thick accent.

"From Guthy's. Took food to the patrol." I gestured down around the corner, and held up the crumpled sack. No light dawned in the man's eyes. *He doesn't really speak Mercedish*, I realized. *We had all he knows with his first two words.* "I carried food to the patrol on the main road," I said in Keltanese, which I strove to make sound halting.

"Any left?" said the second soldier, licking his lips.

I showed the empty interior of the bag. "Come with me to Guthy's. She has more there." I heard Da's voice echo in my mind: *soldiers are always hungry*. I hated to bring more down on Guthy, but I could not be taken to prison. Or knocked in the head and thrown in the harbour, if that was what they did to curfew violators. Who knew?

The two were considering what they could get away with, when a thin voice came out of the darkness. "Please, may I g-guide him home? He does n-n-not know his way." It was Honni who spoke, she had come out by Wieser's side even though the dog frightened her so.

Now I had to be sure she got back inside, too. "Come," I said, in Keltanese, pointing up the street toward Guthy's. "Ale and meat pies." This trumped whatever they had been eating, because the first one let go my shoulder and pushed me in the back in the direction of Guthy's. I walked to Honni and caught her arm. "Just keep quiet now," I said in her ear. Wieser blessedly walked along with us like a commonplace dog, and did not try to wolf down the two men for the rest of her dinner.

I brought them in by Guthy's, where the keeping room held crying women and old men still smoking clay pipes and talking about what they would have done about it all when young. Jaws gaped at our appearance, and before Virda and Guthy could fall on us weeping, I said loudly, "Here's two more, and I promised them ale and meat pies." Virda and Guthy fairly raced Honni to the kitchen, and turned up panting with five cold pies in a wooden trencher. I meantime took one of the pitchers from the mantel, went to the keg and pulled the tap. I pushed the brimming pitcher into the hand of the nearest soldier.

They grinned wide when I opened the door for them, and swaggered out into the night. I shut the door behind them, leaned my back on it and asked Guthy, "Does this have a lock?" The bar appeared in an instant, and I had to jump out of the way as she slammed it home.

I endured embraces from Virda and Guthy, and claps on the back from the bent old men. How did skin get like the creased brown leather of their faces? I escaped into the kitchen with Wieser, and found Honni standing by her pots shaking head to foot. I sometimes felt the same way after escaping with my life.

"What is this I hear about no meat pies left for tomorrow?" I said.

"Your dog," she pointed. "S-she waited like you s-s-said, I heard you but they didn't, and then she started sc-scratching at the door, and they were all talking and carrying on and d-d-didn't hear her. And she started clawing it and barking. I didn't know w-what to do! She ran to the b-back door and I let her out. I had to go with her, in c-case you were t-taken …"

"I expect they got even more worked up when they found you

were gone, too. Thanks for coming after me. That was brave."

She waved a hand impatiently. "Those old salts kept talking, but they did-didn't *do* anything."

"They are old, truly. What's a salt?"

"Old sailor. Too old to sail and usually too stove up to work much. They c-come here to relive old times with the others, and Guthy makes over them. She listens to their tales no matter how many times they're t-told."

Honni's trembling calmed. Her stutter came less often. Wieser licked her hand and got her to smile, before padding over to her abandoned bone to renew her gnawing.

"Do you think I've fixed it so the night watch will turn up here to be fed every day?" I asked. That made her smile again.

"We'll just have to see. I hear there's been a r-run on meat pies."

###

In her relief, Guthy shifted me to my own room next to Virda's, where I was to have an actual bed. My pallet was assigned to Wieser's use, instead of her having bare floor planks for her bed. I hissed to Virda, "How much is this going to cost?" but she shushed me and said not to worry. *Maybe we'll be gone when Guthy has the watchmen at her door each night,* I thought as I settled my head on the goose-down pillow. *Guthy might think of charging us then.* I fell asleep by my next breath.

CHAPTER 24

ome morning, Honni fed us eggs and sausage until I could not hold another morsel. Even Wieser had eggs for her breakfast. I told her not to get used to it, but she was too busy gulping them and wagging to have heard, I'd wager.

We were alone with Guthy at the big table, and I asked after the six old fellows from last night, thinking they must be sleeping in after the excitement. "Do they all board here with you?"

"Half of them shelter with Guthy, the others have rooms nearby. They're all down at the wharves by dawn each day. They watch what ships come and depart, see the cargo loaded and unloaded. Talk to the crews and their old mates. Keeps them feeling in the sea-going life, somewhat."

Did they, indeed. That sparked a thought. They wanted to be able to do something about the invasion, but being too old to fight thought they were useless. It could be there was a use for their eyes and ears, yet. They knew what they were seeing on the waterfront better than any.

I reminded Virda that we needed to take the pelts and seek to trade them for tools. My real intent, however, was to be at the doorway midmorning where I might meet up with the young soldier. I had not decided what I might ask of him, and continued to ponder while we made ready to set out.

Honni rushed us at the door, pushed a paper parcel into my hands, blurted, "Molasses cakes," and fled back to the kitchen, face flaming. I opened my mouth, but she disappeared before I could speak. Virda chuckled as she wound her scarf across her shoulders and tucked it in.

"What has possessed her?" I wondered aloud when we crossed into the bright spring sunshine.

"Why, anyone can see she is sweet on you," Virda said.

I stopped in my tracks, and was bumped from behind by a lady leading a goat. More of the tide of folk split to go around us, when Virda stopped as well.

"Sweet on me? What can I have done to deserve that?"

"You showed such courage with the soldiers, and you were kind to her when she worried about her da and brothers. And you talked to her about living with Guthy, and all." Virda probably thought that sounded reasonable, but it didn't to my ears.

"She's maybe eight years old, Virda!"

"No, Guthy told me she is nearly your age."

"What are you and Guthy talking about our ages for?" I said, exasperated. "You might as well say Morie was sweet on Ticker the smithy's son."

"No need to make such a to-do. Enjoy your cakes. Let's press on."

"It seems to me women run mad about half the time," I told Wieser, as we fell into step in Virda's wake.

Virda took us to the fur traders first, as I thought to get money before trying to scare up some woodworking tools. I would be limited to planes and drills small enough to carry home, could such even be found. I chose to barter with the furrier, since Virda could not claim much knowledge of the worth of the pelts. I was out of my depth, too, considering I had never been to market with Wils and Da, but I had not made a habit of letting that stop me.

We found the fur dealer's storehouse down near the tannery on the edge of town. Gevarr was not exaggerating about the stink.

The grizzled, jut-jawed proprietor pawed through my lynx, wolf and hare furs, muttering. He licked a stubby finger and sorted through some papers on his counter.

"Well, son," he said finally. "They are not too good, are they? And this is hardly the season for folk to be needing furs, you see."

I did not have time to waste while he tried to swindle me. It took longer to walk to his shop than I thought, and I had my midmorning appointment. "More fool me," I said. "Collecting pelts in the winter when they're heaviest. Should I just hang onto them until autumn comes round again?"

"Now, no call to be testy. I can make you an offer, just let me figure a moment." More muttering and paper rustling. He offered me less than half what I knew they were worth, based on Gevarr's reckoning.

"Double it and done," I said.

He made a gagging noise and then began to cough. Virda had to step behind the counter and pound him on the back. When he regained his breath, he squinted at me with watery eyes. "Where's your da?"

"Prison."

Virda started to say something, but shut her teeth at my look. The man scratched his nose, then studied his papers. "All right, son, double. Though that will mean I turn very little profit, but you are a nice boy, and we'll call it my good deed for today." He counted out my coins slowly, lingering over each one. We would have to run to my meeting. I ground my teeth.

"Thank you, sir, and good day!" I called, stuffing the coins into the pouch around my neck, pushing through his door as fast as I could manage. Virda and Wieser came after.

"Look, Virda, I know the way back to the doorway where he'll be. Do you feel safe if I leave Wieser with you and run ahead?"

"You take Wieser, and go on. I'll catch you up. Only please don't get into trouble and leave me to explain it to Wils. Don't let the man take you back to the close, it's too dangerous. Thieves and cutpurses."

I raised a hand to show I heard her, already sprinting.

No soldiers tried to waylay me, or even wondered why I ran through the streets, as far as I could tell. Surely if I had been a man full grown, it would have drawn their notice. I would be sure to tell Wils about my foot race, in support of my contention that boys are mostly ignored.

I stopped at the corner, to catch my breath and see if he waited across the road. I saw the brown hood of the cloak, and walked past, remaining on the opposite side of the street, to make sure the right man wore it.

The familiar face looked up and down the way. I crossed over and walked past him, and saw him push off from his doorway to follow. So where to lead him? I recalled a public well up the street, and walked there at a purposeful clip with Wieser. He shadowed me.

When we reached the well, I told Wieser, "Watch for Virda, and guide her here." Wieser padded away into the stream of people. No one else was drawing water, so I sent the bucket down. The soldier came and stood beside me.

"Here." I handed him my packet of molasses cakes, and his eyes widened in evident delight. I wound the crank to pull up the bucket. "What's your name?" I asked, for lack of a better next step.

He licked his lips. "I'm Joren Delyth."

"Are you in contact with any of our soldiers?"

"I've just tried to lay low here. I've watched for anyone I know, but no luck. I don't know if I can evade the patrols much longer." He looked around furtively.

There's what will get you noticed, I thought. *Looking like they ought to check what you're up to.* "Maybe you'd be better off coming back to our place. My brother is home, and trying to get things organized." *Don't make me be too specific, please.*

"Back to the country?" he puzzled.

"You could meet us on the outside of town. We'll leave early tomorrow, on foot. If you don't think it safe to travel with us, do you remember your way to our place?"

"How could it be safe to leave town?"

"It's safer to leave than to stay and be taken prisoner, I reckon. And the Keltanese are more set on keeping folk out of the town than keeping them here. You should see the wall they're building." I set the full bucket on the ledge, and a young woman who favored Annora in fair hair and deep-set eyes stepped up with a clay jar to fill. I poured the water for her, while Joren looked thoughtful.

"Why do you want to help me?" He asked when the woman went on her way.

"I was hoping you could put me onto more of our troops. That not being the case, you can be most useful by coming to our place and aiding our cause from there."

"You are ... something different, I'll say that. I'll meet you on the road where the way to Roicer Village comes off the main route."

"There is a shrine to the Earth Goddess under the tallest oak on the north roadside. We'll look for you there a couple hours after sun up." Wils might have some remarks about this turn of plans. "Can you drive a cargo wagon?" I asked, inspiration striking.

"Yes, I've done it often. Do you have a wagon?"

"Not yet, but we will have need of experienced drivers if all comes aright."

I left him then, and met Wieser bringing Virda up the street to the well. "Let's go find the toolmaker, now. Town life keeps us as busy as farming, I think!"

We came back to Guthy's in good time, with a pair of planes and a hatchet. I had angled for a drill, but it cost too dear. A hand saw completed my purchases for the day, and Wils would be pleased. I hoped.

My next task I dreaded. I planned to talk again to Honni, and ask if I might meet her friend who worked in the harbourmaster's house. I thought it could be possible to have her smuggle

169

information out, or help us contact the harbourmaster to aid our espionage.

After what Virda had told me that morning, I was loath to approach Honni. I couldn't have the girl thinking me anything like sweet on her in return.

Be brave, I told myself, *you're leaving in the morning*, and tramped down to the kitchen. Honni sat plucking a chicken on the back steps. More hens clucked and scratched in a crate coop beneath the stairs.

"Thanks for the molasses cakes," I said. My tongue felt thick of a sudden. "I remember you telling me about your friend who worked for the harbourmaster."

Honni looked confused by the disconnected comments, but said, "I'm glad y-you like them. What about Orlo? He's my friend."

I assumed her friend was another kitchen girl. "What does Orlo do at the house?"

"He blacks the b-boots, and cleans the fireplaces, goes to market for cook, all s-such like errands. His mum keeps the nursery for the little grandson. Well, not now, since the boy was t-taken away by the soldiers."

"Do you think I could talk to Orlo? I'm trying to find out all the news I can to carry home to the country."

She paused plucking and looked me in the eye. "You can't get him into trouble and then g-go away home."

"No, I wouldn't. I'm looking for a way to help all of us," I protested.

Honni pursed her lips. "You c-come with me in an hour. I'm going to the fishmonger for m-mistress Guthy. We'll see Orlo then."

I didn't think Honni acted as strange as she had in the morning. Maybe she just needed to be kept occupied.

I went to tell Virda I would be going out without her. She made me squirm by patting my hand and saying, "See, it's not so terrible a thing for a young lady to take a fancy to you." I let her think Honni and I were going for a courting stroll, if that made her less likely to argue against my being out in town without her supervision.

"I need you to do something while I'm gone, if you would. Could you talk to Guthy about whether she might let the messenger hawks and owls come to her place? I'll take items back to guide them here if she consents. And her old salts, can you ask if they would observe at the harbour, and report by the messengers? We will use code, which they will be taught if they show willing. I know they would be taking risks they may want to avoid. Just talk to them without giving away too much, and tell me what they say."

"I believe you'll find them more than willing to fight, each in their own way." she said, straightening her skirt. "Just leave it to me."

CHAPTER 25

I led Wieser back down to the kitchen to meet Honni for the trip to the fish monger. She carried a flat basket over her arm and wore a shawl loosely around her shoulders, in town-fashion. She smiled as I came through the swinging door, making me feel as if my feet had grown suddenly a hand-span longer, and I did not know how to set them down and walk. I managed not to stumble, and nodded to her. For who can say what girls have in their minds when they smile like that?

"Let's be off," she said briskly, and went out through the back door. As I followed her down alleys and between buildings, I saw a much different Bale Harbour to what I had walked with Virda. Plenty of folk still came and went, but most at a slower pace, as if the business they attended to was not so pressing as that of the crowds on the main streets. Patrolling soldiers were more scarce. Some men carried draw-neck bags of heavy canvas slung over their shoulders; Honni said these were sailors with sea bags. Many women and girls scurried or sauntered with parcels and laden baskets, depending, I supposed, on whether their masters demanded quick work or cared not how soon the tasks were done. Here and there, men gathered by twos and threes to play at cards or cups. I was astonished to see filthy barefoot boys picking up dog piles and placing them into small pails. A couple of them followed Wieser, arguing over which would have rights to any she provided, until Honni shooed them away.

"The fresher the better, Donatta!" one shouted. "It looks like it could make one worth my time, huge old thing!"

"For the tanners," Honni told me, for I must have looked curious. "They get coppers for a pail-full." That did account for some of the smell at the tannery, then. Honni greeted folk here and there, some asked after her family, and several waited to see if she would say anything about my presence at her elbow, but she never said a bit. And stuttered seldom when she did speak.

When we drew near the wharves where the fish mongers' calls could be heard, she said softly, "Let me see where Orlo is, and t-tell him you want to talk to him. He may not wish to, since he doesn't know you."

"Wieser and I will look at the sea fish. There are many I've never seen before," I said, and wandered toward a booth made of stacked crates topped with planks where the fish were spread out in the sun. They were accomplishing a fine stench; I thought Wieser's nose might be overwhelmed. Mine nearly was.

Wieser and I stood gaping at a large flat-bodied fish with two cloudy eyes on its back and a slit mouth underneath, as a matron lifted it into her basket. "How can it swim?" I mused to Wieser, and heard a choked laugh behind me.

I turned to find Honni standing beside a lanky, shaggy black-eyed youth who looked me up and down with cocksure amusement. "A person would never know *you* were new to town," he said, baring his teeth in what didn't really look like a grin.

I didn't care to be mocked, but kept my eyes friendly. Wieser put her nose in the air and sniffed in his direction, giving no sign of concern. Honni pointed at me, and said, "Here's Judian. Come walk along while I get what Mistress G-g-guthy wants."

I fell into step with Orlo as Honni moved into the crowd, and we trailed her in silence with Wieser padding between us. Near the end of the pier, Honni found the vendor she wanted and began selecting slim silvery fish that looked more like the ones I caught

174

in mountain streams.

"Do you smoke the flesh, as we do at home?" I asked, by way of starting some exchange.

"We can get them fresh every day, why would we want to preserve them?" Orlo answered for her.

"I can get them fresh every day I want to go fishing," I said evenly. "I don't have anybody to do my fishing for me."

"We will have fish stew at Guthy's. I make it often as the old salts like it well," Honni murmured, paying coins into the merchant's outstretched hand. She turned and pinned Orlo with a meaningful look.

"He's not even asking me anything!" he said.

"Out here?" I swung an arm out to encompass the busy pier, and nearly caught a maidservant carrying a long fish with a sword on the end of its snout. "Have a care!" she snapped.

Honni sighed the way I do when Noda the goat upsets the milk bucket. "I need to take some of my wages to Mum. Come along and t-talk behind doors, if that suits you better."

We trailed in further prickly silence as Honni paced along the alleyways until we reached the back gate of a dirt yard. Here a grubby-faced boy about the age of Morie shouted with joy at the sight of her, and more tattered children poured from under the back steps to surround Honni, pat her hands and pull at her skirt. Honni laughed at them all talking at once, and allowed them to draw her through the gate. They evidently knew Orlo, and grabbed him around the knees and pestered him equally, but Wieser and I received only a few shy looks from under tousled hair.

The uproar brought a ruddy-cheeked woman as round as Honni was spare, who looked out from the top half of a cut-door with a genial wave. "Come on, come in!" she called, and we made our way across the yard as the tumble of children would permit.

Donah Emeral enfolded her daughter against her roundness, and stroked her hair. "How are you, love? Not too worried about our men?" Honni clung to her mother for a moment, and made me think of my own mum and how much I missed her still.

"I've brought Judian from Guthy's, Mum," Honni began, standing back from her mother's arms. We were directed to sit on the bench alongside the kitchen table. And without a stutter, she told all the tale of my adventures with the patrol last night, leaving out her own courage in coming after me, so as not to worry her family, I suspected.

Orlo especially seemed caught up in the story, and bounced one of the youngest on his knee without looking at him. He kept staring at me instead.

The other children came closer and closer, until I had one on each knee and another sitting on my left foot. Honni's mum was round-eyed and breathless on hearing what a hero I was, which made me heartily wish Honni hadn't put such a slant on things. Donah Emeral served me cold buttermilk and a great slab of buttered bread; Orlo's portion was not half so large. He chewed thoughtfully, while Honni counted out some coins and pressed them into her mother's hand. I shared my bread around with my stick-tights, who took the pieces reverently. *I should have Honni come to tell Wils about my trip to town*, I thought. *He could never be put out with me then.*

"We'll see if Guthy still thinks so high of me when she notes she is short a pitcher, a trencher and four tankards," I said. "Or when every hungry patrol in town turns up on her stoop." I wished there was something I could do to divert that from happening.

"Aye, there are so many of them to feed, it's true. They take their rations from the goods coming into the town, mostly. Yet they always seem to be looking for more." Donah Emeral shook her head.

"My da says soldiers are always hungry, and not just for food," I put in. This remark stirred up a discussion of the men who were absent, my da included, and how they might be faring wherever they were. I offered them some of what Wils had told me on his return, mostly what news supported that the non-uniformed

176

troops had not been in the way of the invasion force. This caused Ma Emeral and some of the children to cry; not the intended effect. It was Orlo who told me, "Don't worry, they cry when they hear good news as well as at bad." I gave him a grateful look.

At the conclusion of the brief visit, Honni stood and slipped her basket of fish over her arm. Wieser waited at the door, a model of patience. I smuggled her a bite of my bread and butter. We left the way we had come, with what seemed dozens of pudgy hands waving at us until we turned up the next alley out of sight.

"So, what did you want to talk about?" Orlo asked, stooping to pat Wieser's curly black head.

CHAPTER 26

Orlo accompanied us all the way back to Guthy's, pointing out the alleys best avoided and the back doors where a handout could be cadged "if you know what you're about." He sat with me on the back steps when Honni went in to start the fish stew.

"Do you work at the harbourmaster's house still?" I asked first.

"Not as I did, else I'd be there now. I bring the coal, and am sent to the market since I can read and count change. But they do not need me every day, since the rest of the family is not at the house."

"Honni says you were there when the soldiers took the family away. Any idea where they are kept?"

He shook his head, staring into the middle distance. "The old master is fair frantic. I keep my ears pricked, but no word on where they are."

"The soldiers make him run the harbour as before? He keeps track of all the ships and cargoes?"

"He must do, as the ships come and go just as before. Or, no, not just as before—Guthy's old salts have been saying far more ships carry goods away than bring cargo into Merced since the occupation."

"Where do all those ships take their loads to? What country is their destination?"

"Well, not just one country. There are hundreds of ports in as many countries. The world is large, farm boy." His grin was real this time, and I did not take offense. "But they say much of the goods go to Scythera, where there is drought and famine."

"That's where the mages come from, isn't it? The ones the sailors call weather-workers?"

"How did you hear about the weather-workers? I've heard the sailors talk about them, in the public houses. But if they can magic the weather, why don't they cure their country of drought and make the crops come right?"

"I wonder. Maybe the King hired all the mages away, to get him his deep-water harbour, so there's none left for their own land. But then, why does Keltane send Scythera all the goods? Are the Scytherans so rich they can buy it all?"

Orlo shrugged as he plucked a stick from the woodpile and poked the tip into the dirt at our feet. "That's not the kind of thing any of us in the back alleys would know. We worry more where our next meal can be scrounged, and whether the roof we managed last night will still be over us tonight."

"Do you not want to be rid of the Keltanese?"

"Sure, but mostly we work around them … they're not too quick-witted."

"How do you work around them? Everyone must to be off the streets at curfew every night, and violators are never seen again, Honni says."

He laid a finger aside his nose and tapped it. "There are ways to be abroad and not run afoul of any patrols. We've been avoiding patrols for years, with the local constables and guardsmen before the soldiers."

"Say on," I urged.

His expression turned evasive, eyes shifting aside. "What's it to you how we live here? Honni says you're bound for home come morning."

"My brother and I are looking for a way to divert enough to keep our home folk well provided and aggravate the Keltanese, but not so much as to make ourselves worth pursuing avidly," I temporized. "To do it, we need some way of knowing what cargo is coming our way and when."

"You'll find it does not do to be fat and happy when privation shows all around you."

"No, no. The village folk are smarter than that, considering we're farmers." That drew a quick flash of his teeth. "Can you tell me how such information can be gotten, without putting the one who gets it at undue risk?"

"I don't know why you would want to go to that kind of trouble, when you could just use the smugglers to get what you want. As long as you can pay, you can get anything you like."

An unexpected turn, which left me feeling I had just stepped in a puddle far deeper than I thought. "Smugglers?" I echoed stupidly.

"All ports have smugglers. As long as too much doesn't go missing at the docks and warehouses, the port guardsmen don't raise a hue and cry. Or they make enough noise to get their cut, if that's their way." He raised his shoulders. "It's just how shipyards work."

"If my brother wants to go that way, can you put us onto the ones we need to talk to?"

"I can make inquiries."

"How do they manage to take goods from under the noses of the Keltanese? Are the soldiers in on it, too?"

"Nah, I told you, they're not too bright. And they don't know anything about harbours and all. See, the smugglers use the tunnels below the streets and the caves in the cliffs, have for years." Orlo warmed to his topic now, wanting to show what he knew. He did look about him, though, as if to check for anyone else in earshot.

"Is that how you get around after curfew, using the tunnels?"

"Quick for a country boy, I'd say," he said with a dip of his head. "Maybe you want to see tonight?"

I rose to the air of challenge in his tone. "Yah, I can tell my brother better what we are considering. Will I meet you here? I have an errand before sunset."

It appeared from his expression that he had thought I would not be brave enough to come out to the smuggler's tunnels. But then, he had only just met me. "Sure, you come out after you have your fish stew, eh? I'll be here in the back."

I nodded and stood, and Orlo rose as well, and lifted a hand as he turned to the gate. "And don't tell Honni," he said before he was more than a couple of paces away. "She's prone to worry."

I acknowledged this with another nod, and went into the kitchen. "Did you t-two get on?" Honni asked from the fireside.

"Sure, thanks for bringing me to meet him. Is Virda in with Guthy?"

She pointed to the keeping room, and I found the two women by the fire with mending in their laps and mugs of tea to hand.

"Judian, you missed your noontime meal. Have Honni give you a bite of something," Guthy said.

"I will. I want to go up to the chapel where my brother was married last fall." Virda began to rise, but I motioned her back to her seat. I had not told her I planned to go and check if the messenger hawk Annora sent had found the apostate, and whether anything had come of it. "Uphill is harder for you, Virda. Wieser and I can make the climb, I'm sure I know the way. It won't take long."

I won't say Virda did not have misgivings about me heading out alone, for she looked uncertainly at the door to the street. She said no more, however, and I took the packet of cheese and brown bread Honni gave me and set off with Wieser to walk up the hill to the chapel.

The streets continued as crowded as ever, and I wondered idly where folk were bound for—the sailors with their gear, the matrons with children in tow and determination in each footfall.

Aside from sailors, not many men—unless old or young like me. The conscription had taken so many of an age to fight. Now the Keltanese guardsmen were the only men of majority age on the streets, except, as I noted, for the sailors who came and went dockside without interference from patrols. The smugglers couldn't be women? Or, maybe boys like Orlo, who looked maybe two or three years older than me.

I would find out tonight.

The chapel stood just as I remembered it, down to the crows in the oak tree. I had reason to pay more mind to crows since Gargle came to me, and paused to peer up into the branches. Eight crows stared back, cawing at once like watch dogs sounding the alarm. Wieser looked up as well, tail up and waving like a flag.

"There's no need for that," I said, not really intending the crows to hear me, just an absent-minded remark. The cawing stopped at once, though, and a pair of crows flew down from the crown of the tree to a branch that jutted just over my head. "Did I call you two? I seem to have developed a knack all unawares ..."

Both regarded me with the same inscrutable look that Gargle used. When I walked on toward the chapel door, both heads swiveled to follow me.

I was surprised to find the door secured; chapels were generally open for worshippers at all times, so offerings could be left and rites performed. I raised my hand and knocked, and saw my two observers had silently come to perch on the top of the sign affixed beside the door frame. "Will I find him within?" I asked them. I swore, both of them nodded. I just commenced wondering whether I had lost my senses when the apostate swung the door open a hand span—and no further.

"Who is it?" he said in the lispy voice I recalled from the joining day. He applied his eye to the crack.

"It's Judian Lebannen. You remember when I was here for my brother's wedding? The day the men in town marched for the western border?"

183

He made a wary nod, but the door opened no more.

"May I come in for a bit? I wanted to speak with you."

"How fares the young couple?" he said, but still he did not swing the door aside.

"Please, may I come in?" I gave him a steady stare, and finally with a breath through pursed lips, he pulled me in through the threshold. I signaled Wieser to stay, and saw her settle on the stone step with her paws outstretched. All was dark shadows within, where usually fine beeswax candles burned at the altars for each of the gods. He followed my glance, and said with bitterness, "Yes, the tholdiers took all my candles. Bullying heathens! Come down to the thellar. We can thpeak there."

He *was* hiding in the cellar, as I had suspected on the mountain when Annora dispatched her message. It looked as if he lived there instead of in his rooms behind the chapel proper, for bowls and spoons and a kettle on a small grate showed he cooked within the gloomy room, and a long bench along one wall had a wad of blankets at one end. I was lucky he had heard me knock.

"I don't have much to offer," he looked about as if food might volunteer itself, "perhaps thome broth?"

I shook my head. I hated to take any of the little he appeared to have. Instead, I held out what remained of my cheese and bread from Guthy's, as Honni had been generous. He looked longingly at it, but did not reach out to take it, so I set it on the bench. "I wanted to ask, holy brother, if …" Better to waste no time, I decided. "If you received a message we sent from our hiding place on the mountains by the northwest pass?"

His jaw worked for a moment, without sounding out a word. He sank onto his bench, and put his face in his hands. "The gods did not thend the hawk to me?" he said after a long moment. He left his hands over his eyes.

"I cannot say how it was guided to you, that may have been divine, at least in part. But the message was written by my brother's bride, sent the morning after I saw that the troops had

184

come through the pass. The enemy may have been well on their way to the coast before we knew. Were you able to get word to our troops here?"

I saw tears leaking between his fingers. "I did try. I went into the threets and found thome of our men working to build the barricade. I told them the Keltanes were coming from the near pass, that the gods themselves had thent word. They thought me a panicky fool, I could thee. I don't think there were more men who could have been brought in, anyway. We were thin, thin. We were overrun in mere hours." He lifted a tear streaked face to me. I had given him short shrift, and regretted my earlier certainty that he would do nothing out of timidity.

"It is true our men were too few, most of our troops had been lured out into the western territory. The Keltanese used mages from Scythera to achieve their victory here. I believe the sorcerers delayed the winter to keep the nearer pass open. At least I wanted to know our message reached you. You did everything you could. I thank you for trying. We only hoped our warning might have made a difference, but it came too late."

He nodded slowly. "Your father, he theemed to know thomething was upon us."

"He and my brother went with the troops that marched west that day. My brother has returned, but my father is under siege at the border fort, Hasseron. Our fight continues there, to keep the Keltanese from controlling the western pass unopposed."

The apostate brushed away the wet on his cheeks, and pushed his hands on his knees to stand. "What's next for us, I can only wonder."

"I came to make sure our delivery method worked, holy brother. We need a way to send information between Bale Harbour and our farm, and our troops to the west, at the fort. Could you help us?"

"Me help?" his voice went faint. "What would I do to help in a war?"

"I don't expect any of us to fight them. What our country needs is a courier network to ensure that our soldiers have the critical information at the moment it's needed. My brother came back to try to set up such a network, but we haven't been able to contact our troops. I found them imprisoned in a warehouse on the waterfront, but can't get word to them."

"What can they do from prithon?"

"We must work out a plan to free them. I don't even know how many there are, or how many are wounded. That's the kind of information I need to get and pass on."

"I—I—" he swallowed with a loud gulp. "I could athk to vithit the prithoners. To offer thpiritual comfort."

Yes, if the Keltanese can understand your lisp and if they care about their prisoners' spiritual distress. I had nothing better to suggest, however. And he was showing a brave heart.

"Please try. I'll send the hawk again, and if you can set it free with your message tied to its leg, I'll have it return to us ... er, well, I have to learn how to do that, first. Annora sent the hawk to you by feeding it some holly leaves from beside the chapel door and saying a spell. May I take some more of the leaves? And I have some of the foliage from home for you to keep."

"I have no facility for thpellcathting," he confessed, extending his hand for the packet of leaves I took from my jerkin.

"I'm only just learning. I'll make sure you are taught what's needed, one way or another. It's only twelve miles from our farm to here. I can come back at need. Brother, do you know Guthy's place near the water?"

"Where the old thailors go? I think I do."

"I've been thinking a hawk in the town at Guthy's might be noted. Up here at the chapel, it would not be so unusual, perhaps be thought a divine messenger, no?"

"I doubt it would be even theen, little do folk come up my hill nowadays."

"The old sailors are being asked to send us information, too.

186

Could you walk to Guthy's, maybe every few days, and bring what they provide back here to send along to us? I think it would spread the risk better than having a hawk arrive at Guthy's door so often. Are folk accustomed to you walking about the town?"

"Yeth, I go here and there. I will do what I can. The gods mutht be on our side, against invaders tho cruel."

He clasped my shoulder, and I took my leave. Wieser and I paused at the door to collect some of the holly leaves. I took some extra so Annora could save some for a wedding remembrance. I knew she would like that.

The pair of crows left their tree to fly along above me, just as Gargle had done. "I cannot afford to draw attention," I told them quietly. "You must stay higher, or lag further behind. I have to figure out how I call all these creatures!" They flew higher, circling like the gulls which screeched and swooped overhead. No passers-by on the street gave them a glance. Wieser paced beside me, back downhill to Guthy's for my next task: meeting the smugglers with Orlo.

CHAPTER 27

I thought during my walk about the coming night, and the soldiers turning up again to demand food and drink from Guthy. She would be unwise to refuse them, even if she wanted to try it. And if she could not afford a nightly raid, then what? I stewed about it as I strode along, and tried to think of a way Guthy could both give them what they wanted and make the soldiers not want to take from her any more. Wieser crossed in front of me, nearly tripping me up, and I saw as I stumbled that my pair of crows were perched calmly on the sign which hung just where I had been halted. The sign's letters declared "Emoryn's Herbarium."

"What do I want here?" I mused to the trio of animals. But I pushed open the door and went in. Wieser came by my side, the crows remained on the gently swinging signboard. Inside I found ranks of jars with corked tops and labels inked in spidery script. Bunches of drying herbs hung from the rafters.

"Hullo," came a pleasant voice from beyond a drab curtain hanging behind the counter. "I'll be right out."

A woman about the age of the smith's wife back home pushed aside the curtain and stepped out smiling. She had dark auburn hair and pale blue eyes that looked first at Wieser and then at me.

"What are you looking for today?" She placed her hands flat on the counter and waited, seeming in no hurry.

I really did not know. My lessons in herb-lore from Annora had not gotten far. Perhaps my crows knew best … what had I been thinking just before they stopped here? How to make the soldiers not want Guthy's food. "Is there something that can make men not want particular food?"

She wrinkled her brow for a moment. "Not want to eat a certain food at all, or not want to eat it again?"

"Not want it again, but not harm them so they wanted to have revenge on the person who gave it to them. If it made them ill, perhaps, but not deathly so."

She nodded and moved to the row of jars on the highest shelf behind the counter. She plucked two clay jars from the shelf and mixed their contents on a square of paper, stirring the powders with a broom straw. "How many men?" she asked as she considered her pile.

"Perhaps a dozen," I hazarded.

She looked up at her rafters, and pulled several stems from a straggly, dusty bunch over the window. She stripped off the leaves and crushed them between her palms, then let the scrumbled bits fall onto the powders and stirred them in.

"Mix this in the food you wish to put them off, shortly before it is to be eaten. In other words, do not include it for the entire time the food is cooked. No strange taste will be noted, but within an hour, they will have cramps and puking. No real damage, just like eating food that's turned. But they will also not be able to think of eating the same thing again without bringing back the sick feeling. Will that do?"

"I think it sounds exactly suited for my needs. What does such a thing cost?"

"For you, three coppers. Between one with the gift and another, special prices are struck."

I must have looked flummoxed, as I did not think of myself as either gifted, or looking so. I opened my mouth but could think of no words, and drew a throaty chuckle from her as I stood gaping. I turned hot in the face and fumbled for the coppers. She accepted them, still smiling, and tucked them in her pocket. She folded the paper carefully to contain the powder and handed it to me.

"Did you think your dog would seem just an ordinary one? Or that I could not feel the power in you?"

"I don't know what to say to that. If I have power, I wish I knew how to use it. There is much I would do about present circumstances."

"You are doing much, already. And will do more, I'm thinking. Please do come back if you can use anything else I have here," she said, and returned to her curtain. "Good luck with the soldiers." She slipped back into the room beyond.

"I never said anything about soldiers," I told Wieser, and left her shop with the skin on the back of my neck crawling. To the waiting crows, I said, "Come on then." I thought about the encounter as I walked the rest of the way back to Guthy's, and concluded that soldiers would be obvious candidates for sickening, in an occupied town. *Take your allies where you find them*, I could imagine Da saying.

The crows already perched on Guthy's gable when Wieser and I pushed through her door. Happily, I had not the least bit of trouble getting Guthy and Honni to agree to set aside food for the night watch, and to dose it as the herbalist had directed. If we waited until the patrol came calling, the concoction would not be wasted from mixing it in too soon. I put Honni in charge of my packet, and went upstairs to wash for supper.

I found Virda had lain down for a nap while I had gone to the chapel, and was only just waking. "You are wise to rest," I said. "Annora says you are not fully recovered yet. I was cautioned not to wear you out."

"Tiffle-toffle. I'm as good as I ever was." She followed me to the window, where I poured water from the cracked pitcher into a shallow bowl for washing. The two crows stood on the ledge and regarded us through the wavy diamond-shaped panes in the little window.

"You've collected more advisers?" Virda asked.

"At the chapel. I wonder if they'll follow me home tomorrow? Gargle doesn't seem the hospitable sort to me. These two did get me to a good idea for dealing with the night watch, though." I told her about my side-trip to Emoryn's, and her offer to help further at need.

Virda chuckled. "Annora could not have thought up a better plan, with all her knowledge."

"I don't know about that," I said, toweling my face and neck. "But at least I may be able to leave without worrying every night about the soldiers coming back here demanding all Guthy has. Now, I need to talk to you about something else."

"I've not seen the old fellows yet, to ask about messages," Virda said.

"No, I expect them back nearer supper time. While you talk to them after we eat, I will be going with a friend of Honni's. He has people I need to meet, so I can tell Wils all our options." The dismay on her face shone clear to see. "I'll be careful, and only gone as long as I must be."

"But if you're out after curfew—"

"Orlo says there are ways to work around the curfew patrols. He does it all the time."

"And if he's just bragging to a country boy? What then? I should hate to go back to Wils and … Oh, it doesn't bear thinking about!" She twisted her skirts in her hands.

"Virda, you must believe by now that I can see to my safety. With Wieser, and now these other two helpers," I gestured to the watching crows, "I'll be able to use my gift to find out what we must know to reach our goal." I hated to play the card of "use my gift," since I had no clear idea how I was using it now. But neither could I have Virda interfere with what I came to do.

"Oh, I am grown too old for all this intrigue. What will your da say when he comes back? I wonder now why I felt this was wise, coming here with you."

"You came here because you are brave and want the Keltanese back where they belong. Remember, I just went to the chapel and back with no trouble," I said, with much the same placating reasonableness I would use with Morie.

"But that was daytime!" she answered back.

It took me until supper to calm her and get her focused on her task for the evening. The old salts came back from the waterfront and took their places around the table. The stew was rich and tasted wonderful, but I ate quickly so I could meet Orlo as arranged. I claimed I felt tired out, and took my bowl to the kitchen. There, I told Honni I was meeting Orlo, and slipped through the back before she could raise much objection. She must have thought we planned to talk back by the chicken coop again. I had not brought my cloak, so as not to look as if I prepared for an excursion. Wieser left her bowl of scraps and came along by my side.

"Here," came Orlo's voice from the shadows by the neighboring building.

I walked to where he waited, leaning on the wall and chewing on a bit of straw. He wore dark clothes, darker than mine. A haar fog rose thick from the harbour, though, so I hoped I wouldn't stand out in my lighter-colored tunic and trousers.

"Your dog will have to stay unless you can guarantee it will keep silent."

I spotted my two crows on the roof of the back porch, and gestured to them to stay, but about Wieser I said, "She only makes noise if I need warned of trouble. And even then she is quiet about it. She won't call attention to us."

"Will she go below ground without hesitation?" he said, squatting to pat her head. Wieser wagged her tail like a simple, friendly dog.

"That won't be a problem," I assured him. He stood and waved a hand to tell me to follow him as he turned into the alleyway.

Though we kept to the shadows as we walked down toward the wharves, no night patrollers were in the back streets, and rare townfolk. Between the fog and the coming darkness, I was glad to trail after Orlo. I was not sure I could find the way again, since I could see so little. Wieser would be able to follow her nose, and return us to Guthy's if need be, I consoled myself.

Orlo led us in silence to a crusty stone wall along the bottom of a steep slope, then put out a hand to stop me. Still saying nothing, he ducked into the bushes at the near end of the head-high stones, and I could hear him pushing at the branches. In a moment, he stuck his hand out and pulled me into the brush with him. I found we were standing on a shallow step cut into the stone behind the wall, with a course of descending steps just visible in the fog and gloom. Wieser stood beside me, and we went down behind Orlo, feeling our way a bit as it became darker at the bottom. He stretched out his arm to move thick vines aside, and shouldered through a narrow arched opening. When we came after, he crouched by a lantern, striking a flint to light it. The flame began to glow, and the shadows fled down the passage deeper into the hill. Four more lanterns waited at the passage wall by our feet.

"This will be enough light," he whispered. "You take one unlit, in case we need it farther in." I swung the closest lantern up by its handle, and crunched after Orlo on the sandy tunnel floor.

I was thankful for Wieser pacing at my side, because after a dozen twists and turns of the passageway, I could no longer keep track of which way we had come. Tunnels opened off our path every twenty or thirty paces, and forks where a choice had to be made came several times as we rounded curves. The tunnel was tall as a man, and ran narrower and wider by turns. Orlo showed no hesitation in his route, he must have been down below many times. I admired his certainty. Of course, I could have led him all over our mountain with equal confidence, and no danger of losing the way. That was my place—this was Orlo's.

I couldn't say exactly how far we walked, when the way opened wide, and we stepped down into a cavern as big as Guthy's keeping room. More lanterns within showed a dozen young men and women, and half that many boys hard at work shifting crates and barrels, with one swarthy, heavily bearded man seated on a wide-bottomed keg, smoking a curved pipe.

He took the pipe from his mouth and rose on catching sight of us. "Well, scald me," he said with a smirk, "look what's come to town."

CHAPTER 28

Orlo spoke next, while I was still considering how to respond to the man's sneer. I met his gaze as Orlo said my name and where I hailed from. The man looked like one of the Traveller folk, who lived in caravans and roamed all about the provinces doing small jobs. And thieving, if the village gossip was true. Not a bad way for smuggled goods to be handled, maybe? Wieser sat at my side, and sniffed the air with interest, but did not give any wary looks to the man before us.

"What did you bring us your hayseed boy for?" the man asked Orlo.

"He and his brother want to get supplies for their village. And aggravate the Keltanese, but not too much," Orlo said.

"We actually want to send the Keltanese back where they came from, but that's not our first step," I said.

"Haw, we can help you with part of that. Though you won't find we see much difference between council constables and Keltanese patrollers. If you can pay, boy, that is what makes a bargain. I'm Zaffis. What needs does your village have?"

"Some supplies of food that keeps. Raw materials for the forge and lumber to rebuild what the invaders burned and stole. Buyers for villagers' woolens, milled grain, leatherwork—rather than giving it to the Keltanese." I scratched my head. "And I need a wagon," I added. "Ours was burned in our barn when we were overrun during the invasion."

A few of those laboring stopped to look curiously at me as I spoke, and Zaffis growled at them and pointed his pipe stem at their waiting work. "And do you want all this at once?" he said, turning dancing eyes back to me.

"No, I'm heading home in the morning. I just need to know if all of it can be gotten here. My brother and I will return if we decide to use your … services."

"*Services*—Haw! I like that. Makes us sound like the merchants we are, eh? You'll need to bring a heavy purse of gold for all you want. Do you and your brother have coin?"

"If we start with a wagon and a load of dried beans, plus lumber, how much might that run?" We had some gold at the farm, and the villagers had some as well, I had to think.

"You'd need a team to pull your wagon? Or do you plan to clip clop into the harbour on your plow horses?" He play-acted holding reins high and bouncing along.

Orlo sniggered at the sport he made of me. I said, "For the right price, maybe you'll drive our new horses and wagon to Roicer Village with the load of goods. It's only seven miles walk back, and that's just a good stretch of the legs for country folk. If we can agree, I'll bring a third of the gold to you here, and you'll bring the wagon to us in Roicer and get the rest of the gold on delivery."

"Being a countrified boy, you probably don't realize, that's not how this is done. You don't tell me what's to be. I tell you."

"Being a smuggler, you maybe don't appreciate I want to be out only a third of my money if you don't come through," I said, trying to copy Da's affable way of talking. As if haggling with smugglers was something I did whenever I took a break between chores. Like pipe-smoking, for instance. Though I had smoked a pipe as often as I had bargained with smugglers, or never.

"I'll have to charge enough to cover my risk, see. A wagon and team don't readily fit beneath the streets. That part will have to be … arranged and then loaded. What if I say 200 gold pieces? 'S war and occupation, after all. Drives prices high."

"Has to be worth your while, that much is plain. I'll carry the price back to my brother and his men. If they agree to the bargain, I'll get back to Orlo, then?"

Zaffis shook his head side to side like a horse trying to shoo flies. "What mad creature have you brought me, cousin?" He spoke to Orlo, so I surmised that was their relation to one another. Did that mean Orlo was a Traveller, too? He had the dark looks of one. "I'll stand by my price if you don't wait overlong. I'll need to hear back by the waning of the moon, so we can load and deliver at dark of moon. Later than that, your deal is no good."

"My brother will decide without wasting time. Our time nor yours."

"Yah, be off before I realize I'm selling too cheap by half." He turned to his cavern of workers, but he was grinning.

I followed Orlo as he withdrew, and wondered if the whole village could come up with 200 pieces of gold.

By the time Orlo had led me a roundabout return path to Guthy's back yard, I had been struck with an idea to help the harbourmaster, since my previous thoughts of how much money might be kept at home, and with our neighbors, had no ready answer.

"Orlo, do you think when next you are at the harbourmaster's house you could get some clothing from the grandson, and the parents and the harbormaster's wife, too? Something they have each worn, or some of their bedding? Something with their scent. I think Wieser could track them to where the Keltanese are holding them."

He paused mid-stride, and faced me. "The laundress might could help me do it."

"Needs to be worn clothes, not washed, to have a good scent."

He looked at Wieser, who sniffed the sea breeze and licked her chops. "If I can get such as that, and bring it to Honni at

Mistress Guthy's, you'll have the dog try when you come back to bring the money?"

I nodded in the fog, then thought he might not be able to see my gesture, and said, "That would be the best time, no? Then she can start with the little boy, in case they are held in separate places."

"And the benefit for you, of relieving my master's mind?"

"I want him on our side, so he sees I've done him a favor if it comes to pass that he can do one in return."

Orlo accepted this as sufficiently sensible, and said, "I never saw Zaffis cut a deal like yours, or so quick."

"He wants rid of the Keltanese, even if not as bad as I do, that's my take on it. And, he looks to get 200 in gold for about 30 coins' worth of goods."

"You could be right," Orlo said, and led us smack into Honni on the porch. She held an iron skillet, and had blazing murder in her eyes.

"Orlo Suerat, you better hope you have brought him ba-back whole!" she said, and hefted her skillet with real menace.

"Aww, Honni, they only took one of his ears. He has the other still—Hey!" He yelped as he vaulted off the porch beyond her reach. She had a mighty swing for such a scrawny girl. The weight of the skillet swung her right around until she faced me again. I pulled back my hair on either side of my head, to show two ears, while laughing fit to bust.

"And you!" She pointed her skillet at me. "You never said you w-were leaving with Orlo! I thought the patrols had taken you both off the s-stoop." Her glare was truly fury. She would have seemed scary, if not so bony and frail.

"Did the patrols come? And get their dose?" I asked to divert her. Orlo climbed over the porch rail and smacked dirt from his trousers, collected as he rolled on landing below.

"Hmmph! Yes, one bunch of the same o-ones, and more we hadn't seen before. What are we supposed to do if more c-come calling? There's no more of your packet left." She sniffed and tossed her head.

"I'll give you the money and tell you where to go for more. It would be wise to have on hand. Tell the lady at the shop the country boy with the dog sent you. She'll remember."

"Oh, you j-just think you know everything," she said, and carried her skillet into the kitchen, slapping it on the hearth with a clang. I looked up into the mist, and could barely make out the pair of crows where they perched on the porch roof, watching.

It's not me that knows everything, I thought. *Here's hoping they do*. I clasped hands with Orlo, and went into Guthy's warm kitchen. While the fire burned toasty, Honni's back turned to me seemed as chilly as the clinging fog outside. I soon felt called to go upstairs and see how Virda got along with Guthy's old sailors.

I suffered a hug, the price of safe return, and asked after her errand. She lit up as she shared her news.

"I thought they'd be proud to help us! Only one of them knew my Davini, but I was once a shipmaster's wife, and that carries weight no matter how much time passes. Some know what ships carry what sort of cargo, and can send word when what we want comes in. Then when it's loaded to go west, they can tell us which wagons and the number of guards—everything we need. No one will question them watching, as they have always done. They even have an idea for the code to use, so the messages do not go into wrong hands even if they go awry. The ships use lanterns. From deck to deck, short and long flashes of light. The Keltanese will not know maritime code!"

"But how can we use lanterns, Virda? Flashes of light can't travel as far as what we need. Over flat water is one thing. Up the mountain is another."

"Laroot, he was one of the signalers when he sailed, he suggests writing our messages of one and two-syllable words, to make up the code letters. Then if the enemy reads a message of, I don't know, farm news or how someone's baby is getting on, they won't have anything to make them suspicious of another meaning."

"I like the plan. Maybe we could carry some messages back and forth, just like regular letters instead of using the messenger birds. Use the birds only when speed is most vital, so they do not attract attention by flying to and fro frequently." Wils would like the plan, too, I thought. I felt lifted up by hope of getting help to Da soon. "I remember you said you doubted coming here with me was a good idea. I could never have got the old salts to come round as you have! Great work, Virda. Only you could have done it."

She said, "Oh, well, now, I don't know if it was all that … " and pushed at her hair to tidy it. But she was pleased to hear what I told her, I could tell by the spots of color on her cheeks.

"I don't suppose you can guess whether there's 200 in gold at home?" I said, and told her about the smuggler's dealings.

She sucked her lower lip. "Such a sum! I mislike to bargain with criminals, but dire times make dire needs. And dire deeds, betimes. There may be that much coin amongst several families. He didn't say it had to be Keltanese coins? Because none at home will have that."

"He never said. He likely melts it down, and trades in gold ingots or such, so it's harder to trace."

"You found out a lot about them, it seems."

"I'm only guessing. But he never said what currency we had to have. Gold is gold."

"I'll be glad to be out of this town and back where we belong!" Virda said.

While I missed the mountain, I would have been glad to stay longer. I liked the way something new to me seemed always happening here. But now, I did want to travel home and get our plan to help Da at the fort fixed in place.

CHAPTER 29

W e woke as early as the old salts the next morning. My hand fairly ached from being shook so often—some of them were not as creaky as they appeared and had a grip in them yet. They set off for the dockside with more bounce to them than I had seen previously. *Feels good to be of use*, I thought as I watched them filing out. One of them pinched Guthy on the backside as he passed. She swatted at him with her table-wiping cloth, but didn't mean it as serious as Honni had meant her skillet-swinging, as far as I could see.

Honni thawed overnight, and did not grumble at me further about going off with Orlo. While Virda and I hurried to eat bread and tea, she packed sliced pork and onions for us, with a hunk of cheese and bread. I protested we would be home by evening, unless slowed by the weight of her food package, but she only smiled. Guthy crunched my backbones in a smothering embrace, then flung her arms about Virda.

"Do not leave me lonesome for you so long again!" Guthy said, dabbing at her eyes. I had hoped to come with only Wieser for company next trip, but it looked as if Virda coming along would be required to minimize female fussing.

The fog still pressed against the windows and swirled through the open door. Though nearly dawn, the light was diffuse and the haar as thick as Honni's fish stew outside. Virda walked out with confidence, since she knew her way, and Wieser and I followed her toward the edge of town.

The wall the soldiers were building at the main road had grown far higher over the short time we stayed in Bale Harbour. Many Keltanese labored on, replacing Merced's hasty wooden barricade with rough cut, keg-sized stones. Two gates stood open, one for travelers coming into the town, and the other for those making their way out. I saw with relief that only those wishing to come in faced a quartet of sentries. Both the gates were wide enough to accommodate the broad drays that carried heavy goods, which would have made them difficult to secure. But, the Keltanese had more knowledge of barricades than we did. The iron gates set into the wall at each opening could be swung shut to bar any onslaught from without or within. I would have to be sure we avoided this route when we rescued the imprisoned troops of Merced. Perhaps a sea escape?

There remained a great deal of stone still stacked at the worksite, dim hulks in the fog. Likely they planned guard towers and a walkway above, such as the walled city drawn in one of Da's books at home. Keltanese might not know seacraft, but in warcraft we were not their equal. A disheartening thought.

I felt further dismay after we passed through the exit gate and onto the road west. Marching eerily out of the mist to meet us came a column of some forty men. Merchants and farmers conscripted by our troops, I guessed from their lack of uniform. Keltanese surrounded and herded them as the men trudged home. Some bore severe wounds, and leaned on their fellows as they stumbled along. Others had slings or bandage-wrapped arms, some limped with canes and crutches. One fellow with grimy rags about his head was led by the man beside him. His eyes open, he appeared either blind or addled. All were dirty and downcast. I hoped Honni's da and brothers were among their number, and marching under their own power.

"Will they be sent back to their families?" Virda said in my ear, voice soft and somber.

I shook my head. "I think it more likely they'll be taken to the warehouse we saw. I hope the apostate is allowed to visit them there, so he can tell the families." I drew her over to the side of the road, where we stood in the gravel to let them pass. I wondered if some of Roicer Village menfolk would be among these captives, or if they might have filtered away into the countryside when the invasion came. There were more troops unaccounted for, too. The men Wils and Da had found camped at the western pass, who Da had sent on their way east to meet the enemy. Surely those men had not all been killed or captured? There would be uniformed Mercedians among their number. More difficult to hide among the citizens, for them.

"Let's keep count of our troops we see marched to the harbour. When time comes to free them, we'll need better numbers, of course. But I think it would be good to know a rough amount," I said to Virda as we walked along. Wieser kept pace, and though the fog kept me from seeing them, the caws I heard above us told me the pair of crows followed us, too.

As the morning wore on, the climbing sun began to burn away some mist, plus our road began to rise until behind us a bowl of milk-white marked the harbour. By the time we reached the road that came off the main way and headed to the village, we had counted another fifty of our men. So, almost a hundred walked down to the sea this morning. How long would Keltane feed them, if feeding their own troops was their priority? How many made the walk every day?

We saw wagons coming and going with typical loads of goods, and one curious wagon I paused to watch go past us, headed west. It carried a load of men, sallow-skinned and with long dark hair fixed in hanging plaits. The wagon's canvas panels were rolled up, but packed tight in the bed, the men scarcely looked about them as they jolted along over the stones and ruts. I turned to

Virda and saw her make the warding sign as she gazed at them going by. "Slaves," she said, shaking her head. "Gods' mercy be on them. My boys have told me of Scytheran slave traders. It's a bad business."

"Are the slaves being taken to Keltane?"

"Only too likely. Mercy be, mercy be." She drew her shawl closer about her head, turning to resume our journey. I stepped out as well, wondering what work needed slaves in Keltane. Forced to work in the mines? Tend the fields and crops? Leaving more Keltanese men to bear arms against us, maybe.

We drew up to the Earth Goddess shrine in good time. Virda pulled out some of our cheese and bread for an offering, but I persuaded her to save the cheese, since those at home had been without. We mounted the three stone steps that led to the moss crusted granite pillar. The rock was generally woman-shaped, with crude features chiseled in to represent eyes and mouth. Other supplicants had left foodstuffs, grain sheaves and stoppered water or wine jars at the base of the statue. These offerings were never disturbed; it brought the vilest ill-luck to trifle with the Earth Mother's due. It appeared even the invading Keltanese respected the shrine, if indeed they had passed exactly this way. Did Keltane share our same beliefs? I would ask Wils and Gevarr.

Virda knelt and said her prayer as I looked about for Joren Delyth. We waited just beneath the tallest oak on the north side of the shrine, where I had directed him to meet us. I wondered if he had found it more trouble to leave Bale Harbour than I had led him to expect. He might not even have attempted to come.

But Virda had just stood to brush the dust from her skirt when I heard a soft hiss from the bushes behind the Earth Goddess. I did not think She Herself courted our attention, and Wieser at once poked her nose into the branches while wagging her flag of a tail. Joren emerged grinning.

"Hullo, well met." He pulled a sea bag out, and extended his hand to me after touching his forelock to Virda.

"I didn't know you were a sailor," I said as we clasped hands.

"Truly," he said with a sidelong look about him, "I'm not. I saw how the sailors went about town without being bothered by the patrols. A sailor came to the close for a cheap bed, asked me to help him hang onto his Double Jack winnings until he sailed. I told him I'd see to it he left with his cash if I could have his bag, less the gear. It suited him better than sharing the money, and I walked out the town gate without drawing any remark!"

"Clever," I said, and meant it. We could use the ruse more than once, I reckoned. Eventually the Keltanese would learn how to sail, and not have to be so respectful of the men who already had that skill. In the meantime, our way in and out of Bale Harbour could be smoothed.

We shared our meat and onion in the shade, with cool water from the seep that trickled down the rocks above the shrine. Wieser and Joren both especially relished the pork. My crows had some of the remaining bread, more politely than Gargle would have done. Then, with wind picking up from the west, we set out through the village proper and on up the road to home. Joren insisted on relieving Virda of her burden of yard goods. Just as well, since the way grew steep ahead. I would not let him carry my tools, though, I'd have felt foolish.

The villagers still kept to their houses, and actually I was thankful. I wanted to get to the farm and tell Wils all we had learned in town. I did feel a twinge when we passed by Annora's Uncle Werrel and Aunt Lorneh's place. Yet, it looked undamaged, and they had not stirred themselves to come up and ask how she or any of us fared in the invasion. I supposed she was right to leave them be. I did not imagine it would profit us to appear at their door asking for gold coins to pay the harbour smugglers.

I could see when we approached home, Wils and the others had been busy these three days with framing the new barn. Though roughly half the size of the old barn, it took shape as practical space for animals and storage. And, he had left part of the stone foundation cleared for future expansion. In truth, he was doing a better job of managing this part of our new life than I would have done. I thought to tell him so, as he walked out to meet us, but the first words out of his mouth were complaint.

"Your stray isn't of much use on a farm," he said, tight-lipped. I did not think he referred to Gargle. I reckoned Gevarr must have done or said something to rile Wils. After giving me a dark look, Wils then glanced over at Joren, and added, "Have you brought us another? This isn't one of your sons, Virda."

"No—" Virda started to say.

"I'm Joren Delyth," my new stray said, while setting his burdens down and extending a hand. "You must be the husband of the pretty Donah."

I maybe should have told him that a remark about fair Annora would not prove a way to win Wils's regard.

My brother scowled at the proffered hand. "Why do you know my wife if you're a seaman?"

"He's one of our troops, the bag is a disguise. You remember you were keen to find some of our army?" I said. "Joren was with the fieldmaster who came to us before the invasion."

Wils grunted and gave Joren's hand a brief shake, before turning on his heel and walking toward the house. "He's also a good wagoneer," I called after Wils.

"I don't see a wagon for him to drive," came the sour response. So, I sighed and made my way to the house, to tell Wils how we were planning to come by our new wagon.

Gargle waited on the porch railing. As I had feared, he fluffed his feathers and lowered his head to glare at the pair of crows who hopped along the ground at my feet. Much muttering, and a new call that sounded like "clock, clock" ensued, then all three flapped madly into the sky and away. "They'd better be coming back," I told Wieser. "If they know best, we're going to need them now more than ever."

Joren I introduced all around, and Morie fussed at me for not

208

bringing her anything from Bale Harbour "because Da and Wils always bring me a present when they go to town."

"I guess I am a bad brother, then. I brought tools home, that's all."

Morie nodded. "And another soldier. I bet we have the most of anybody, now." She led Joren about showing him her doll and books. I tried to rescue him, since he was too mannerly to refuse her, but he said his sister had little girls and he didn't mind.

It did keep the two of them out of the way while I told the other men what I had seen and learned in town. Virda shared her news of the old sailors and the code methods. Annora joined in the group, but Gevarr was still behind the quilt in the corner. I would have to mention him to Joren. I thought Joren would probably be polite about it, running true to his habit.

Joren was not, though, in the event. He noticed Annora held Gevarr's Keltanese uniform tunic, and asked how she came by such a thing. She told him our story of rescue of the wounded enemy, and indicated the quilt hung by the alcove. "That's where he sleeps."

Joren swept Morie up in his arms, and backed away from the kitchen. "You cannot mean you allow him in the house with you! What danger to the little one!"

"Oh, he's mostly mean and grumpy," Morie told the fearful man. "But Judian and Annora made him mind. And now Wils does. He won't hurt you."

I smiled to hear her so reassure Merced's quavering warrior. Our cause might have been lost even without the sorcerers imported by Keltane.

Annora explained she was repairing the tunic to be used when we attempted to hijack a wagonload of goods on the road. Joren's eyes showed white all around like a spooked horse, but he set Morie back on her feet.

Annora continued, "We only have the one. I've tried to dye some fabric to match, using wine—"

"A sorry waste of wine, that," Perk said.

"—but the color doesn't last." She gave Perk an austere look.

"We can steal some more from the wagon's guards. Can you sew sea bags?" I asked. I pointed to the one Joren had brought. "Men can pose as sailors and move about town more easily, carrying one of these."

Annora looked over the bag Joren placed in her hands, and Virda put in, "I've fashioned plenty of those over the years. Annora and I should be able to churn out a fair number quickly."

"How do the lessons in Keltanese come along?" I asked as I took a piece of dried apple from the bowl on the table, and handed another piece to Joren. Gevarr was instructing the others in rough language used by soldiers and wagoneers. What Wils and I had learned under Da's instruction was used more by gentle-folk, Gevarr told us.

"Morie picks it up quickest. Though she is not allowed in the lessons, somehow she hears the swear words. And forgets none of them." Annora said this from behind her hand, and so softly I had to strain to hear it, but I saw Morie's eyes flick in Annora's direction. So, when Da came home somebody would have to explain why Morie swore like a Keltanese laborer.

When all the others were fed and settled for the night, Wils took me upstairs. He climbed onto a chair in the loft he and I had used to share, and felt about on top of a corner rafter. He handed me down a piece of dusty wood roughly a hand span square, then a drawstring sack of equal size but heavier weight. I found it stuffed with gold coins, the clinking muffled by carded wool. Wils and Da must have hollowed out a space in the rafter to hide money inside.

Wils put his finger to his lips when I started to speak, and held out his hand for the wood. He replaced it above, then led me out to the barn with the bag tucked under his tunic. Once we were out of sight of the house, crouched in a pool of lantern light, he said, "Let's see how far short we fall. Count it."

We had 110 gold coins. I goggled to think I had slept with

such a sum overhead. "How did you think to put it in the rafter?" I asked Wils.

"Da said thieves and other searchers seldom think to look up. He showed me the place once before he went to market alone, so I would know where we had cash if needed. So, we have enough for the down payment, and a bit of time to scrounge the rest before delivery. If you truly think we won't be handing our money into a deep well never to be seen again?" Wils gave me a stern, assessing look. He was trying to seem in charge like Da, I supposed.

"I don't think Honni would have put me on to someone she did not trust, or that Orlo brought me to his cousin Zaffis as fresh meat. Beyond that, I cannot say. I have not thought of any alternative but stealing a wagon and team here ourselves, but then the Keltanese would be able to find out who we were more quickly, if we waylay them so near the harbour and home. This way, Zaffis and his folk are the thieves the enemy guard will be seeking."

"If the smugglers come through for us," Wils said.

"If you have another plan, let's hear it," I answered back.

"No," he sighed. "I do feel we should hold back some of our coin, though, for our own future needs. What if we pay the third down, and then make our total investment seventy-five. Cobbel and I will start going about the village to get contributions, while you take the down money to Bale Harbour and see it gets in the right hands."

I nodded, and could not help suggesting, "Take Joren Delyth with you. He is well-spoken and one of our troops, besides. His manners could help loosen purse strings."

Wils agreed, despite it being my idea. We walked toward the kitchen door, where I found all three crows lined up on the roof's edge. They watched Wils's and my progress across the yard, heads turning in unison. Though difficult to be certain, I thought Gargle must be the largest. I would have to set Morie to naming the other two.

"Do they always stare at you like that?" Wils said with a shiver. "They look like mourners watching a funeral march."

An ugly thought that sent a chill down between my shoulder blades. "They seem more cocky than solemn to me," I answered. "I only wish I knew how I am calling creatures."

"I was hoping you knew well enough that you could come on the road for our highwaymen strike, and tell the enemies' horses to stop. So that Annora will leave off pestering me to bring her," Wils said, lifting his lantern to see the trio of crows better.

Here was I, thinking I had a lot of fast talk ahead of me to be included in the journey. "I'll be able to do that well enough," I said quickly. *Just so long as Annora can teach me before we set out*, I added to myself. I sent a wish to be gifted in communicating with horses. I had sent up so many wishes and prayers already, what was one more?

CHAPTER 30

Wils and Miskin prepared a test message to be sent to Guthy's: "ready here." Annora and Virda coded this into a brief note which reported Virda's safe return to her home. A Keltanese reading it would not suspect any subterfuge, surely.

We sent the note tied to a young goshawk, whose departure was accompanied by a flurry of caws and flapping from all three of our resident crows. Annora watched the uproar, and said, "You'd almost think they wanted to go in her place. You may be right, Judian, about a crow being less noticed in town. They are harder to enspell, though, with the delivery instructions. Being generally strong-willed."

I had to agree with her. "Maybe we should send the hawks and owls to the chapel, and try to send a message to Guthy's with Gargle. Or one of the other two crows, if they might know their way better to the harbour and back." All three fluffed up their feathers and shook their open beaks at me. "I'll set off in the morning to take the money to town, and check that our message found its way to the right house. Maybe we could send one with Gargle today? We'll know at once whether we've succeeded, if Guthy has two notes in hand tomorrow. I'll be home the next day, after I see if Wieser can find the harbourmaster's kin. Provided Orlo can get the clothing to track them with."

"Oh, I'm so in hopes she can find the little grandson, especially. I knew Wils would never say you nay about seeking them," Annora said. I had not been so sure, but Wils had not denied the harbormaster's favor would be a good thing to possess.

Annora wrote a second note then fixed Gargle a dose of what I called "destination potion" in my palm-sized leather book. I wrote down in its pages all she taught me since we returned from the caves. Written beside the recipe were the spell words to be spoken to the messenger to send it on its way. My little folio was more than half full, I noticed when I looked up the sending words.

"You call them and see which comes for this," Annora said, handing me the nugget of meal mixed with leaves and buds from Guthy's backyard. "You speak the sending words, too. It's time you advanced your skill."

I swallowed my nerves, and took a step to the porch rail. I laid the portion on the wood, and looked each of the crows in the eye, where they perched on the pump handle. "Which of you is going to town?" I asked.

Gargle flapped across the short distance to take the dose. I had suspected he would, and that's why I laid it on the rail. He is not gentle. I held my right hand toward him palm out, and spoke the words Annora taught me, muttering under my breath as she did. The rising and falling inflection of the words was a part of the spell, and it all must be spoken on a single breath. She nodded approval of my attention to technique. Next, I took the duplicate note Annora placed in my hand, and Gargle stuck his leg out, standing on the other foot and half-spreading his wings to aid his balance. He waited while I secured it to his scaly leg with strips of suede, then mounted to the sky, calling loudly.

"It would not do to try to send him when stealth counted," I said as I tracked him east with my hand shading my eyes.

His two compatriots regarded me from the pump handle. Morie chose that moment to appear with Murr in her arms. Both birds spread their wings on catching sight of the cat, but neither flew off. The vision of them sent Murr shooting over Morie's shoulder into the kitchen. Though he was twice their size, there were two of them, and their display convinced him he was no threat to them. Rather the reverse.

Morie rubbed her shoulder and scolded the crows for being mean to the cat. She did not find it funny when I laughed, and stuck her lower lip out. To make peace, I said, "Have you thought of their names yet?"

"Mean and meaner," she said, but then relented and told me. "One is Tock and the other is Clock. It's what they say."

"Which is which?"

"It doesn't matter. Each of them says both."

I was still puzzling over this when Wils, Cobbel and Joren came out to walk to the village. To the benefit of our fund drive, smithy Bar Estegg had returned home. He told all the folk how grand grateful he was for Annora's help with birthing his new daughter, and mine in setting his boys to hiding the village's goods from the soldiers. He pledged to help Wils and the others rout out currency from the folk who could spare it. We nearly had enough, and without putting in our last coins we hoped to keep.

###

It was a soft, breezy dawn when I set out for Bale Harbour the next morning. Spring peepers sang in the ditch water along the road. Da had showed me one once, a tiny little frog to make such a racket. *Something so small can make such a dent in the peace of a morning*, I thought. *I hope I can make as much of a dent in the Keltanese peace of mind.* Wieser walked with me, and I carried sacks of spun yarn for a reason to be coming to town. Our coins were wound into leggings under my boots. I'd been told I was too young to carry a seabag, as I wished to do. Virda said boys my age went to sea, but had to earn the right to carry gear by learning the rigging and sails, and how to steer by the stars. I would have liked to learn such things. Perhaps I would one day. But for now, I had another goal: to get my da home safe.

Wils and Annora had taken up for me regarding Virda not coming along this time. A short turnaround, they argued, and she had already shown me my way about the harbour. Thus, Virda helped sow the garden while I walked the harbour road. I did miss her company a little, though I would never say.

I counted thirty of our troops being marched along the road to the harbour, and the passing of seventeen wagons bound to town, and thirteen outbound. Each wagon had its complement of two mounted guards riding alongside. We were going to need more horses.

Guthy and Honni were happy to see me, though thankfully I only had to endure an embrace from Guthy. She showed me both copies of our message, so the goshawk and Gargle both found their way. Gargle in fact remained, squabbling with the chickens and waiting, to all appearance, for a reply to be sent.

"I'll bring him back with me," I laughed. "Unless there is news to send?"

"I won't know until the sailors come back at supper," Guthy told me.

I copied out the recipe and the sending spell for her, and she studied it earnestly. However, when I coached her in the cadence of the speech, she became more and more flustered.

"I have no talent for this! Only some people have the way of it—not Guthy!" she despaired at last.

"If you truly cannot master it, I know someone who will help." I told her about Emoryn at the herb shop, and her offer of any aid we needed. "She is one who can do sending and other spells, I'm certain. Honni knows the way, I sent her there for more potion to keep the guard away from your larder. How does that go?"

"The same ones are never back twice, more's the blessing. None came last night." Guthy wiped her brow in relief, whether at being delivered from soldiers or the learning of magic, I could not say.

I made another copy of the sending spell for the apostate,

which Honni said she would carry to him at the chapel. I asked her to put him on to Emoryn for aid with the spell, since he had already said he had no talent for it. My yarn I left for Guthy to trade in the shop Virda and I had visited, and told her to keep the goods she got there to pay for my night's stay and all her help.

"Oh, tosh and that. 'Tis little enough Guthy does if it will help be rid of these brazen thieves that infest us." Guthy said, but she did take the yarn and tuck it in her apron.

I bade Gargle wait at Guthy's back door while Honni took me to her mum's again to wait for Orlo. The passel of children had not forgotten me yet, and this time greeted and hung on Wieser as well. She tolerated all attentions paid to her ears and tail, and finally lay on her side to be petted by all. Donah Emeral insisted on feeding me lentil soup with bits of smoked meat in it, and black bread. I scraped the bowl clean.

Into this domestic scene breezed Orlo, grinning as usual. He carried a small bundle of clothes he said belonged to the hostage grandson, which the laundress had not washed. I set this aside. We conducted our business indoors and away from young eyes. Once he counted the coins, we bound them up in the leggings to make a packet that would not clink while carried. I asked him to tell Zaffis we would wait for delivery at the village smithy, since for a wagon to turn into his yard would seem natural, even at night. When he set off with a slab of bread and butter, he was whistling, our packet slung around his waist under his shirt.

I undid the twine that held the bundle of clothes, and saw that the boy was smaller even than Morie. A nightshirt and trousers of good cloth were rolled together inside. I called Wieser away from the children, and said, "Find this boy, Wieser. Lead me to him." Wieser buried her nose in the clothes and snuffed deeply, then went to the door.

I thanked Donah Emeral for the food, and told Honni I would return to Guthy's by curfew. Wieser and I went out, with me hoping she understood and *was* leading me to the boy.

I followed her up, down and around street and alley for most of two hours. I had begun to doubt her grasp of our errand, when she sat and barked outside the sawyer's on the southern edge of town. The mill's noise assaulted our ears, loud with shouting men peeling logs, stripping off branches and sawing planks. Straining teams of mules dragged the heaviest logs across the yard, while chains and pulleys hoisted others. The sharp smell of pine sawdust swirled everywhere, my nose could detect nothing else, but Wieser would not budge from her calm regard of the site.

Where would a small boy be best kept? Out of sight, and surely no one able to hear him with all this noise. I could see the largest central building which housed the saw works, but men walked in and out of it constantly. Two smaller shacks stood behind, one farther up a slope and surrounded by stacks of wood. I spoke to Wieser, and told her we would check the farthest shed first. We made our approach by circling around from the back of the property.

No Keltanese guards were in evidence, but I saw the door had been secured with a heavy hasp and padlock. The sawyer might secure tools and such within, I reasoned. But when I looked to Wieser, she commenced sniffing under the door and wagging her tail. I checked to be sure we were still out of sight of the men working below, and came around the side to pull myself up to a tiny window. Cloth had been tacked up as a curtain, but I could see inside through a gap at the bottom. In the dim interior, I could make out three shapes, one smaller and two larger, huddled on straw on the floor. A strong odor of pisspot leaked through the gap.

I let myself down from the window, and went around to the side closest to the huddled forms. I crouched there and knocked on the wall. "Psst," I called, none too loudly. "Are you the harbourmaster's kin?"

A moment passed, then, "Yes, yes. Who's there? We are his wife and his son's wife. And grandson, too."

"I'm Judian. I've come to help you get away. I'll come back at dark—"

"No, the guards come at dark when the mill stops. They gag us then, so we can't call for help in the quiet hours."

"I'll have to get you out now, then. I'll be right back." I told Wieser to stay, then walked back around and into the mill yard through the front entrance. I tried to look as if I knew my destination, walking with purpose and not wandering. I looked for some tool to break into the shack.

I found a pry bar, and had just picked it up when a sour-faced, jowly man called out, "Boy, you!" and pointed at me. I went over to him, what else could I do? He shoved a fistful of papers at me.

"Take these to that blockhead Nagmus. And tell him not to take all day sending them back to the ship after he's done with them!"

I took the papers and set off toward what I prayed was where a person might expect to find Nagmus, within the large building. This seemed to be right, because the man called after me, "And don't tell him I called him a blockhead!"

He won't hear it from me, I thought.

I set the papers under a jug of water on the first workbench I passed, and left the building by a different door, carrying my pry bar. I made my way to the backside of the shack without further trouble.

Once there, I set about pulling away the boards to make a hole large enough for the prisoners to crawl through. In only moments I saw three anxious faces peering out.

"You are the answer to all our prayers," the older lady said, weeping.

I couldn't have that. "You must be quiet, please. We are going to sneak off the property here, but then we have to walk through town to a safe place."

I saw with a sinking heart as they emerged one-by-one that they were in their nightshifts and light shawls. Perhaps they had been taken away from their beds when the soldiers came. "I have trousers for the boy," I said, handing them over. "You ladies will have to wrap yourselves in your shawls as the country women do, and tuck them round the middle. Here, rub some soil on the shifts so they look more gray than white."

They did as I bid without speaking, the boy timid but silent as his mother helped him into his breeches. If luck and the gods were on our side, we could be taken for country peasants making our way through town on some errand. The ground around the shack was hard packed, but I made sure no dog prints could be seen. It would not do to have the Keltanese seeking a dog involved in the prisoners' escape. I had seen too few large dogs about town to think Wieser and I would not risk being identified as potential culprits.

I bade them gather sticks when we passed through the brush on the slope, and carry armloads of them as we walked. The boy held his mum's hand, and carried a handful of sticks as well. I took him to be nearly three years old, and small for his age. Wieser walked beside him, touching him gently with her nose when he dawdled.

About half the way back to Guthy's the boy had enough. He began to cry, his feet hurt. He had on some sort of cloth shoes that rich townfolk must wear in bed. The ladies' version of the flimsy shoes began to fall apart, but they walked on hugging their sticks to their chests with their eyes downcast like proper country matrons. I picked up the little boy, and while I carried him, I told him my dog was named Wieser and she was taking us to a place he would like. He left off crying and just sniffed now and then, keeping an eye on Wieser over my shoulder.

We turned up on Guthy's back stoop, and I felt I could breathe again. "I did not really plan this," I began as I ushered the three past an astonished Honni. The little boy went at once to peer over the edge of the kitchen table where brown loaves were cooling. Honni managed to stammer out a call for her mistress, who came trotting in response to the urgency in the girl's voice.

As the next moments involved a lot of female gibbering and wailing, I cut a hunk of bread and slathered it with butter. This I gave to the boy, saying, "What's your name, then?"

"Toohe," he said around a mouthful. "Mummy," he pointed. "And Granna." I led him to the hearth to sit by the fire. Wieser came and sat beside him, and I heard him say to her, "I do like it here."

Guthy became a ways undone, and could not decide whether to offer wash water or food to the women. I watched her dither for a short time, then felt her indecision had continued long enough.

"We'll need clothing for them, and serviceable shoes of some sort. Maybe you can find something? Honni can give them a bit to eat, and then they can wash up," I said, since nobody seemed able to sort it out. This at least set folk in motion, Guthy bustling above stairs and Honni setting plates on the table.

"Do you know anything about where my husband is?" the boy's mum asked.

"Really, Madelon, we must thank the young man first for rescuing us. We have been in such straits, we forget our manners. I do apologize," said Granna.

"I'm afraid you're not wholly rescued yet. We must still get you away from here. I don't know about your husband, Donah. My dog tracked the boy by his scent on the trousers, and found you besides. If I can get something with your husband's scent, we can seek him next," I said.

"The soldiers would not leave him with us, they thought he could break down the door or escape some other way. They said he was too valuable a hostage to throw in the harbour, but—but—" Here she broke down in sobs. Guthy reappeared with skirts draped over her arms, shed them instantly on the end of the table and came to pat the mother on the shoulder.

"Here now! Judian will find him if anyone can," Guthy soothed her.

"See, it's Wieser who—" I started.

"How are you getting them away?" Honni wanted to know. "You c-can't think to walk them out the town gates?"

"I cannot leave without my husband!" Madelon cried.

"Now, he said he just needed some of Nevra's clothes. How did you come by Toloun's trousers?" asked the older lady.

"I thought he said his name was Toohe? Is that just a fond name?" His mum nodded to me. "Anyway, Orlo Suerat brought me the clothes."

"Nanny Suerat's boy? The one who runs errands for cook? Does he know how my husband fares?"

"Vonna, you must calm yourself, you've been so worried about all of us," said Madelon in her turn at comforting.

"Orlo says your husband is frantic about your safety, but well enough himself," I managed to put in. There came a rapid triple knock at the back door, and Honni rushed to open it. Orlo stood on the stoop, and I had the pleasure of seeing his eyes bulge at the sight of the ladies and boy.

There was a blissful moment of silence before all the women started talking at once, but this time they were buzzing at Orlo and not me. He put up his hands and tried to back away, but Honni took hold of his wrist and pulled him the rest of the way into the kitchen.

"Donah Folio, Donah Folio," Orlo said, nodding to each in turn. "Yes, I can get some of Donar Nevra's clothes for Judian. And I will ask cook to put some message in with Harbourmaster Folio's food tray that you are safe."

"Tell nanny, too." Toohe added.

"I will. She's been missing you plenty." Orlo looked at me. "Tell me later how you managed this. What are you going to do with them now?"

"Can they be smuggled out of town underground?" I asked.

"That may be possible. I could get them below tonight, and see from there," Orlo said.

"Get me the man's clothes, and I'll go out with Wieser while they clean up and rest. I'll help you get them to the tunnel after dark." I looked at all the faces staring at me as I spoke. How had I waded into this? I resolved to consider my actions more carefully, in future.

By the time Orlo returned with another bundle of clothes for Wieser to smell, the newly washed ladies had been dressed in plain dark skirts and shawls less fine than their own. Each wore simple slippers of sturdy leather, though Donah Vonna's were quite snug. I told her how to go about stretching them, but by the quizzical look she gave me, I judged such things were done for her, not by her.

Honni slipped out to her family's house for a shirt and rough weave trousers for Toohe. She said he would draw less attention barefoot, at his young age, which scandalized the ladies but suited him.

I left with Wieser as soon as I gave her the scent, since it was late afternoon already. If we had to do another rescue, time would be short to get it accomplished before we needed to escort the others to the underground. It did not take her nearly as long to find her target this time, though. She led me to the back of the warehouse where our soldiers were held. I surmised she did not take me to the front because of the Keltanese guards leaning on the doors, watching the street.

"It's no good," I told the others when I returned to Guthy's. "We plan on setting the men free from there, but I can't do it today. We need a better plan than what I came up with at the sawyer's. It's bricks and mortar, not wood, and there are guards besides. We don't even know how many are held there."

Young Donah Folio despaired the most at the news. The harbourmaster's wife now remained stoic though it was her son who was imprisoned still. Orlo said in my ear that it could be possible for the smugglers to tunnel below the warehouse and get the men out that way. He laid a finger to his lips as he moved away.

The old salts filtered in from the waterfront as the sun began to sink. They were enlivened by word of the rescue, and deferential to the harbourmaster's lady-folk. One of the sailors set about carving a wooden ship for Toohe, while the others sat with me in an upstairs room to compose a reply message. The one who had been a signal master was able to quickly render their report as short and long strokes to say: two guards each wagon.

It was not that we didn't know all the wagons we had seen so far had two guards, but that we didn't have our wagon yet to travel and ambush the wagon carrying what we wanted to steal. We did not need cargo information until later, and tonight's message was more for practice.

It took them longer to convert this missive into an innocuous letter, to be decoded at home. After much scratching at grizzled chins, a particularly toothless fellow took up his quill to write of his regard for Virda, and how he longed to see her again soon. The message was cleverly embedded within. What he intended Virda to make of the accompanying sentiment could only be guessed at, but the man's eyes twinkled.

I took the message down to Gargle, and tied it to his leg as before. Guthy and Honni had fixed the pellet to send him home, and I spoke the words carefully while old sailors, Guthy, Honni and the freed hostages all watched from the kitchen window. Gargle found this audience only his due, and strutted up and down the porch railing. "Just you fly home to Annora, now, and enough showing off," I finished, poking him in the shoulder as he passed. He gave a look at my finger and then a look in my eyes before flapping away. I would not say he appeared chastised. More like sulky, I reckoned.

We had all been fed and it was dark out under the waning moon when Orlo came to guide us below. Toohe had fallen asleep clutching his toy boat, and had to be carried by his mum. Guthy found a bit of old counterpane to wrap about him, since the sea breeze had grown chill. Vonna Folio may have been a grander lady than most, but she still clasped hands with all the old sailors and hugged Guthy, and Honni, when we left. Madolen Folio, burdened with her son, spoke warm words of thanks to each in turn.

Orlo moved with especial caution as he led us along the alleyways. Tonight no fog concealed us, and so we kept close to the walls in deeper shadows. We stopped once, breaths caught and backs pressed against the stones, while a pair of guards went stomping past. Orlo waited until their guttering, flaring lantern light faded around the corner before we traveled on.

When all were safely in the tunnel mouth, with Orlo lighting the lantern there, I took my leave. "Will you find your way in the dark?" fretted Madolen.

"I have Wieser to guide me," I said, petting the black head at my side.

"Words cannot express our gratitude, young Judian. When we are reunited with my husband, you can be sure he will reward you and yours," Donah Vonna said.

It would have been rude to say I was counting on it. So instead I said, "May you be reunited soon, gods' willing. Keep safe and I will do what I can to speed Donar Nevra on his way to you all." Orlo rolled his eyes at me, but followed that with a wink. He led them down the passageway.

Wieser and I evaded more patrols on the return journey to Guthy's, but none spotted us as we practiced fading into the darkness like wolves. Wieser no doubt better than I, being entirely black.

I found Honni angry with me again when we arrived. "You will m-make me run mad, I do swear. I've been sure you were dead half a d-dozen times already tonight." She scrubbed furiously at the kitchen table.

"I've only been gone just as long as it takes to walk there and back," I complained, and Wieser whined at my side.

"Easy for y-you to say!" she snapped, and wheeled away to go into the keeping room. Wieser and I exchanged glances, mine the more puzzled, and went up to bed.

As before, Honni's anger spent itself overnight. She fixed food for my journey home and said she was sorry I had to leave so soon. I gave up looking for sense in her, and made my farewells to Guthy and the old salts brief, so I could get on my way.

Next, we would wait until dark of the moon in hope of our wagon's delivery.

CHAPTER 31

A s fate and the gods would have it, rain fell the night our wagon was to be brought; one of those chill spring rains that seep down the neck of a tunic and soak from inside out as well as outside in. Wils and I had trudged down to the forge with Miskin and Beckta, leaving Perk, Joren and Cobbel by the fire with Gevarr and the women. I told Wieser to stay by the hearth, but brought the trio of crows along as spotters. We carried the remaining gold we owed in a leather pouch, which Wils had charge of, being bossy as Gargle at his worst.

Bar Estegg the smithy let us in to stand out of the weather. He told Wils on returning home that he saw nothing of any battles, and tonight talked further with us about his experience with the troops. He marched west with them, and then back east, and when the Keltanese proved to have beaten them to the harbour, his portion of the conscripted army had fragmented and scattered to make their way to their separate homes as best they could. He heard no news from the fort on his route, and had not been with other local men. The miller had not yet returned; Bar believed some had been taken captive, but didn't like that to get about for fear the miller's wife would hear.

Ticker wanted to come out and wait with us, but his mother said he was too young to truck with smugglers and shooed him inside. She watched through a crack in the door, and I caught a glimpse of her baby, grown fat and with more teeth than some of Virda's old salt admirers.

At nearly midnight, Gargle called and the others pecked at the window. The wagon rolled through the mud around to the back of the forge, the team's harness jingling. Bar waved the driver into the bay with his lantern, and we all stared. Even in the weak lantern light, the wagon almost glowed, a bright sky blue. Black and yellow curlicues chased and twined along the sides. It appeared to have a hut built on the back, rather than a plain bed. The sort of wagon the Travellers lived in on the road. Except those I had seen were pulled by one horse. This larger wagon was pulled by a pair of tall, heavy legged, feather-hocked golden horses, with flaxen manes and tails. Though soaked and muddy, they were clearly an especially distinctive team, and a bit too large for their harness.

Two outriders on plain bays followed the wagon in, and the driver, who proved to be Zaffis, threw off his oiled-wool cloak and jumped down into the wagon. He reappeared at the back, swinging open the small door, and swept aside a canvas covering to reveal the kegs of beans and our load of lumber.

"Where's my young bargain-striker?" he boomed. "Ah, there you be, amazed at what we've fixed for you. Which is your brother?" He rubbed his hands together and looked at us standing on the straw.

Wils found his tongue first. "Mothers of earth and water and all else that's holy. We'll certainly be noticed about the countryside in this rig!"

"Wait," I said. "It looks new and sturdy. It can be painted."

"Are we painting the team, as well?" Wils said, walking around the back to get the full view of our purchase.

"It isn't like putting in your order at the wheelwright's, see." Zaffis did not sound offended by Wils's remarks, for a wonder. He extended a three-step wooden ladder from the door, and hooked the top over the threshold. The bottom reached the straw and he stepped down to join us. "Traveller folk are not drawing much attention from the Keltanese these days, I'm told. This may serve you better than you think at first glance."

Wils looked less than convinced. "And the horses? Is no one seeking a pair this fine, gone missing?"

"Sought they may be, but no one will be seeking them *here*," said Zaffis with a wink.

"Yah, Wils," said Bar, straightening from his inspection of the horses' rumps, which bore no brands. "I have been shoeing these two for your da these five years past. So I'll say to any who might inquire."

I went round to their heads, where they both lipped my outstretched hand and flicked their ears at me. Both mares; we could have a herd if we bred them to Halvor Billen's stallion. If he still had him after the invasion came through, that is.

"Sure, Donar Estegg. I've brought them down myself to be shod," I agreed. "This is Cider, and the other is … Honey."

Zaffis stood with his arms crossed, while Wils completed his circuit of the wagon and team. He checked the lumber and kegs of beans, picked up the horses' feet, then looked in each one's mouth. "You'd better say you've been shoeing them these three years past, Bar. They're young yet." He wiped the horse slobber on his trousers, and came back to face Zaffis.

"Much finer than expected. Worth the price in these times, I reckon." Wils took the pouch of gold from his tunic and handed it to Zaffis, inclining his head to him. Zaffis hefted it judiciously, and tossed it to one of the outriders, who began to count it. He passed handfuls of counted coins to his partner, who tucked them about his saddle and stuffed some in his boots and tunic. When he drew aside his oiled cloak, I saw a small crossbow at his back and a knife strapped to his leg. He noted my glance, and gave me a wolfish grin.

When Zaffis got the sign all was in order, he extended his

hand to Wils. As they shook, he said, "Happy to do business again, my lad. We're finding our trade somewhat constricted of late as the Keltanese fools try to learn how a harbour is run. We welcome your efforts to harass them."

"Our ultimate aim is to banish them," Wils said. "We may call on you for aid in freeing our troops held on the waterfront."

"Judian already has my folk working to burrow under the warehouse," Zaffis laughed. "Orlo says he knows how to get word to you when we are ready to break through."

All eyes turned to me. Had I forgotten to mention this when telling my tale of the rescue? "It was Orlo who thought of it, tunneling under. Good news in any case," I said lamely. "Are the captive women and child well away?"

"Aye, far and away. I'll not say where, as the less you know the less you can tell, eh? I was glad you thought to bring them to me once I thought it over, a little like your brother had to think over his wagon and team, see. But you're right, it's good to be owed a favor from a man with the harbourmaster's influence. Though I wish I could see his face when he finds out smugglers, the bane of his life's work, helped his family escape trouble."

With a loud guffaw, Zaffis pulled on his cloak, mounted behind one of the riders, and raised a hand to us in parting. The two men pulled their mounts around and kicked them back out into the rainy night.

"I don't think we'll need Joren Delyth to drive this rig," I said, to head off discussion of who had set a troop rescue in motion without consultation. "May I try driving it home?"

"Joren will be driving the heavy wagon we steal. As you well know," Wils said with an air of dignified resignation. "I can see Zaffis' point about this wagon. We can hide men within as we travel. I had wondered how we could keep our numbers secret."

Miskin and Beckta, silent looming presences through the encounter, now began to laugh and congratulated me for finding Zaffis and Wils for his handling of the exchange.

230

Bar would not hear of us setting out for home yet. "Let them get some road behind them returning, in case anyone did note their coming." He brought us in beside his hearth to dry out, while he gave our new team a bit of grain and water. Gefretta and her mother Nellen told us to take our wet boots off and have a hot cider toddy. It was getting onto hard cider, but Wils did not say I shouldn't have any on account of being too young. And after all in a few months, I would be thirteen, so was nearly a man.

Gefretta studiously ignored Wils, which was only fitting with him being a married man, but I could tell by how she went about it that she wanted him to be wounded by her disregard. I don't think he noticed. Beckta and Miskin both noticed Gefretta, though, and paid her all the attention she could wish. I supposed she was pretty, in kind of a crisp, tart way. But it seemed to me she was someone who always wanted things her way and no other, and no reluctance in telling anyone if they displeased her.

Wils drove home when we left. Though the rain stopped, the track ran steep and muddy, he said, and the team might not be used to mountain roads. They drove well together, we found. Still, a relief to pull into our own yard, and unhitch our own horses. Wils put the wagon behind the barn, and I took Cider and Honey into their stalls, newly built. Dink whickered to them amiably from his loose box. Beckta and Miskin worked together to treat the wet harness, so it wasn't too long before we could find our beds. Dawn would come soon enough, and there would be more work ahead, making ready to be highwaymen.

In the morning, Gevarr had a laugh at our fancy wagon, but then, like Wils, allowed it would be good for concealing our load of armed men. Morie loved it and wanted to live in it with Murr, full of crabby remarks when I told her we had to take it to do work instead of leaving it for her playhouse. "Da would let me have the pretty wagon!" she shouted at me as I walked away. That was what came of her being everybody's pet, a girl and the youngest.

Those villagers who had put in money, as tracked by Wils and Joren, were invited to share in the beans and lumber. Wils's reputation was fixed as a fair-minded man. Folks were appreciative and he encouraged them to tell their neighbors who hadn't shared their gold. So, maybe next time we asked, the hold-outs would remember the benefit, Wils told me aside.

Wils tasked me with restocking all the caves. "Where else are we going to house the troops if we can free them?" he said. "Or had you thought of what to do with them all? We don't even have a fair idea of their number."

"I hope to hear from the apostate, or the smugglers, how many there are all told. The caves are not so large, the ones I used. But there are more, the mountain's full of them. I think they must all be connected, if we explore further." I feared he would suggest exploration for my job, too, and I wanted to go to the border fort with him, to Da. "Of course, I could do the exploring, but then I wouldn't be here to learn the animal craft from Annora …"

"I'll set Miskin, Cobbel and Beckta going deeper in, once you're sure they can find their way up and back without going astray. Pack the pickaxe and shovel on Dink with the other supplies. They'll likely have to excavate as they go."

Probably he did see through my wheedling, but if it went my way, why should I worry further? As soon as I had escorted the men enough that I was confident they could get back to the house, I pestered Annora to teach me horse-lore with Cider and Honey. I needed to make myself essential to our mission.

Annora watched me practice for hours in the pasture, calling the mares to me, sending them away, all without a word. With a mere nuance of gesture, she could send them in separate directions, at differing paces, and bid them stop and stand far across the grass. Wieser and the crows lined up by the fence to watch, and Morie and Murr came sometimes, too. Morie generously told me she liked the mares' names; I had expected her to pout since I usurped her job of naming new animals. She did see fit to contrast my horse directing efforts with Annora's, saying, "I don't think you're doing it right. They *like* going where Annora tells them."

"How do you know they like it?" I said, sweaty and harassed by flies.

"'Cause they look happy," she replied, stroking Murr.

I looked at them cropping grass, immense gleaming beasts, almost seventeen hands, the pair of them. Happy? Equable, maybe. Docile enough. How could I direct them in a way that made them happy to obey? Did Annora make them happy because of her happiness, with Wils home and productive work to do—that made sense to me. I tried to send out cheerful thoughts for my own part, with our plans for rescue and all I was learning about magic making me useful. I took a deep breath, and gestured Cider to come to me.

She lifted her head from grazing, ambled over to me and pushed her forehead into my chest. I scratched her forelock and she heaved a great sigh.

"See, like that," Morie said, satisfied.

"Indeed. I see," I said with a smile.

I tried to explain my revelation to Gevarr as we worked on griming the wagon to make it less flashy. Annora had suggested we rub it with rags dipped in ashes, and Gevarr's hands worked well enough for that. He could not grip a weapon yet; maybe never would again, according to Wils. Gevarr listened to my tale of better communication with Cider if I set positive intention, and paused in his rubbing.

"If you become as skilled as Annora, will your brother take you along? And give over his foolishness about taking her with him?"

"It's she who wants to go, he doesn't want to take her. That's why I'm to learn animal lore."

He grunted and resumed with his rag. "I had a war horse, laid his ears back to everybody. I called him Snake, because that's how he would lash out and bite anyone in reach. I wonder if you or

233

Annora could have made him happy to do your bidding." He laughed without humor. "I have to think not, and he wouldn't have been much good in battle if made tame, anyway."

"What happened to him?"

"Don't know. I lost him when I lost my rank. He's someone else's problem now. Or fed to the dogs."

Afternoon lengthened into evening. Gevarr and I turned to loading the wagon with sacks of grain for the team. His strength was coming back, if not his grip, and I passed him the burlap bags as he stood behind the wagon's seat. He stowed them below the bench. I had just handed up the last one when we heard a sudden cry from the east field. Wieser didn't look up, but Gevarr and I froze. It came again, Annora's voice, but crying out in laughter, not fear. She appeared on the path to the back gate, skirts pulled up in her fists, running fast. Wils came pelting after, and caught her up at the gate, with an arm slung around her waist. She gave a little shriek, but turned in his arms to twine her own arms about his neck and kiss him. He swept her up after a moment, pushed through the gate and carried her up the stairs into the house, still kissing her.

Gevarr stood stock-still, watching. Muscles bunched in his jaw, but he did not look away or put down his burden. I did not like to guess what he was thinking.

"He's her husband," I said at last.

"I'm clear who he is." He turned his back to me to shove the sack under the seat. It is a wonder the bag didn't burst.

I called Wieser and walked to the garden, trying to sort out whether I should get skilled enough to leave Annora home. It could be better for her to come with Wils, than stay home with Gevarr. Or, maybe I would suggest to Wils that Gevarr be shifted to the caves to live with whichever of the men stayed up there while we were gone.

I told Wieser, "It's wearing on me to be in charge of everybody. Da coming home can't happen too soon for me!" She

234

licked her muzzle and wagged her tail.

###

Next morning, I walked into the barn to find Wils and Gevarr having a blazing row in Honey's stall. Both had their fists balled up at their sides, but with several feet still between them, I did not think they had come to blows. Yet. That looked to be coming next.

"If she was my wife—" Gevarr ground out, voice getting louder word by word.

"As she's *my* wife, I'll be the one to say where she goes," Wils growled, feral and fierce.

"What do you know about war!" Gevarr shouted. "You have no idea what you'd be carrying her into. Have you ever seen a woman used by troops in blood-lust? Used to the death? I have." Here he flung out a hand toward me. "Even your boy brother had sense enough to keep her as far away from soldiers as he could!"

"Leave me out of it," I said.

"Sure, he kept her away from soldiers until he took one into our house. I'm still trying to figure why!" Wils glared in my direction, but kept facing Gevarr, every muscle taut.

"I'm a trained warrior and you are not. You cannot think to keep her safe. Have sense," Gevarr growled in his turn. Abruptly he ran a hand through his hair, and shook out his arms. "Just let me keep her here with Morie and Virda. Leave me one man, and I guarantee I—we will keep all harm from them until you return. We'll even go up to the caves now to make sure. Be a man. Don't put her at this kind of risk because you're afraid you can't keep her heart."

Gevarr would likely have been successful but for his last remark. Wils had begun to listen up until then, I could see. As soon as Gevarr suggested Wils could lose Annora, Wils's face shut like an iron gate.

"You'll hear my final decision when I am ready. And live with it," Wils said, and strode out.

"Stripling fool," Gevarr muttered to his departing back. "Can't

235

you make him see reason?" he said, swinging around toward me.

"I said, leave me out of it. You know he can see how you feel about her, why would he want to leave her in your care?"

"Because I can take care of her, and he can't. I would not … trespass, even if the lady would allow." He gazed off toward the house.

"Maybe you'd better tell him that, then. Your tongue does not serve you overwell."

"I'm a soldier, not a noble," he grumbled.

"If a noble is someone who can keep their feet out of their mouth, then you're right. That's not you." I stomped off to get Dink ready for a trip to the cave, which is what I'd been going to do before I got involved in their own private war.

I did not need any uncanny sight to see Wils agonizing over whether to bring Annora or no. Growing more desperate to show proficient in the animal lore, I went to the village to try my horse skills with the smithy's cob, and any other horses there getting shod. I saw no point denying, Annora had the greater skill with horses unknown to her. I did well enough with those familiar ones at home which knew me. I was not so reliable with any others.

Annora helped her cause by not pleading, pouting or crying. She only said she would not want to be parted from Wils again, having endured it once. Then she held her head high and went pleasantly about her work.

While I stretched the too-snug harness and added extra leather, I overheard Wils tell Perk, "It would be easy to bid her to stay if she carried on about going. She acts a better soldier here at home than many we passed on the road. Merchants and farmers whining about sore feet and empty bellies."

Perk agreed with him, but added, "She hardly looks a Traveller, though, with all that fair hair. You and I and Judian can pass, but not her."

"A woman's hair can be hidden, under cloak or shawl. That's

not what worries me ..." and they walked off together, still murmuring.

Virda heard them talking, too, and looked over at me as I watched them pace away. "Don't take it so, Judian. Wils will make a wise choice. Your gift with magic and animals he may not have, but he has a gift of his own. He's like your da. People come to him, and follow him, look to him for what to do. Why do you think these men came from the fort with Wils, when they had only known him a short time, and knew nothing of where he was from?"

"Because he asked them to be couriers," I said, but I hadn't really thought about it before. They were just Wils's men.

"Because of his way with people. Your da has it, too."

I thought about it for a bit, then said, "He doesn't seem to have much of a way with Gevarr."

"He keeps Gevarr subdued enough, considering how taken the man is with Annora. Did you think I was too old to notice?" she teased, when I feigned shock at her remark.

"Never," I said, though Morie once wondered aloud why Da and Virda did not marry, since they were both old. "Because Virda has sons as old as Da," I had told Morie, who was puzzled why that was a hindrance.

As soon as we received word from our watchers in Bale Harbour, describing the off-load of a heavy cargo of oats destined for Keltane, Wils declared his roster. Virda would take over the messenger birds, flying between the farm and the harbour and us on the road. Morie of course would stay with her. Cobbel and Gevarr would remain and do the farm work, and take everyone to the stocked caves if danger threatened.

Annora and I would drive the wagon, with Wils, Perk, Miskin, Beckta and Joren Delyth within, armed with the weapons from the cache Gevarr had shown Wils in the winter. Wieser and my crows would accompany us as sentries, and to fly to and fro with messages as we ran ahead of the oat wagon to stage our ambush.

Wils's look as he laid it out dared Gevarr to comment, but the man kept silent, if pointedly so.

We carried out final preparations for early morning departure.

CHAPTER 32

hy oats?" Joren Delyth asked me as we loaded our remaining gear, plus all the arrows from the arms cache.

"Because oats can be cooked with just water, which they have aplenty in the underground cisterns, or ground into flour and baked. And also fed to horses. Unless they've eaten all their horses and are living on rats by now." I could not claim to be at my most polite early mornings, and never as polite as Joren.

"And are we sure the Keltanese soldier,"—for he never called him by name—"taught us the proper words to use, and not nonsense that will betray us at once?"

"Both Wils and I know enough Keltanese to be certain of that," I said.

He still seemed wary, and I prayed he would keep silent and out of the way until we stole the cargo wagon for him to drive.

Wils took charge of the maps, and had relieved me of Da's sword. I still had my knife, and I saw Annora still had Gevarr's knife at her waist. She wore a skirt, but had shown me a pair of Wils's trousers she packed in the event she needed to conceal her gender. She confided that Gevarr had shown her some tricks of hand-to-hand combat, going for the eyes or windpipe, using an attacker's motion and weight against him.

"Do you mean he put his hands on you?" I paused, holding a frying pan as I looked for space in the cook box.

"How else would he show me what to do?" She creased her brows at me.

"I wouldn't mention it to Wils. Gevarr's opinion about you coming along is a sore place between them." I jammed the pan in the box sideways, and decided to say no more.

Tock took wing to Guthy's to carry a message that we were setting out. Gargle and Clock took it in turns to ride on the peak of our wagon hut or circle above, scouting the road.

We made good time through the village, waving to Bar and Nellen Estegg as we passed. Gefretta ran alongside to hand up a loaf, "for Beckta and Miskin" she panted, then stood in the road waving. I handed her loaf into the back, warning, "Don't let it drop on your foot," as it was a brick. If she thought to impress the men with her baking skill, she would have to try again.

I had been wondering if we would be able to spot the battlefield where our troops fought the invaders near the village. We found it not far west along the road. Though our fallen had been buried long since, the expanse of grass was marked with rock cairns, perhaps a hundred of them, one cairn standing over each grave. At the far end of the field, a bonfire had been made of other bodies, those of the enemy, I guessed. Flame-blackened bones stuck out of the ash. I felt a moment's gladness that Gevarr's were not among the bones there.

I spoke to the others in back. I knew they would want to see. Everyone looked out, and we passed by in silence. Just at the edge, Annora called out, "Wait!" and hopped off to stand in the grass. She raised a packet from her herb bag, and let the golden contents drift away in the breeze, carried over the cairns. "For their peace," she said when she grasped my hand to climb back into the wagon. I clucked to the team and we rolled on.

From time to time, Wils stuck his head out to survey the road ahead. "This will be a bit too much like our trip home, I think, though I must say I prefer riding to walking. We will have to camp off the main road, since we can't all sleep in the back." Indeed, the interior was stuffed as tight as an egg in its shell. "I have some places in mind."

"Will we stay in any of the inns?" I asked.

"No, that's where the drivers and guards will be staying. Or, in stretches without inns, they camp in groups. We saw some of them when we made our way back home. We will need to make ourselves scarce until we come to the right place to strike."

We swayed and bumped our way along all the day, passing some wagons and being overtaken by others, meeting a goodly number headed east as well. We didn't see any other Traveller rigs. We ate Gefretta's bread while we rolled, and only Annora and Joren did not complain it was tough.

Wils peered ahead, shading his eyes from the lowering sun, until he consulted his map a last time and said we would turn off the main way and continue a couple of miles south to camp by the Cisca River. All the country to the west we had covered was new to me, though it didn't look too different from home yet. Annora also said she had not been this far west before, and Wils allowed he didn't think the countryside had much to recommend it. He was still wondering if he had made the right choice in bringing her, I reckoned.

Wieser had lain in the back with the men when she wasn't sitting between Annora and me. She looked to be as glad as any of us to climb down and walk out the cramps in her legs. She and I took charge of the horses' feed and water, and I groomed them while they tugged at haynets. Wils rigged a line between two trees to tie them for the night.

We made what Perk said was a fine form of a Traveller encampment, since he had seen some in his journeys. Annora cooked over the fire. Supper was settling fine when Wieser barked gruffly once, and then walked stiff-legged down the track we had followed. I could just hear wagon wheels rumbling and hoof beats.

Next a faint chingle of harness drifted on the breeze.

"Company," I said. Annora covered her hair, Wils gestured to her to step up into the wagon with the other men, and I sat by the fire. He joined me there, saying, "I thought we were far enough off the main way to be alone."

"Maybe just a farmer on his way home from market," I said. I prayed so.

A laden hay wagon with lanterns hung on either side trundled into view, the horse plodding with fatigue. A lone man drove, face obscured by shadow under a broad-brimmed hat. He raised a hand to us and reined his horse to a stop.

"Hallo," he called. "Are you bound for Everton Lake? There's work to be had in the fields there. So few of our men folk have come home from the war as yet."

"Our way lies farther west, but we'll tell others we meet," Wils said. "I thank you for the news."

"Don't know what we'll eat this winter if we can't get crops in," grumbled the driver. "The Keltanese have turned our lives arse uppermost."

That made me laugh, and Wils poked me in the ribs to shush me. "Yah," he agreed. "They have done well at that, it's true."

"Send any and all our way!" the man said, and clucked to his horse. It shook its ears and strained against the collar to get the wagon rolling again, and they creaked on into the night, trailing the sweet smell of hay. When we could no longer make out the swinging lanterns, Wils let the others come down by the fire.

"Is it the same story through the whole of Merced, do you think?" Perk asked Wils. "Taking the harbour may have been their first goal, but if they've dissolved the government and council, that means the enemy is far and away south in the capital, too. There must still be an entire army occupying not just our province, but all others, as well."

"It will be years before we know the sum of what has taken place, I fear." Wils rubbed a hand over his eyes. "I aspire no higher

242

than getting my da safely home, then routing the Keltanes from our home province. I'm not ready to take on clearing the whole country of them. Perk, you have first watch. I hope I haven't picked us a spot at an all-night crossroads." He looked at Wieser, then up at the crows perched above the wagon's door, but they gave no warning of further passersby.

Wieser and I took our bedroll to a flat spot under the wagon, and it wasn't long before she fell to snoring. I followed her into dreams soon after.

###

We built a rhythm of daily travel and camping, keeping ahead of the cargo wagon we planned to waylay. Wils told us to expect to travel for three weeks to come to the valley below the fort. He had marked a desolate, hilly stretch of road as the best place to hijack the wagon. We could then drive it into the valley where the tunnel entrance led into the fort high above the valley floor.

"We better unload and then send the wagon on beyond the entrance," I said one day as we drove. Wils sat beside me, maps on his knees. "Otherwise we'll have led any pursuers to our way in."

"You're not wrong there," he admitted. "I thought to get the sacks into the tunnel as quick as we can, then run the wagon on down here, see?" He pointed to a river that wound across the map of the valley. "We can make it appear we have sent the goods downriver by raft, if they track it there."

"We'll have six horses and two wagons at that juncture. Our team and the heavy wagon's team, plus the two guards' mounts. If Joren takes the cargo wagon to the river, and we hide ours nearer the fort, how will we get back together?"

"While you've been back and forth to Bale Harbour, I've been working all this through. My thought is to send you with Joren—"

"Think again! I'm going in to Da with you!"

"I have to stay with Annora outside, I can't bring her into the fort or leave her unprotected in the valley. The others will go in and carry the goods up. If Da won't come out with the men, I'll go

243

in to see him and find out what he wants to do next. My suspicion is he'll want to find a way to close the pass—loose the rocks. He was preparing to see to it when the siege began."

"Why didn't he have you do that when you left?" I wondered.

"It's not like tripping the string on a deadfall trap. There are boulders along both sides of the pass held back by giant timbers and networks of iron chain. You need a crew of a dozen men on each side to let it loose." He sighed. "It has to be done, for it will take them many months to clear, and require a great many men. Plus, all their trade would have to go miles and miles out of the way to the southern trade routes."

"They won't be able to use the northwest pass by us for any of it?"

"Not for wagons, only pack trains. Just a trickle compared to what's going through this pass ahead of us." He nodded toward the western horizon.

Annora put her head out of the back, and handed us each sacks of dried fruit and nutmeats, then a jug of mead. Wils leaned round and brought her hand to his lips as he took the jug, and she smiled up at him.

"Maybe you could act that sappy when I don't have to watch," I suggested, but I smiled, too. Wils gave me a poke in the ankle with the toe of his boot, though I saw he was grinning when he turned to face front again.

In due time, and after a bout of sloppy weather that seemed endless but was actually three days all told, we came to the stretch of road where Wils planned to lay our trap. The way had started to narrow and climb, so drivers had to be attentive to what lay over the next rise or curve, being unable to see far ahead. There was room for two wagons to pass side-by-side, but only just. Drivers could only go ahead, not turn around anywhere.

We arrived a day ahead of our quarry, according to our messenger crows. Wils scouted a high place for Annora and me to be situated so we could see the approach of a dark red wagon drawn by a gray and a sorrel. Wils planned to hide our wagon off the road where the valley opened out farther ahead, and walk back with all our men to wait hidden in the trees and brush on the slope below the roadside. Gargle was to fly above and squawk when Annora and I saw the target come into view. She and I would then work our magic to stop the team and the guards' horses, and our men would attack. Once the wagon was commandeered, and the soldiers' uniforms taken, Joren would drive the team on, while Beckta and Miskin donned the stolen uniforms and rode alongside like guards. On past the ambush, Wils showed us where the wagon was to turn off and make for the tunnel entrance in the valley. Annora and I were to climb down and drive our wagon to the tunnel entrance following the stolen wagon. If we were lucky, we could get all accomplished before another wagon came upon our skirmish; if we were unlucky, we would have even more men, and horses, to contend with. I prayed to all the five gods, Earth, Fire, Water, Air and Ether, for good fortune in our plan and its execution. *Smile on us this day.*

Wils armed me with a crossbow, and asked me to be careful not to shoot anyone on our side. I said, "Mayhap I could chalk a big "X" on your rump, so as to remind me." He was past joking, though.

"Are you killing the driver and guards?" Annora wanted to know.

"If I have to. If I can get them away and trussed up so they'll raise no alarm for a while, that is another possibility." He frowned as she turned to rummage in the cookware box. She took from it a long length of braided cord and held it out to him.

"This is strong, and enspelled to knot tightly and resist fraying or cutting. If you use this to secure them, they will be kept out of the action for some hours. Maybe even a full day."

Wils played it out between his hands. "Enough for how many men?"

"Six at least. Judian will have to lend you his knife to cut it, though."

Both of them turned to me. I reached into my boot and grudgingly withdrew my knife in its sheath. "You'd better return it as you found it."

Annora shook her head. "No, you have to give it willingly, Judian, or trouble will follow. You can let another wield it if you lend it with the proper intention, but the kavsprit magic can come back on those who are greedy or act with malice."

"It's not malice to attack men and steal a wagon?"

"It's not malice to tie men up instead of kill them," she said.

I held out my knife to Wils. "I loan you this gladly so it keeps you from being haunted the rest of your days by doing murder."

"I accept it and will remember who I borrowed it from," he said with equal solemnity. "But you understand," he said to Annora, "I'll do what I have to do."

She handed him cloth for gags from her cook-box. "I know."

All of us were wound up too tight to sleep that night. I lay awake and reviewed horse-lore in my mind for hours. *We're coming to help you, Da* I thought over and over. I was still awake at dawn when Wils came to get me.

Annora dressed in the trousers she had packed, with a hooded cloak to cover her hair, since a shawl and trousers didn't do together. She handed me a skin of water, and more of the nuts and fruit to carry up with us to our perch. Beckta, Perk and Miskin shouldered quivers and swords, while Joren and Wils checked knives and crossbows were ready to hand. I set Wieser to guard our wagon and hobbled team, and signaled Gargle to come with me. Clock hopped up and down on the wagon roof. "You wait," I told him. "We'll have a message for you to carry back later, if all goes as planned."

Annora and I clambered up the rocks to overlook the road. The sun grew warm before long, and black flies began to plague us without mercy.

"Eat a few of these, can't you?" I said to Gargle, as I waved them away from my head. He watched them buzz for a bit. "Wieser would try, if I asked her."

He looked at the flies, considering, then shrugged his wings and hunkered on the rock. As if to say, "All right for some, not worth *my* time." Too much trouble to catch, perhaps, for a lazy bird.

Six wagons we didn't want rumbled through by midafternoon. Then Annora pointed—it was the red wagon mounting the rise. I dispatched Gargle, who flew down into the hollow where Wils and the others waited, cawing as loud as I'd ever heard him.

Annora and I had agreed she would stop the guards' horses, while I concentrated on the team. That way, mine were harnessed together so if I got one to stop, the other would stop perforce. I licked dry lips and tried to bring my mind to bear.

The guards' horses took several increasingly stiff-legged strides before halting altogether. Their riders sawed at the reins and cursed. When struck on their hindquarters with quirts, the two mounts laid back their ears and twitched tails in fury, but did not pick up their hooves.

My team slowed as if distracted by deep thought, and did not quicken to the driver's clucking and waving the whip above their heads. But they did not stop. I cursed under my breath and redoubled my effort. If I could not halt my pair, the wagon would be too far away for Wils and the men to attack the driver and both guards all at once. I could not be the cause of failure, of failing Da … and as my doubt in myself grew, the team below stepped livelier again.

Blast all! I covered my eyes, and drained my mind of any vision except the sorrel and gray standing as if carved of stone. I called on all the gods to make my mind's eye true on the road beneath us. With a deep breath, I drew my hands away from my face, and dared to look. The pair stood still, gazing placidly around while mouthing their bits. The driver rose and cracked his whip, but they ignored him utterly.

Wils and the others burst from cover. First they dragged the two soldiers from their mounts, before either could draw a weapon. Perk hauled the driver down by the belt while Joren climbed the other side of the wagon and swung into the seat. When he took up the reins, I released the team, which startled and drew the wagon forward as if they woke from a daydream, with much head shaking. Annora kept the outriders' mounts standing still while their struggling riders were carried into the bushes. Some minutes of muffled shouting ensued, before Beckta and Miskin emerged dressed in the Keltanese tunics. I saw they had appropriated their boots as well. The gods were smiling on us so far, as everything seemed to fit well enough. Both men mounted the standing horses, Miskin smoothing his rumpled sleeves, and Annora released the two to follow after the wagon.

It wasn't until our crew paced well up out of the hollow that another wagon crested the rise.

We had done it!

Annora and I clasped hands wordlessly, and she gave no sign of awareness that I had struggled so hard to do my task. I decided not to say how near a thing it had been, and we began our climb down the rocks. Gargle appeared in front of me, and received a congratulatory hunk of cheese from my pocket. Much tastier than flies, it appeared from his eager pounce.

Wils and Perk had the three men trussed with the enspelled cord and gagged. They lay in the shade under the brush, well down the hill from the road. The soldiers glared, but the driver looked resigned to his fate. I saw Wils and Perk had kerchiefs tied over their faces to disguise their features, and thought belatedly that Annora and I should have done the same. Of course, it had just now occurred to me that I should have practiced stopping horses *while* someone else was trying to get them to go; it was indeed the gods' pleasure that everything had gone as well as it had. A near thing, truly.

After they dragged the soldiers farther down the slope, and separated them by greater distance, Annora and I pulled the driver to a spot by a seep so he could wet his gag and not go entirely thirsty. He blinked and nodded thanks, as I took it.

We gathered the weapons, and Beckta's and Miskin's clothes and boots, and set out for our wagon and team. Not until we were some distance from the scene of our triumph did Wils clap Perk on the back and vent a quiet "well done!" my way. He kissed Annora on the cheek, and whistled tunelessly as we walked on. And that was Wils when something suited him, well and good.

Wieser greeted us with extravagant wagging, and we soon had the team harnessed and set off to follow the hijacked wagon to the tunnel mouth. Annora sent Clock with a message for Virda about life on the road, with subtext of our success.

Dusk was falling when we arrived at the valley floor. Wils made quick work of steering us to the far side, where we found Joren, Beckta and Miskin busily shifting the sacks of oats into the tunnel. We fell in with them at once, Wils organizing a line of us to pass the bags along all the faster. As soon as the wagon was emptied, Joren rolled up and tied the canvas cargo cover, mounted the seat with a lantern, and made for the river midvalley.

Wils and Annora wanted to take our wagon to hide it where the trees were thickest, as the slope rose to the pass. First, we had to unload the arrows we had brought from the Keltanese stockpile by home. As we shuttled these into the tunnel, I began in earnest to chew on Wils's ear about being allowed to go up to the fort with Miskin, Perk and Beckta.

"I can find out what Da wants to do. I can be more use carrying some of the oats up and seeing what's going on within than I would be out here with you. I'll come and report to you—"

"Enough and more! I should have sent you to help Joren make it look like the cargo was sent downriver. Still, you *are* underfoot here, I imagine," Wils continued, with a sidelong look at Annora.

She looked to me to be on my side, when she said, "Wils, he

249

hasn't seen his da for so long …"

"See you do not annoy everyone into distraction, eh?"

"You mean I can go? I'll never forget this." I felt my smile stretch wide.

"I'll wager none of us will. Try not to set the place on fire, or topple the ancient stones on all the fort's men. Be a credit to Da," Wils admonished. I was scarcely listening by then.

I shouldered my as-yet-unused crossbow, and called Wieser from lookout to join me. "Shall Gargle wait with you, to be dispatched to bring Joren and the wagon back?" I said, and saw Wils stood holding my sheathed obsidian knife out to me. That made me think of the spirits, and I added, "Have you left any offering for the kavsprit in this cave? I can give them some oats. Give me some of the nuts, as well."

Annora quickly put nutmeats in my hand, while Wils secured the other two horses' reins to the back of our Traveller wagon. Beckta handed me the lantern, and allowed as how he could carry more if I held it instead of him. We ducked inside before lighting it, and I waved farewell in the last of the evening light to Wils and Annora boarding the wagon. Miskin grunted as he hoisted two bags of grain, one on each shoulder, while Beckta gathered armfuls of arrows with Perk. I managed one bag with the lantern, and we set off deeper into the tunnel. Wieser sniffed the air warily, and walked beside me.

I found a place by a seep for the kavsprit offering, and as I knelt to make the sign, could swear I felt my knife almost thrumming, restored to its spot in my boot. It vibrated like a plucked string. Perhaps it greeted the folk below the earth who treasured it before gifting it to me. I still had so much to learn about magic ways.

The passage was as Wils had described, natural in some places and bearing pick-marks and strewn rubble in others where men had enlarged the way. Miskin had to put down his sacks and drag them through after him at the snuggest areas. We would have to make many trips to shift the whole load to the fort. I should have brought along more lantern oil.

The lantern light picked out flashes of pyrite, quartz and mica, and a time or two I thought I saw reflected eyes in the darkness, small and green.

The air grew chill the deeper we walked into the mountain, and at times we had to clamber over water-slicked rock to gain the way higher. The fort sat overlooking the road through the pass, so we had to climb without pause the last half of our journey. All of us were winded when we reached the great cisterns in the cavern beneath the fort.

We surprised two guards on the far side of the cisterns, drowsing at their post, lulled by the sound of streaming water. They sprang to their feet as Miskin, Beckta and Perk laughed.

"You'd be sunk if we were enemy soldiers come calling," Beckta snorted. That's why, I realized, they had taken time to change back into their own clothes, and left the outrider guards' tunics at the entrance. He freed a hand to grip the arm of the shorter of the two men, and nodded to the other.

"By the gods, it's good to see you," said the short, bandy-legged man. "Have you brought Wils and an army with you?"

Miskin put down his sacks. "No army yet, we're working on that. We have brought you food and arrows, though."

"Keltanese arrows, by the markings," said the other man, bending to take a closer look at Beckta's burden. "Wonder what they'll think when we fire these at them?"

"My brother thought you might be running low, since once you shoot them, they're gone for good." I stepped up to set my bag with Miskin's, and Wieser sat at my side. "There's more oats and arrows at the mouth of the tunnel. I'm Judian Lebannen. Where's my da?"

"Ahh, young Judian. Charged with the safety of the new bride and the little sister. Did you all fare well?"

"Well enough, but I need to find out what Da wants us to do

251

now. Wils is waiting outside."

"I'm Rews. Come on with me, we'll find your da and get some men to carry up the rest of this welcome load," said the short guard, taking up a tallow candle. They had been making do with only candles for light in the vast dark of the cavern, I saw, not lanterns.

He led me to the steps, and we left Perk, Beckta and Miskin with the other man, beginning their story of what had befallen them since they left the fort months ago.

I understood what Wils meant about the fort being built on the bedrock—we went up twisting stairs carved out of the walls. We climbed a long ways before the bare rock gave way to dressed stone blocks, and the stairs stretched further still.

"Who made this place?" I asked Rews.

He glanced back at me. "It was so long ago, who knows? The ancients built it, long before there was Merced or Keltane thought of. Stone meets stone, enduring on." He laid a hand on one of the immense rough-hewn rocks as he passed. "We've all been grateful for the old ones' craftsmanship, keeping us safe from the enemy."

"Has there been any damage from the siege?"

"They have flung the biggest rocks they could load and it has not shifted a single stone. They keep us penned within but have left off trying to come in after us!" He sounded as cheerful as a farmer describing a soft soaking rain on newly planted fields.

When we emerged at length into a sunken kitchen, I was amazed to hear the sound of a feddle and flute coming from the courtyard a few steps above. A hearty male voice joined in, and the music swelled and ebbed. I had been expecting all to be in despair from their long isolation.

"Where's the paladin to be found?" Rews called to the merrymakers.

"Out watching the night take shape," answered a soldier with a bristly red beard. "Find him above the main gates. Who've you got there?"

I reckoned a new face would stand out, since they had all been cooped here for months despite the apparent size of the place. "I'm Judian, his younger son."

"In truth? I look forward to hearing how you've come to join us. We'll see to it your bow gets some use!" For I carried it still. Others waved from across the yard, and called out greetings. No one seemed grim.

"Can your dog climb a ladder?" asked Rews, steering me to the north wall.

"I expect so, though I can't say as I've ever seen her try. She's not likely to want to wait below unless I bid her to."

"She is … unusual to look at," he said.

"In more ways than looks, she's something unusual."

We wound our way up enclosed stone steps until we came to the ladders that led to the top of the crenellated wall. Wieser thoughtfully watched Rews climb, then mounted the rungs when I told her to follow. It did not look easy for her, but she met me at the top with her tongue lolling when I came up behind.

Dozens of men lined the battlements, illuminated by only a few torches placed low. I picked out Da readily as the tallest among them, and was off to his side as fast as I could push through the others.

"It's Judian!" he cried when he saw me, and lifted me up to squeeze the breath out of me. A dog less aware than Wieser might have thought this a bad thing, but she seemed to know it was what I had been wanting for months. He wore a full beard, and smelled of wood smoke and sweat, but all seemed right with his strong arms about me. Still, I could not act the child in front of his soldiers. I hugged him back but then straightened my arms, and he set me on my feet.

"How have you come? Where's Wils?"

I told him all in a rush and tumble. Wieser came and nosed at his hand as I spoke, and he petted her absently. I heard Rews take his leave from another man who bid him go organize men to carry up our delivery. Da nodded, much pleased to hear what we had brought.

When my tale ran down, Da drew me to look over the wall at the field below. Campfires dotted the grass in the distance, surrounded by the humped shapes of tents. Men gathered on the flat ground immediately outside the fort's gates where the road cut through. All were grouped around an open area where two robed men carrying long sticks paced to and fro, accompanied by two other men who held lanterns aloft to light the way. When the lantern-bearers passed close to the encircling men, I could see that the group bore weapons aimed our way.

"What do you make of that?" mused a deep voice beside us.

"Mages," I said, my voice sounding hollow. "Plotting the ley lines in the earth."

CHAPTER 33

D a and the other man both stared at me.

"What do you know about mages?" the deep-voiced man asked.

"I know the Scytheran mages came to our province to hold back the winter so Keltane could invade us through the northwest pass," I said, meeting Da's steady gaze.

Da turned to lay a hand on the shoulder of an officer behind him. "Watch closely. Send for me at once if they begin to do anything different from what they're about now. We'll be in the fortmaster's study."

He waved a hand at me and the other man I had answered, so we fell in behind him, with Wieser behind me. There ensued a bit of dither at the ladder, for Wieser could not make out how to climb down it. I was trying to coax her to start backwards, when a pair of strong fellows collared by Da lifted her into a giant bucket and lowered her with rope and pulley. I clambered down the ladder beside her. She licked her nose often as she descended, but sat still and did not tip the bucket at all. She wasted no time hopping out by the stairs, while I thanked the men. They chuckled and waved at me from the height.

Da led us deep within the fortress walls, where corridors intersected and arched doorways led to a plethora of passages. It would take long and long to explore this place. Da spoke to many men as he passed, but the other man walked silently, head down. Both Wieser and I had to trot to keep up.

At last, we went through a thick door of peeled logs, into a rounded room with a banked fire. A broad slab table stood by the hearth, with a trio of chairs pulled up to its map-strewn surface. Da used the tallow candle he carried to light the candles on the table, while the other man shut the door.

"Sit here, Judian, and tell us about the mages. This is Fortmaster Cochren Luppes." Da pulled out a chair for me, then he and the fortmaster sat in the others. Wieser crawled under the table to lie at my feet.

I cleared my throat, and told what I knew of weather-workers from Virda, and how I had seen them marking out the lines of power when we were hiding in the mountain caves. "Have you never seen them at this pass before?" I asked Da.

"No, only Keltanese troops. Though during the build up to the invasion, some heard rumors the mages were responsible for the illusion of enemy forces beyond their true number."

"I have always seen two mages at a time. Well, both at home and tonight. Whether they work in pairs and there are many of them, or just two traveling the country, who can say?"

"I have not heard of or seen any uncanny weather or unseasonable occurrences such as you describe," said Cochren Luppes, his bass voice rumbling. "Are you sure the snows did not come late naturally?"

I had no patience left for being thought only a boy who knew nothing. "The enemy soldier I captured admitted as much," I said, which changed his doubtful expression to one of shock, "but I have not had chance to get a confession from a mage, no."

Da was biting his tongue inside his cheek, by the way it looked. "Can you speculate what they might have come here to do?"

"Eliminate your threat to the pass. Take the fort. Through some form of magical attack, is my wager. You need a plan to loose the rockslides before the sorcerers make it impossible, somehow." I felt more certain as I said it.

"This isn't even your grown son," protested Fortmaster Luppes.

"He knows more from traversing the countryside than we know from months behind these walls. I can think of a plan, using your stolen cargo wagon and uniforms to get a team of men to the other wall of the pass."

"We sent the wagon to the river, as I said." I went on, ignoring Luppes's scowl, "I can go back outside to summon it and bring Wils and Annora within. How soon can you act?"

"Two teams of men are already chosen and trained, but we must have light of day for the climbing on both sides of the pass. Will the wagon hold a dozen men under the cargo tarp?"

I nodded. "Yah, it's one of the big rigs meant for hauling across the mountains."

"We'll load the team at the tunnel mouth, then send the wagon across the valley to join the roadway headed west. I'll school your driver where to leave the road to let the men off to begin their ascent. We'll need to time carefully, Cochren," Da said, including the fortmaster at last.

"What about the team for this south side of the mountain?" I asked.

"They will have to leave by the tunnel and climb up behind the fort, which will take longer." Da pulled a map toward him, and pointed to the pass.

"We haven't been able to get men to the north side, y'see," Cochren Luppes said, an edge of defensiveness to his low voice. I recalled Wils had not held a high opinion of him, for wanting Da to stay and do the job of closing the pass. "Now we can move at last, if all comes together."

"We'll make it come together," Da said, and pushed the map under Cochren's gaze.

A quick rap at the door, and a breathless soldier entered when

Da said, "Come."

"They're doing something queer, sir, the mages." He paused for a gulp of air. "Chanting, and the wind is rising fast. You'd best come …"

We all rose at once, and went as quick as we could to the top of the wall. This time I bade Wieser wait at the bottom of the ladder, and climbed up with my crossbow slung behind me. The air had grown cold and black clouds billowed above, driven by a fierce wind. The mages moved farther from the gates, and stood some distance away, still surrounded by the cadre of Keltanese soldiers. A bonfire burned in the field beside them. By its light, I could make out a pale flapping shape spread out on the grass that looked like a ship's sail, and was of similar size to the sails I had seen at Bale Harbour. Men worked beneath it, slinging ropes and tying a dark shape about as big as a pig to the underside.

The ropes led to a giant wooden wheel, like a thread spool. Half a dozen men stood beside the wheel, holding the ropes. I pointed to them, and said, "Can you see, the wheel—there's rope wound all around the middle!" I had to shout over the keening wind.

"This is not what I expected for an attack by magic," Luppes called in Da's ear.

"No, it's the wind, that's the magic," I answered, but felt the whip of the air carry my voice away into the night sky.

Da reached out and caught a soldier by the arm, and pulled him near so he could cup hands to his ear to shout over the wind, "Get down to the cisterns and send Beckta and Miskin out the tunnel to get Wils, and tell them to call the wagon back. Go now!"

The man sprinted over the stones and down the ladder at once.

Next Da pointed at me and then the ladder. I shook my head. I knew he wanted me to get below for my own safety, but I could not leave him. I could not make my feet move.

"I can do magic!" I called out in desperation. "Let me stay! See if I can help!"

Da was lifting his hand to point at the ladder again, when the officers began to shout, "It's flying! It's in the air!" waving their arms frantically at the field to the north. I rushed to the wall with Da, and saw the snapping, jerking sail rise into the howling wind.

The mages strode out to stand beneath the sail as the men by the wheel strained to hold it in place in the air, hauling on the ropes. They looked to be shouting to one another, the sound drowned by the gusts.

I could only just see the mages in the firelight, raising their arms; each held a long staff in his right hand. Wind whipped their robes about them, as they faced each other and struck the two staves together over their heads, loosing a shower of bright sparks. A shaft of golden light sprang from the crossed staves to strike the underside of the sail, where the dark object I had watched them tie in place earlier was held.

A boom I felt in my belly echoed off the sheer mountainsides, as the shape exploded into flame.

The men straining to hold the sail now let it fly up, over the fortress wall, fire raining from beneath. Soldiers on the battlements screamed and fled, trying to escape the streaming flames. Da and some others drew bows and let fly at the wings of the thing, but how could they hope to bring it down in a wind so fierce? I had to turn my eyes southward so I could open them wider than mere slits. I saw the purpose of the attack then: wooden roofs within the fort, over the stable yard and more. Thatch and haystacks, too. I looked for Da to tell him, but I was shoved aside by the soldiers jostling, seeking some way to fight the great winged thing.

I turned as I fought for balance, to see a huge dark hawk, buffeted by the gale, but still pounding its wings against the roaring air. It swung wide and rode the air over the wall, then circled the courtyard. The pale fabric wings followed its curving path—the hawk was leading it. No—the hawk was guiding the wind to carry it! And with a sudden jerk of shock, I knew a mage looked through the hawk's eyes to find his target in the fort. I could *feel* him doing it.

None of the men seemed to have noticed the hawk. I cocked and loaded my crossbow with shaking hands, shouting, "Bring down the hawk!" though I knew they could not hear me over the wind and tumult. The fire splashed onto the thatch and shingles below. Flames shot high, whipped by the frantic torrents of air.

"The hawk!" I cried again, and let fly a bolt and a prayer for it to find its mark.

It was too dark to see my quarrel's path, but I saw the bird spin and tumble in the air, surely struck. It did not fall, instead beating harshly with its broad wings, it righted itself, and flew straight toward me.

I scrambled to reload. Da appeared beside me, and I gestured with my bow at the rushing hawk—"The mage is in it! Kill it, bring it down!" He fired as the bird drew in its wings to dive, talons outstretched. Da's bolt flew wide of its wing, and I loosed mine to strike through the neck. The bird crashed onto the battlements at our feet.

The wind began to drop at once, and the soldiers around us leapt up to grasp the ropes that hung from the false firebird, sinking now without the fury of the magic-driven wind. They pulled it down and doused its fire with dirt and sand from buckets on the walls by the torches.

Fires roared in the keep below, with masses of men struggling to put them out. I could hear the echoing screams of panicked horses. Da prodded the body of the hawk with the toe of his boot. Not yet dead, it locked eyes with me, panting, its dark blood spreading on the stones. I trembled so hard I could scarcely keep my grip on my crossbow. A bitter chill clawed at my chest. Then, just as suddenly as I had known the mage was in the hawk, I felt him flee. A breeze ruffled the feathers across the crumpled body. The bird's eyes turned milky, and its breath ceased. I no longer sensed the mage inside it—his mount was dead but he lived.

I ran to peer over the wall into the field to the north. Both sorcerers stood stone-frozen in the light of the bonfire below. And I swore both of them looked directly at me as I stood on the walkway above. What would they do now? Now that they knew me …

Da's hand on my shoulder jerked me back, and I found I had been leaning out over the edge, on the brink of tumbling over. My ears buzzed and I felt distant, disconnected from my eyes and feet. "I'm taking him down below," Da told the officer at his side. "Find me in the infirmary if anything changes."

I did not speak, and let him lead me to the ladder. Wieser leapt and barked at its foot. I wanted to tell her I was all right, but I did not trust my voice not to quaver.

Someone pulled my crossbow out of my feeble fingers, then Da helped me place my feet and hands on the ladder rungs. My muscles felt like sodden noodles and I fought to make them obey. I was loath to ride down in Wieser's bucket, despite my wobbling. Once on the ground, Da's great warm hands steered me through yard and corridors past the firefighters with Wieser walking at my heels.

We came to a long room lit by guttering candles, lined with narrow beds and reeking of smoke and burnt flesh. A white-haired man of the Order of Healers looked up from sluicing char off a man's shoulder. His initial squint at me caused him to point to one of the cots. "Put him there. What happened?"

Da aided me to lie back, and my teeth began to chatter, then my whole body to shake so that my limbs ached with it. The healer told an assistant to put salve on the man's burned shoulder, and crossed to me, wiping his hands on a cloth.

"This is my son. He slew a possessed creature on the battlements, and seems stunned somehow by the magic released," Da told him.

I tried to speak, but could not for the violence of the shaking. The healer passed his hands over my limbs and peered in my eyes. "Get him warm. It is perhaps some reaction to the attack, the boy is not used to battle."

Someone covered me with a blanket warmed by the hearth. *Idiot*, I thought, *I'm not cold and that wasn't a battle. The mages have seen me, and now they are hunting me.* I could feel them touching my mind, small glancing brushes at my thoughts. "A-Anno-nora," I managed. She would know better what to do than this fool of a bone-cutter.

Da dispatched one of the soldiers at once. "Bring Wils and his wife directly here when they arrive through the tunnel." The man saluted and sped away. Wieser sat at my bedside, and Da pulled a stool next to her and captured my quivering hand in his. "I would hear more about you and doing magic," he said. "When you can speak more easily."

I nodded and closed my eyes. I would have sworn I opened them only a moment later, but when I did Annora was seated on the stool, holding a steaming cup of one of her concoctions, looking down at me with worry-creased brows. Da and Wils stood at the foot of the cot in quiet conversation. Wieser alone had not moved. I found my shaking had ceased.

"What time is it?" I asked.

Annora plied me with the cup. "Nearly dawn now."

"How is it I feel the mages trying to touch my mind?"

Annora waited to see me take a gulp of the brew before she answered, "You recognized what the hawk was doing, and struck it down. So, the mage felt the magic in you, then he saw you through the dying bird. They look for you now to assess what you can do to thwart them. How strong you are."

I wish I knew. "Don't tell me any more about any plans, just carry them out," I said to Da and Wils. "I have no idea if they can know what I know by my thoughts."

"If you remember, I told you *not* to set the place on fire," Wils said, trying to muster a grin.

Do I look as bad as all that? I wondered.

"I tried to keep them from touching it off, didn't I? Are the fires all out?"

Da nodded and drew Wils away. The healer stopped at the foot of the bed and sniffed. I heard him mutter "hedge-witch" as he ambled on to the next cot. Annora and I traded smiles, and I finished my cup.

"Should I have needed an arm cut off," I said, watching the healer's stiff neck, "I'd still rather have you do it." Annora stifled a laugh and took the empty cup.

"Get me out of here. I can't stop my thoughts from going to Wils and Da and what they're doing. Let's go to the stables and see the damage. See if Da's grey stallion Wils thought so high of is still there." I grew restless now I felt better, and could feel less intrusions from the mages when I was talking.

Annora, Wieser and I followed our noses to the stable yard; a place where stock is housed being familiar enough to a farmer. Much of the roof had burned, and dawn's light shone through the blackened beams. The size of the fort continued to amaze me. We passed extensive gardens on our way from the infirmary, and a vineyard. Several kitchens were busy at daybreak, and we cadged a loaf at the baker's and a hunk of goat cheese at the dairy. I shared this out as we stood looking at the stables. There had to be space for forty horses, at least.

"How many men do you suppose there are here, all told?" I said, then added quickly, "No, don't answer. I have to watch what I have in my head!"

We went inside, and walked from stall to stall, greeting the occupants. Annora spent a little time with each one, soothing them after the fire had stirred them up so. She soon had them nuzzling and calm, investigating Wieser and me without tension. Some larger stalls had two horses within, whether debris and damage from the fire required the doubling up, or usual practice, I could not determine. But the fine grey head I sought came out over the stall half-door ahead of us, followed by that of a dun plow horse that must have been Wils's mount on the autumn journey here.

Both whickered softly to me.

A bow-legged man with a straggly beard stumped up the passage toward us, two haynets slung over his shoulders. This must be the horsemaster who put Wils onto the tunnel to the valley, I realized. "Hullo," I said. "Is this my da's stallion?" I petted its cheek, and its stablemate's, too.

"Yah, that's the rogue, full of himself, as usual," came the answer, but his voice was fond. "You'd be the paladin's younger son, then. I heard you brought down the mage's spirit hawk in that roaring gale last night. High magic, that." He spat and slung one of the nets over the door and onto its hook.

I knew I shouldn't ask—I had come to the stables to get away from thoughts that could betray me, after all. But still I blurted, "High magic?"

"Mmm. Weather-working, sendings, possession of animals. Shooting a bolt true through wild gusting wind. Such as that."

"Which is different from?"

"Low magic," supplied Annora. "Such as you see me do. Keeping ground fertile, healing folk and animals, preserving crops and fixing broken household things. Working in rhythm with the world. Are we supposed to be talking about—"

"No. Not at all." I made myself change subjects. "He surely is a fine horse. If we had him at our farm, we could make a profit from stud fees, I reckon. Is his stallmate the plow horse Wils rode in on?"

It was a knobby-kneed gelding that I could easily believe to be as rough gaited as Wils had said. It wuffled at Annora until she came and rested a hand on the broad forehead. She spoke gently in its ear, and it sighed and half-closed its eyes.

"You'll be young Wils's bride, I wager," said the old man. "I'm Senner Brayman. And aren't you every bit as pretty as he said. How he pined, down here brushing that grey. I'm that glad he made his way home to you. And now you turn up here!"

"She won't be staying as long as I did, so don't get too

attached to her," Wils said, striding up.

"Can I keep her to settle all my nervy horses? They're that spooked from last night," grinned Senner, hanging the other haynet so he could clap Wils on the back.

"No, I need to fetch her to teach—" here he looked at me, and amended, "—to come and do something else. Judian, can you wait for me by the door?"

Wieser and I dutifully walked away, but I still heard Wils. "We need two dozen readied to ride out before noon. The grey for the paladin, and please something more vigorous than this leg of mutton for me." I saw him pat both horses out of the corner of my eye; sorry to be disparaging the mount who brought him safely here, probably.

So, they were riding out, and to where? I slapped myself on the leg to interrupt the thought. *Stop now!* I scolded myself. Wils walked up with Annora, arm in arm, and pointed out into the courtyard.

"She's coming with me. You're to go down to the cisterns and wait for her there. When she joins you, go out and get the Traveller wagon. She'll tell you where to drive it. And take care of her!"

"I'm more used to doing that than you are, having done it for longer." Maybe churlish, but I did not care for being kept in the dark, however necessary it might be.

He made no comment on my sour outlook, and turned away with Annora. Then, swinging back, "Can you find the cisterns?"

"Wieser can," I said as I waved them on their way. And I would have more time to explore the fort, while Annora performed her errand, since it appeared I would be leaving the place later today. Who could say when I would have another chance to see a fort? I hoped to occupy my mind with poking about.

Wieser and I found several weapons stores, or armories. The soldiers working at them told us the proper term. I saw the wisdom of not keeping all the weapons in one place, they were less vulnerable spread out as they were—*Stop thinking!* I spotted some of the Keltanese arrows we had brought in one cache. I asked a friendly soldier who put me in mind of Cobbel if I might have a crossbow, since mine had been left on the battlements, maybe. He found one with a full complement of bolts, and gave me a short sword besides. "Are you riding out to engage?" he asked eagerly.

I saw the error of my choice in coming to the armory then, and said, "No, just keeping prepared, thanks." We instead went back to looking at foodstuffs and kitchens. Wieser liked that choice better, since no one could resist giving her a bit of meat or a broth soaked crust when she turned up. I accepted gratefully a cup of honeymead and an egg and onion stuffed in a hand-sized loaf so I could eat it as I walked. Relieved to know that men here had not been going hungry, I wondered if that was why they all seemed so resolute. We made our way past budding fruit trees and bee hives to the side of the keep where the way below to the cisterns lay.

We were gifted again passing through the sunken kitchen on the way to the stairway. Biscuits and honey, tender as could be. I wiped my hands on my trousers, and took up one of the tallow candles. As I struck a light, crouched over the wick in the curved stone entryway, Wieser began to whine. I looked about quickly for the cause of her unease, but found no person near. Peering deeper into the passage, I saw a shadow-shape, with nothing to cast it. I had the same sensation as I had in the forest months ago, of being watched. Hairs prickled on my arms and neck.

The wick caught, and I held the dancing flame before me, leaning in to see. The dark shape formed roughly the outline of a man, with a head and shoulders as of a man in a cloak. Where a face should be was only shadow. The image seemed to waver in the air, and I could make out the mortar between the stones behind it. It seemed Wieser saw it also, so it was not only in my mind.

Was this a Sending, a sorcerer walking abroad without his earthly body? Or some spirit of the ancient builders of the fort? It did not seem aware of Wieser and me, though I would be hard pressed to say why I thought that the case. As I stood still with caught breath, the figure drifted deeper into the hallway and dissolved into the stones as if passing through them.

A voice behind me startled me so I dropped my candle. Annora, drawing her shawl about her, saying, "Why is it so cold here?" She looked at my face in some alarm, then.

"Do not say I look as though I had just seen a ghost, because I think perhaps I have. I saw … something." I retrieved the candle and lit it again, and told her what I had encountered. "Mage or spirit, do you think?"

"Certainly I can feel echoes of the past in this place, ancient as it is," she mused. "I thought a Sending looked solid, and resembled the sender. Tangible enough that two can talk to one another, across distances."

"A useful skill to learn, seems to me. But why can I see such a thing as a spirit today? I never have before. Bah! Let's away to the wagon. Don't say where we're bound until I have the team ready." I took a deep breath before leading Annora and Wieser down the passage, but the shadows within all behaved as shadows should, when we passed by.

CHAPTER 34

I found we had been left the team from the hijacked wagon, when Annora brought me to the Traveller rig. Honey and Cider must have been hitched to the larger wagon, traded in case the ambushed soldiers had worked their way free to report the theft. *Do you think you can stop now—thinking thoughts that betray our plans?* I scolded myself.

I harnessed the two, and climbed up beside Annora and Wieser. "Where can I carry you, Donah?" I teased.

"To the river where Joren Delyth took the wagon yesterday. Did you see on the map?"

I nodded and clucked to the team. I tried humming as we crossed the valley, so I could keep my thoughts from the soldiers climbing up to loose the rockslides, from Da and Wils riding out the gates to attack the enemy soldiers to divert them from the climbers, and from whether Joren would be able to get back to us or be trapped on the far side of the pass, or where Perk, Beckta and Miskin were now ... ahh, it was maddening! I next tried whistling loudly, until Annora begged me to stop. She taught me a rhyming question game, and that was more successful at occupying my mind, for I had to focus on her clues.

We were perhaps halfway to the river, and could just make out the tall trees that followed its course across the valley, when a reverberating, grinding crash came from the distance behind us.

Deep rumbles and groans followed, and the earth of the valley floor seemed almost to tremble. I swung the horses around so we could look back, and saw a rising cloud of dust mounting above the pass, thickening as we watched. It bloomed so wide and steep, it looked as if another mountain had been birthed over the pass between the peaks.

"I hope no one was hurt," Annora said at length. It looked to me as if there were many ways to be hurt in such an event—I had no idea the pass closure would loose such a large amount of rock. I sent up a wish for all dear to us to be unscathed, and turned the wagon back on route.

Gargle found us a short way further on, and took up his post atop the wagon's peaked roof. He bore a cloak of pale dust, only his eyes shone dark, and he set about frantic preening.

"You must have helped with the close timing—" I started, and then bit my tongue.

"Yours is an active mind to try to keep still," Annora said. She held aloft a handful of nutmeats, and Gargle took some in betwixt his feather cleaning. I noticed he was careful not to jab her hand with his beak, unlike when he took food from my hand. Annora's heart drew out the best in us all, I reckoned.

When we reached the intended river bend, where I could see signs that the stolen wagon and team had visited, I pulled into the trees on the bank and halted. "Are we to set up camp? Or just lay low?" I asked, watching the broad riffles of clear water.

"They'll join us and we'll move on, though not to the main road. That's likely to be busy." She hopped down. "A meal wouldn't go amiss, though. Then they can eat when they come."

She had fine trout frying in what seemed no time at all, while Gargle washed himself in a pool and enjoyed the results of the gutting, letting nothing go to waste. I would have liked to practice calling fish from the cold sparkling water, but feared I might draw ominous attention by using magic. Thus, I felt useless, so groomed the team and let them graze awhile, shepherded by Wieser. All the while, I could not shake my feeling of being watched by something outside of the world I could see around me.

The feeling of spider webs brushing my thoughts had ceased since I left the fort; this differed in seeming to surround us, as if the very air was … *attentive*, somehow. Several times as I worked on the horses, my nape hair rose and my obsidian knife suddenly felt hot and heavy in my boot. I kept my sword and crossbow close to hand, uneasy.

When I asked her, Annora claimed to sense none of it, and paused to close her eyes for a bit to try. She reopened them shaking her head, "I only hear the water rushing, and the birds in the brush. That little snake in the rocks, there. Sometimes I feel as you describe when magic is being cast abroad, but I don't feel it now."

She walked the bank collecting fiddlehead fern to steam, and when she returned to the wagon, said, "You were heavily touched by the mage's spellcasting last night. Then you saw the spectre today. Perhaps you have been opened to the worlds beyond ours. My gran said some folk can see or feel the others who exist with us but are out of the sight of most. They are all around us, all the time, but unseen. The ability to sense them is a gift, like the ability to do magic."

"If that's so, will I always be able to see them?"

"It might not be permanent, but just an after effect of slaying the possessed hawk."

"I regret that," I said, and though I knew I should stop there, could not help continuing, "It wasn't the hawk's fault. I wish I had known a way to cast the sorcerer out of it, instead."

"The goddess forgives," Annora said. And as she spoke, rising behind her in the shade of the tree, I saw a flicker of a green-robed woman, arms stretched up like the branches. A blink and the image was gone.

"Are the gods about us all the time, too?"

"Of course. They are the world, and the gods together balance us all on the turning wheel of life so we do not go awry. Do you see them, as well?"

"I may have done," I said, considering. I helped myself to a plate of fish, and made sure to thank the fish for being our sustenance and the gods, every one, for every other aspect of life. One could not be too careful where the divine was concerned.

Annora and I took turns watching across the valley the way we had come, and I was doing my stretch on our wagon roof when I saw a wagon with mounted men alongside. I called to Annora, picking berries a short ways away, and she rushed to climb the back ladder to look, too.

"It is them!" she cried. "Oh, gods be praised forever!"

"Can you see that far, it's not Keltanese soldiers coming?" I could not say for certain, myself.

"Why would they pursue us with a wagon?" came her sensible reply. It proved to be Da and Wils who drew up to us on mounts, with Joren on the wagon's bench seat, and Beckta and Miskin returned to their disguise as Keltanese guards.

Perk was nowhere to be seen. My stomach gripped hard.

"Please, where is Perk?" Annora asked before I could. Wils rode to the side of our wagon and helped her from the roof to sit behind him in the saddle. He rode across to the cargo wagon's bed. I scrambled down the ladder and ran to look into the bed with them. Perk lay on scumbled blankets, a wide blood-stained bandage wrapped around his left thigh.

"He took a sword blow while mounted. The bone is not broken, but the muscle is deeply cut." Wils aided Annora over the side of the wagon. She knelt at Perk's side. "The healer at the fort sewed him up, but perhaps there is more you can do for him?"

"Aye, if you could staunch some of the pain, I'd take it as a favor," Perk said, voice tight.

I sped to our wagon's shadowy hut, and snatched up Annora's pouch of herbs, then grabbed a bottle of mead as well. I handed her everything quick as quick. She bent over Perk's wound and caught her lower lip in her teeth.

"Judian, would you see to boiling some water?"

I nearly fell over my feet racing to set the kettle over the coals.

"Make ready to head downstream, we'll follow the river to the next town and then take the long route home," Da directed the others. He would let no one tell any more of the morning's tale, only that the pass had been closed. They did make time to dismount and polish off the fish and greens. I fetched the team as soon as I handed Annora the kettle.

"Wait," called Wils around a mouthful, "Trade the teams out again, to confuse the descriptions being told where we've been seen passing by." Da nodded approval, and Beckta came to help me. We both froze when Perk cried out as Annora worked on him. Wils stood in the silence that followed, but then we heard Perk tell her, "Go on, go on. Just give me another pull on the bottle first, eh?"

The wagons stood ready when the food was gone, and Annora finished with Perk at the same time. She bade Wils and Da transfer him to the back of our wagon, in the hut out of sight. Perk grimaced when they lifted him, his teeth hard clenched. As they carried him past me, he held a fist aloft, and gave a pale shadow of his wide, easy grin.

I saw Wils had been put up on a springy-hocked bay mare with black stockings, not the quality of Da's mount but a fine horse, none the less. Instead of thinking about Perk's wound and whether jostling in a wagon would set it bleeding worse, I imagined the herd we would have when we gathered all these horses at home. The barn would have to be enlarged sooner rather than later. *Perhaps I should not think about home either, lest I help the mages find me there?* I wondered.

Da and Wils rode alongside Annora and me, looking like Travellers, we hoped. Beckta and Miskin continued as Joren's outriders with the cargo wagon ahead of ours. I strove to lag behind them enough that we looked like two groups, not a passel of folk together on a journey.

The first village we reached was no more than a hamlet around a ferry crossing. Wils found it on the map and told me it was called Pilsberry Crossing, before I reminded him nobody was supposed to tell me anything. "Treat me like a mushroom," I said, "Keep me in the dark."

"Should you also be fed a diet of manure?" Wils joked, for that was where the best mushrooms sprouted in the caves, where an animal left scat.

"If Annora prepares it, I will give it a try," I said. "Make no mistake about me trying any you turn your hand to!"

I steered our blue wagon down the single dirt track between the handful of stone houses, after waiting to see that Joren and the others had pulled out. None of the occupants of the drowsy place had heard any news of late, Da learned when he stopped to buy supplies. They had little enough to offer, though they eyed his coin avidly. Da bought some smoked venison, and a couple jugs of cider. He offered, Traveller-like, to do a job or two, but they refused. It seemed if we didn't want to be ferried across the river, they wanted to see us move on.

"I should have had a chain," Da said as we went along. "Travellers melt gold into chain links, and twist off so many for a purchase. I hope those folk don't remark to the wrong ears that I used Merced coin."

"Maybe the Travellers do that more with each other. Zaffis was only too happy with our coin," I said.

"Mmm, Wils has told me some of your enterprises in my absence. You've both done me proud with all this," he nodded toward the wagon and horses, and the cargo wagon up ahead.

I felt my heart swell to hear it, but could do no more than dip my chin. I didn't want to seem more a boy than a man, with my birthday only a short while away. I concentrated on driving the team, watching the faint track between Cider's ears.

###

We fell back into our prior rhythm of rolling along during

274

daylight hours and camping at night. Perk could not bear weight on his leg, but Annora insisted he get out and walk of an evening with a crutch she fashioned—"To keep the breath clear." She dressed and redressed his wound, with stinking poultices that made my eyes water. Yet, she said the gash progressed toward healing. I wondered if he would always limp. Perhaps for a horsemaster, a limp had little consequence. Perk, for his part, took care to only look grim and pained when he thought no one watched him.

We saw nothing of Clock or Tock, so sent Gargle home with word that we would be returning soon. I overheard Wils telling Annora what to say, so she could code it. I also heard him tell her that Cochren Luppes had not wanted Da to leave, or to let any of the men depart. "As if I'd send you home with Judian alone. Luppes will just have to act like a fortmaster and fight the Keltanese himself, when they try to clear the pass."

"The men at the fort all seemed strong in their mission, and I could not see they lacked for anything," said Annora.

"That's Da's doing, he took over the running of the place during the siege. Kept everyone lifted up and doing their best. Luppes is better since his wine ran out, but he's not the leader Da is. And he knows it. I'm sure Da will want to keep sending the fort arms and other supplies, since you taught them to use the code so we can keep in touch. I hope the enemy doesn't find the tunnel."

I hoped not, too, so I forced the tunnel site from my mind at once.

Gargle returned two days later with far more news than I could be told. Woven beneath Virda's words of how the garden was coming on and the twenty chicks she got for helping birth twins for the wheelwright's wife, Wils read out to Da by the fire that night the real word from the farm. It felt like when we used to read by the hearth at home, except that I was banished to check the horses and unload bedrolls from the wagon.

"For my own good," I grumped to Wieser, but proximity let me hear that the warehouse prisoners were arriving in dribs and drabs from the cliffs, and being shuttled to the caves on our mountain by Gevarr and Cobbel. Whatever else was revealed made everyone equally happy, as far as I could tell by their reactions, and it was not until a week later that Tock arrived with the letter that changed everything.

CHAPTER 35

W e kept to lesser roads and tracks to make our way toward home undetected, so the summer rains mired us more than once that week. The men had got quite good at levering up the axle with a pole while Annora and I put flat rocks under the wheels. I tried to do the muddiest work to save her from it. That day I was just scrambling to my feet swearing, covered to the chest in black muck and rotting leaves from under the cargo wagon, when Tock alighted on the hut roof.

Maybe he thought I tried to take on his plumage color, because he bobbed his head in what appeared to me to be approval. Annora took his message to decode, while I tried to wash off some of the worst of the slop in the stream next to the road.

Every face that came round to me when I returned looked as bleak as snow-dusted rock.

"You'd best tell me what this one says." I wrung out my shirt front, sinking onto a log at the edge of the wagon ruts.

Annora held out the paper for me. Virda had sent a scrawled market list, which in code beneath said tersely, "Stay away. Soldiers taking magic folk."

"Taking them where?" I said into the silence.

Da had an answer first. "No matter at present. Wils, you take Annora and Judian and head south. Delyth drives the wagon to our place, with me, Beckta and Miskin. Perk, you'll have to ride with

Wils." The men began to move, gathering gear and shifting it from one rig to the other.

I felt my home sliding away over a cliff while I could do nothing but watch. "Why can't I take Annora up to the caves? Not go through the village but go around the backcountry way instead?" I tried.

"And if they've tracked you to home by your thoughts?" Wils said.

"I have not done one scrap of magic since I shot the hawk!" I said, and this was true. But I had thought of home.

"We don't know if they're looking for Judian specifically," Annora said, tugging at the rain-swollen wagon door.

Da jerked it open for her. "They only have to know they are looking for my son," he said."The whole fort knew who I was, and who Judian was after that night. Finding my home will not be difficult for the enemy. I'm well-enough known as former paladin."

Wils brought the maps out. "It will be better to continue north, and pick up Grebble Road southeasterly. Better for fast travel." Da looked over as Wils traced the route. I tethered Wils's bay to the back of the Traveller wagon, and climbed up on the seat.

"Yes," Da said. "It's not far to the junction. Mount up."

All of us did as we were ordered, which is what people always do when it's Da doing the telling. We had three more miles of rough track to cover to reach the crossroads.

Wils's expression grew so empty as he drove. Annora sat beside him with me at her other side. Wieser sat on the floor behind the seat but stretched forward to lay her nose on my boot. I could hear Tock call, circling above with Gargle.

I could not stop wondering if Morie and Virda were safe. Gevarr and Cobbel would take them away to the caves, unless at the caves themselves, situating the refugee soldiers. And would Virda be taken, since midwifery was a sort of magic? Who would care for Morie, had they left her alone at the house? How I wished

278

I could fly home with my crows and see.

Wils started to talk, and I listened to him to keep my thought away from magic and home. "I never knew what Da could do until I saw him fight, when we rode out together. Somehow he knew just where to send men to drive back a surge of enemy. Then he swept around like a holy fire. I had practiced long days with sword and axe when we were stuck at the fort, and I thought I could handle weapons. But he ... how he made his sword ring through the air. It was his own sword, I gave it back to him and took another. I was staggered to see him wield it." Wils swallowed.

"What is the best thing to do in a battle?" I asked, for I might need to know soon.

He shifted his shoulders. "Be somewhere else."

"Did you have to kill anybody?" I persisted.

"Yes." It seemed at first he would not say more, but then, "I saw six fall to me, but maybe not all of them died." Annora put her hand over his on the rein, and settled her head on his shoulder.

I did not know what to say. Was it wrong to feel I would have liked to see my da fight? But what Wils said rang true—better to avoid a battle than seek one. Did Wils already carry the ghosts of the slain men with him? It could have been because I was thinking deep about what Wils said that I did not notice the sky darkening before us. Canyons and cliffs of black cloud seethed above before I chanced to look up and see them roiling.

"Queer weather of a sudden," I said. *Not queer, uncanny,* came into my mind unbidden. I had just opened my mouth again when Gargle and Tock flew in front of our faces, in a fury of flapping and cawing. We rolled out of the canopy of trees and onto the wider crossroads, with Wils cursing as he tried to fend the birds away from Annora's head.

Emerging from the trees on the opposite side of the main road was a squad of Keltanese soldiers.

I could see the back of our stolen wagon continuing north, with Miskin and Beckta in their Keltanese garb as escort. Da had pulled his grey stallion to a stop on the rise—watching to see us turn aside to the southeast.

"Take arms but stay," Wils murmured to Perk in the back of our wagon. And why had I not thought to ride in the back? Wils gave the barest glance to the soldiers and swung the team onto Grebbel Road. I looked to where Da had been and found he had vanished into the woods. Ten foot soldiers, I counted as we turned past, with two more in the trees holding horses. One closest to the road stepped out toward us with hand upraised.

I could see on Wils's face the conflict—stop as if Travellers abroad, or make a run with Perk shooting from the rear? The desultory way the soldier held his hand up, and the fact that the others did not charge forward … he pulled the team to a halt.

In stilted Mercedish, the soldier said, "We be seek a boy and the father. Home near here."

"We are Travellers, come from far away," Wils said, looking at his boots.

"And isn't she a pretty piece I'd like to ride," the man said under his breath in Keltanese. Wils gave no flicker of reaction, though I knew, too. The man wasn't talking about the bay mare. "You be?" the soldier pointed at me, switching back to his clumsy Mercedish.

"Cousin," I said, for Wils and I looked much alike. The soldier squinted, as if he did not know the word.

"Egorace." Wils pointed down the road, naming a town some twenty miles ahead. "Find field work." The soldier looked blank. "Work," Wils repeated, and I made motions of digging as with a shovel.

This appeared to reach him, and he nodded and waved us on. I cast another look at the sky, which now bore green-tinged clouds ringing the hills we approached. A looming thunderhead shaped like a smithy's anvil capped the crest of the hill. As I watched, streaks of cloud began to rotate slowly. Thunder rolled over us.

"We should stop," I said to Wils.

"Some distance from them, first."

Da rode down the road bank out of the trees. He had crossed behind the soldiers to rejoin us. "Keep going, but do not rush," he said to Wils.

I said again, "I think we should stop," and pointed to the strange sky before us.

Annora said, "I don't know as much about weather-workers as Virda, but I think that has to be their doing. Judian's right."

"Perk, look out behind. Do they follow?" Da risked a look back, too.

"No," came from Perk, and Da nodded.

"Are there more crossroads ahead?" I asked, and Wils handed me the map. I felt my nerves start to thrum and taughten. A crack of thunder made us all jump, and the team lurch forward. Even Da's obedient mount jittered and sidled.

I looked feverishly for some lesser track to turn off the road, away from what lay ahead of us. Nothing—no other roads to take. "Give me Wils's horse and I'll go crosscountry," I said, grasping at any idea, now.

"I do not want us separated. Climb in back." Da kicked his mount ahead, cantering around a curve. I clambered over the seat to join Perk in the hut.

"What can you see?" Perk asked, for he could see ahead only a little from inside.

"We're headed into some kind of foul weather. It seems like what the sorcerers would call up." I licked dry lips. Wieser crept in to curl beside me. I could feel her shiver from time to time. *If she is frightened, I'm done for*, I thought. Wieser had shown no fear, in any of our adventures.

Perk held a cocked crossbow along the length of his good thigh, aimed toward the back door, and his sword lay next to his side. I started to pull my bow toward me to do the same, but he put out a hand. "I'm worried enough I'll shoot you or myself bouncing over a rut. Let's have just one ready," he grinned.

"Have you been in lots of battles?"

"A fair few. Mostly minor scrums with brigands and thieves until I was posted to Fort Hasseron. There I trained as cavalry."

"I can see why the fortmaster didn't want you to leave, being trained and all."

He grinned again. "He didn't oppose your da in sending me with Wils the first time. So, maybe I wasn't as good as all that." He continued to peer out a slit in the back door.

We rolled on accompanied by rumbles and crashes from the clouds, and a heaviness to the air that made me as twitchy as Wieser. When Gargle and Tock set up a chorus of caws, I had to poke my head out to see what stirred them.

We drew up to a Traveller encampment, set up among trees just off the road. The crows were loudly directing our attention to a grouping of five wagons similar to ours, with a large fire in the center under a jutting rock overhang. Horses stamped, tied to lines in the shaded woods. Da waved Wils to steer off the roadway toward the men gathered at the largest wagon. Wils gave me a push to send me into the rear again, but I could hear Da address the men when we stopped.

"You are well met, with this storm brewing. Do you object to us joining you to shelter here?" Did Da sound like a Traveller? I would have liked to see the men's faces, but had to settle for hearing them grunt assent. Our rig was no more colorful than theirs, in my brief glance round. Perhaps we would fit in with the group, to Keltanese eyes. Then I had the chilling thought that maybe Zaffis had stolen our wagon from these Travellers. *Gods forefend.*

Da and Wils sussed out who the leader was, and soon walked off with the man and his two sons. Annora found a young mother by the fire who had a fretful, feverish baby. That was her means of making herself useful; she boiled a tincture and rocked the dosed infant to sleep while the mother drowsed over a dish of porridge. Perk, balanced carefully on his good leg, chopped fuel for the fire, shedding his shirt in the sultry heat. This won him admiring glances from some of the girls, for he was well-muscled and fit. I stood about like a chicken with thumbs after caring for the horses. Wieser still quivered and panted at my side, and the crows glowered from branches above our wagon. The storm hung overhead, bringing early darkness to the heavy air. Lightning began to flash from cloud to cloud.

The Traveller women were roasting several fat ducks, and Annora was quick to contribute what we had left of our root vegetables. An old woman cackled as she mixed flatbread with bent and twisted hands. Annora became the center of attention for the half-dozen younger children, who clustered round her feet and stared silently as she chopped and stirred.

The clouds broke open just as Da and Wils returned with the other men. Even impeded by the trees, so much rain sluiced from the sky that we could scarcely see the wagons scant feet away. The group huddled under the rock overhang, watching muddy water run over the lip above and splash on the ground at our feet.

"The road may wash out to the south," said the wiry leader, lighting his pipe with a twig from the firepit. "We'll make for the stone bridge at Nygaard. I do not trust the wooden bridge at Egorace to survive this. Debris will likely take it out, even if there is no flood." He offered Da a clay pipe, accepted gladly. Soon they were both puffing.

The rain pounded down while we ate, and while we cleaned the pots. It never let up throughout the bottle being passed man-to-man while the women mended clothes by the firelight and the children played at Stone Toss. The sick baby awoke with a cool forehead and a fresh appetite, fixing Annora's acceptance into the family group. I still could not relax.

My mind worried at the rain like a ratter at a nest. Did the mages know we fled, and so drenched the road to slow our progress? Would that not also slow pursuers? Did our presence endanger the Traveller band, and had Da told them we were wanted by the enemy? I could not think he would deceive them, or that they were not shrewd enough to see we were not really Travellers. We were maybe three days ride from home, if we turned toward it now, longer with the wagon to drive. How I wanted to go home—and how I feared to!

Winds lashed the rain this way and that, blowing wet gusts to invade our shelter. Gargle and Tock blew in on such a burst, and found a ledge to perch on, splattering me as they shook out their feathers. The old woman stared at the crows and hummed to herself, rocking slightly. That would have my sanity as its price, if I had to listen to her every night.

The men usually kept watch by the fire, while the women and children bedded down in the wagons of a night. Thus, Da and Wils settled by the fire with Perk and the other men, and Annora and I made a dash through the deluge to the backdoor of our wagon. Wieser came with us, so to contribute the odor of wet dog to the close air within.

Over the noise of the rain pelting the roof, I told Annora that Wieser and I would sleep closest to the door. She nodded, and shifted the load about to make room for herself toward the front. The rain continued drumming, but the thunder and lightning began to sound more distant as we made ready for sleep.

I knew the men were on watch and not me, but still I could not make myself close my eyes. I spoke into the dark, "Annora? What if we cannot go home?"

"I know you don't mean because of the rain," she answered.

"No, because of the magic folk being rounded up. It may be uncharitable of me, but I do not think Gefretta Estegg will waste any time telling the Keltanese you and I do magic. She is still smarting that Wils didn't choose her to marry, despite how you see her making over Miskin and Beckta."

I could hear a smile in her voice, though I could not see it in the dark. "I cannot say I would put it past her, though her father and mother would be mortified if she did betray us to the enemy."

"I expect she would conceal it from her folks if she did tell."

"My aunt and uncle are others who might speak about me, to deflect trouble from their own door."

"Would you come with me, take Wils's and Da's mounts, and ride away to another route to the harbour? We could meet up with Wils and Da there, or get away to the underground with Orlo's folk." I was spinning out my thoughts. Looking for any path at all out of our current quandary.

The only sound was the rain thrumming for a bit, then, "Do you mean leave now? Because they are on watch, and in the storm and dark, we'd never get horses saddled and away without them knowing."

"No, no. At dawn perhaps? We'll have to convince Da and Wils to travel with this group while we break away, just the two of us to confuse ... the searchers."

"How do you think to get into Bale Harbour?"

"No one is looking for a boy and a young woman. Then maybe Da and Wils can come to town with seabags and seem sailors ..."

"They would have to go home to get the bags, no? And if Fenn is sought at his home, he'll be taken. As paladin, not for magic-work. You're worried about Virda and Morie, too, I know. But Cobbel and Gevarr will take them to safety as arranged, if enemy soldiers have come to the mountain."

"I don't know enough!" I burst out. "I do not know how to fight the mages. I only work magic in lurches and spurts. What good am I?"

"Enough good to shoot their hawk out of the sky. How did you come to the fort on the one night when the mages' magical attack would burn our men out—after months of the siege being at a standstill? The apostate told you he believed the gods are on our side. I think they are using you to fight the mages."

"Then they must be finding me wanting. Where is the Goddess of Sea and Water? And the God of Air, while the weather-workers wring the clouds dry? We do not have unrelenting torrents like this here. Da has books that tell of places far away where rains like this come every year, but not here."

"I do not think the gods reach into the world with their own hands. I think they empower us with magic to do their work here."

"Do they also empower the mages, those who use their power for ill?"

"I do not know what bargains mages may make with darker forces, in order to feed their ambition for conquest. Both good and ill exist in all worlds."

Wieser sat up with a thump of her tail on the floor of the wagon, and I heard a knock at the door. I opened it on a sodden Wils, who stuck his head in to say, "We have to move to higher ground, the waters are rising. Da wants us up the hill ahead."

The Travellers readied to move as well, and we aided one another as we could. I began to wonder what it would feel like to be dry as the chill water overtopped my boots.

"All in all, I believe I prefer tending goats," I told Wils as we put our shoulders into the back of a Traveller wagon.

"You used to complain about that, too," he grunted.

Dawn found us on top of the hill, wagons scattered this way and that with horses tied wherever we could hitch them in the dark. The rain spluttered to a stop as I stood watch with Da. I did not figure I could get any wetter, so might as well be outside.

"I am thirteen today, did you remember?" I said, watching the sun struggle to shine through thinning clouds.

"Yah, in fact I did. If we were home we could celebrate your coming of age properly. As it is, I will tell you I have something of your mother's for you at home. Have I told you I could not have done a better job of rescue myself?" I shook my head, throat catching. "Well done, Judian."

Wils came up, scratching his neck. "What's he done now?" he asked on a yawn.

Da and I laughed loud at that. "Make ready," Da said, wiping his eyes. "We roll for home today. We cannot go further south, I know the country that way. There will be flooding and mudslides to block our path."

"Are they herding us home, then?" I said.

"If so, I have surprises in me yet. Call me one of your messengers," Da said, with a grim smile.

We parted from our friends of the wet, wild night. The baby Annora helped was bright-eyed and sassy, and batted its arms at us. The old crone hobbled to my side still humming, and pressed a circle of pale stone into my palm. A looped leather thong threaded through a hole in its center, and she gestured I should put it around my neck.

"For the strong magic," she quavered as I picked it up from my tunic front to look at it closer.

"It gives me strong magic? Or it protects me from strong magic?"

She smiled and tottered off. *Queer old thing*, I thought. "Thank you!" I called after her. I showed it to Annora when I climbed onto the wagon seat beside her.

"Oh, a moonstone," she said at once. "Powerful talisman. She gave it to you? Did she know today is your birthday?"

"How would she know that? I didn't know you knew."

"I've been saving back some cherry mead for you, now you are of age. I'm thinking she knew you had magical gifts because of the crows and Wieser."

"Do you know what this is for?"

"Protection mostly, such as keeping you from the sight of those who would do you harm." She touched it and murmured a few strange words. "Keep it always with you. Good fortune to have it now, I would say."

To be sure. Da told me to settle in the back, and Perk took the reins with Annora by his side. Wils rode ahead to scout, and Da rode his stallion, which I named Storm in honor of what we had weathered. We set out north toward home.

As miles passed, I noted we were headed more toward the coast than to our mountain. The first night's camp, I dreamed of a snow-white owl circling and searching. I was told to stay in the wagon, but the voice came from inside my own head. I held tight to my moonstone and obsidian knife. As a dream, it somehow made sense that I was sleeping curled within the wagon and also watching the owl wheel above fields and treetops with wings silvered by moonlight.

When I woke at dawn I found Annora sitting beside me. Warding signs chalked on the floorboards surrounded us both. "Was I dreaming the owl?" I asked first thing.

"Not a dream, a vision. I saw her, too. She could not see us, between your stone and my spell."

I pulled my leather booklet of magic-lore from my tunic and set about copying the signs from the floor. "If sorcerers can send creatures to seek us, why not send gangs of them in all directions? And by day as well as night?"

"One mage for one creature at a time, I think. And they cannot ride too long or they risk losing themselves to the wild nature of their mount. However many sorcerers are in Merced, I do not think all are solely occupied with finding you. They communicate with one another by Sending. They must have done, to explain the speed with which your capture is their goal, and the soldiers told to seek a boy and his father."

"They overestimate me. I am sure of that, if of nothing else."

The second night, a white wolf appeared in my dream. *Where's the owl?* I wondered in my sleep. The wolf made a more restive host for a mage, and whipped about with snapping jaws as if to dislodge something from behind its ears. More time was spent chasing its own tail than loping through the firs. I could almost sense the frustration in the sorcerer's mind, and thought, *Do not pick the pack leader, then. He chooses his own path.*

By day we began to encounter cargo wagons flanked now by

four Keltanese outriders rather than two, all journeying south to find a way to Keltane beyond the mountain range. "They will have far and away to go," Da said with satisfaction. "The Aganetha Mountains run more than a thousand miles along the borderlands, and passes are few."

The closer we came to the West Road, the more squads of Keltanese troops appeared, setting up checkpoints to question any wayfarers besides those accompanied by their troops. Once, we were ordered to climb down and stand beside the road while they searched the back of our rig, but between my moonstone and whatever Annora was humming under her breath, none of the soldiers took particular notice of either of us. One of the officers coveted Da's horse, until it bit him on the ear when he tried to feel its foreleg. We were waved on our way while he pressed a cloth to his bloody cheek.

"Did you make Storm do that?" I asked Annora.

"He wanted to, anyway," she smiled in return.

Clock came to us at the campfire the third night, and Da and Wils translated the message he brought with barely contained glee. I longed to know what was afoot, and received sympathetic glances from Perk and Annora as I moped about my day's end chores.

My dream vision that night was of a broad-winged heron, bluish in the starlight, with long legs trailing as it flew. *They pick mounts poorly*, I thought in my sleep, for the bird beat its wings rather than stretching them to ride the wind currents, and only looked down when going over lake and river. *Perhaps finding me has been relegated to the least adept among the mages.* Still, I took comfort in my talisman and ring of protection. Tonight I had renewed the symbols myself, with Annora's guidance.

Da sent a message away with Gargle at first light, and we traveled on toward the coast. I was granted a reprieve, and allowed on the wagon seat instead of in the back, thus able to see an approaching red cargo wagon drawn by a matched pair of golden horses. Perk was driving our wagon, his eyes alight with mirth when he glanced at me. I made out Joren Delyth's face as the other wagon drew near, and he winked at me from the driver's bench. Four in Keltanese tunics accompanied the rig; in addition to Miskin and Beckta, Cobbel and Gevarr rode alongside. Gevarr raised an eyebrow at me when he passed, but his expression betrayed no recognition beyond that. I saw their horses were some of Bar Estegg's from the smithy; so the villagers were in on whatever Da had set in motion. The tarp spread taut over the wagon bed, tied securely to the cleats. What were they hauling?

Once past us, Joren swung the wagon about in a wider section of road, and followed us from some distance back. Wils reined in his bay to come beside us and tell Perk to pull off to the south at the next creek crossing. Once under the trees and out of sight from the road, Da ordered the teams switched between the wagons. It was short work with so many men, and when we were ready to set off again, Da told me, "We make for Bale Harbour. Wils, Perk and I will walk in through the gate with seabags Joren has brought. Our horses will be tied behind your rig, and you and Annora will follow the other wagon to a warehouse on the waterfront. Drive the wagon within and stay there until I say different, understand?"

"I'll do as you say." *But I wouldn't say I understand, exactly.*

Da and Wils dismounted about a mile from the harbour town gates. Perk handed the team's reins over to me, and I asked him quickly, "Do you think you are healed enough to walk a mile?"

He pulled his crutch out from beneath the seat and clambered down. "I'll hobble in or they'll carry me. Don't worry."

"The enemy has built such a fine wall for us, I hear," Wils said softly to Perk as he tied the horses to the back. He chucked the saddles through the back door, and the three of them shouldered their seaman bags. Though the canvas sides bulged, I did not think it was with sea gear. I hoped sentries did not look in sailors' bags.

Da, Wils and Perk naturally fell behind us on foot. We covered ground faster, and came to the town gate just behind the red wagon being waved through by the guard. "I hope none of them recognize Gevarr," Annora said, giving voice to my fear. None seemed to note him as in truth one of their own, left for dead.

The sentry waved me to a halt where the stone wall cast a deep shadow. Bowmen paced the walkway above. "What business?" he said brusquely. His Mercedish was quite good. I supposed that was why he had gate duty.

I tried, "Relatives live here. We carry them to work at Everton Lake."

"Women for the vineyards and orchards there," Annora added, eyes downcast. I saw her hands twist in her lap in a curious gesture. Joren slowed ahead, and Gevarr looked back.

Whatever Annora did, the sentry shrugged and waved us through the iron gate and onto the cobbled street. Joren clucked to his team, and I rolled behind him.

My only experience driving a wagon and team in town traffic was the day Wils and Da marched away, and at that time we had not been in the tangle of streets near the waterfront, but more at the edge of town. Today I felt I would sideswipe passersby even in my narrow wagon. How Joren navigated his wide rig so easily, I could not but attribute to his skill as a driver. We were lucky to have him turn up. Or perhaps the gods knew we would need him.

Wieser sat behind the bench seat, and Annora sat beside me equally as calm as Wieser, but I felt my jaw tightening more and more the deeper we went into the town. I said to Annora, "There are far fewer patrols about than I remember."

She nodded. "Many have been sent to find magic folk or guard transports on their longer journey. That's why your da—" she stopped abruptly. "I have to remember not to talk too free."

Joren Delyth had been instructed where to take us, I reckoned. Maybe this was the favor from the harbourmaster? I would ask Da once I could be told things again. I followed Joren up a ramp and through wooden doors slid wide apart, into an echoing warehouse interior, empty but for our two wagons and four riders. Or, no, a few crates lurked at the far end, stacked this way and that as if discarded. Joren swung about to face the doors, and so I did the same, as Beckta and Miskin dismounted and rolled the sliding doors shut.

Gevarr ambled his horse to our wagon's side, and said to Annora, "I'm told you have been kept from harm?"

"Never threatened, so I did not have to fight anyone," she said crisply. "And if it is not too much like bragging, I was needed to teach the code and message sending at the fort."

"No doubt you were essential," he said with a glint of amusement. "And you and Judian eluded capture by being elsewhere when the troops came for magic-gifted." Here he nodded to me.

"How is it you are trusted enough to come along? And how do Virda and Morie fare?" I asked, a touch put out to be such an afterthought for him.

"Cobbel and I took them up to the caves when we heard of your success blocking the pass, and it was just in time to avoid the sweep of troops looking for any who were known for magic. I gather some in the village pointed Annora's way." He frowned at this. "So, Virda is installed as cook for the hale troops of Merced who have been arriving, and healer for the wounded who have been coming more slowly. Morie has been working hard to aid Virda, and talking everyone's ears off their heads."

From Joren came a call of, "Gevarr!" and a wave to bring him to the cargo wagon. It was the first time I had heard Joren use his name. Gevarr touched his forehead to Annora and went to the back of the cargo rig, where the other men were untying the tarp over the bed. As the heavy canvas was rolled back, soldier after soldier in green Mercedian tunics clambered to the dirt floor of the warehouse, stretching their backs and legs. I counted thirty men, all fully armed.

One of them proved to be Fieldmaster Behring, who strode over to our wagon and sketched a salute to Annora and me.

"Donah Lebannen, young Judian, isn't it?" he said. "You have been many places besides where I thought you were bound when I took my leave at the mountain."

Nettled, I said, "Yah, and I hope you are finding my messenger birds and our code a better way to send information than your couriers. Still, I am glad to see you have been rescued from prison by us. What is going to happen now?" For I could feel tension building in all of them.

"Wait—we are not supposed to tell Judian the plans. The sorcerers are seeking him since he foiled them at the fort," Annora said.

"*He* foiled them? That's a tale I would hear when this night is over," Behring allowed with a raised brow. "Is Paladin Lebannen far behind you?"

"Not far, just slower coming on foot. They will arrive before long, I think."

"Judian," Miskin called from the crates in the corner. I hopped down and went to him, hoping the crates might be full of weapons hidden for our use. Something was coming together, whether I was given a clue or no.

Miskin had me shift a couple of the crates with him, and we uncovered a loop of leather strap sticking up from the dust. He pulled it, and a trapdoor rose with a cascade of the covering soil mounding at the back. A dark hole in the floor with a crude wooden ladder lay beneath, and as I watched, Orlo arrived at the bottom rung with a lantern and a hearty wave.

"Hah, you made it back! I've got some more troops for your battle!" He ran lightly up the ladder, followed by a broad-shouldered soldier who lumbered up with a knife in his teeth, and more men behind him.

Miskin had evidently not been reminded to keep me uninformed, because he grinned, "We take back the harbour tonight."

CHAPTER 36

I brought Orlo to our wagon and introduced him to Annora, since I had no other role to keep me occupied. All around us, officers directed by Fieldmaster Behring formed the emerging soldiers into ranks. They made no chatter, a Keltanese patrol passing outside would not hear the rumble of men's voices.

"When the paladin comes, then the attack can commence," Orlo told me, eyes bright. Annora shushed him and said he should not tell more.

So, I asked, "Did the harbourmaster's son make it to freedom?"

"Yes! You have never seen a man more happy, Zaffis says. Harbourmaster Folio aids us now—" he broke off at Annora's click of tongue and upraised hand. "Tell me what befell you on the road west," he continued instead.

"Cannot tell that, either, until after … whatever this is," I jerked my head at the massing troops.

"Ask your da if you can come with me when it starts. I'm to make sure as many women and children and old folks are below in the tunnels as possible, to keep them out of harm's way."

"Only you?" I said.

"Me and the rest of the smugglers," he said. "Zaffis claims we're practically law-abiding, of late."

I caught sight of Perk and Wils slipping in from the street, followed a few moments later by Da. Soldiers fell on the seabags they carried, extracting torches and oil. Behring flew to Da's side in an instant, saluting before clasping both hands around one of Da's and smiling wide. A murmur spread through the gathered men, then they silently saluted, fists over hearts, in Da's direction. He answered with a salute, and walked off with Behring to the tailgate of the cargo wagon, where maps were spread.

"That's my da." I nodded toward him. Then, "That's my brother," I said to Orlo, when Wils strode up and embraced Annora and kissed her.

"I'd kiss her before any other business, too," Orlo said with a wink.

Wils turned to us, and said, "You and Annora are to go into the underground until the fighting is over. Take Wieser with you, but we need all three crows to carry messages. We'll find you when the danger is past."

"You mean I do not get to do *anything?*"

"He means you will not go out and engage trained warriors in a street fight," Da said, walking up to us. He continued to Wils, "We will wait until curfew would have everyone except patrols indoors, so empty roads do not seem amiss. I need a crow to send to each of the other warehouses and the sawyer's yard, so I need a runner to go to the chapel and make sure the apostate rings the bell to signal the troops who cannot see the fire."

"Joren Delyth will know his way best," Wils began.

Orlo stepped forward. "I can go most all of the way underground. Just tell me when to have him ringing, and I'll see it done."

"This is Orlo, I told you about him," I said to Da. "Let me go with him. Annora can come as well. The chapel will be out of the way of the fighting, surely."

"I'd have to call him brave," Behring said at Da's side.

Da looked at me with arms crossed. "That's one thing to call him."

"The apostate knows me. I went and asked him for help to start with."

"That is true," Orlo nodded. "When we released the soldiers, the apostate helped us get the wounded out first, and had the able men take the place of the infirm until we could take all the rest at once. He said Judian asked him to come to their aid in the prison."

Da made his choice. "Once the fire is lit at the sawyer's, you will see it from the chapel across town. That is when the bell is to be rung seven times. After you see to that, the three of you return to the tunnels and wait for us to come for you. You will do nothing else!"

We all agreed vigorously that we could be counted on to be obedient. No one laughed outright, these being serious times. Wils did draw me aside and say in my ear, "Be told: You let no harm befall her from you playing the hero, eh?"

"I just want to help, and she does, too. I'll take utmost care."

"See you do," he said, and moved off with Da and Behring.

Perk helped us by lowering Wieser down the hole in one of the empty crates, and we were outfitted with torches and a lantern. I carried my bow and short sword, but as Orlo was unarmed, I shifted the sword to him and carried my obsidian knife instead. He whistled softly when the torchlight touched the black blade. "I have only heard of those in legend. You'd best save a lot of time to tell me your tales when this is over."

"He does have tales to tell," Annora agreed, and we set off into the dark shadows.

We were soon enough peering from behind bushes at the midpoint of the chapel hill, where an exposed road led up to the chapel itself at the top of the rise.

"I thought you said we could go most of the way below ground," I complained to Orlo.

"This is most of the way. It's just up there."

"But we have to go right out in the open to get to it."

"We could go below and tunnel into the chapel cellar—by midwinter."

Wieser looked from one to the other of us. "At least if we had dark cloaks or something—" I started.

"Do you smell wood smoke?" Annora interrupted. "Could they have started the fire already?"

"Town always smells of wood smoke, what else?" Orlo answered back.

It was just dusk, barely so. They shouldn't be lighting their diversionary fire yet, it would be too hard to see, I reckoned. "We have to cross the road and go up. I'll go first, then you come over with Wieser when I signal," I told Orlo. "Annora, I'll send Wieser back for you."

"I think she should wait in the tunnel," Orlo argued.

"I think we should all walk up to the chapel like supplicants, right now before it is past curfew. Surely that is less out of the ordinary," was Annora's whispered opinion.

I closed a hand around the moonstone at my chest. "So be it. We go now."

We all tried to walk up the road, instead of scurry like granary rats when the farmer shines a light on them, and made it to the chapel door. The apostate ushered us in, shushing us although we said nothing, and that with his lisp made Orlo and me laugh. "Thuth!" he said again, severe. It may not have been kind to make sport of him, but he might have chosen to say "keep quiet" instead. I said sorry, and Orlo dipped his head also. He barred the door to the street and drew us deeper within.

Annora kept presence of mind enough to tell him our task. We were to watch for the fire to the south end of town at the sawyer's, and ring the chapel bell exactly seven times when we saw it ablaze.

"You thent me the firtht hawk," he said to her fondly. "Has your young huthband fared well?"

"Yes, brother. By the gods' grace."

He led us to the bell tower and up the steps, and I bade Wieser wait at the bottom of the ladder to the belfry. We could see across the entire town and out over the harbour from the high vantage point. In the fading light I could make out the top of the wall the Keltanese had built. It looked beyond breaching, broad and thick. Torches lit the walkway, and wagons still rolled in and out of the town gates. The streets were otherwise emptying of folk except for the pole lanterns that marked the enemy foot patrols.

"What do you think, Orlo, are there half as many night patrols as before?" I asked, looking round at him.

"If that. When word came that the pass was blocked, they doubled the outriders at once. When you were here last, there was a Keltanese soldier for every third citizen, Zaffis said. Many fewer now."

The apostate spoke, voice tight with outrage. "After the prithoners were found mithing from the warehouse, they marched the new arrivals to thips and anchored them out in the bay. I hate to think what our men are enduring there."

"My da will set them free. The Keltanese have let themselves be spread too thin and he will turn it to our advantage."

The sea winds shifted as the sun went down, and we four watched to the south where I knew the sawyer's mill to be, high on the slope. We burned no light, so our eyes could accustom to the darkness that crept across the sky.

Annora was first to point to a growing glow on the slope, and by the time she lowered her arm, the fire had doubled in size. The men must have lit dozens of fires at the same moment. As quick as we could make our feet and hands find the rungs, we were down the ladder. The apostate gripped the bell rope, and gave a mighty yank. Orlo and I seized it with him, and together we tolled the great bell seven times, letting the ring fade between to set each apart for clarity. The sound was near to deafening, so close to the bronze giant.

Orlo barely let the last toll fade before clambering back up to the belfry. He called down to us, "Come see, our men are flooding into the streets!"

Maybe just a quick look, I thought as I mounted the ladder. *Before we go back to the tunnels.* Annora and the apostate followed. A rushing torrent of men carrying torches neared the gated wall. Wagon teams reared and plunged on the road. Some horses bolted into the crowd of soldiers, scattering them like pebbles from our high view. We could see less of what was happening at the waterfront, but could see torches aplenty all around the docks. Shouts and sounds of running men carried on the breeze. Street to street, our soldiers overtook patrols while the fire blazed at the south end of town. At the city wall, our men gained the ladders. Some pitched over backward as the enemy sought to repel the onslaught, by knocking the ladders away. More and more came behind the fallen, swarming up onto the walkway to overwhelm the guards with wave after wave of men. How had we achieved such numbers? Then I realized, the enemy had marched our men down to the sea, rather than leave them in the countryside. Keltane had consolidated our numbers for us. All the able escapees must have trekked back from the mountain, to fight at Da's command.

We stood above the melee, gasping in turns and pointing to skirmishes the others might have missed.

Annora seized my hand. "Oh, Judian, I think we will win!"

"Gods be praithed!" echoed the apostate.

Where were Da and Wils? They had not told me what role they were to play. Attacking the wall? Rounding up the patrols? Fighting on the docks? "Do you know what Wils and Da are doing?" I asked Annora.

"Fenn set the plan, but I think Behring conducts the attack. Wils and your da were to roust the officers at the harbourmaster's residence, and obtain their surrender."

I turned to Orlo. "Can you get us there underground?"

"Oh, aye."

"Oh, no. Gods keep us!" said Annora, but I took it as more of a remark than a true protest.

"You'd best retire to your cellar," I advised the apostate when we took our leave moments later.

"I think tho, too," he nodded, and I heard him set the bar back in the chapel door as soon as it shut behind us. We asked Wieser to lead us across the road to the tunnel entrance when it was safe to leave the shadows, for we dared no light. Once within, all was quiet, and I lit a torch to hand to Orlo so he could lead the way. He did not hesitate, but cautioned, "We have a fair walk ahead."

"Do you go underground to your work?" Annora asked, for of all of us, she seemed most discomfited being below ground.

"Nah, I just know all the tunnel network," Orlo said, tapping his temple.

We went by twists and turns, and found caverns where women and children sat with their backs to the rock walls, waiting for word from above. We told them from what we had seen, the battle looked to be going our way, and this was met by joyful gestures but little sound. All seemed to feel it fitting to be quiet in the underground. Finally, Orlo slowed at one group, looking at faces until he found the one he wanted.

"Cook!" he said. "Have our soldiers come to the house?"

"I let them in the kitchen just as you said," she answered, arms hugging her thick waist. "There was a dozen or more of them. I lit out for the tunnels as soon as they were through the door."

"Annora, wait here. We should go up and see if they need help," I suggested.

"I wager you would, too," came Wils's voice from behind me. "Da is turning everything over to our officers. We won the day! Or the night, more so." Annora caught him round the neck in a fierce embrace. He laughed as he kissed her.

"How did you know to look for us here?" I said.

"I was only starting here, when we finished at the harbourmaster's house. Zaffis brought me down." He jerked his head, and I saw Zaffis grinning behind him.

"I told you I would like to see Harbourmaster Folio's face when he learned smugglers were part of his salvation," said Zaffis. "Well worth the trip!"

Wils said on, "We are all to climb to the cliffs above, and walk home from there. Others are set to bring the wagons and horses."

"I'll take you far enough you won't get lost," Orlo offered. "Then I need to show my mum and the Emerals I'm still in one piece."

"Did Honni's da and brothers make it home?" I suddenly remembered she had not had any word of them last I knew.

Orlo's face clouded. "They were in the warehouse. One brother suffered a bad shoulder wound, but it may yet come right. They've all had too little food and too much filth."

"Tell her ... tell her I said hey, will you?" What should a person say in such times?

"Don't give me too much sentiment to have to remember to her," he scoffed.

"I think you can remember hey."

"And I am sure it will warm her heart," he said.

"Why should I want to warm any of her?" I could feel my color rising, and was glad for the weak light. "And give my regards to her family, and Guthy as well."

Zaffis foraged lanterns for Wils and me, and Orlo kept his torch for the walk back. He led us through more of the web of tunnels, past caches of crates and barrels here and there. Smuggler's stash, I reckoned. Wieser walked alongside, ever patient with where I took her. I kept up a steady stream of narration to Orlo, telling him about my knife from the kavsprit, and our trip to Fort Hasseron to rescue Da. Wils had to fill in about closing the pass, since I was told few details at the time. He and Annora walked behind, holding hands. Her smile lit the passage almost as much as his lantern.

Our tunnel's floor began to rise steeply. I had to watch my steps with care to avoid rolling an ankle on the rocks. "Are we near the cliffs yet?"

"Not yet. We had a time getting all those wounded soldiers up and out, I can tell you," Orlo puffed. "Zaffis had to have some of them nursed below in town 'til they could walk. No litters through here!"

At last, Orlo stopped and pointed ahead. "Keep to this way, there are only smaller side tunnels from now to the top of the cliffs. As long as you stay in the wider passage, you will not get lost. Fare you well, and gods keep you safe until you come to town again, country boy!" He waved as he turned away.

The way was not as rough as the last climb, to the cisterns at the fort, but I was still glad when the floor began to level. We strode more quickly in the flickering lantern-glow, and though we still had a far piece to walk from the cliffs to our farm, it felt as if we were almost home, in a way.

So, doubly cruel when Wieser's hair rose and she lifted her lips to show white teeth in the lantern light. I put out my hand to stop Wils and Annora, and lifted my light high to peer ahead. A whispery crackle raced toward us out of the dark, then a flash of blinding light erupted overhead like a lightning strike. I threw an arm over my eyes too late, and could only blink, too dazzled to see, while I heard approaching boots crunch on the tunnel floor.

"This cannot be you, at last? Only a boy?" said a voice that seemed to grind on my bones as it passed over me. Strange bright colors still burst across my vision, but gradually I could make out a tall man with a close-trimmed black beard, dressed in a black robe. He held a staff nearly as tall as himself. Around him stood five Keltanese soldiers, swords drawn.

I half-dropped my lantern at my feet as I fumbled in my boot top for my knife, and said to Wils, "Run!" I could see him from the corner of my eye, sword before him and Annora shoved behind him, her own knife out. "Take her and RUN!"

He cast me a desperate look, then wheeled and pulled Annora away, pelting back the way we had come. The soldiers started to follow them, but the sorcerer said, "No, with me. They do not matter, others will take them."

He took a step toward me to look closer at my blade. "How did you come by that?" he said sharply. Wieser leaped from my side to block him from coming any farther. His voice scraped at my ears, and with all my heart I did not want him nearer. Foul, acrid scent wafted from him.

Da always told me it is better to keep quiet and be thought a wood-wit than to speak and dispel all doubt. I held my tongue. Wieser rumbled deep in her throat. The mage narrowed his eyes and held up his hand, palm facing me.

"And you wear a moonstone. No wonder we have not seen you well. Who was it thought low peasant magic would save you? Who has trained you?"

I only wish somebody had ...

He leaned forward. *"You will tell me all, in the end."*

Despite the hammering of blood in my ears, I heard faint sounds like wind-rustled leaves. Flashes of green in my vision did not seem to be the clearing of the mage's light-strike. My hand began to tingle where I gripped the obsidian knife. The bone handle grew warm, then hot.

"Take the knife from him," the mage directed the nearest soldier. Wieser stiffened and drew a breath to renew her growl.

The man hesitated. "I thought we were finding escaped prisoners, not shepherd boys." Wieser snapped her jaws.

"Go on. It's only a dog," said the soldier behind the first, giving him a shove toward us.

"You think so?" sneered the sorcerer.

"What's your name?" I said to the mage.

He gave a derisive bark of laughter. "So you can use it in a spell against me?"

I would if I knew any. "No, I have seen some of your fellows from Scythera, and I was just wondering. Were you at Fort Hasseron of late?" The knife seemed alive in my fingers, aware.

Something was going to happen, and I bargained for time.

"What are you about?" His eyes raked over me, suspicious.

"Usually I see a pair of you together. Where is your partner?" I had a sudden thought. "Are you a Sending? Is that why you don't take my knife?"

"Disarm the boy!" the mage snarled and banged the butt of his staff on the rock. Dust rose from the impact; he must really be here. The soldiers looked at each other and shifted their feet.

"You do not want to take by force what the kavsprit have bestowed," I said with brittle cheerfulness. The air began to buzz, as if hornets swarmed.

"Bah! You lie! No human would be given such a gift by the spirits of the deep dark." He began to hear something too, it appeared, for he looked about as if seeking the source.

"Maybe Scytheran kavsprit do not like you overwell. Our Mercedian spirits are different. If you honor them, they hear you. If you want their help, you've only got to say." *Hear me, I'm saying now*, I pleaded in my mind. *Or, tell me how long before Wils might return with help for me?*

Distant caws echoed from behind the men, and Gargle soon flapped in to pass above them and drop something from his claws—something writhing. Three long black snakes, twisting as they fell. I could see they were a harmless sort, no venom, but a shock nonetheless. Soldiers leaped and cursed, swatting them away. Even the mage jumped.

And turned the serpents to ash with a word and a pass of his staff.

"Good try," I told Gargle when he lit on my shoulder. "Pit vipers next time?" He muttered and took up a perch on the rocks beside me.

A second mage arrived to push his way past the unnerved soldiers. His robe and staff were like that of the first, and his jaw jutted hard in anger. His voice was worse to hear because of what he said: "Kill the dog, fools."

One of the men cocked his bow and aimed. He would never miss her from this close on. Still I lunged with my knife when he loosed the bolt, and felt it smack my blade and spin away to clatter on the stones. My hand flashed out faster than I would have believed I could move, and sliced the bowstring as it vibrated. The soldier fell back among his fellows, gibbering.

I pointed the blade tip at the first mage. "You want my knife come and take it."

Both of the mages glowered in livid fury. I heard pattering from the shadows, and the buzzing grew louder. I could feel it on my skin. My hand remained rock steady, though I cannot say it was because I felt no fear. I met their eyes and hoped my thoughts did not show on my face.

"Who trained him?" asked the second mage.

"He has not said. Yet."

"Enough of this. We will stun them both. Take some care not to kill the boy, I will know more from him." The second mage shot his wrists out of his trailing sleeves, and turned to face the first. Each raised his staff and began to speak guttural words that made my heart knock wildly in my chest.

Wieser began to whine as their voices rose. Her body twisted and she shook so hard. I shouted, "No!" and raised my knife, trying in some crazy way to cut their words from the air. Wieser's whine rose to a shriek of agony. I could not bear her anguish, and cried out as well, falling to my knees. As I fell, blackness exploded from the knife blade just as light had burst in the tunnel from the mage's spell. Inky darkness blotted all light, thick, burdening the air, which came alive with the chatter of thin whispery voices. Men screamed. I felt about me for Wieser, and closed my fingers in her curly coat.

She was so still.

I felt as if a thousand bird feet scrabbled over me, as the pattering sound swelled to fill the tunnel. Boots blundered and scuffled nearby, with incoherent cursing and piteous cries that did not come from me, this time. I could feel I still held my knife before me, but I could see nothing at all.

How long the blackness held sway, I do not know. When gradual lifting of the oppressive dark began, at first I did not recognize what seeped in at the edges of my vision as my lantern's light, so absolute was the dark in my mind. I prayed to the gods to feel some stirring within Wieser, heartbeat or breath. The dark retreated as it had come, contracting into the knife blade, though it receded more slowly than it had burst forth. Gargle hopped next to me, gurgling and shaking his wings. I looked up to see the five soldiers sprawled about the passage. I knew they were dead. Of the mages there was no trace.

The sound of pounding feet came from the tunnel behind me. I turned my head to see Wils and Annora, and Da and Orlo. And so many others, all bristling with swords and panting heavily. Da looked at me, kneeling in the dust with Wieser at my side, and swallowed hard. He pointed his sword at the dead soldiers, and I saw Cobbel and Miskin, both ash-smeared, go to turn them over and check for signs of life. There would be none.

Wils said, "What happened? Did you kill them all? Where is the sorcerer?"

But I could not summon the will to speak.

Annora knelt by Wieser, running her hands over her—just as she had done for the sickly kid on the first day Wils and I ever saw her. She bent to press her ear against the broad furry chest, and smiled. I felt my own heart falter in its rhythm, then.

"Lift her head." And when I did so, Annora cupped her hands around Wieser's muzzle and blew in, long and slow. As she took her hands away, Wieser's pink tongue flicked out. Annora never said a word when the tongue flicked out again, to lick off the tear that fell from my eye onto the black muzzle.

To Wils she said, "She's been shocked by magic, stunned. It will wear off, but it takes a while."

"What about Judian?" Wils said, brows furrowed deep.

"I'm not stunned. But I am ready to go home."

CHAPTER 37

I found I wanted to avoid bright sunlight for the next few days. I spent most of my time by the hearth with Wieser, as she gained strength. No one asked me to do any chores. That would not suit me for long, but it suited me fine for the time being.

Morie alternated between pasting herself to me and then to Da. "What sort of language have you been using in front of her?" Da wanted to know. "She would make your crows blush." Gargle, Tock and Clock exchanged glances with me at that.

Virda set food in front of me regularly, and *tsked* and reverted to calling me poor lamb if I did not polish the plates clean. I did my best to do justice to her meals, since she had been called from coddling the wounded soldiers to coddle me instead.

Gevarr came down from the cave barracks to see how I fared. He told me gruffly he had never seen me more useless, then pronounced himself a mercenary rather than a turncoat traitor. He got on wonderful well with Da. "I still can't think of a reason to leave," he said to me, with his usual insolent flash of teeth. I took more cheer from his visit than any other.

I asked Joren Delyth what had changed his mind about Gevarr enough to bring him as outrider, and to the harbour battle. "Cobbel told me how he would have lain down his life for Virda and little Morie, when he was here while you all were gone to the fort. How he watched over them. He has a good heart, in his way. And he fought hard in the harbour, led a squad of our men. A natural commander, Behring says."

I also received a visit from Behring, who had charge of a garrison by the lowest cave. They were to guard the northwest pass and prevent its use by Keltane. He thanked me for what I had done to free the soldiers from the warehouse. I only nodded, I had given over telling folk it was Orlo's idea. He told me the troops from the prison ships had all been brought ashore. "And if I were your da, I'd skin you twice over," he said as he shook my hand.

Every day some of Merced's officers came to see Da, including the marshall he had pursued west. Freed from one of the prison ships, the man's uniform hung on his bones and his hands trembled like autumn leaves. Virda fixed him a heaped plate of food at once. He relayed plans to move captured Keltanese troops from Bale Harbour, transporting them by wagon to scattered camps about the country to work in our fields. "I know another one they could take," I overheard Wils say to Annora, but she shushed him.

Da was often called to the harbour, but did most of his business by messenger bird, still using our code. Annora kept busy training a cadre of our soldiers in the system, so each could train a dozen others. For though we had been victorious in our province, the rest of Merced endured occupation still. Our army had much yet to do.

Wils did every sort of work around the farm without complaining. I could have watched him all day. And did. Annora tried not to laugh at me with my boots up while Wils chased chickens in the evening to shut them in the new coop.

Annora gave tender care to Wieser, fixing her broths and brushing her coat. We had to carry her home that night in a cloak sling, from the cave tunnel to our hearth. She could walk a bit, of late. Murr often came to sleep at her side, which I supposed a gesture of affection rather than just looking for a warm place. Anyway, Morie insisted it was so.

What I mostly did was try to avoid thinking about mages. I had no way of knowing if the two from the cave had escaped or been killed by the kavsprit. What happened to a mage's body when he no longer inhabited it? Were they still mortal men? If angels came from good folk ascending to the gods, what did a mage become? In any case, there had to be more than two Scytheran sorcerers in Merced. I figured I would be sought more than ever now. Da thought so, too.

He came to me by the fire late evening, after the others settled for sleep. I had taken to sleeping beside Wieser's pallet, so she would not be lonesome in the night. Da walked over to sit in his chair. He carried a wooden box I had never seen before, deeply carved with leaves and vines.

"I never gave you your birthday gift," he said, setting it before me.

I opened it to discover a book with a tooled leather cover. It looked as if every kind of animal, bird and plant was depicted, each merging and mingling together in a web of life. The intricacy amazed me. I lifted the cover to see page after page of magic. Spells and drawings, potions, remedies and lore of every kind, and more whose meaning I could not guess. Some pages were in languages I did not know. I looked up at Da.

"This was your mother's. She told me the night you were born, you would be the one to have her gift. Wils like me, you like her, and Morie," here he smiled, "like no one else, exactly."

"Mum was a witch?"

"More than that. A sorceress. She was not from Merced, though you might not know that. I met her as a young officer, away to the South War. She was from an island country far across the ocean—"

"But not Scythera," I broke in.

"No, Lohr Island, nowhere near Scythera. She emigrated with her family to Merced's riverlands. Elyn. My first look at her sealed my heart to any other. I brought her home to the mountain." He paused and looked at his hands in his lap. "I miss her daybreak to sunset every day, and in my dreams."

I did not know what to say. I had thought always more about my loss than of his. I was not even sure I had known her name was Elyn. I just called her Mum.

He looked up. "I think it best you go to her folk on the island now, to be trained in magic."

"I do not want to be a sorcerer, like those two in the tunnel."

"Like all of us, you have a choice to use your gifts for good or ill. You need not be like them. But you could learn what you need to fight them. They will come for you. I fear I cannot keep you safe here, Judian. And I would have you safe."

A log hissed and settled in a shower of sparks as I considered what he said. For an instant, I thought I saw a face in the embers. The God of Fire? My mother's book seemed heavier in my lap of a sudden. "I would take Wieser with me." I laid my hand on her head; she gave a thump with her tail. "And Gargle should come with me, but Tock and Clock can stay to carry messages, they'll prefer that."

Da nodded. "I have spoken to Harbourmaster Folio, he thinks to get you aboard a ship that carries cargo that way. If Wieser can travel, can you be ready to leave for the harbour tomorrow?"

"If I am going, better sooner than later. I do not want a dose of carrying on from everybody. I'd rather leave even before they all know I'm gone."

"Do you want to go to the harbour through the cliff tunnel?"

"No! No. I don't want to go back there. But see to it— please—that an offering is left there for the kavsprit. A generous one, renewed always." His eyes told me he would see it done. "Wieser can ride in our Traveller wagon. You might drive us down to the sea, if you would."

"I will," he said, and rose to blow out the candle beside his chair.

I packed my folio of magic in the box with my mum's book. I

found one of the canvas seabags Virda had sewn, and put the box and all my clothes inside. Did Lohr Island have seasons like Merced, if it was so far away? I took winter cloak and scarf anyway. I still had room for stylus and paper, so I could write folk at home. Though I did not suppose Gargle could carry a letter across the ocean. Perhaps ships carried such to and fro? If they didn't, they should, and I would look into that.

How would I find my mother's people on the island? Was there a school for magic, such as fancy folk had to teach their children their lessons in the capitol? Or tutors, as some country folk engaged in our province? Da always taught us.

I did not want to sleep. I had not had dream visions of pursuing animals since the cliff, and tonight would be an ill time to find the mages' search renewed. Da found me sitting beside Wieser with my packed bag when dawn only hinted. He gave me a sack of gold and silver coins, startlingly heavy, and a thick folded vellum he said was a letter of introduction to a master mage who would take me as apprentice. We went out to harness a team while the rest of the house still slumbered. Wieser rose to follow us out, though she walked stiffly yet.

I bade farewell to Dink and Murr, and chose Cider and Honey for the drive down. Da and I just finished hitching them to the wagon when Annora appeared at my side. Silently she handed me a leather pouch with a long strap for wearing over the shoulder. Within were all manner of labeled paper packets of herbs and such. When I looked up, I found her eyes brimming.

I had never seen her cry.

"You cannot be starting that now," I said, my own voice thick. She shook her head and kissed me quickly on the cheek before fleeing back to the house.

Da lifted Wieser into the back, and we rolled out of the yard with Gargle on the roof, though I glared him into silence when he looked to be drawing breath to gloat to the other two crows perched on the peak of the barn. I waved to Tock and Clock, and they took wing, circling above the farm until we were out of sight.

I kept turned in my seat until I could not see home any more. It did not seem fair that all I had worked for was to have us safe at home as before, only to have to leave when Da, Wils and Morie, and Annora and Virda too, were finally ready to resume some kind of life like we had been living before the invasion. I understood now what was meant in Da's books about "war torn" countries, because I was being torn from my home.

We rode without speaking, but it did not feel strained. As day broke about us, I tried to note every bird call and scent on the breeze so I could remember home while I lived away. Blueflax and sunny white bonnets nodded in the tall meadow grass as we passed. The village was barely stirring when we rolled through. No other folk travelled the road with us. I enjoyed the quiet and peace, which I usually don't, being more inclined to want something happening all the time. Perhaps because I was a man now, I would have more patience. The full-grown always seemed to me to have the capacity to sit still and do nothing for amazingly long stretches of time.

Both town gates were shut tight and guarded by Mercedian sentries when we reached Bale Harbour. Da was waved through with no delay by men who smiled and raised hands to us both.

"Is it true they all know you?" I said, waving back.

"More all the time, it seems," he said, nodding their way.

He knew the ship he sought on the quay, and halted by the tallest. The name on its side was *Moon Road*, which joggled in my memory a bit. I found out why when we hauled Wieser and my bag up the ramp, or gangplank as it is called, Da said. The man who met us at the top, on the deck, I was hastily schooled, not the floor, was Virda's son Lichan Tedesch.

Da handed him what must be payment for my passage. "If it was up to my mum," Lichan allowed, "we'd carry this one all around the world for naught. She thinks quite high of him."

Da smiled. "You'll see he finds the proper folk at the port? My wife's people will not know to expect him."

"Oh, aye." Lichan must favor his da, Davini Tedesch, for he was tall and angular, with a square jaw. None were Virda's features. I could remember him a little from his visits home over the years, but he was one of her older sons, and had been at sea longer than I had been alive. His cheeks did not yet look like boot leather, though.

Gargle came to perch on my bag, and peck at it looking for food, which reminded me of my stomach and Wieser's. "I haven't eaten, should we get something on the street?"

"As this is your first time aboard ship, you'll want to stay empty to start," Lichan said. "Some landfolk take seasick until they get accustomed to riding the waves." He lifted my bag to his shoulder.

I turned to Da. He pulled me to his great chest for just a moment, then shook my hand, engulfed in both of his. "You'll do well," he said, and strode off down the gangplank. I thought his voice had been just a little thick, at that. I know mine would have been, if I tried to speak.

"A quick farewell, that's the best," Lichan said, watching him walk away. "Let's stow this below. We set sail on the tide, and the tide does not wait!"

I did not know what that might mean, exactly. *Below what?* "Come, Wieser. Gargle. Let's go see where our fortunes will carry us now." And off we went, together.

The End

About the Author:

Aimee L. Gross loves to tell stories. When she was nine years old, she noticed an advertisement for The Famous Writers School in the back of a magazine, and wrote a letter at once, since she planned to be a famous writer.

She received a kind reply from the school's director, telling her that students must be grown up before enrolling. He advised her to keep writing, and she always has.

She lives in the Midwest with her husband. They share their home with an adopted Cairn Terrier named Kizmet, and Norbert, the orange marmalade cat. Many crows live in the hedgerow, and often suggest she increase their allotment of corn.

Readers are her favorite people. She welcomes followers on Facebook as Aimee L. Gross, author and artist. Or connect on Twitter @Aimee_SanG. Send a message anytime at agross9999author.com.

Judian, Wieser and Gargle will continue their journey in the forthcoming *No Mercy From Crows*, summer 2015.

www.ingramcontent.com/pod-product-compliance
Lightning Source LLC
Chambersburg PA
CBHW030419180626
46812CB00005B/2078

* 9 7 8 0 9 9 0 9 6 8 1 0 8 *